The

EVASLIFE'S

Cathy l   o others.
She find   l it gives
her gre   nothing
like see   h loving
care ha   o being.'
Cathy l

Also by Cathy Sharp

Halfpenny Street Orphans
The Orphans of Halfpenny Street
The Little Runaways
Christmas for the Halfpenny Orphans
The Boy with the Latch Key
An Orphan's Courage

Children of the Workhouse
The Girl in the Ragged Shawl
The Barefoot Child
The Winter Orphan

East End Daughters
A Daughter's Sorrow
A Daughter's Choice
A Daughter's Dream

Button Street Orphans
An Orphan's Promise
An Orphan's Sorrow
An Orphan's Dream
The Lonely Orphan

The Evacuees
The Boy with the Suitcase
The Lost Evacuee
An Orphan's Story

CATHY SHARP
The
EVACUEE'S PROMISE

HarperCollins*Publishers*

HarperCollins*Publishers* Ltd
1 London Bridge Street
London SE1 9GF

www.harpercollins.co.uk

HarperCollins*Publishers*
Macken House, 39/40 Mayor Street Upper
Dublin 1, D01 C9W8, Ireland

First published by HarperCollins*Publishers* Ltd 2025
1

A catalogue record for this book is available from the British Library

ISBN: 978-0-00-868020-6 (PB)
ISBN: 978-0-00-868021-3 (TPB)

This novel is entirely a work of fiction. The names, characters and incidents portrayed in it are the work of the author's imagination. Any resemblance to actual persons, living or dead, events or localities is entirely coincidental.

Set in Sabon LT Pro by HarperCollins*Publishers* India

Printed and bound in the UK using 100% Renewable
Electricity by CPI Group (UK) Ltd

This book contains FSC™ certified paper and other controlled sources to ensure responsible forest management.

For more information visit: www.harpercollins.co.uk/green

CHAPTER 1

London, May 1940

'Leave 'im alone! I've told yer once afore. Leave 'im be or I'll bash yer!' Georgie Greene glared at the bully who had been pushing Billy around the playground.

'Yeah, you and whose army?' Mick Bailey demanded aggressively. He was a few inches taller than Georgie and heavily built, his stance combative. 'I'll squash yer if yer try anythin', Georgie boy.'

'I ain't afraid of yer,' Georgie said, standing his ground. He brought his fists up in the way his older brothers had taught him. 'I ain't a bully like you, Mick Bailey, but I can fight.'

'We'll just see who can fight!' Mick took a step forward and then the bell rang for the end of playtime and two male teachers came into the playground.

'Come on, you two,' one of the masters summoned. 'You've been told before – fighting in the playground earns the cane across your hands.'

'This ain't over . . .' Mick hissed as he pushed past Georgie. 'Just you wait till I catch yer alone.'

1

Georgie didn't bother to answer. He knew a fight was coming whether he wanted it or not. Mick bullied most of the younger lads into giving him their sweets or pocket money and, thus far, no one had been brave enough to stand up to him, but Georgie wasn't going to let him get away with hurting Billy. Though only a year younger than Georgie, Billy was his nephew and small and thin for his age. He was full of life and happy when he wasn't being bullied, but he was afraid to stand up for himself. They were friends as well as relatives and Georgie felt protective of him.

'Thanks, Georgie,' Billy whispered as he followed him into the school building. 'He's always picking on me. I don't know why.'

'Mick Bailey picks on all the lads that are smaller than 'im,' Georgie said. 'When we leave school, just stay close to me, Billy. We'll walk 'ome together same as always.'

'Ain't you goin' ter Aunt Kate's fer yer tea tonight?' Billy whispered.

'I'll see you 'ome first,' Georgie replied. 'Hurry up or we'll be late.' They parted inside the school to go to their different classrooms. To look at them you'd think them at least three years apart in age, but Georgie was a few months from his fourteenth birthday and Billy twelve and a half. It was just the difference in stature. Billy's pale fairness made him look even younger while Georgie's shock of russet hair and his stocky build put him a head and shoulders above most in his class – in fact, the only boy bigger than him was Mick Bailey.

'You're late, Greene,' Mr Thompson accused as he entered the classroom.

'Yes, sir. Sorry, sir.'

'Take your seat then and be quick about it.' There was a snigger from the back of the room where Mick Bailey sat watching. Georgie ignored him. It was a maths lesson, one of his favourites. Kate, the younger of his two sisters, was a teacher and she said he had a good brain, especially for working out problems, but was too lazy to use it.

Georgie thought schoolwork was a bit of a waste of time. He enjoyed some of his lessons, others he just switched off and gazed out of the window. There was a hedgerow just outside, blocking the school from the busy road, and he watched as birds went in and out, often with bits of grass in their beaks. Building nests, he reckoned. He liked seeing them and sometimes looked for the nests, fascinated by the intricacy of them, but not during his maths lessons.

He sat straight in his seat, waiting for the lesson to begin, but when the master began to speak, all the boys were surprised by what he had to say.

'I don't know if any of you lads have heard,' Mr Thompson began, 'but I have been sent my papers and I shall be leaving at the end of this week – I'm joining the army.'

There were murmurs of surprise because he wasn't a young man, perhaps in his early forties and most fit men had joined as soon as the war between Germany and Britain and the Allies had begun.

'Wish you weren't going, sir,' one of the lads said and Mr Thompson smiled.

'I shan't be doing a lot of fighting, Simpkins, so when this nonsense is over, I'll probably be back to

3

plague you all again.' A ripple of laughter greeted his words. 'However, they need every man they can get and I've got a good head for figures and keeping track of things so I'll be in an office organizing stuff and getting supplies from one place to another.'

'Someone needs to do it, 'cos they're in a bleedin' mess at the moment,' a voice piped up. 'Me dad says they've never got enough of what they need – half of 'em ain't even got a gun yet.'

'Yes, well, I've heard that kind of rumour as well, but I think that is mainly for the Home Guard,' Mr Thompson told him with a smile.

'Dad's Army,' one of the boys ribbed. 'His dad is in the bleedin' old fogies!'

'That will do,' Mr Thompson quelled him with a look. 'The Home Guard is struggling with lack of equipment because the fighting men have to come first but remember, this war was forced on us because we had to stand up for what was right in the face of German aggression. We didn't prepare for it for years and that's why we're finding it harder than was thought at the start. It is also why every able-bodied man is needed.' He smiled. 'I volunteered at the start but was turned down because of my flat feet – but now they've changed their minds. I'll be doing work that a fighting man is currently occupied with and that releases him to fight.'

'All my brothers are in the forces,' Georgie said. 'I wish I were.'

'Don't wish your life away, Georgie,' his teacher replied. 'You have a good brain. There's lots you could do with your future – if you work hard.'

Georgie bit his lip and sat back. Mr Thompson looked around the room. 'That was my first piece of news – the second is that the school will be closing shortly. We have kept going with a reduced staff because many of our pupils have already evacuated to the country but now we understand that there is to be another Government directive to parents who have not yet sent their children to the country to do so. As you know, the war has intensified and although London has not been affected yet, it may happen soon, because of the way things are going overseas. You will all get letters for your parents, telling them what is happening and when.'

There were exclamations of dismay all round as the children looked at one another. Those who still attended this school in London's East End had all resisted a move to the country and so this was bad news. Mr Thompson was speaking again, 'You will need your gas masks for a drill later today. I hope everyone has brought theirs?' Mr Thompson glanced round at the guilty faces of those who'd left theirs at home. 'I know it seems a lot of nonsense at the moment, but please do try to remember them in future. If a gas attack comes, they could save your life.'

He waited for the groans to subside and then nodded. 'Good, now we'll turn to page ten in your books and everyone will do exercises five to seven, except Georgie Greene. You will turn to page fifteen and do the exercises there please.'

Georgie nodded. He had done all the exercises in the book up to page fifteen, because he was quick and could calculate in his head. He smiled as he opened the book and bent his head over his work. Mr Thompson's warning about the new directive didn't bother him, because he knew his mother wouldn't send him away. When he'd refused to go last time she'd supported him, said she wasn't going to let her family be torn apart by the war so that was all right.

A smile touched his lips. He was looking forward to having tea with his sister Kate after he'd seen Billy home. She was fun to be with and always had something nice specially for him. To be fair, his mum did, too, when she could, but Georgie and Kate were the closest in age of all the brothers and sisters. It was a big family, with three brothers in the army and Vera, his elder sister's husband Bob in the Royal Navy. Vera had a daughter Jenny, a year older than Billy, and there was a big gap between her and Kate, because she was the oldest of the family. Vera was all right and lived with Georgie and his mum and dad, while Bob was away at sea. Georgie didn't get on with her, at least not the way he did with Kate.

Georgie raced through his exercises and then turned to look out of the window at a blackbird in the hedge. He didn't take much notice when his teachers told him he was wasting a good brain by not trying, because he knew exactly what he was going to do when he was old enough. He would be a train driver like his dad and for that he only needed to get his school certificate and that was just too easy.

CHAPTER 2

'Kate, I'm home.' The man's voice was raised with excitement and brought the sound of running footsteps down the stairs. A few moments later Kate ran into the kitchen of their small, terraced house and straight into his arms. 'My love, my love. I missed you . . .' Steve Silvester's voice was hushed and deep with passion as he buried his face in the softness of her fair locks, just now tumbling about her face and shoulders, as she raised her face for his kiss.

'Not as much as I missed you,' she murmured when their kiss ended and she could breathe once more. Her green eyes were shining like stars as she gazed up at him. 'Oh, Steve . . . it's seemed like a lifetime without you.'

'Steady on, old girl,' he said huskily. 'It's only eight weeks since I joined up.'

'That *is* a lifetime,' Kate insisted, laughing up into his handsome face. 'We've only been married six months and—' Her laughing complaints died on an indrawn breath as she realized: they were not alone. Meeting his eyes, half in alarm, half in wonder, Kate waited.

'Oh, sorry.' Steve glanced over his shoulder and grinned at the man standing hesitantly in the doorway. 'I forgot about Chuck for a minute – he's a new friend, Kate, and has nowhere to spend his leave so I invited him here. You don't mind?'

'Of course not . . .' Kate moved back from her husband's embrace and looked at the man. He too was wearing the uniform of the British RAF but against Steve, tall, dark, and broad-shouldered, he looked insignificant with his pale almost silvery hair that was short and waved back from his high forehead – though his eyes were the bluest she had ever seen. He was nearly as tall as Steve but thin with white skin. Not as handsome as Steve but . . . intelligent was the word that came to her mind as she offered her hand. 'You are welcome to stay, Mr . . .'

'Flight lieutenant,' Steve said. 'Flight lieutenant Charles Durrant. He is one of our instructors. Chuck, this is my darling wife, Kate . . .'

Charles took the hand Kate extended, pressing it briefly as he thanked her. His touch was cool and firm and the smile in his eyes banished any doubt she might have had about a stranger in their home.

'Please, call me Chuck. And I can go to a hotel if it isn't convenient, Mrs Silvester. I am sure you must be wishing me to Jericho.'

'Not at all,' Kate said, 'and call me Kate.' She looked at him curiously. 'Forgive me – but that isn't an English accent. Are you American?'

'Canadian,' Charles replied. 'My mother was born in Texas but she met my father and moved to Ottawa

8

with him when they married. I was born there – so maybe there is a mixture of both.'

'I have an uncle by marriage who lives in Canada – in Halifax,' Kate told him with a pleased smile. 'He and my aunt, who emigrated out there, came over a couple of years ago and I thought I recognized the accent, though it isn't quite the same as Uncle Mo's.'

'Chuck doesn't have any British relatives,' Steve said as Kate moved away to put the kettle on the black range. It had recently been polished and gleamed, as did the pots and pans standing on its surface. Heat came off it in waves, because it was a warm spring day and despite the back door being opened into a small yard, it was very hot in the kitchen. It had to be kept alight because the house didn't have gas yet, though there had been plans to update it before the war put everything on hold.

'Why don't you take Chuck into the parlour, Steve?' Kate asked. 'I'll bring the tea through when it's ready.'

'Yes, it's too hot in here,' he agreed and led the way through to their sitting room. Unlike most of the front rooms in the terraced houses of Brook Street, Kate's parlour was used. Not for her the hard, seldom sat on sofas, or a cold, neat place that no one was ever comfortable in. Kate's parlour had a large, very old but comfortable sofa with long-fringed Spanish shawls tossed over the back and lots of soft cushions. At one side of the room was a dining table with drop-down sides, pushed up against the wall and just now loaded with piles of exercise books. One wall had bookshelves from floor to ceiling and as many books as could be crammed onto them. Nothing in the room was new, including the rugs that gave it its comfortable feel; they were Chinese washed-silk in various shades of pink and green, but had been picked up from a second-hand shop, and one had a small stain that wouldn't come out. A pair of pink slippers stood by the fireplace and a few knickknacks graced the windowsill.

'Kate's a teacher.' Steve indicated the exercise books with a jerk of his head. 'Too clever for me – but I beat all the others off who wanted her, sent them all running so she had no choice but to take me.'

Coming in at that moment with a tea tray, Kate heard his comment and laughed, one eyebrow quirking in mockery. 'Ignore him,' she advised Chuck. 'We went to school together and he was always top of the class when it came to maths and sciences, the best in all sports and most things he wanted to do but he doesn't want to be behind a desk all day so he went into the building trade – and then the war started . . .' For a moment her eyes darkened.

'He beat quite a few of his class in the exams for our lot,' Chuck told her, looking amused. 'Your husband hasn't told you, Kate, but he's well on the way to becoming a pilot. Just one more exam, which he'll undoubtedly pass. He already has most of his flying hours in.'

Kate looked at Steve. He grinned but made no comment. 'That's wonderful, Steve,' she said quietly, but there was a quiver in her voice that she couldn't quite control. 'You'll be flying missions soon . . .' Something in his eyes told her that he already was, probably as co-pilot. 'Congratulations. I know it's what you wanted.'

'Kate . . .' Steve gave her a quick apologetic smile.

'Your husband is going to be a first-rate pilot,' Chuck told her, unaware of the current beneath the surface. 'God knows we shall need them all if this war goes on for as long as the last one.'

Kate had set the tray down and busied herself with the tea things, asking Chuck how he took his tea. 'With a little milk and one sugar,' he replied and grinned. 'I never drank tea until I came to England but the coffee is so damned awful over here!' A red flush crept up his neck. 'I beg your pardon!'

Kate laughed and shook her head. 'This is the East End of London, Chuck. All the kids at the school I went to used far worse language, I promise you.'

'You should hear some of the chaps at the base,' Steve said and accepted his own tea, hot, strong, and sweet. Kate had provided a plate of plain biscuits. She offered them to their guest with a look of apology.

'I'm sorry. I haven't baked this week. I don't bother too much unless Steve is home or if Georgie comes over and he was here to tea yesterday and ate all the sponge I'd made.' Her eyes sparkled suddenly as she said. 'Georgie is my little brother – and a right little tearaway. He's eleven years younger than I am, just thirteen. Mum thought she couldn't have any more and then Georgie turned up and has been causing mayhem ever since.'

'Georgie's all right,' Steve said. 'Always into mischief I grant you, but he's a great kid. I hope we have a couple like him one day.'

Kate gave a shout of laughter. 'You wait until they fill the house with noise and start breaking the neighbours' windows every other day.' Suddenly the laughter drained from her face as she thought of something. 'They're talking of closing his school for the duration, and mine. A lot of children have already been evacuated and if the numbers drop any lower, my school will amalgamate with another and I'll be out of a job.'

Steve looked at her, hearing the suppressed distress in her voice. 'That's bad luck. What will you do?'

'I'm not certain. If I want to stay in teaching, I may have to relocate to the country. That means . . .' She sighed and shook her head. 'We'll talk about it later.' Transferring her gaze to their guest who had drunk his tea and eaten two biscuits, she smiled. 'I always keep our spare room ready in case one of my brothers wants to stay. Georgie is the youngest of us but I have three brothers older than me, all in the army, and my elder sister and her three children live with my parents as her husband is in the Royal Navy and so my brothers come here to stay when they're on leave. Steve will take you up if you'd like to unpack and have a wash or something. We have an upstairs toilet but no bath, I'm afraid – we usually bring a tin one into the kitchen. Steve is going to build us a bathroom out the back when he gets a chance.'

Steve stood up and led the way upstairs. There were three bedrooms. Two were a nice size, the third no more than a boxroom, where cases and junk were presently stored. The bedroom Steve led his friend to was clean and bright with a white candlewick bedspread, blue rugs on a stained wood floor and blue-and-white curtains at the windows. Beside the bed, there was a mahogany chest, a wardrobe that vaguely matched and an oak washstand, which had a blue-and-white set of basin, jug, and soap dish.

'It's not much of a place,' he said, slightly awkward now. 'We wanted to get married and it was all we could afford. When the war's over and I'm back at work I'll be looking for something better.'

'This will suit me fine,' Chuck said, looking about him. 'It's a bit like my grandparents had when they were younger – except they had land at the back that they scraped a living from. They were dirt farmers. Hadn't a cent to bless themselves with when they started, but Grandpa pulled himself up by his bootstraps, made a bit of money and sent my dad to college.' He grinned at Steve. 'I much prefer this to a hotel – but are you sure I shan't be in the way?'

'You're fine,' Steve said. 'We'll all go to the pub this evening – I'll introduce you to the family on Sunday. Most of them will be here for lunch. You might meet Georgie before that, though.'

'Thanks.' Chuck nodded. 'I'll invite you and your wife to Canada one day. Meet my folks. We're still farming folk, but bigger now – and Dad has a few extra interests.'

'Sounds great,' Steve said. 'I'll bring some hot water up in a couple of minutes. Leave you to unpack . . .' He went out, closing the door behind him.

Kate looked up as Steve walked into the kitchen. She had a kettle of hot water and a can of cold standing on the pine table. 'That was a surprise. I wish you'd told me you wanted to bring a friend.'

13

'I only asked him last thing. He said he was staying on the base because he had no one to visit. I didn't think you would mind?'

'I don't,' she said. 'I'd have done more shopping if I'd known but I can go tomorrow.'

'Chuck bought a bit of stuff on the way here. Tinned, mostly, tea, sugar and he got some fresh steaks. Don't know how, but he has a way with him.' Steve took a paper bag of groceries from his kitbag and put them on the table. 'He's a good bloke, Kate. Helped me a lot. I'm not sure I'd have got through my primary exams without him. They were tougher than I expected, but he gave me a bit of extra coaching, because he says I'm good in the air. I'm OK at maths, though paperwork isn't my favourite thing, but Chuck got me through it. He's very clever.'

'Then I'm glad he's your friend,' Kate said and moved towards him. He took her into his arms and kissed her long and hard, then looked down into her face. 'Are you all right? You look a bit tired, love.'

Kate hesitated and then a little giggle escaped her. 'I wasn't going to say just yet, but I went to the doctor last week and . . .' She took a deep breath, 'He says I'm about nine weeks gone!'

'Nine—' Steve stared at her in shock. 'You're having a kid? But that wasn't what we planned. We were going to wait for a couple of years, until this stupid war is over.'

The smile died out of her face. 'I thought you'd be pleased,' she said. 'You like children – or so I thought . . .'

'Yes, I know but . . .' He sighed, running his long fingers through his dark hair. 'It just wasn't what

14

we'd talked about. We were going to save, work hard and find a nice house in the suburbs before we had children!' Steve sat down, stunned, and disbelieving as his dreams seemed to crumble about him. 'Oh, Kate, I'm sorry.'

'I'm not. Mum and Dad are over the moon. You'd think with all our lot they would've had enough of kids. Mum has offered to look after the baby for me when I'm ready to return to teaching . . .'

Steve looked at her, suddenly seeing the hurt in her face. 'I'm a bloody fool!' he said and jumped up, reaching out for her again. 'I'm sorry, Kate. It was just so unexpected. Of course I want our children. You know I do. I just thought it would be a while yet.'

'Well, I did, too,' she agreed. 'I was shocked too for a start, because we'd been careful – but we weren't that night you got your papers. We both had a few drinks and . . .'

Steve nodded. 'It was my fault,' he said and grimaced. 'I was in a funny mood that night, love, excited and yet reluctant. I only applied to the RAF because I knew they'd put me in the army if I waited to be called up.'

Kate inclined her head. 'I know, Steve. If the war hadn't happened . . . Oh, we had so many plans! I know you want your own business and a lovely house for us and all the rest, but it isn't so bad here. Which is why I'm going to try and find work in London if they close the school. If we give our home up and put our stuff in store, goodness knows what we'll find when it's all over. Most of the houses we looked at were far worse than this and you've done a lot to it.'

15

Although they rented their home, Steve had done endless little jobs – repairing things and putting in a new toilet upstairs, besides decorating and repairing some of the guttering and even plastering one ceiling. Because he could turn his hand to almost anything in the building trade, he'd made their home into a comfortable place she was happy to live in for as long as necessary.

She smiled, indicating the kettle and water jug. 'You'd best take those upstairs or the water will be cold. We'll talk later, when you've had time to think.'

CHAPTER 3

Georgie Greene put his fists up. 'Come on then. You think yer can pick on anyone, but I warned yer the other day to leave our Billy alone! So put 'em up!'

'Stupid little runt!' Mick Bailey was the son of a docker and both his parents spent most of the money they earned in the pub of a Friday and Saturday night. His clothes were torn and rarely patched, his shirt worn and dirty round the collar and one shoe had a hole in the toe. Used to being given the belt for any misdemeanour at home, Mick liked to take it out on anyone he could at school. 'I'll teach yer a lesson yer bloody well better not forget.'

Challenges laid, the two lads went at it hammer and tong, punching, kicking, scratching and, in Mick's case, biting Georgie's ear. Georgie was giving almost as good as he got, but the bigger boy was bound to win in the end. However, before either of them had really got into the fight an avenging angel in the form of a girl in the top class came charging in and gave Mick a hard clout round the ear with her satchel. As the attack came from behind and the satchel was heavy with books, Mick was taken off balance and went down on his knees. Seeing his chance, Georgie gave him a boot in the side, which winded him. He lay for a moment, glaring up at the girl who had floored him.

'Bitch!' he snarled. 'You wait until I tell my dad what yer did – he'll come after yer and yer'll be sorry.'

Jenny Rush tossed her fiery red hair and looked at him in scorn. 'He'll more likely take his belt ter yer fer fighting, Mick Bailey. If I hadn't stopped you two, you would both be reported – and you know you're both on a warning. Do you want ter be thrown out of school? It's what my mum says will happen if yer don't stop these fights.'

'He was picking on our Billy again,' Georgie defended defiantly. 'Kicking him – and he pinched the tuppence your ma gave him for his lunch money. And school's closing anyway!'

'You just shut it. You're nearly as bad as he is,' Jenny told him, looking at her uncle with annoyance. 'If you took Billy's money, Mick Bailey, you can just give it back. My Aunt Kate's husband Steve is home on leave and he'll speak to your dad if you don't. Then you'll be for it!'

Mick's eyes sent daggers at her but reluctantly he produced the two pennies from his pocket, giving them to her. 'I was goin' ter give 'em back termorrow,' he said lamely.

'Yeah?' Jenny's eyes flashed with temper. 'Good thing I told yer to then.' She rounded on Georgie as he snorted his pleasure at his enemy's routing. 'You needn't snigger, Georgie Greene. You should've told me or a teacher, not taken it on yourself to get it back.'

'It's my tuppence,' Billy piped up suddenly. 'I said Mick could have it – so it's his.'

'What?' Jenny rounded on her younger brother.

'He said he 'adn't 'ad no breakfast nor no supper neither. Give it back to 'im, Jenny. I ain't 'ungry.'

'Yer never are,' she said, a look of concern chasing the anger from her eyes. Billy was pale and thin, and often suffered from a racking cough in the winter. 'That's Mum's money. She works 'ard for it and if yer don't spend it, yer should give it back to her.'

Georgie was staring at Mick. 'Is it true yer ain't 'ad no breakfast nor supper?' Mick stared at him hard but gave a slight nod. 'Give it 'ere, Jenny,' Georgie said and snatched it from her hand. He handed it to Mick. 'Mum always gives me sandwiches fer me lunch – if yer 'ungry another day I'll share. Just don't take our Billy's money.' Mick stared at him and then took off down the street, running as if he feared they might snatch the coins back.

'What did you want to do that for?' Jenny demanded. Georgie shrugged. 'I thought you 'ated 'im?'

'Sometimes I do,' Georgie replied. 'Ain't nice ter be 'ungry. We're lucky. Mum says we should try to help folk what ain't as well orf as us.'

'Gran's too soft-hearted,' Jenny scoffed and then grinned and reached out to wipe a smear of blood from his ear with her handkerchief. 'You'd best get cleaned up before yer ma sees yer.'

'I'm goin' round our Kate's fer tea again,' Georgie said. He looked at his nephew. 'Do yer want ter come, Billy? Steve's home and he's brought a friend. Chuck's a pilot and an instructor.'

Billy hesitated, his face lit for a moment with interest, but Jenny held out her hand to him imperiously. 'Come on,' she said. 'Mum wants you home. We're 'avin' sausages and chips ternight.'

Billy went with her, sending a regretful glance after his uncle. Georgie shrugged and started to run. He had no idea what Kate would have for their tea. It might be bread and jam, but the lure of stories told by Steve and Chuck about their flying experiences was stronger than his partiality for sausages and chips.

'So we got home on a wing and a prayer,' Chuck said, finishing his hair-raising story of an attack in the air, he and his squadron had survived when surveying German ports. 'I thought I'd had it for sure when we were hit, but somehow we made it back.'

'He landed on one wheel and ended up in a ditch,' Steve chortled. 'Got out all right, all of them, but the plane was in a bit of a mess.'

'Cor! That's excitin',' Georgie breathed, looking at Chuck with awe and respect. He turned to his brother-in-law. 'Steve, you're flying with Chuck now, ain't yer?'

Steve grinned and nodded. 'I'm still training, Georgie, but I've sat in as co-pilot on a couple of reconnaissance missions.'

''Ave yer been shot at, too?' Georgie asked, but Kate had come in with the tea tray and Steve just shook his head. Tea was strawberry jam sandwiches and buttered toast with some sliced tomatoes, followed by seed cake. Georgie wolfed his down and eyed the last piece of cake hungrily. It should have been Chuck's but he said Georgie could have it if it was all right with Kate.

'Just this once then,' she agreed. 'Then you'd best get home or Mum will worry.'

'Nah, she knows I'm wiv you so she won't,' Georgie replied. He glanced at the two men. 'Are you goin' ter the pub ternight?' His hopeful glance disappeared as they nodded. 'I'll walk part of the way wiv yer then.'

'We've got time for a kick about in the street first,' Steve said and laughed as Georgie's face lit once more, knowing full well how much he liked to play football. 'Come on, then.' He glanced at Kate. 'You don't mind?'

'I've got marking to do,' she said, 'after I wash up.'

Steve nodded and he and Chuck led the way out into the street. It was a pleasant early summer evening and several of the local lads were just hanging around. They all looked towards the newcomers, faces beaming as they saw that Steve carried a football. Georgie wasn't the only one who idolized the men in RAF uniforms. Steve had introduced Chuck the first day they were home and now the lads hung on their every word, following their heroes down the street, and wanting to be around them. And it wasn't just because Chuck handed out cigarettes and bubble gum for them to share, though that didn't come amiss. Whether their mothers would have approved of the cigarettes was dubious but the lads, most in their teens, were no strangers to snatching a crafty fag when they got the chance.

As yet the war hadn't truly begun to bite here. Everyone knew it was going on, of course, and some families had already lost sons to the fighting overseas; the papers had been full of it when Norway was lost and Britain had tasted the sourness of seeing a neutral country overrun without being able to stop it, but here, in this quiet little back street, nothing much had changed yet. Now and then a siren would sound but it was always a false alarm and no one bothered to run for the shelters. Apart from when the young gods of the RAF, or other services, came home for a visit, to the boys of Brick Lane, the war was far away – something their fathers might be involved in but not their mothers, younger brothers, and sisters. As yet it was just a dark cloud gathering for the storm.

As the youngsters formed sides, choosing to play with either Steve or Chuck, they were oblivious of how soon their lives would take a turn for the worse or what fate had in store. Charging up and down the street, yelling their heads off as they jostled for the ball, they enjoyed their game and were soon joined by more lads, plus a couple of men home from the docks and ready for some fun.

Georgie had been chosen as a goalkeeper. He watched avidly as the opposing team came towards him and, as Chuck kicked, dived to save the goal. Laughing, because he landed on the ball and managed to keep it safe, he then jumped up and kicked it as far down the street as he could, happiness surging through him. Life was good and although he didn't know it, that night was one he would remember for most of his life.

CHAPTER 4

'Good grief!' Kate's mother cried as she saw the stark headlines in the paper. 'Dunkirk, the last stand of the British Army! That's our lads there, Kate.' She looked up at Kate, fear in her eyes. 'Tom and Derek, that's where they are.' John, the youngest of the three brothers was still training but the elder two had been in the fighting from the start, because they were regular army.

'You don't know that, Mum,' Kate said, trying to reassure her, though her own heart had caught. 'They might be anywhere. We haven't heard a word for months, not since Derek was home on leave.'

'He knew they would be in the thick of it,' Mrs Greene said. 'They're both regular army so they'll be in France.' She shook her head. 'They were so certain the line would hold – thought the Ardennes were impregnable.'

'It looks as if the Allies got caught with their pants down,' Kate agreed, taking the paper her mother had been reading to scan the article. 'It says we're planning a rescue mission, Mum.' She reached for her mother's hand and held it tightly. 'If I know my brothers they'll have made it to the beach.'

'It's getting them off the beach,' her mother said and took a large clean handkerchief from her pocket. She blew her nose hard. 'I just pray they get them all off – but it must be hell out there.'

The newspaper had written a jingoistic article filled with upbeat rhetoric about how a massive rescue was under way. It seemed that besides the Navy's gunboats and destroyers, an army of little boats manned by fishermen and private citizens had set out to get the stranded men off the beach but both Kate and her mother knew what the reality must be. The ships would be under attack from enemy planes and the men on the beach exposed to raking fire as they scrambled through the water to whatever help presented it itself.

'All those men!' Mrs Greene said and tears were trickling down her cheeks. 'It's most of the British Army. If they don't get them back . . .'

'We'll all be speaking German by this time next year,' Kate said, attempting to jest but the look on her mother's face stopped her. 'It won't happen, Mum. They'll get them home and Tom and Derek will be with them. I promise.'

Her mother nodded, swiping the tears from her cheeks and blowing her nose on a crumpled handkerchief. 'I hope to God you're right,' she said and then looked at her. 'So what are you going to do then, Kate? If your school is closing because most of the kids are in the country . . .'

'Don't know.' Kate sighed. 'I've been given a choice: either I evacuate to the country – and they've offered me a job in a junior school – or I leave and find myself some war work.'

'It's not right,' Mrs Greene said. 'Why should you have to leave London or lose your job? You've worked so hard, all through college – and the nights you sat studying when other girls were out havin' fun.'

'It seems a bit unfair,' Kate agreed. 'They need extra teachers in the country since a lot of the city kids are there now and they don't need me here in London. You know they're urging those parents who haven't sent their children away to do so?' She met her mother's distressed gaze. 'What about Georgie, and Vera's three?'

'Georgie refused to go, you know he did,' Mrs Greene said defensively. 'I know you think I ought to have made him, but he didn't want to go – but Vera's thinking about going and taking the children with her.'

'How long has she been saying that?' Kate was surprised as her sister had consistently refused to discuss it.

'Since someone told her that we're going to be invaded very soon and London will be one of the first places they take.' Mrs Greene looked grim. 'Vera thinks we'd *all* be safer in the country but your father's job is here. He's in a protected job, driving for the railways, and he couldn't leave so I'll stay here with him. Georgie doesn't want to go – but if they start sending the kids off again, I'll try to persuade him. He might feel differently if Vera takes her kids to the country. He could stay with them and be fine.'

'Yes, that would certainly be a better idea than letting him go to strangers,' Kate agreed. 'You could go with them, Mum. I'd look after Dad . . .'

'Decided you're stayin' then?' She inclined her head. 'Your dad will be upset – wastin' your education like that, Kate. You know how proud he is that you went to college.'

'It's only for a while.' Kate smiled at her. 'You know I'll be taking leave soon, anyway, Mum because I'm having the baby – but it won't stop me going back to teaching as soon as I can.'

'I suppose that's true.' Her mother smiled but looked a little sad. 'I thought you'd have a bit longer – time to get yourselves organized. You seemed so certain you could manage your lives, but I've told you often enough; babies come along when you're married, whether you're ready or not.'

'I know.' Kate smiled and put her hands on her belly. 'I'm pleased now, I really am – and Steve was too, when he got used to the idea.'

'It will put a damper on all your big plans, love.'

'Only for a while – and the war did that anyway,' Kate said. 'It's going to be rough, Mum. I've already had to queue at the grocer's for my fruit and veg. Mr Samson is rationing what you can buy now. He'd got some bananas in but says it may be the last for a long time. He let me buy two.'

'I got three,' her mother replied with a laugh. 'He's always had a soft spot for me, and he knows your dad likes a banana. Georgie isn't bothered. He likes a tin of peaches or mandarins, but when we'll get any of them again, I don't know – now they've started bombing any ships that supply us.'

Kate nodded, looking serious. 'Some of the shops already have big spaces on their shelves. I'm not sure if they're holding stuff back or they've really run out of tinned goods.'

'Hoarders,' Mrs Greene said with a shake of her head. 'That's what your dad says, Kate. Some people went out and spent all their savings on tinned food and sugar, filling their attics. The Government have clamped down on it now and we'll soon have everything rationed, but for a start it was a free for all with greedy folk making sure they were all right.'

'And be damned to the rest of us,' Kate said but laughed. 'You've got a few bits put by if I know you, Mum.'

Her mother agreed she had, but not boxes of it in the attic, as some folk had done just before the war started.

Georgie arrived then, demanding to know if his tea was ready and Kate took her leave. She walked the short distance to her home, through narrow, often dirty streets, the gutters littered with debris. Some of the houses had paint peeling from the doors and the area was generally rundown. It was where she'd grown up, but it wasn't where she and Steve had planned to spend their lives. Both Londoners, they didn't want to move into the country, even though it was undoubtedly cleaner, but they were determined to find a better area. Perhaps one day even own their home rather than renting, as their parents always had – but the war had put everything on hold and Kate was in a quandary about what she ought to do.

She still had weeks to go before she'd even feel her baby move, months before the child was actually born, and she would be entitled to take leave and return to teaching when she could. Once, she wouldn't have had that chance, but conditions had improved and she looked forward to carrying on with her job when her child was old enough to be left with her mother. Mrs Greene was willing to take the baby whenever Kate was ready but if she was in the country that couldn't happen. No one – not even Hitler – would move her parents from their home. It might be an end terrace but her mother's step was scrubbed white each day and the lace curtains at the windows were spotless. Inside, it was clean and neat. Like Steve, Kate's father didn't bother asking the landlord to do repairs, which he would have ignored. He just got on and did them himself, as did a lot of other men in the back streets of the East End. It was the only way if you wanted a decent home. Landlords were notorious for ignoring requests, so best just keep your mouth shut and do it – if you said a word, it just meant your rent got raised.

Kate couldn't see the point in moving to the country for a few months. She would have to take leave of whatever job she was in when her child was born. Besides, as she'd told Steve, she didn't want to give up their house. So she would have to find some other work in London. The problem was, what could she do? Not many employers would want to take her on, knowing that she would be leaving in a few months to have her baby.

Some of the local lads were out in the lane playing football as she approached her home. She stood for a moment, enjoying the warmth of the evening sun, before inserting her key in the lock and entering her home. Kate dumped her heavy bag on the kitchen table and put the kettle on. She'd brought her marking home again as there never seemed time to do it in class. Her pupils were bright and eager and loved the lessons she set them. Kate taught both history and literature and of late had also been setting sums because the maths teacher had gone off to join the army.

The kettle boiled as she made herself a sandwich of cucumber and tomatoes. The cucumber had come from a pupil's father's greenhouse and he'd sent it in for Kate as a thank you for getting his son through his exams for the higher-grade school. Terry Grant was a bright pupil but had been a bit lazy until he moved into Kate's class. Adding a pinch of salt to her sandwich, Kate had just bitten into it when she heard the knock at the front door. She went to answer it, swallowing her first bite and wondering who it could be at this hour – unless it was Jess from next door on the cadge again, though she always came to the kitchen door when she wanted a cup of sugar.

Opening the door, Kate's heart caught as she saw the youth there in his navy-blue uniform with his red bike. Instantly, she knew it was a telegram and she could hardly breathe as he handed it to her.

'Sorry, missus,' the boy said as he cycled off.

Kate stood staring at the envelope. She felt sick of a sudden and her hand trembled as she shut the door and returned to the kitchen. Who would send her a telegram? Unless . . . it had to be bad news.

She went into the kitchen and sat down, staring at it. Her mouth was dry and she took a gulp of her tea, not wanting to open it. If she didn't read it, it wouldn't be happening . . . But even as her mind warned her not to look, she was reaching for that horrid buff envelope and tearing it open, her eyes catching the most relevant words.

Sorry to inform you . . . Derek Greene was killed in action . . .

Tears sprang to Kate's eyes and the words blurred in front of her. Her throat caught with emotion and she gave a little cry of distress.

Her brother Derek had been killed in action. He wasn't one of the survivors on the beach at Dunkirk and he wouldn't be coming home.

Kate wept. The hard choking sobs wracked her body as she thought of her cheerful brother, always smiling, always looking for the bright side of things. He'd chosen the army as his profession straight from school, starting out as a proud cadet and working his way up to Sergeant. Killed in action. That probably meant no body would be returned – in the retreat to the beaches the dead would have been left behind.

What would her mother do? Kate's tears dried as she thought of her mother, so loving and proud of her sons. She would be devastated.

Getting up, Kate washed her face. She looked at her tea but knew she couldn't face it. She had to go and tell her mother the awful news. Mrs Greene would wonder why the telegram had come to Kate, but Kate knew. Derek had told her he'd put her down as his next of kin.

'You'll break it to Mum if the worst happens,' he'd told her as he'd given her a brotherly hug. 'Besides, I stay with you so it makes it easier giving them just the one address.'

'You'll be back home before you know it,' Kate had assured him as she hugged him back. 'Just keep your head down and don't be a hero.'

'Trust me for that,' he'd laughed and whistled as he left. Now he wouldn't be coming back.

Georgie was out in the street with his mates, playing rounders. He saw Kate and ran to greet her. 'What's up, Kate?' he asked as he saw her face. 'Dad's home havin' his tea.'

'I've had some news,' Kate said, reaching for his hand. 'You'd better come in, too, love.'

'Is it Derek?' Georgie asked and she nodded. 'I had a bad feelin' . . . is he . . .?' Kate nodded again and saw his face crumple with grief. Tears sprang to his eyes but he knuckled them away. 'Go on, I'll be there in a bit . . .' he mumbled in a thick voice.

'Don't go too far. Are you all right?' she asked.

Georgie nodded but didn't speak. He walked and then ran off down the lane. Kate wanted to call him back but didn't. Perhaps he couldn't bear to witness his parents' grief. It would be hard enough for her.

Kate's mother looked up as she entered. She took one look at her face and gave a moan, sitting down abruptly on a chair. 'Which one?' she asked.

'Gracie . . .' Kate's father said, looking at her anxiously. Then: 'Kate?'

'The telegram came to me,' she replied. 'Derek told me he'd given my address because he stayed with me these days.'

Kate's mother bowed her head, covering her face with her hands. She was weeping, deep, silent sobs that wracked her whole body and then she let out a wail of despair.

'I knew it,' she muttered. 'When I saw that headline, I just knew it . . .'

'If Kate's had the telegram, it must have been a while back,' her father said heavily. 'In all that chaos happening now . . . no, it must have been a week or two back.' He looked at Kate. 'Does it say?' It seemed that he needed to know the date of his son's death so she gave him the crumpled paper she'd screwed up in her hand. He read it and nodded, seeming satisfied. 'It was last month – three weeks ago by the date.'

'I didn't read it all,' Kate choked, her gaze on her mother's ravaged face.

'Says he's to be commended for bravery . . .' Her father looked at her and she saw pride along with grief in his eyes.

'Oh, Dad,' Kate whispered and went to put her arm about her mother's shoulders, but she shrugged her off. 'Mum, I'm so sorry . . .'

Her mother gave a huge sniff and then wiped her face. She straightened her body and looked up. 'It's what the lad wanted – to be a soldier. Well, he got his wish. I'm just glad he didn't have a wife and kids . . . he didn't have much life at all.'

'Gracie . . .' Kate's father said. 'Don't let it make you bitter. Derek was doing his duty. He was happy to do it . . .'

Gracie got up, ignored both her daughter and

husband as she shrugged on a coat. 'Where are you going, Mum?' Kate asked.

'For a walk,' she answered without looking at them. 'Just leave me be – both of you.'

Kate looked at her father as she went out. 'Should I go after her – or you?'

'She wouldn't thank you for it,' he replied with a sigh. 'Just leave her be as she asked, Kate. She'll come back when she's ready. If she needs to be alone it's best to let her.'

Kate sat next to him. 'She's hurting. I know she's been worried sick for them all – but he isn't the only one. They all had to go and a lot won't come home.'

Her father reached for her hand. 'We're all hurting, but you're right – a lot of our boys won't come back.' He cleared his throat. 'I'm proud of my boys. None of them would have got out of it if they could. Derek's gone, lass, but he won't be forgotten.'

'No, he won't,' Kate agreed. 'Do you need anything? A cup of tea?'

'Nay, love. I'll just sit here with my pipe for a bit,' he said and she thought he suddenly looked aged and tired. 'If you see our Georgie, send him in.'

'Yes, I will,' she agreed and dropped a kiss on his head as she stood. 'I need to get home, Dad. I've got work to do . . .'

'Aye, you get off home . . .'

Kate left him sitting there. She knew his heart was breaking but he wouldn't let on. He would keep it inside and hold his memories close.

Walking home, she thought that settled it. She

couldn't leave London now even if she wanted. Her family was grieving and the dreadful thing was there were still two brothers who might be in danger at any time. How her family would bear it if any more were killed, Kate just didn't know.

CHAPTER 5

'I shan't go,' Georgie stated, a mulish look on his mouth. 'You can't make me. I'm stayin' 'ere wiv me family.'

'Well, that's where you're wrong, my lad,' his mother said, giving him a firm look. 'Vera's off next week and she says you can go with her. Billy, Jenny, and baby Sally are goin' with her so you'll be with your family.'

'You ain't comin' nor Dad nor Kate,' Georgie cried stubbornly. 'I don't like Vera as much as Kate – she hits me round the ear and she's got a spiteful tongue.'

'Your sister only hits you if you cheek her,' his mother retorted. 'I want you gone to safety and I won't let you change my mind. I've lost my eldest but I won't lose my youngest to this damned war.'

'It ain't my fault that—' Georgie held back the words. His mother couldn't bear to hear Derek's name spoken. She'd gone a bit quiet after the news and Georgie thought she acted strange sometimes, staring into the distance, and talking to someone he couldn't see. He wondered if she was talking to Derek but daren't ask, because she would get angry and shout at him if he so much as spoke of his dead brother. Kate and his father said she was grieving and would get over it, but Georgie, grieving himself, resented that she didn't seem to want him around any longer.

'Your dad's puttin' one of them shelters in the back yard,' his mother said. 'But they don't look as if they'd stop a bomb to me – and, besides, your school is closing this weekend. It's off to the country with your sister you go, Georgie.'

Georgie stared at her in silence. He knew that once his mother made up her mind, she wouldn't listen to him. She'd always been fairly easy going, letting him play in the lanes until dusk and not getting angry unless he went off somewhere without letting anyone know. She'd changed and he didn't much like it. He wanted his mother back the way she'd always been, loving and happy, always laughing at something Dad or Kate said. Georgie hadn't seen her smile since the news came. It was as if a light had switched off inside her, and he knew his father saw it too. The puzzled look in his eyes was just the way Georgie felt. As if they were no longer important and the only one that mattered was Derek.

'I'll ask Kate if I can stay wiv 'er,' he said defiantly but his mother just shook her head. Georgie's heart sank. She would send him to the country with his sister Vera and his nieces and nephew – who were all right – but Vera was always getting at Georgie for something. He didn't want to give in, but he knew his father would just look sad and tell him to do as his mother said so it was no use asking him.

'You'll do as I tell you,' his mother repeated, and Georgie kicked the leg of the kitchen table sulkily. He had a good mind to run off. That would show her.

'Why? There ain't no bombs,' he said, fighting a losing battle. 'Might never be any.'

'Oh, it's comin' all right,' his mother said. 'If we don't all starve, they'll blow us to smithereens.'

Georgie knew there were shortages of everything. You couldn't get an iced bun at the corner shop and some foodstuffs just weren't on the shelves. No dried fruits or sugar, even, on some days, and though folk were digging up their gardens to grow vegetables or rear chickens and pigs, there was a fear that the food would run out. Everything was either rationed or about to be, according to the newspapers.

'They've got more food in the country,' his mother told him. 'Vera has taken a farm cottage so you'll get a fresh egg for your tea like as not down there.'

Georgie muttered something rude under his breath and she glared at him. 'It's what's right for you,' she told him in a voice of finality. 'You'll thank me for it one day.'

'When do I go then?' he asked sullenly.

'Next Monday. You'll go on the train with Vera and the others – it will be fun. It's better than goin' to strangers.' Georgie nodded and turned towards the door. 'Where do you think you're off to?'

'I'm goin' to see Kate,' Georgie replied. 'I shan't run off – not yet, anyway.' For a moment he glared at her, disliking her for the first time in his life. 'But if I hate it down there, I shan't stay . . .' He went out before his mother could answer.

'Why can't I stay here with you if Mum doesn't want me around?' Georgie asked Kate as she spread a slice of

37

bread for him, half margarine, and half butter. They'd all had to start using margarine now; it wasn't as nice as butter but it was OK. 'I don't like Vera as much as you, Kate.'

'Vera's all right,' Kate said but smiled, because she knew her little brother and Vera didn't always get on. 'Mum is just worried sick something will happen to you. She even tried to persuade me to go with you though she knows I've just got a job at the library in Oxford Street – well, just off it, but not far away.'

Georgie nodded. His dad had said the same. 'Will you like being at the library, Kate?'

'Not as much as teaching, but the head librarian is trying to get some evening classes going. She thinks it's somewhere for kids to come with their mothers. We'll be giving them a cup of tea and a biscuit so it might work.'

Georgie looked at her. 'What sort of classes? If it's boring stuff like history no one will come.'

'History isn't boring.' Kate shook her head at him. 'I think we're starting with English literature. It will be a sort of a book club, I suppose. It's just a way of trying to help folk. Not everyone has a home to go to, Georgie, and a lot of women must be feeling lonely with their husbands away.'

'Like you?' Georgie said, looking at her, his eyes bright. 'You miss Steve, don't you?' She nodded, her eyes sad. 'I'd be a bit of company for you, Kate – couldn't you ask Mum to let me stay with you?'

'If they start bombing us, my house is just as likely to get hit as anyone else's,' Kate told him. 'Mum wants you to go to the country to be safe, Georgie.'

'I know.' He shrugged. 'She's gone queer since Derek was killed. I don't think she cares about the rest of us anymore.'

'That's not true,' Kate told him sharply. 'She's just grieving. Derek was her eldest boy but she would be just as upset if it was any of us.' Kate's eyes rested on his face for a moment. 'I know you feel shut out, love – I do, too, just a bit, and I think Dad feels the same. Mum is hurting so badly she can't think of our feelings for the moment, but she still loves us.'

'OK, I'll go if you say I have to,' Georgie conceded grudgingly. 'But if I hate it, I'm coming back. I don't care what anyone says!'

'Give yourself a chance. You might find it fun. There will be animals on the farms, perhaps horses. You liked riding on a pony when we went to the seaside. Do you remember when Steve took us, just before I got married?'

'Course I do,' Georgie said. 'I hate bloody Hitler! It was fun when Steve was around. He was going to take me with yer when you went on holiday to Clacton this summer.'

'We shan't get a seaside holiday this year,' Kate told him. 'I doubt we'll get one for a while but Steve won't forget. He'll take you like he promised – you'll just have to wait a while.'

'Yeah, I know.' Georgie finished his bread. 'Thanks, Kate. I like comin' to you. I'll miss yer . . .' He sniffed, wiping his nose on his shirt sleeve, the suspicion of a tear in his eyes.

'I'll try and come down one weekend soon,' Kate told him. 'You're not going to the end of the world,

Georgie. I can get on a train and visit – and it's only until things settle down.' A look of anxiety creased her brow. 'With all this talk of invasion everyone is jittery. We never thought the British Army could be beaten the way they were.'

'It's a miracle they got most of the soldiers off the beaches,' Georgie said. 'There were some aerial pictures in Dad's paper. It looked as if one of our ships was being attacked and there were men queuing in the water.'

'At least Tom got taken off safely,' Kate said. 'Mum had a letter from his captain. He's in hospital somewhere at the moment. None of us can visit yet, but they'll let us know when we can go.'

'Maybe Mum will feel better when she sees him,' Georgie said. He stood up. 'I'd better get back. She'll be wondering where I am.'

'Yes, she will,' Kate agreed. She reached for her purse and took out a pound note, offering it to him. 'Don't spend this, Georgie. Keep it safe and it'll get you home to us if you really can't bear it down there with Vera.'

'I love you!' Georgie flung himself on her and hugged her. 'You're the best sister in the world.'

'Thanks!' Kate's eyes sparkled with amusement. 'But give it a go, Georgie – there's a good lad.'

He nodded, grinning as he stuffed his fortune into his trouser pocket. He'd never had as much money in his life, even on his birthday. A pound would buy bags of sweets and— No, he wouldn't spend it, not yet. He would keep it like Kate said in case he really needed it . . .

CHAPTER 6

Georgie's father took him for a walk by the river on Sunday morning. They found a nice spot away from the docks and the warehouses, sitting on a patch of grass in the June sunshine, watching a couple of swans drift by, seemingly with no effort, though beneath the water their webbed feet must have been working like mad.

'Your ma isn't very happy just now,' Georgie's father said after they'd been sitting in harmony without speaking for a while. 'She's sending you away because she's afraid the enemy will invade England at any moment and they'll make sure of London if they do.'

'Then why don't we all go to the country?' Georgie asked, looking at him. 'If they drop bombs on London, you could be killed.'

'I've got a job to do,' Mr Greene said and drew on his pipe. 'I can't desert my post, Georgie. They could lock me up if I did – and it would be cowardice, see. I'm fighting for my country same as the soldiers but in a different way.'

'I'd rather stay and fight, too. I could leave school and get a job.'

'Nay, lad. Labouring is all you'd get – if anyone would take you on. You need to finish your schooling and do something worthwhile, like our Kate.'

'I don't want to teach a lot of boring lessons. I'd rather drive a train like you, Dad.'

'Well, you need to be a bit older to do that,' his father said, still in the same calm voice he always used. 'You might get some Saturday and holiday work on the farm, though. I reckon strong lads like you could do the work of men what have gone off to fight.'

Georgie hadn't considered this and he looked at his father with interest. 'Would they let me drive a tractor?'

'They might if they've got time to teach you,' his father said. 'I'm not sure just what goes on – I'm a Londoner bred and born – but it might be all right, and it's just until you can come home safe. Once all this talk of invasion is over, I'll persuade your mum to let yer come home.'

'Promise?'

'Cross me 'eart and 'ope ter die.' His father smiled at him then reached into his pocket and brought out a ten-shilling note. 'This is for pocket money, Georgie. Don't spend it all at once.'

Georgie hesitated. 'Our Kate gave me some money but she said to save it in case I needed it.'

'Well, this is for spending. Vera won't give you any pocket money so you'll need to do a few jobs, earn yourself a couple of bob now and then.'

Georgie took the money, slipping it into his pocket. He felt a bit nervous having so much and decided to take great care of it. His dad worked long hours for his money and most of his life they'd done all right,

42

never having a lot to spare but always food on the table and decent shoes and clothes. His Mum hadn't gone to work since she married. Dad would have been ashamed to let her.

They got up as a party of young people arrived, intent on a picnic; it was three soldiers in uniforms and their girls, all wearing pretty summer frocks and sandals. They were laughing and talking a lot and the peace was shattered.

Georgie's dad gave him a bit of a wink and they walked off, turning back homewards in time for lunch; it was going to be a special one, because it was the last Georgie would have with his parents for a while.

Reconciled to his lot, if not yet happy about it, the boy walked in silence with his father. His dad never talked that much as a rule, but when he did it always helped, and Georgie felt better. He would still rather stay home but now he was accepting.

Vera had a mountain of luggage. She'd arranged for someone she knew to fetch them all in his van and transport them to the railway station and Jock McBride shook his head as he looked at all the suitcases.

'You'll never manage all them on the train,' he told her, his deep voice carrying the burr of his Scottish heritage, though he'd lived in London for the past ten years or more.

'Yes, I will,' Vera insisted. 'I'll carry the two big ones. Jenny can carry two of the smaller ones and Billy can take his satchel. Georgie will carry his own stuff.'

'What about baby Sally?' Jock asked.

'She'll be in a shawl tied round my chest.' Vera

replied. 'Stop fussing, Jock. This is only a half of what I'll need for a long stay. Dad says he'll bring more down one weekend if he gets time.'

'I reckon I'd best take you all the way,' Jock said. 'I'd never feel right in my mind if I let you get on a train with all this.'

'Oh well, if you're going to take us all the way . . .' Vera handed the baby to Georgie. 'I'll run in and fetch that other suitcase . . .'

Jock watched her go, shaking his head at Georgie. 'She's a rare one, that sister of yours, Georgie. Why she needs all this stuff . . . but I promised your brother-in-law I'd look after her and the kids and I will. To be honest, I thought this might happen and I stocked up on petrol in case.' He jerked his head at his large van. 'Climb in the back, kids. There's a couple of cans of petrol in there so it might smell a bit, but I couldn't be sure I'd get any on the way so I'm taking it with me. I've got a full tank but I ain't certain it will get me there and back.' Jock worked on the docks in a reserved occupation and he'd promised his best friend he'd look out for his family.

Georgie did as he said, still holding the baby in one arm. Jenny scrambled after him, settling on the blankets Jock had put down for them.

'Ugh, it stinks of petrol,' Jenny said with a grimace. 'Here, give me the baby.' Georgie handed her over willingly and Jenny nuzzled the warm bundle, which smelled of talcum powder and soap.

'I thought we were goin' on a train,' Billy grumbled as he scrambled in after them. 'It smells horrible in here and you can't see nuthin'.'

The only light came from the front of the van. It was also a bit squashed and airless when Jock had finished packing in all the suitcases and a basket of food that Georgie's mother rushed out with just before they left.

'I packed paste and jam and some cake,' she told them, giving the basket to Georgie. 'There's half a banana each and a bottle of ginger beer, oh, and some water. I thought you might get a drink on the train but Vera says you're goin' in this van.'

'It stinks in here, Granny,' Billy wailed. 'I don't like it in 'ere.'

As Jock shut the back doors on them, Billy screamed. He screamed so loudly that the doors were opened by a cross-looking Vera, who grabbed him and the baby and pushed them into the front seat with her and Jock.' She called over her shoulder to the two in the back. 'Just behave and we'll soon be there.'

'It's all right for her,' Jenny said resentfully. 'I'll be sick before we get there. The smell of that petrol is awful.'

'I just hope it doesn't spill over,' Georgie muttered, because he was the one nearest to it. Although the cans rocked a bit as the van moved off, they were secured and the tops on tight so no liquid spilled.

Folk often travelled with spare petrol in cans, because they were never sure these days whether the garages would have any in. Government sources published that stocks were adequate but with ships getting bombed on the Atlantic run, it was obvious that they wouldn't last forever. So even if you'd got coupons, it didn't mean there would be any to buy.

Georgie felt a bit sick, too. The smell was very unpleasant and sitting in an airless van for mile after mile, bumping over every little dip in the road, was very uncomfortable, but instead of constantly moaning the way Jenny did, he simply put up with it.

'You OK back there?' Jock asked after they'd been driving a while.

'I feel sick,' Jenny retorted. 'I shall be if I don't get some air.'

'I'll open a window,' Jock said and did so. 'There – that better . . .?'

It did help a little, though Jenny continued to complain. Georgie started to get a headache but he wasn't going to say. He gritted his teeth and got on with it – like his dad said a man had to when things were bad. All he hoped was they would have a few stops on the way or he was sure Jenny would make things worse by casting up her breakfast all over him.

Jenny was sick about an hour after they left London. Jock had stopped the van at the side of the road so that she could get out and vomit on a patch of grass. It was a quiet stretch of road, winding through villages and they decided to go on a short distance and find somewhere they could all get out, walk around, and eat their food.

Jenny continued to complain even after they'd had a break of half an hour, but Vera made her get into the back of the van once more. Georgie thought she might have offered to change places with her daughter for a while, but she didn't. Maybe it was because she had to nurse the baby and keep an eye on Billy. He hadn't said a word since he'd got to ride in the front. Naturally, it was better riding up front where there was more air and you could see what was going on. Had they gone on the train as intended, it would have been much nicer for everyone. It was all Vera's fault for bringing too much stuff, Georgie thought. In his opinion, Vera never thought about anyone else but herself. Hearing her laughing with Jock up front, his blood boiled. She was flirting like mad and his brother-in-law Bob would be furious if he knew.

'I hate this,' Jenny muttered through gritted teeth. 'I'm never goin' ter ride in a van again.'

'It's probably all right in the front,' Georgie told her. It was the stink of the petrol that was making him feel bad. He thought his mum would go mad if she knew they'd been forced to ride like this for so long with petrol cans rattling beside them. He could just imagine what she'd say: 'If there's an accident that van could go up like a bomb and they'd all be killed!' She would never have let them go if she'd known about the petrol cans.

Georgie let his thoughts dwell darkly on the likelihood of an accident making the van go up like a bomb. What would it feel like to catch fire?

It couldn't be much worse than he felt now, he reckoned. Every bone in his body ached from being cramped and jolted over endless ruts in the road. They hadn't been aware of them so much in town but once they got on to the narrow country roads it got worse and worse.

'Gran wouldn't have let us come if she'd known,' Jenny said, shooting a venomous look at her mother's back. 'I reckon Mum planned it just to get a day out with her fancy man.'

'He ain't – is he?' Georgie shot a look at the back of the adults in the front. Could they hear what Jenny was saying? She would catch it later if so.

Jenny leaned towards him confidentially. 'Dad thinks he comes round for him when he's home but he fancies her. I've seen them making eyes at each other – and I saw something else.'

'What?' Georgie asked curiously but Jenny wasn't telling.

'How much longer?' she sighed. 'If we don't soon get there, I'm goin' ter be sick again!'

They finally turned on to a road with a sign that said The Isle of Ely and then a bit further on – Witchford, Sutton, Witcham, Mepal. It was here that Jock started to look for the names of roads and he finally found the one he wanted – Chatteris. 'Nearly there, kids,' he said over his shoulder.

'About bloody time,' Jenny muttered and her mother turned to look at her sharply.

'That's enough of that,' she said then looked at Jock. 'Do you think we're goin' the right way – those signs aren't pointin' the way my map shows.'

Jock pulled over and looked at the piece of paper she'd been given. 'Damn it!' he swore. 'Looks like we took a wrong turning back there.'

'Someone has switched the signs all round to confuse

48

the enemy,' Georgie said. 'Kate said a lot of places had taken their signs down or made them point the wrong way.'

Jock studied the hand-drawn map and then his road map. He muttered a few curses but did a three-point turn on a narrow road with steep dykes on either side and followed a road that was not signposted at all but seemed to be leading to nowhere.

'Bloody hell!' Vera was frustrated, tired and fed-up because the baby had cried and screamed for the past few miles. 'I never thought it was out in the wilds of nowhere. I thought there was a village or something close by.'

'There is,' Jock told her. 'About a mile or so further on from where we turned off, there's a small town – well, not much bigger than a village according to my book – but they call it a town. It has shops and a train station, and about fifteen miles the other way there's Ely – pictures there and I expect there'll be a bus now and then.'

Vera didn't say anything. Georgie thought she was shocked to discover how far from anywhere they were. 'There's a farm over there!' Jock said suddenly. 'Fen View . . . Well, that's right enough. We're in the fens. You can see for miles around; it's all flat fields and a couple of trees.'

'I was told to ask at the farmhouse and they'll give me the key,' Vera said as they stopped outside a gate with a big Keep Out notice.

Jock came round and opened the door so that the children could jump out. It was nearly dusk and there was a swirl of mist over the furthest fields. Georgie shivered. He wasn't exactly afraid of this alien country but it felt a bit creepy. Jenny grabbed his arm tightly.

'It's horrible,' she muttered. 'Mum must be mad to bring us here.'

Georgie thought he agreed, but kept his silence. He watched as Jock opened the gate and Vera marched up to the farmhouse, her heeled shoes making her progress difficult in the rutted earth that had dried hard in the summer sun but must be just mud in winter.

Billy was sitting on the grass at the side of the road, tears trickling down his pale cheeks. 'What's wrong, mate?' Georgie asked. Billy shook his head, sniffed, and scuffed the tears away.

'Maybe it won't be too bad,' Georgie said. 'There's plenty of space to play football – and a couple of trees to climb. If we can borrow some bikes we can go exploring. Might get a bus and go to the pictures one day . . .'

Vera came back bearing a large metal key. She didn't look very happy. 'It's about half a mile further down – Lovesedge Cottage.'

'Right-ho,' Jock said. 'Good job I brought you, Vera. You would never have made it here with the kids and all that luggage. Cost you a fortune for a taxi and I ain't sure how often the buses run.'

'Mrs Baker told me there's a good service,' Vera told him. 'They run every few hours to Chatteris and March, and the other way to the villages we passed and Ely. There's one to Cambridge but that's only twice a week and just one there and one back. Not that I want to go there . . .' She seemed to have cheered up a bit and when they got to the cottage, which was pretty with a nice front garden and a bigger one out the back, Georgie saw why. Inside was clean and neat and there was a fresh loaf on the table, together with some other foodstuffs that had been hard to get in London in the pantry. A basket with six eggs, a pat of farm-fresh butter – a little melted, despite it being cool inside – and a pot of soft white cheese, together with a brown paper bag of tomatoes that smelled wonderful. Also, some large potatoes and a piece of home-cooked ham together with a freshly picked lettuce and some other vegetables that had clearly come from the farm.

'Well, at least they've made you welcome,' Jock said. 'It was good of them to provide all this food – did you have to pay them?'

'Not as such . . .' Vera said and looked a bit guilty. 'I'm going to help Mrs Baker in the kitchen and dairy and . . .' She looked at Georgie. 'I've promised that the boys will help on the farm on Saturdays. In return Mr Baker will take the kids to the end of the drove to catch the bus for school in the mornings. He has to leave the milk churns there so . . .'

Georgie looked at her. 'That's the first I've heard about workin' on the farm,' he said, giving her a look of dislike. 'What if I don't want to?'

'You can walk to school in the mornin' then,' Vera told him bluntly. 'Billy can't do much but he can collect eggs and feed chickens and pigs – and you can help in the dairy, too, Jenny.'

Jenny looked at her mother sulkily. 'I'm not stoppin' 'ere,' she announced. 'I hate it – it's scary and lonely!'

51

She shuddered. 'I'm goin' back to London with Jock. I can live with Gran.'

'You'll do as I tell you!' Vera said sternly. 'I know it's strange but it won't be so bad once you've had something to eat and settled your rooms . . .'

'I ain't 'ungry,' Jenny declared. 'I don't care where I sleep. I'm not stayin'.'

'You will stay if I have to lock you up,' her mother said.

'Shan't! I know what you do and I'll tell Dad!' A sharp gasp followed by a slap made Jenny yell and then burst into tears. She whirled round and dashed out of the house, running back the way they'd just come.

'Jenny! Come back here!' Vera called after her but she just kept running. She whirled round to look at Jock. 'Go after her, please?'

'Nay, lass. Where can she go?' Jock said. 'I'm thinking she'll be back soon enough. She has no idea where to go and she won't stay out there in the dark.'

Georgie went upstairs. He found two bedrooms and a tiny boxroom that had a camp bed in it. One of the larger rooms had two single beds and the other had a double. He and Billy could share a room but that left just the box room for Jenny. Georgie didn't think she would be too happy on the camp bed. He tried sitting on it and it wasn't very comfortable. Frowning, he went back down to the kitchen.

'Jenny won't like her room,' he told his sister. 'There's a double with two single beds Billy and I can share and a room for you and the baby, but the other one just has a camp bed. She won't put up with that.'

'That one's for you,' Vera told him shortly. 'Jenny

52

shares a room with Billy at home. Your gran hung a curtain up for privacy – but half the time Billy gets in bed with his sister. You'll prefer a room on your own, Georgie.'

'Want to share with Georgie,' Billy piped up. 'Jenny's mean to me.'

'Oh, for goodness' sake!' Vera was exasperated and burst into noisy tears. 'Can't you kids ever behave?'

Billy was shocked into silence by the sight of his mother in tears. Her face went red and patchy. Jock patted her shoulder kindly and tried to comfort her.

'I did it for the best,' she said between sobs. 'I'm scared to death the Germans will invade and take London and we'll all be shot or thrown into prison camps. Down here – well, I doubt they'll bother to come lookin'.'

'That's right, you'll be safer here,' Jock told her and gave her his handkerchief. 'I'd best leave, because it will be dark soon and I've a long way to drive.'

'Couldn't you stay overnight, to see us settled in?' Vera asked him, the look in her eyes giving Georgie food for thought. Jenny might be right about them getting together.

'I'd like to, you know that,' Jock told her and squeezed her hand, 'but I have to be back to work in the morning, love. I'll come down when I can get a couple of days off and stay overnight then. I can sleep on the settee . . .' He'd looked in the parlour. 'That's comfortable enough. Jenny could sleep there if she doesn't like her room. It might be best if she had her own now.'

Vera nodded. She went outside with him and closed

the door. Georgie started to carry the cases up the stairs. He'd put his own things in the smaller double room and Jenny's in the boxroom. She might kick up a fuss but she'd probably be subdued when she came back later and just agree to it – though Georgie was sure she would have enough to say when she got over her fit of the sullens.

CHAPTER 7

Jenny wasn't back by the time it was dark, which was almost nine o'clock. Vera glanced at her wristwatch every so often and grumbled to herself, muttering the things she'd do to her daughter when she got back, but she was busy unpacking and it wasn't until Georgie asked if he should go and look for her that she looked a bit worried.

'Have you got a torch, because I haven't?' she said crossly. 'Billy it's time you went to bed. Georgie should be there, too, but . . .' She sighed. 'Just go out and call for her, Georgie, but don't wander off. It's not that cold. If she's got lost it's her own fault . . .'

Georgie shrugged his jacket on and went outside. The daylight had faded and for a few moments he couldn't see much, but then, as if by magic, a cloud rolled away and there was enough moonlight to see where he was going. He walked a few yards down the narrow track that had brought them to the cottage; it wasn't a proper road. The farmer's wife had called it Fen Drove and he thought it was normally used just by tractors and horses – or a wandering cow. He'd seen cows in the flesh for the first time that afternoon and he thought he could hear sounds of lowing somewhere, though he wasn't sure which direction it came from. Perhaps a meadow nearer the farm so they would be easier to bring in for the milking.

Georgie cupped his hands about his mouth and called Jenny's name. He called it over and over for several minutes. 'Come on, Jenny! Your mum is worried. Don't be daft . . .'

He listened but there was no answering cry. He'd thought Jenny was just sulking but now he wondered if she'd hurt herself, maybe fallen into one of the steep dykes that he'd seen on the way here. Yet it had been light when she went out. Surely she didn't intend to stay out all night?

Glancing back at the cottage as he heard his sister call his name, Georgie turned and walked back to her. She was standing in the doorway and had an oil lamp in her hand. It was the only form of lighting in the cottage, apart from the candles he'd seen in the bedrooms.

'Do you think she's fallen and hurt herself?' Georgie asked his sister when he got back to the cottage.

'How do I know? She is the most provoking girl!' Vera said, looking annoyed. 'It's time you and Billy were in bed.'

'If you give me that lamp, I could walk down to the farm and see if she went there,' he suggested.

'Why would she do that?' Vera asked. 'Jenny knows how to look after herself. You and Billy go to bed. I'll sit up in the kitchen and wait for her.'

Georgie hesitated, but although he could see when

the clouds parted, they had a habit of obscuring the moon and he couldn't find his way to the farm without the lamp. He went back into the cottage. Billy was sitting on a chair reading a comic. He looked up as Billy came over to him.

'Where did Jenny go?' he asked in a whisper.

'Dunno – maybe to the farm. I saw some barns on the way 'ere. She might 'ave crept in one.'

'Yeah.' Billy glanced at his mother, keeping his voice low. 'She didn't want ter come, said she would make Mum let her go back to London. I reckon she's trying to frighten us.'

'Yeah, mebbe,' Georgie agreed. Jenny was fiery and apt to tantrums if she didn't get her own way. 'I wouldn't want to be out there on my own all night, but Jenny might have somethin' planned.'

'What do yer mean?' Billy asked.

'Tell yer upstairs,' Georgie said. 'Vera, can we have a biscuit and a glass of milk, please?'

'There's only enough milk for a drink in the morning. You can have a glass of water – and there are some digestives in that tin. Now go up to bed. I've got enough to worry about without you pair playing up.'

Georgie thought that was unfair as neither of them had been any trouble but he helped himself to a couple of biscuits and drew water from the tap over the sink. Pushing Billy in front of him, he clattered up the stained wood stairs. There was a single oil lamp burning on a table at the top of the stairs. It wasn't as bright as the electric they were used to at home, but they found their way to the bedroom easily enough. Once there, Georgie lit the candle he'd seen earlier with a match from the box of Swan safety matches that lay beside it and then shut the door.

'Jenny has enough money to get back to London,' Georgie told Billy when he was sure his sister Vera couldn't hear. 'She said if she hated it here, she would go straight back to Gran and I reckon that's what she's done. She'll have gone to Chatteris which isn't more than a couple of miles or so once you get back to the main road. If she went to the station and there was a train she might be on her way home now.'

'Lucky her,' Billy said in a small voice. 'I don't like it here much either, do you, Georgie?'

'Not much,' he admitted. 'It's the middle of nowhere and a bit strange but I promised Dad, I would give it a fair try and I shall.'

Billy nodded solemnly. An owl hooted nearby, making both boys jump. 'What's that?' he asked nervously.

'It's a bird, an owl I reckon,' Georgie told him. 'There's a lot of queer noises here – animals, I think. Cows and other creatures, but they won't hurt us, Billy. If the Germans invade London, they'll probably kill us, that's what your mum and Gran think. So even if we're miserable here we might be better orf.'

Billy looked at him thoughtfully. 'Can we push them beds close together? I'm a bit scared . . .'

'Course we can,' Georgie agreed. He got one side of the single bed nearest to the door and pushed. It took a bit of shoving but after a couple of minutes he had them together so that one bed was right up against the far wall and the other touching it. 'You climb over into the one near the wall,' he told Billy. 'I'll protect yer, but there really ain't nuthin' ter worry for.'

'Thanks, Georgie. I'm glad you're 'ere.'

Georgie grunted and slipped into bed beside his nephew. Neither of them had taken off their clothes. It seemed colder than they were used to, though the day had been warm enough; or maybe they just felt safer that way. Everything was strange and different and the only adult they had to turn to wasn't the sympathetic type. If approached because they were nervous and unsettled, Vera would simply tell them not to be daft or get cross.

'I hope Jenny's all right,' Billy said as Georgie blew the candle out.

'Yeah, me, too,' Georgie replied. 'Get some sleep. Yer mum will be busy sorting out schools and things tomorrow. We'll 'ave ter be ready for all sorts.'

'Night, then . . .' Billy settled against Georgie, snuggling into his body for warmth and comfort. After a very few minutes, he was gently snoring, sound asleep. Georgie lay wakeful for a while. He hoped Jenny was safe and on her way home. She'd been miserable all the way here and, although she'd talked wildly of running away, he'd only half-believed her.

Georgie would like to go home on the next train himself, but he'd promised his dad to give it a try – and there was Billy and the baby. Vera was set on staying, despite the cottage being much more isolated than they'd expected and Georgie knew he was the man of the family here and he felt a bit responsible for them. He couldn't just hop it. Vera had taken on more than she'd looked for, in Georgie's opinion. She might get fed up with being stuck out here on her own and take them all home if he was patient.

Georgie's mum needed a little time to grieve for her eldest son. Maybe in a few weeks, when she felt better, she'd be glad to have them all back . . .

A cock crowing woke Georgie as soon as it was light. Billy was still curled into his side under the blankets, fast asleep. He'd been very tired and Georgie had slept well too, better than he'd expected. Slipping cautiously from the bed, he crept to the window and looked out. A faint mist had been lying over the land the previous evening, but it had gone now and the day looked as if it would be fine. It was still a bit chilly, though, and Georgie rubbed his arms, looking round for his jacket. Pulling it on, he decided to go downstairs and investigate.

Trying not to wake anyone, he trod softly down the stairs, wincing as one of them creaked. When he got to the kitchen, he saw that his sister was sleeping on the daybed. The oil lamp had burned itself out and the stove was cold too. There was no sign of Jenny. Obviously, she hadn't returned or Vera would have gone to bed.

Georgie went to look in the stove. The fire had burned very low but it was still smouldering. He took a couple of logs and inserted them into the fire, giving it a gentle stir with an iron poker. Although he tried hard not to make a noise, his sister sat up suddenly and looked at him.

'Jenny?' she asked, and as he looked at her, he saw her reddened eyes and realized she must have been crying before she slept.

'I haven't seen her,' he said. 'I didn't look upstairs . . .'

'Go and look, just to make sure,' his sister requested

and so he did, returning to shake his head at her look of hope.

'She didn't come back,' Vera said in a resigned voice. 'I expect she's on her way to London by now. Well, if that's the way she wants it, she can stay there – if her gran will have her.'

'Mum will have her, because Dad will tell her to,' Georgie said confidently. 'She'll only run orf again if they send her back. She was miserable all the way 'ere and it ain't much of a place, is it?' He gave his sister a straight look. She stared at him for a minute or so and then shook her head, looking defeated.

'No, it isn't,' she admitted. 'The cottage is fine but I thought it was closer to a village or a small town.'

'It isn't far to Chatteris once you get to the end of the drove,' Georgie said, trying now to comfort her. He didn't like his sister that much, but he realized she was feeling shocked and upset. 'I 'spect we'll get used to it after a bit.'

'I might try and find somewhere closer to a town or village,' Vera told him as she got up from the settee and went over to the range. She opened the door and saw that the logs he'd put on were beginning to catch. 'I should've made it up more last night. I was too upset over Jenny running off.'

'She might come back yet,' Georgie said. 'I could walk to the farm and see if she's anywhere around.'

'Can you fetch some milk?' Vera said. 'By the time you get back I'll have the range ready to cook some food – and then we'll find out what time the buses run and see about a school for you and Billy.'

'You're stayin' then?'

'Until I find something better,' Vera said, decisive now. 'I still think London will be overrun within weeks. They're bound to come now they think we're so weak after Dunkirk. We'll be safer down here.'

Georgie didn't argue. He picked up the milk can they'd brought from the farm the previous day and left his sister to get the fire going. He walked at a steady pace towards the farm, knowing he had only to follow the drove. There were no turnings so he couldn't miss it. Now, he could see the cows he'd heard the night before. They were a couple of fields over, and just down the road and round a winding curve, there was the farm. He could see people moving around in the yard.

He was standing outside the gate, trying to see how to open the latch, when a man came up to him, a middle-aged man, thick-set with a tweed cap and a patched jacket, his trousers pushed into long leather boots.

'Hello there, lad,' he said, smiling broadly. 'You're up nice and early. Come for some milk, have you? Well, come to the shed and see how it arrives.'

'Are you milking them now?' Georgie asked, his interest aroused, as much by the friendliness offered as anything. As he walked towards the long shed, he caught the smell of cows and their excrement. It was strong and made him wrinkle his nose a bit.

'Yes, they do stink until you get used to it,' his new friend told him. 'My name's Jim Baker, by the way. Your mother met my wife Muriel last night but I wasn't around. We work long hours these days – not enough labour.'

'She's my sister,' Georgie said. 'There's Billy, me, and the baby – Jenny too; she's a bit older than me. She went off in a temper last night, sir – did she come 'ere?'

'Not to my knowledge.' Jim Baker frowned. 'It's a pity you didn't come and tell me last night. I'd have gone out to look for her.'

'I reckon she'll have gone straight off to catch a train back home,' Georgie said. 'She didn't want ter come.'

'There was no sign of her as you walked here?' Jim asked, looking more anxious than Vera had. 'I doubt she'd find much harm hereabouts, unless she fell in a ditch – but I don't like to think of a young lass out all night on her own.'

'Her mum says she'll have gone back to London and I think so too. We're goin' ter see what schools there are after breakfast . . . Are there any buses today?'

They had entered the fug of the cowshed. It smelled of the animals and hay as well as straw, but Georgie was fascinated as he watched a young lad not much older than himself bringing milk from a cow's udder with his fingers. The milk flowed warm and sweet into a spotless pail. When it was filled, the lad got up and tipped it into a large metal churn.

'We'll have a little of that,' Jim said and the lad saved some and brought it to tip into Georgie's can. 'That's right, Benny. You can milk Primrose now and Daisy – but leave Jezabel to me. She's a right kicker.'

Jim turned to Georgie. 'Take that back to your sister, then, lad. I'll keep an eye out for young Jenny when I'm away down the drove this morning but I daresay you're right. She's a town lassie and it doesn't always suit them in the country.' He gave Georgie a speculative look. 'Are you willing to lend me a hand when you're not at school? I can teach you to feed the cows and pigs – and if you've the knack for it, mebbe the milking. You could help with that before you catch the bus mornings if you're always up this early?'

'I wouldn't mind 'elping sometimes if I can,' Georgie said. He was torn by uncertainty. He didn't want to spend all his free time working on the farm but was interested enough to think he might give it a go.

'Get yourselves sorted first,' Jim advised. 'You'll mebbe want to look for Jenny. Ask at the booking office if a young girl bought a ticket for London – there won't be many old Mr Johnson doesn't know by sight, so he'll be bound to remember a newcomer.'

'I shall – and thank you for the milk. My sister will pay your wife . . .'

'No, it's part of the arrangement,' Jim told him. 'Milk and whatever food we have goin' spare on the farm and your sister and you working a few hours.' He smiled and waved at Georgie as he walked off with the milk.

Georgie frowned. By the sound of that, he might not get paid for his work. He'd been hoping to earn a few bob so that he and Billy could go to the cinema now and then, without dipping into his savings. He wanted to keep them, just in case he decided to follow Jenny and go home.

CHAPTER 8

'What are you doing here?' Kate asked as she saw her niece standing outside the house when she got home that evening. 'I thought you went down to the country with your mum and the others yesterday?'

'I did – but it was awful,' Jenny said, looking guilty. 'We went in the back of Jock's van – he's dad's friend – and I was sick all the way. When we got there . . . oh, Aunt Kate! It was terrible. A horrid little cottage in the middle of fields far from anywhere and Mum got on to me – so I ran away and came 'ere.'

'Jenny!' Kate looked at her in dismay. 'Your mum will be worried to death by now.'

'No, she won't,' Jenny cried dramatically. 'She doesn't care about me – only Billy and the baby, and herself!'

Kate hesitated before answering. It was on the tip of her tongue to tell Jenny that of course her mother cared about her, but she realized that platitudes wouldn't help. Vera had always been a bit selfish, a little self-serving. Kate had never got on well with her.

'So why did you come here?' she asked Jenny now. 'Why didn't you go to your gran?'

'Gran would send me straight back on the next train,' Jenny told her. 'She's been acting strange since Uncle Derek died . . .' She faltered, then raised apprehensive eyes to Kate. 'I hoped you might let me stay with you? You could give me lessons and I'd help you. As soon as I can I'll find a job.'

'You're not old enough to work yet,' Kate said thoughtfully. 'You need to finish your schooling – but I could give you lessons myself . . .' She hesitated, uncertainly.

'Please, say you'll let me stay?' Jenny begged and Kate felt herself weakening.

'I'll let you stay for now,' she agreed. 'I'll send your mum a telegram to say you're all right and want to stay with me but if she insists you have to return to her, I can't keep you, Jenny. Your mum has the right to demand you go to her and I'd be breaking the law if I defied her.'

Jenny sniffed. Kate gave her a handkerchief and she blew her nose, before wiping away her unshed tears. 'If she doesn't, you'll let me stay?'

'Yes, for a while,' Kate replied. 'When Gran is better, she'll probably want you to live with her, but we'll see what happens.'

'Oh, thank you!' Jenny said and flung her arms around her. 'I know I can get a job delivering newspapers in the mornings and evenings and I'll do all the lessons you set, because I want to work in a high-class dress shop when I'm old enough and I need a proper education or they won't take me on.'

'You could do better than that,' Kate told her. 'Why don't you take a course in shorthand as well as my lessons? You could find work in an office then and that might be better paid.'

'It'd be boring, sitting in an office all day,' Jenny said, smiling now she'd got her way. 'I like clothes, Aunt Kate. I've never had many nice things. Mum buys me nearly-new from the market and I'd like to work with pretty clothes, even if I can't afford many of them.'

'We could make you a nice dress,' Kate said, thoughtful again. 'We can buy the material on the market but choose a stylish pattern and make it up ourselves.'

'Have you got a sewing machine?' Jenny asked, brightening.

'No, but a friend of mine has and she's told me I can borrow it whenever I wish. She doesn't use it as much now, because her children are grown up. I've asked if she'll lend it to me to make some things for the baby and her son is going to bring it round at the weekend. Rodney works on the docks. He wanted to join the army but they wouldn't have him because he has flat feet. He does important war work anyway, and also does fire watching.'

'What's that?' Jenny inquired, her interest stirred.

'It's in case arsonists try to set fire to important buildings or ships in the docks, even stores: there could be fire from bombs, too, if an aerial attack ever happens. And the IRA set off a bomb recently and you never know who will try to cause trouble. People you'd never suspect are sympathizers with the enemy so at night, men who can't be in the forces because of their age or slight infirmities, go on fire watch.'

'Do women do it, too?' Jenny inquired but Kate said she hadn't heard of any.

'A lot of women and girls are doing things like mobile canteens for the service men, driving ambulances and fire engines – all kinds of things.'

'That sounds interesting,' Jenny said. 'I'll be fifteen next birthday – and that's only September. I can join things then and do an important job.'

'You could start to look for work then,' Kate agreed. 'You won't be able to drive anything for a few years yet, but you may be able to take first aid classes and help out when the trains come in with the wounded – or just be there to offer a mug of tea or a cigarette.'

'Do you do anything for the war, Aunt Kate?'

'Yes, I help with a mobile canteen for the troops,' Kate told her. 'I was at the station when some of the wounded from Dunkirk were brought in. It was heartrending, Jenny. Some of them were too ill to want food or even a sip of water. One soldier was dying. All he wanted was a last puff of a cigarette . . .'

'Oh, that's sad,' Jenny cried, her eyes moist with sympathy. 'It must have been awful to see them come home like that?'

'Yes, it was, but to tell the truth, they were just glad to be home. Most of them thought they'd had it and when the little ships turned up, they couldn't believe their luck.'

'It makes you think you'd like to be a nurse and help them,' Jenny said, making use of Kate's hanky again. 'Except I know I wouldn't be any use. I feel faint at the sight of blood.'

'I'm sure you'd get over that,' Kate said and laughed

at her niece's face. 'But I think the war might be over by the time you were trained – they won't take you unless you're over eighteen.'

'That's no use,' Jenny said in disgust.

'You'll find small things to do to help the war effort,' Kate reassured her. 'Some of the kids who are still here go out collecting old newspapers and books because there's a shortage of paper – and metal. They've taken some of the railings from the park and they say it'll all go . . .'

'Do you think the enemy will invade us like Mum and Gran say?'

Kate looked at her for a moment, then shook her head. 'I don't know why they haven't done it already, Jenny. We were so vulnerable after Dunkirk. I suppose we still are. We lost a lot of men, more still are wounded – and an awful lot of equipment was left behind in France. It takes time to rebuild that, so why aren't they invading us now?'

Jenny shrugged. 'Perhaps they don't really want to?'

Kate laughed. 'You may well be right. The papers said Hitler wanted us to be his allies at the start. So maybe he has some reserve about invading Britain but we shall have to be on the alert in case it happens.'

'I hope it's all just alarmist talk,' Jenny said. 'Why do folk have to fall out, Aunt Kate? All we want is just to get on with our lives and be happy, isn't it?'

'That's what most people want,' Kate agreed. She looked at Jenny. 'It's a good thing I keep the spare bed aired. Did you bring any clothes with you?' Jenny shook her head. 'Then we'll have to see if I've got anything you can borrow until we can make you some new stuff.'

'Some of my things are still at Gran's,' Jenny said. 'I didn't pack as much as mum told me to, because I didn't plan on stopping there.'

'Oh, Jenny!' Kate shook her head. 'I hope for your sake that your mum doesn't demand you go straight back.'

'Tell her you need me here to help,' Jenny suggested. 'You will need help when the baby comes, won't you?'

'Yes, I might,' Kate agreed. She'd been counting on her mother's help but since Derek's death, that seemed less likely to happen. 'I won't use that to blackmail your mum, Jenny. If anything should occur – if we were bombed and you were hurt or killed – I'd never forgive myself.'

'Even if I'd prefer that to living in that awful place?'

'Was it really that bad?' Kate questioned. 'You didn't give yourself a chance to like it.'

'I never would. If Mum makes me go back, I'll run away again – and next time I'll just disappear and you won't see me again.'

'Jenny!' Kate looked at her in disapproval. 'That's a horrid thing to say.'

Jenny looked a bit guilty but set her mouth stubbornly. Kate sighed and led the way upstairs. She went first to her own room. She had a suitcase containing the clothes she'd worn when she left school. Most of them were still usable and she'd kept them in case she could make something out of them, but Jenny's need was the more pressing.

She took it to the spare bedroom. Jenny had stretched out and was sleeping – or pretending to be.

'You might find something you can wear until we can fetch your things from Mum's,' she said. 'Rest now and I'll make us some supper later.'

'You should've sent her straight back to her mother,' Kate's mother said when she walked round to collect a few of Jenny's things that evening. 'Where is she?'

'Sleeping,' Kate told her. 'She thought you'd be angry with her and said she was tired. She didn't get much sleep last night.'

'Serves her right,' Grace retorted. 'She's still a child, Kate. Vera will be angry and I don't blame her.'

'I sent her a telegram as soon as I could,' Kate said. 'If she demands that Jenny goes back at once I'll take her at the weekend but she's told me she'll run away again, and next time she'll go off on her own.'

'She wouldn't last a week before she was back!'

'I'm not so sure. She told me she could find a job delivering papers – and she looks fifteen, especially if she put some make-up on. With the right clothes she could probably find herself a little job in a shop or even a factory. Goodness knows they need workers badly. With most of the men gone and the girls joining the Women's Forces or acting as auxiliary nurses, the factories are crying out for workers. I wouldn't put it past some of the managers to set her on.'

'She would hate it.' Jenny's gran shook her head. 'I know her – all that girl thinks about is clothes and film stars and going to the pictures.'

'Mum!' Kate cried. 'Don't make it more difficult. I

know she ought to do as her mother says – but Jenny can do the lessons I set for her and I'll get her doing some kind of volunteer work too, if she stays. It's just for a while. I can't see Vera staying in the country for long if it's half as bad as Jenny says. She'll come home when she sees there isn't going to be an invasion.'

'It will happen.' Grace was pessimistic. 'Besides, I know Jenny. I'm her grandmother and I've had more opportunity to watch her. She'll neglect her studies and be off with friends whenever she gets the chance.'

'If she does, I'll threaten to send her back to her mother.' Kate laughed. 'Mum, please, try to understand – besides, Jenny might help me when the baby comes.'

'I'll do that . . .' Grace sighed. 'I know I've been neglecting the rest of you, but . . .' She shook her head, choking on the tears that were always close.

'I know, Mum.' Kate hugged her. 'We all miss him – but you're his mum so you feel the worst.'

'Your dad is as bad, but he never says.' Grace sighed. 'Take her stuff, then. She can come here when she wants – but only if her mother agrees. Vera would make all our lives a misery if we kept her and anything happened to her.'

'I know but I'm hoping nothing will happen,' Kate said, crossing her fingers. 'I shudder every time I hear a siren, Mum, but so far it's just a false alarm.'

'Let's pray it stops that way,' Grace said. She looked at her youngest daughter. 'Georgie won't be pleased. He asked to stay with you and I refused him.'

'Georgie will understand,' Kate said. 'Are you sure you don't want him home, Mum?'

'Not yet. I'll see what happens in the next few months. If nothing does by Christmas, I'll tell Vera to stop being so anxious and bring them all back . . .'

'Good.' Kate smiled and gave her a hug. It seemed her mother had come back to them a little. She was still grieving but at least she was thinking again instead of going round in a daze.

CHAPTER 9

The telegram was delivered to the farm and Jim Baker brought it the next morning.

'I wouldn't give it to Georgie, Mrs Carter. It might have been bad news.'

Vera tore the envelope open, scanned the brief message and gave a nod of satisfaction. 'I knew it! That girl of mine headed straight back to London. She's with my sister.'

'Ah, that will be a relief to you,' Jim said and smiled. 'Will you be able to give Mrs Baker a hand today? She needs to make butter and she has a lot of other chores to do.'

'Yes, I'll come down in half an hour,' Vera said. 'I was just packing some lunch for the boys. They're off to school and I haven't arranged school meals yet.'

'I doubt they're very good. Sandwiches are probably just as nourishing as semolina pudding and a vegetable stew. That's what my youngest said they had yesterday. His mum says she'll give him a lettuce and tomato sandwich today. He'll eat that, which he didn't his school dinner.'

'My lot will eat most things,' Vera said. 'Those fresh eggs you sent us were much appreciated, Mr Baker. I saved one for their sandwiches today. With a bit of lettuce and tomato they'll gobble them up and be ready for whatever I've got this evening.'

'We killed a pig this week,' he told her. 'There are some chitterlings and trotters going spare – well, my missus will use them if you can't, but most of the meat has already gone, to family, friends, and neighbours. We always share it if we've got one on the go.' He winked at her. 'What the buggers up in parliament don't know can't hurt them, eh?'

'I'd like the chitterlings and the trotters if your wife can spare them. The kids like chitterlings fried with a drop of vinegar and I love a bit of pork cheese. Those trotters will go down a treat for our dinner.'

'Talk to Mrs Baker. I told her to save them for you. I like the kidneys myself and a nice bit of pork cheek . . .'

Vera nodded and went back into the cottage. She wasn't sure whether it was legal for the farmer to kill a pig and sell it or give it to his friends and family. There were so many regulations about what folk could do with their own things, these days. You could keep a few hens for your own use, but livestock was all supposed to be notified and sold to the Ministry of Food. Not that she was going to tell anyone or refuse a gift horse. Anything she could get from the farm, legal or not, would help to eke out the rations they were allowed.

Vera had got on well with her butcher in London and he always had something under the counter for his special customers. He was old enough to be her father but he'd like to flirt with her so she'd laughed at his silly jests, because an extra sausage or two kept the kids fed. She'd already visited the butcher in Chatteris but he'd offered her only some bacon and a bit of scrag end she could make into a stew. No doubt he'd got a bit of prime steak or pork rib under the counter for his favourite customers, but she was a stranger.

Sighing, she went back to preparing the toast for breakfast. Billy had just made his first appearance and was drinking a cup of milk – that was one bonus of living on a farm. Georgie had returned from the farm with a jug of milk a few minutes earlier, and had already consumed a slice of toast and marge.

'Is there any more?' he asked hopefully.

'Yes, you can have another half a slice,' she told him. 'I've packed your sandwiches, but there's no cake or biscuits. I'll shop again on Saturday and use my ration card then. I'll buy flour and make a fatless sponge. I can use a bit of marge to make a filling, a bit of jam, too, if I can get any.'

'Mrs Baker says she has some plum jam if you want a jar,' Georgie said. 'She made a lot last autumn before all the rationing started and she's got a whole shelf full of it. I told her I like plum jam and she says she'll give us some.'

'I could make some jam tarts,' Vera promised. 'We all like them and homemade jam is usually lovely.'

'Mrs Baker gave me a bit of her fatless sponge,' Georgie said. 'It was smashing.'

'And you're still hungry?' Vera frowned at him as he finished his toast and licked his fingers. 'If you've finished, you'd best be off. Mr Baker is going into

76

Chatteris this morning so he'll likely give you a lift all the way.'

'He's all right,' Georgie said. 'Come on, Billy. You can eat your toast as we walk.' He put both satchels over his shoulder. 'It's a lovely mornin' . . .'

Vera grabbed her son, gave him a kiss, and pushed his hair back from his eyes. 'Eat your sandwiches at lunchtime, Billy. I'll have something tasty for your tea.'

Billy nodded but didn't say anything. He looked scared and pale, and Vera knew a pang of regret. Billy was dreading going to the new school. Luckily, Georgie had got into the same one so he would be there at playtime to help if his nephew was bullied, but Billy might be behind the others in his class when it came to lessons and he would be afraid of a new teacher, who wouldn't understand that he'd had a lot of time off with his health and hadn't quite caught up to where he should be . . .

Billy had a miserable first day. The teacher was giving a lesson on equations and fractions and he didn't have a clue what she was on about; they hadn't done them at his school and he just sat staring at the board in a daze. By the time the teacher realized he'd never done those kind of sums and had no idea what was going on, it was the end of the lesson.

In the playground, he found himself left alone. Georgie had been kept in to talk to his new teacher and none of the local kids came near Billy or asked him to join in their games of tag or ball. The next lesson was reading. Billy was better at that and followed the lesson, though when he was singled out to read, he went pink with embarrassment and stumbled over some of the words. It wasn't that he didn't know what the words meant, he just found the long ones difficult to say. Hearing sniggering from some boys at the back of the class, he felt hot and uncomfortable.

At lunchtime he found Georgie waiting for him and they chose a spot at the back of the hall to eat their lunch. A teacher came up to them as they were eating and asked why they weren't having school dinners. Georgie explained that his sister hadn't got round to asking about them yet and the teacher said he would send a note back with them that evening. He then said there was milk or orange squash and they could each choose a glass of what they wanted. They both chose the orange drink as they had milk at home, but a lot of the boys drank the milk; some had both if they could get away with it.

The afternoon was better for Billy, because they had a games period and the teacher put him in the blue team; they all had a blue band to wear and it was a ball game, each player throwing it to someone in his team and trying to keep it until they reached a net on a pole and threw it up to score. Billy caught the ball and managed to dodge round all the other players and throw it successfully through the net. After that the lads on his team started throwing it to him and he scored another two goals during the period and so his team won, as the red team only scored once.

At the end of the games period, they all went in and were given a glass of water. The teacher then read them a story about a hero called Hereward who had fought the Normans when they invaded the Fens, and, too soon for Billy, the bell went to announce it was time to go home.

Georgie asked him how he got on as they walked to the bus with the other kids. They chose a seat together near the front of the bus and, apart from Billy having his hair pulled by a boy in the seat behind, their journey was short and uneventful.

'It was all right in the afternoon,' Billy admitted. 'I hated it all morning but then it got better. How did you get on?'

'It was all right,' Georgie said. 'We had science and French. I don't like French, can't understand what they're on about most of the time. In the afternoon we went to a field and played cricket. I liked that.'

Billy nodded. 'We had games too, in the playground. I scored some balls in the net – but I didn't like the maths teacher. He looked at me as if I was stupid – but I'd never heard of sums like that.'

'They're daft anyway,' Georgie told him. 'You need to add up and subtract – and be able to measure, that's all. Can't see the point in all those fancy things they do. Shouldn't let it worry you, Billy. If the invasion turns out to be just scaremongering, your mum will take us back to London soon.'

Just then they heard a loud noise in the sky and looked up. Two planes were flying low and they could see that one of them was British because of the markings but they weren't sure about the other one until it started shooting at the ground, narrowly missing them. The boys dived for the ditch at the side of the drove, as the British plane fired at the enemy and lay looking at each other, frightened. For several minutes the planes soared and dived overhead, firing at each other and then they heard a stuttering sound. Raising his head to look, Georgie gave a cheer as he saw that the enemy plane was on fire.

'It's going to crash,' he told Billy. They both stood up and waved at the British plane, which dipped its wings and then flew off, following the damaged enemy aircraft until it suddenly fell from the sky and there was a loud crash and flames exploding into the air.

It had flown quite a long way, too far off for the boys to see clearly what was happening, but the smoke and flames must be visible for miles around.

'Do you think the pilot's dead?' Billy asked, his face white and scared.

Georgie was feeling shaken himself. 'I dunno,' he muttered. 'Serves him right if he is. He could have killed us, Billy. I never thought we'd see anything like that down 'ere.'

'Nor me,' Billy said. 'Our plane must have chased him from somewhere else. I was really scared, Georgie.'

'Yeah. There's an airfield at Mepal and another in Witchford,' Georgie said in an awed voice. He'd been scared too but he felt exhilarated now that the enemy plane had been downed. 'I reckon they must have fought off an attack from the air.'

'Mum will go mad if she knows we were shot at,' Billy said and looked at Georgie hopefully. 'Do you think she'll take us back home?'

'She might if we tell her,' Georgie looked thoughtful. 'Do you think we should? If there's goin' to be a lot of fighting, I reckon more of it will be up there. What happened just now – that might never happen again. I ain't sure, Billy. I didn't want ter come, but it ain't that bad. I reckon it might be all right, if we give it a go.'

'I'll stay if you do,' Billy said. He was feeling better now and the sun was warm as they walked towards the farm. 'We've only got a few weeks left until the end of term. It might be fun playing round 'ere – but only if we're both 'ere.'

'Yeah. I like 'elpin' on the farm. I didn't think I would but I'm learnin' ter milk a cow. It's all right. Collecting the eggs and feedin' the hens and pigs is fun.'

'Can I help, too?' Billy asked, looking at him as they walked the last few steps.

Farmer Jim, his wife, Benny, and another lady as well as Vera were standing outside the house staring across the fields towards where the wreckage was still burning. Vera darted towards them as she saw them.

'Did you see it?' she asked. 'We think one of our planes shot an enemy plane down.'

'Yeah, we saw it happen,' Georgie told her. 'We dived in the ditch when we heard them shooting at each other and lay watchin' 'em.'

'Thank goodness you had the sense to take cover,' she said, looking at Billy as if she expected to see a hole in him somewhere. 'I never expected anything like that down here.'

'I was telling Vera there are bound to be dogfights sometimes,' Jim said in a reassuring way. 'We've got a lot of airfields round here and the enemy knows they have to deal with our air force first if they intend to invade us.'

'We're all right,' Georgie told her. 'We waved at the pilot after he downed him and he dipped his wings to us.'

'I thought the countryside would be safer . . .' Vera said, looking worried.

'We're much safer than the towns,' Jim put in with a chuckle. 'Never seen that happen before, Vera, and I doubt you'll see it again while you're here.'

'I hope not,' she said and then turned to Georgie. 'I've just got a job to finish for Mrs Baker and then I'll be home. You can make yourself a cup of tea and there's a couple of jam tarts for your tea. Mrs Baker gave them to you so thank her.'

The boys did as they were bid, and then Georgie looked at Jim. 'Please, sir, can Billy 'elp out on the farm too sometimes?'

'Yes, of course he can,' Jim said and beamed at them. 'We need all the hands we can get come harvest. My eldest boy is in the RAF. He could have got an exemption to work on the land, but he joined up as soon as war was declared. He started helping out when he was about your age, Billy. In the meantime, you can help feed the animals. That's a regular job come rain or shine.'

'Thank you, sir,' Billy said shyly. 'I saw some horses on the way 'ome – are they yours?'

'Yes. Shires, they are, and bred for land work. We've got tractors but with things the way they are, it's the horses we rely on for pulling the wagons. You never know when the fuel will run out these days. Got plenty of hay and oats for our Shires.'

'Can I ride them?' Billy asked.

'No, of course you can't,' his mother said crossly. 'Don't be a nuisance, Billy. Mr Baker has work to do.'

'When the time comes, I'll give you a ride,' Jim promised. 'But best you get off home now. Have you got homework to do?'

Billy shook his head, but Georgie groaned. 'Yes. I've got sums and a short essay to write.'

'Get off then – and be on time in the morning.'

'Do you want help with the milking tonight?' Georgie asked but Jim shook his head.

'Benny is here – and my daughter Jess will give me a hand. You be nice and early in the morning – and bring Billy if you like.'

Georgie grinned and took Billy off. 'Come on,' he said when they were past the farm. 'I'm going to do my homework quick and then see if I can get to the wreckage. I'm not sure if I can, but I want to try.'

Thick black smoke was still pouring into the sky as Billy looked towards where they'd seen the plane crash. 'It's a long way,' he said. 'I don't think I'll come. What shall I say if Mum comes and you're out?'

'Just tell her I went for a walk,' Georgie grinned. 'Save some tea for me. I shan't be long . . .'

CHAPTER 10

'There's a letter for you,' Kate said, bringing a small bundle of post into the kitchen that Saturday morning in late July. 'It's from your mum – I know her handwriting.' Nearly three weeks had passed since Jenny's return to London and this was the first they'd heard from Vera. Kate watched as her niece reluctantly opened the envelope. 'What does she say?'

Jenny scanned the brief note and then breathed a sigh of relief. 'Nothing much, except she's cross with me for leaving the way I did. She says for two pins she'd disown me but if I want to go down for a holiday when the kids are off school I can.'

'She doesn't say you have to go back?' Kate took the note as Jenny offered it and read it for herself. 'Looks like you got away with it, then.'

'She knows I wouldn't stop if she made me go back,' Jenny said, grinning. 'That means I can stay with you, Aunt Kate.'

'If I'll have you,' Kate said and then laughed as Jenny's face fell. 'Of course I will, dope! I quite like havin' you here.'

Jenny beamed at her. 'I'm not any trouble to you, am I?'

'No, you've been a help.' Kate nodded. 'I didn't think you'd settle as well as you have – but you got yourself two little jobs and you've helped me with the scrap metal collections the children have been doing.' Anything from milk bottle tops to old rusty nails was being deposited in boxes in the classroom and then Kate and another teacher took them to an area collecting point. The class that collected the most had been promised a penny bar of chocolate each.

'I like living with you. You make me feel as if I'm a grown-up not a little girl. Mum always treats me as if I'm a child – even though I've started my you-know-what's.'

'Your period?' Kate nodded. 'You've started young, same as I did. Not sure that's good. Just means you have to put up with the pain for longer. My cramps were so bad I had to miss school, but you're not going to school anyway.' Kate had been giving her lessons in the evenings, setting her some exercises to do while she was at work during the day. Sometimes, Jenny took her books to the library and did her studies there. She was interested in fashion through the ages. Kate had shown her some Regency fashion plates and they'd talked about how they were made and the long hours the seamstresses must have worked. It had surprised Kate how interested her niece had been to learn that kind of thing.

'I wish you'd been my teacher at school,' she'd told Kate after one of their evening sessions. 'Your lessons aren't boring.'

'I think it's best you learn about life rather than a lot of stuff you'll never use,' Kate affirmed.

They were getting on well, enjoying each other's company, making clothes together, and Jenny was turning out to be quite a clever seamstress. Kate had told her that the ability to do alterations might make all the difference when she applied for jobs in the fashion industry.

'You might even like to work in a clothing factory,' she'd suggested. 'It must be interesting to see the clothes made, don't you think?'

Jenny did, but she was still set on getting a job in a high-class dress shop in the West End. A couple of times on a Saturday, after Jenny had finished her paper round, they'd gone window-shopping in Regent Street and Bond Street, looking at all the beautiful things. Merchandise was becoming scarcer but there were still some beautiful clothes to be seen in the more expensive shops. Perhaps they'd stocked up well before the war started and all the regulations came in.

'I suppose the government has to ration the supplies we have,' she'd said to Jenny as they discussed it. 'If they didn't, folk with lots of money would buy more than their fair share.'

'Yes, but it's a shame all the same,' Jenny had observed when they came out of one store, where the rails were half-empty. This used to be such a busy shop and have all the latest styles.'

'I don't suppose there'll be much in the way of new fashion for a while,' Kate had told her. 'Except I've noticed the new range of jackets has wider shoulders – almost mannish.'

'Do women want to look like men because they're doing men's jobs?' Jenny had asked and Kate had laughed.

'Perhaps that's what it is,' she'd agreed. 'Our new milkman is a woman in her forties. She told me her husband has joined up as an auxiliary, whatever that means. I think he's helping with ambulances and stuff rather than fighting, so she's taken over his round until the war's over.'

'I shouldn't want to do her job,' Jenny had replied. 'She must be up at five in the mornin'. I get up at six and that's early enough for me.'

Bringing her thoughts back to the present, Kate opened her own letters. The first two were small bills and the third was from her husband. She scanned it anxiously and gave a little cry of distress as she got to the end.

'What's wrong, Aunt Kate?' Jenny asked.

'Steve said their planes ran into heavy flak on their last mission. Several of them were hit and they lost two pilots. He has a small injury he got when his plane did a forced landing on one wheel but it isn't enough for him to be sent home. Unfortunately, his friend Chuck has been hurt quite badly and is in hospital in London. Steve asked if I would visit him.'

'You will, of course,' Jenny said. 'I saw him for about two minutes when he was staying with you and Steve and he seemed really nice.'

'Yes. He's a pleasant, quiet man – intelligent I think,' Kate said. 'I'll visit him and take him some fruit – if they'll let me. They don't always allow it if you're not family.'

'Pretend to be his cousin or something,' Jenny quipped and Kate laughed.

'Well, he doesn't have any relatives over here, so I could probably get away with it,' she said. 'I wonder what injury Steve has . . .'

'Didn't he say?'

'No, just that it was slight and wouldn't stop him flying.' Kate was worried and Jenny went to touch her arm.

'Steve will be all right,' Jenny said. 'I know you worry about him, Aunt Kate, but he's so strong and brave. I'm sure he'll be fine.'

'Yes, of course he—' Kate's words were lost as the door flew open and someone burst into her kitchen.

'Kate, you need to come at once!' her father cried. 'It's your mother. I can't do anything with her . . .' He was grey in the face. 'We've had bad news . . .'

'Dad?' Kate looked at him in shock. She had never seen him look so ill and old. He looked to have aged overnight. 'What's happened?'

'It's your brother Tom . . .' he said and his voice broke on a sob, his body sagging. 'We had a telegram from the doctors. He's taken a turn for the worse and not expected to live!'

'Oh no!' Kate stared at him in horror. 'I thought he was on the mend – what happened?'

'Apparently, it was a blood clot,' her father said through his tears. 'The telegram says it happens sometimes. It was unexpected – but then he had a massive stroke. They say if we want to see him, we have to go now.'

'Oh no!' Kate's head was in a whirl, her throat

tight as she fought her tears. It was just one thing after another. First Derek and now Tom. It hurt. It hurt terribly but she had to keep her head, because it was clear her parents were distraught from their shock and grief. 'Who's with Mum? You didn't leave her on her own, did you?'

'Nellie from next door is with her,' Kate's father said. 'And I called the doctor and he gave her a sedative to calm her. Now I think I've done wrong, because we need to get her there today or it might be too late.'

'Have you rung the hospital? Did they give you a number?'

'No – and yes,' her father said. 'I just came for you, Kate. We have to do something . . .' He was clearly lost, needing her help.

'I'll come with you now.' She glanced at Jenny. 'Can you stay here in case I need you when I get back? I know you were planning to meet a friend later . . .'

'Oh, that doesn't matter,' Jenny said her face white and shocked. 'I'll do anything you want – poor Granny . . .'

'Yes, poor Mum,' Kate said and looked at her father. 'Let's go. I'm not sure what to do for the best . . . Let's just see if Mum is up to making the journey . . .'

When they got to her parents' house, Kate's mother was asleep on the couch in the kitchen. Nellie, her next-door neighbour, was sitting at the table, drinking a cup of tea and looking anxious.

'How long has she been asleep?' Kate's father asked her. 'I need to get her to the hospital.'

'She went off soon after you left, Ned,' Nellie replied.

'If the doctor gave her a sedative, I doubt she'll wake for a few hours yet.'

'You get off, Dad,' Kate said, seeing his indecision. 'You've a train to catch and if you wait for Mum to wake up you might not get there until it's too late.'

'She'll never forgive me,' he said, looking and clearly feeling guilty. 'I should never have let the doctor give her that sedative, but she was hysterical and I didn't know what to do.'

'If you don't go now Tom will die alone without any of his family,' Kate urged. 'I'll wait here with Mum until she wakes. If she wants to catch the next train we will – but try and get a message to us somehow, Dad. I'd rather not bring her down to Portsmouth if he's already gone.'

Her father nodded and went upstairs to fetch some things. He was back down in a couple of minutes and bent to kiss his wife's cheek. 'I'll come back as soon as it's over and I've made the arrangements to bring him home for burial. At least we can do that for him. It's more – more than we could for Derek.'

Kate gave him a hug and he went off to catch a bus to the station and the next train headed in the right direction. Kate sat down beside Nellie at the kitchen table, her gaze resting on her mother who seemed to have just flopped out and looked far from comfortable.

'Fancy a cup of tea, love?' Nellie asked. 'Oh, it's hard on your parents losing two of their boys. I don't know what I'd do if it was one of mine. We've been lucky so far – but they're both at sea.'

Nellie had two sons in the Royal Navy. They were about the same ages as Tom and Derek and had all gone to school together.

'I don't know how she'll bear it,' Kate said, accepting a cup of strong sweet tea, her gaze never leaving her mother. 'It nearly killed her when we had the news about Derek.' She shook her head and cuffed the tears from her eyes. 'It isn't fair – this bloody war! I hate it!'

'We all do, love,' Nellie told her sympathetically. 'War is never a good thing, even though the lads all went off to join up in high spirits. Thought they were in for a bit of fun I reckon . . .' She looked sorrowfully at Kate's mother. 'But this is the reality. They get themselves killed and it's their mothers that suffer.'

'Yes, she'd been suffering for weeks, even before Derek was killed. I don't know what to say to her now . . . two of them. We thought Tom was getting over his wounds. We even had a letter from him and he seemed as if he was all right . . .' Kate gave a little sob, the tears spilling now. Her concern was for her mother but she loved her brothers and it hurt so much to know that they weren't coming home . . . ever. She took out a handkerchief and blew her nose. 'You'll be wanting to get home, Nellie.'

'Ain't got nuthin' spoilin',' her kind neighbour said. 'Ken is at work and there's only us two to cook for so I'll wait and see how your ma is when she wakes up. You'll maybe need a bit of 'elp with her then.'

Kate nodded, feeling too wretched to insist that Nellie go home. She wasn't sure that her mother would want her neighbour here when she did wake, but couldn't find a reason to send her away. Looking round the kitchen for a job to keep herself busy, she could find none. Everywhere looked spotless and tidy. Her mother must spend all her time cleaning. She'd always kept things nice, but now it looked almost as if no one lived there, with everything put away. When Vera and the children were living here there had always been a bit of clutter and Kate thought her mother must be missing them all dreadfully. She'd sent them away for their own safety, but she must be finding it lonely on her own all day, especially when Kate's father worked long hours, as he often did.

He wouldn't get home that evening. Kate would have to stay overnight to care for her mother. She looked at Nellie. 'I'll need to stay tonight at least,' she said. 'Would you mind if I pop home and fetch a few things?'

'You go, lass. I can't see her waking for a while yet.' A loud snore from Grace seemed to confirm that she would sleep on for a while.

Kate thanked Nellie and left, walking quickly through the few streets to her own home. Jenny would be anxious too. Kate wondered what best to do for her niece. Either she had to come and stay with her gran while Kate was there or stay in Kate's house alone.

Jenny was reading a fashion magazine when she got back. She'd washed up while Kate was gone and looked up anxiously as her aunt entered the kitchen.

'How is Gran?'

'Sleeping at the moment. Dad's gone to the hospital alone and I'll have to stay there at least for tonight, maybe longer. What do you want to do, love? Stay here alone – or come with me?'

Jenny hesitated, then, 'Could I come this evening after I've done my paper round? I'd like to go out and see some friends if that's all right with you?' She looked anxious. 'Unless there's something I can do to help?'

'Not at the moment,' Kate told her. 'Nellie's helping me. You go out and come to me at your gran's when you're ready. I might need you to fetch something for our tea. It depends on what Mum has in the larder – and how she is when she wakes. She might want to rush off to see Tom.'

'Grandad'll be worried about her,' Jenny said. 'Why did it have to happen, Aunt Kate?'

'I don't know. It isn't fair,' Kate replied. 'I'm going to pack a few things – if you want anything special, bring it when you come.' She moved towards the hall and then hesitated. 'I ought to send your mum a telegram. Can you do that, Jenny? Take the money from my purse in the dresser drawer. Just say Tom worse and Mum upset. If she feels like coming to visit, she can make her own mind up.'

'She won't come,' Jenny replied with conviction. 'Not unless she hates it where she is – she only cares about herself.'

'Jenny, you ought not to say things like that about your mother.'

'It's true, though. She'll leave it to you to cope, Aunt Kate. All she'll say is that she has the baby and Billy to look after. Georgie might want to come, though.'

'Yes. Well, he's old enough to travel up alone if he wants to,' Kate agreed. 'I'd best hurry and get back, love. Nellie's very good but I can't expect her to cope alone if Mum wakes up and starts screaming again.'

CHAPTER 11

Vera looked at the telegram for several minutes before she could bring herself to open it. They always brought bad news. She hadn't heard from her husband in weeks and was afraid it might be him, so when she finally found the courage to open the envelope, she felt relieved. It was awful that her brother was worse and her mother upset, but she didn't know what she was supposed to do about it. And Kate was only just round the corner. She would do whatever was necessary. Vera had enough to do as it was.

Baby Sally was fractious again. It was her teeth and she'd cried all night and most of the morning while her mother worked in the farm kitchen with Mrs Baker. The farmer's wife had found a little blackcurrant juice and smeared it on a dummy. Sally had sucked on it and quietened for a while as they cooked and cleaned.

Mrs Baker had been busy in the dairy for most of the morning, leaving the kitchen work to Vera. She didn't mind that, because it was a lovely big room with a warm, friendly atmosphere. She'd washed all the pantry shelves down and scrubbed the floor, as well as helping to bake bread and cook a big panful of stew. After lunch, she'd washed the dishes and come home, because Mrs Baker only needed her a few hours each day, sometimes mornings and sometimes afternoons.

Vera did a bit of baking herself. She made bread and a fatless sponge so the boys would have egg on toast for their tea and a piece of cake to follow. Now that they were off school for the summer, they often ate at the farm with the family and Vera found that much easier to manage. She gave her meat ration to Mrs Baker, because she got better meat from the butcher and cooking a large stew meant there was plenty for everyone with lashings of potatoes and vegetables. It made it simple for Vera to give them easy things at home, like toast and sandwiches.

She lifted the baby from her cot and found she was wet again. After changing her nappy, Vera sat down to write to her sister. She wouldn't write to her mother because she didn't know what to say to her. It was awful to lose two sons. Vera felt for her, but she really didn't know what to say or do to help. Better just to tell Kate she was sorry and ask if she could do anything. Kate wasn't likely to ask for help.

Vera had finished her letter when the boys came rushing in for their tea. They spent most of their time on the farm these days, helping with all the jobs that needed doing at harvest time.

'Will you walk down and post this for me later?' she asked Georgie. 'Your mum's upset because Tom has taken a turn for the worse.' She saw his eyes widen and the colour left his face. 'It's all right. Kate will look after her.'

'I want to see Mum,' Georgie said and Vera sighed. She had hesitated to tell him, because she knew this would happen. 'I earned ten shillings helping with the wheat stacks this week, Vera. I'll pay for my fare myself – and I'll come back when I've seen Mum is all right.'

'Can I go with Georgie?' Billy asked, his eyes wide with alarm. 'Is Gran very ill, Mum?'

'I think she's just upset over your Uncle Tom,' Vera told him. 'No, you can't go, Billy. How would I manage here alone with the baby if you both left me? I need you to help me sometimes.' She looked hard at Georgie. 'Don't think you can stay with your sister the way Jenny did. Kate won't have room for you as well, and your mum wants you here with me.'

'I'll come back,' Georgie promised. 'I'm going anyway . . .' He set his face in a mulish expression and Vera gave up.

'I haven't said you can't – just that I want you back.'

'And I've said I'll come,' Georgie told her. 'I promised Mr Baker that I'll help when they cut the barley next week so I shan't be long – but I have to see my mum.'

'All right,' Vera nodded. 'You can catch the first train in the morning. You don't want to arrive in the middle of the night.'

'Yeah, I will,' he agreed. He glanced at Billy. 'Do you want to come down to the post box with me? We'll go and tell Mr Baker I'll be away a few days and you can help him while I'm gone.'

'Yeah, all right then,' Billy agreed.

They went out again, leaving Vera to sort out a few bits and pieces of washing she needed to iron. Georgie would need a clean shirt if he was going home to visit his mum. Working on the farm, she didn't bother with their shirts much. It wasn't easy to boil the water in the copper so she did it once a week and they wore the same shirt at least three days in a run. She sent them to school in clean shirts but it didn't matter when they were just roaming the countryside, because they were always dirty when they got in . . .

'I wish I was coming wiv yer,' Billy said as they walked to the end of the drove where a post box was situated. 'You could've took that if yer goin'. It will arrive after you do.'

'Yeah. Never thought of that,' Georgie said innocently. 'I thought we'd get out for a bit longer.' He grinned at his nephew. 'Don't go getting into mischief while I ain't 'ere, Billy.'

Billy laughed. 'You mean like riding on the back of that sow? Mr Baker was a bit cross over that . . .' Billy had caused a bit of chaos by climbing on to the back of one of the pigs as if it were a horse but it had snorted and bolted with him, tipping him off.

'She's in pig – that means she's 'avin' young 'uns,' Georgie told him. 'You came to no harm, but she could have attacked you when you fell off.'

'You scared her orf or she might 'ave,' Billy agreed. 'She was snortin' and I think she was goin' ter bite me when you made her run orf.' He giggled. 'I smelled bad when I got out of that pile of sh—'

'Don't say it,' Georgie admonished. 'Just think yourself lucky Mr Baker put you under the hose and washed yer down. Good thing it was a hot day. Yer clothes were dry and yer mum never noticed.'

'Mum don't notice much we do these days,' Billy said. 'She's busy wiv the baby or workin' on the farm. Then she goes off shoppin'.'

'Yeah, well, she's got a lot to do,' Georgie said and gave Billy a friendly punch in the arm. 'Yer big enough to look after yerself now, ain't yer?'

'Yeah,' Billy said, swelling with pride at his uncle's praise. 'Yeah, I'm all right now, Georgie.'

'It's done us both good down 'ere,' Georgie said. 'It's a bit like a 'oliday. I reckon. I like it on the farm. I wish I didn't have to go back to school next month.'

'Me too,' Billy said. His face had lost its usual pallor over the last few weeks of the summer holidays. He looked and felt so much better than he ever had since they arrived. 'It's been fun – and that dogfight was good too.'

They hadn't seen any more planes, at least none that were low enough to see what was going on, though they often heard them flying over the fenland during the night. Mr Baker had told them it was bombers going to raid somewhere in retaliation for attacks on Britain, but the boys hadn't seen anything as exciting as when the fighter plane was shot down.

Georgie hadn't been able to get anywhere near the crashed aircraft. By the time he'd got closer, it had been surrounded by police and army officers and they had turned him and others seeking to have a look away. Both boys kept the secret of how they'd been shot at and thought it was the most exciting thing that had ever happened to them, now that it was over.

'I still wish Mum would let me go with you,' Billy said as they turned back towards the farm.

'She won't, so there's no sense in askin'. She'll only get mad at you again.'

'Yeah, I know.' Billy looked at him anxiously. 'You'll come back before we have ter go to school, won't yer?'

'I'll come back when I've seen Mum,' Georgie promised. 'You'll be all right, though. No one bullied you at Chatteris School, did they?'

'A couple of boys tried to hit me but a teacher stopped them,' Billy said. 'Most left me alone, because they knew you'd bash them.'

Georgie chuckled. 'I would an' all. Don't worry, Billy. I'll be back before you know it . . .' He pushed his nephew in the back. 'I'll race you. I'm 'ungry . . .'

CHAPTER 12

'You don't have to stay with me,' Kate's mother said when she woke up to find her daughter standing by her bedside with a cup of tea. 'I'll be all right now.'

'I'll stay until Dad gets back.'

'What about your job at the library?'

'I popped in and told them I needed a couple of days off,' Kate said. 'I'm not leaving you on your own, Mum, so don't argue.'

Grace had been too ill to argue the previous day when she'd finally woken from her drugged sleep. She'd tried to stand, insisting that she wanted to visit the hospital to see her son, but she'd sagged when she'd taken a step forwards and it had needed both Nellie and Kate to almost carry her up the stairs to her bedroom, where she'd collapsed in a fit of weeping again. She hadn't screamed, so they'd done their best to make her comfortable. Kate tried to find words to soothe her but nothing she could say would stop her mother crying. In the end she'd fallen asleep again at about seven in the evening and slept through the night.

Kate had sat by her side for a while then given in and gone to sleep on the couch in the kitchen.

'Your father hasn't come home yet?'

'No, Mum, not yet – and he hasn't sent a telegram.'

'He won't. He says they make you feel worse.' Grace sat up and looked at her daughter. 'It's too late now. Tom has gone.'

'You don't know that, Mum.'

'Yes, I do. Don't argue with me, Kate. Your brother Tom is dead.' Her face was as white as the sheets. 'I dare say we'll all be gone soon so it hardly matters. What does anything matter? You're born and you suffer and then you die.'

'Oh, Mum. That isn't true,' Kate cried. 'Life is good in lots of ways. I know it hasn't been kind to us lately, but you have other sons and grandchildren. You still have reasons to live and be happy.'

Grace stared at her in silence. 'Perhaps *you* have – but I've lost two sons. John will be next – and then I'll be with them.'

'Mum! You've got years yet,' Kate said, feeling a prickle of despair. Her mother was just giving in, giving up. 'You love Georgie and the rest of us . . . and there's this one to look forward to . . .' She placed her hands on her belly. 'Don't you care about my baby at all?'

'You'll care for her,' Grace said, her expression unchanging. 'Perhaps when you're a mother you will understand how I feel . . . as if I've been wrenched apart. My flesh was their flesh, my blood theirs – and now they're dead. I carried them nine months and brought them up right – and for what? For them to die

101

in a useless war!' Her face twisted with the bitterness of grief. 'What is there for me to go on living for?'

'Mum . . .' Kate looked at her helplessly. She had no idea how to answer her. Understanding her pain, she knew it must be unbearable, but life had to go on. 'What about Dad? How would he manage without you?'

Grace shrugged. 'He has his work and his friends. He'll find someone to look after him.'

'Don't you think he's suffering too? We all are!' Kate wanted to shake her mother out of this fog of misery but of course she couldn't. 'You have to try, Mum. Neither Derek nor Tom would have wanted you to be like this. You know they wouldn't.'

'Go away, Kate. Go to work and leave me alone!'

'I'll get you some toast and marmalade . . .'

'I shan't eat it – and you can take this tea away. I don't want anything.'

'That's just daft.' Kate felt anger. 'You can't just lie there and refuse to eat or drink.'

'Leave me to my grief.' Grace looked at her and there was anger in her face. 'Get out! I don't want you here. I don't want anyone!'

Kate stared at her in silence, feeling hurt. Her mother didn't mean it, of course she didn't. She was just hurting and lashing out in her pain.

'I'll be downstairs if you want anything,' she said quietly. 'Don't give up, Mum. I can manage but there are others who can't. Think about John and Georgie if you don't care about me or Vera.'

'John is dead, too,' Grace said. 'I can feel it here.' She put a hand to her chest. 'Just go away, Kate. I'm tired . . .'

Kate left her as she lay back and closed her eyes.

Tears were trickling down her cheeks and the pain in her chest was physical in its intensity. She'd never expected her mother just to give up. It couldn't be allowed to happen. She couldn't lose her, too . . .

Georgie arrived that afternoon just as Kate was thinking about what she ought to do in the morning. He entered his former home, looking apprehensively at Kate.

'I had to come,' he told her. 'Vera thought I'd be in the way – but I won't. I just wanted to see Mum.'

'She's in bed,' Kate told him and smiled and he ran to her to be hugged. 'She's a bit calmer now but she keeps crying and saying things – hurtful things. Try not to take any notice if she's harsh to you, love. I don't think she really knows what she's saying half the time.'

'It's rotten luck. First Derek and then Tom.' Georgie's face was streaked with dirt and she guessed he'd shed a few tears. 'Mum must be devastated. It hurts bad, doesn't it?' He lifted his anxious eyes to hers.

'Yes, it does, Georgie. We all feel it but it must be worse for Mum. She brought us into the world and looked after us when we were little – nursed us through the measles and chickenpox and all the rest. It doesn't feel right that they won't be coming back, ever.'

'What does Dad say?'

'Not much. He rushed off hoping to see Tom before . . .' She took a deep breath. 'Before it was too late. Mum had been given a sedative so she couldn't go. Dad let the doctor give it to her to calm her because she was hysterical and screaming, but it might have been better to have slapped her and made her listen to him.

She may hold it against him if he spoke to Tom at the last and she didn't.'

Georgie was silent. He looked at her uncertainly, then, 'Can I go up and see her?'

'Of course you can, love. Like I said, take no notice if she scolds you.'

Georgie nodded and went out without another word. Kate filled the kettle and put it on the range. She might as well start to get tea ready. Jenny would be here before long and she was certain Georgie would be hungry. It was doubtful whether Vera had thought to pack him any food to eat on the train; she wouldn't have been best pleased that he was leaving her there with just Billy and baby Sally.

Kate wondered how her elder sister was coping, more or less alone in that cottage. It didn't have electricity and was some distance from anyone, apart from the farm. At least that was within walking distance.

Kate listened for sounds from upstairs but didn't hear anything much. It seemed as if her mother hadn't shouted at him – not yet, anyway.

She went to the window and looked out. The sun was still shining. It didn't seem possible that a terrible war in another country had just ruined their lives. As she turned back towards the kitchen table, Kate felt a stabbing sensation in her back and then a gripping pain in her abdomen. She stood like a statue to try to catch her breath as yet another sharp stab made her jump. This one was so sharp that she suddenly went weak at the knees and fell to the floor. A warm, wet feeling between her legs made her gasp. It couldn't be the baby! She had another three months to go. Kate gasped as the pain took over, trying to rise and falling back with the pain, a pushing pain this time.

She was going into labour far too early! Kate started to cry, the tears of fear and regret sliding down her cheeks. She was losing her precious baby. A scream broke from her as she writhed in agony on the floor, unable to help herself. All her natural strength seemed to have left her and she just wanted to curl up into a ball and die with her child.

'Kate, Mum wants—' Georgie came bursting into the kitchen, stopping with shock and dismay as he saw Kate, her knees up to her chest, rocking as the waves of pain went through her. 'What's wrong, Kate?' he asked fearfully.

'The baby . . .' she managed to gasp. 'It's coming too soon . . . much too soon . . . doctor . . .'

'I'll get Mum,' he said and rushed out of the room. Kate heard his feet pounding up the stairs. She tried to call out, to tell him her mother wouldn't help, that she needed a doctor but all she could do was moan and cry.

She was so immersed in her pain as the minutes passed that she was hardly aware when he came back, followed by her mother. Kate opened her eyes and looked into her mother's face. She saw her through the mist of tears, vaguely aware that her mother must have pulled a dress on over her nightdress.

'Where does it hurt? Are you bleeding?' Grace asked, sounding just like the loving mother she always had been.

'My back, my stomach . . . my legs . . .' Kate croaked. 'Yes, I'm bleeding, quite a bit I think.'

'You need to be in bed. Georgie, go and ask . . .'

Grace began just as the door opened and her husband walked in. 'Ned! Help us!'

'Grace, what's happened?' he asked, his face grey with fatigue and grief as he came towards them.

'She's losing the baby,' Grace replied. 'She needs to be in bed where I can look after her.' Without turning her head, she said, 'Georgie, go and fetch Dr Morgan – or his nurse if he's out. Tell them your sister's having a miscarriage and we need help!'

'I'll carry her upstairs,' Kate's father said, looking at his wife. 'How did this happen? Why is she here instead of at home?'

'She insisted on staying though I told her to go . . .'

Georgie left before he could hear anything more. He ran faster than he ever had in his young life, pounding on the front door of the big house where the doctor's surgery occupied the long front room. It was opened by the doctor's wife who listened to his story and told him Dr Morgan was out but the nurse was in the back making up medicines. She'd tell her to stop and send her straight along.

Georgie thanked her and ran all the way home. The kitchen was empty, but he saw a little pool of blood on the floor. He went to the sink and fetched a cloth from underneath, rinsed it in cold water and took it back to the blood, kneeling down to wipe up the mess. The floor was still smeared so he repeated his actions until the floor was clean; then he washed his hands and moved the boiling kettle off the heat on the range.

He stood at the foot of the stairs listening; he could hear Kate moaning and his mother saying something, but couldn't make out the words. Then his father came down. He looked at Georgie and then sat in his chair by the table. All of a sudden, he leaned forwards, covered his face with his hands, his shoulders shaking as he wept.

Georgie couldn't move. He wanted to go to his father and comfort him, but he couldn't think of the right words to say. It was all too awful – like a nightmare. He must have spoken the words without realising, because his father lifted his head and looked at him.

'That's just what it is, son,' he said in a voice so thick with grief that it didn't sound like him. 'If we hadn't already got enough troubles . . . Now our Kate. I thought she was strong enough to hold us together but—' A shriek from upstairs stopped him and then there was the sound of loud sobbing.

Just at that moment Nurse Bright arrived. She was a young woman, caring and efficient and she heard the sounds of grief coming from upstairs. 'I'll go straight up,' she said, nodding to Georgie and his father. They looked at each other. Then Georgie went to the range and moved the kettle back on the heat. He fetched the tea things, made two mugs of tea, and pushed one in front of his father. They both sat and drank in silence.

It was about twenty minutes later that Grace came down, carrying a little bundle in a bloody towel. She placed it on the kitchen sink and then sat down facing Georgie and her husband.

'We'll have to bury the poor mite,' she said. 'Can you find something suitable – a casket of some kind. We'll put her in the garden and say a few prayers ourselves. The nurse thinks she would've been a girl so we'll have to think of a name . . . Kate won't. She refused to look.' Grace bowed her head, covering her face with her hands for a moment. 'It's my fault. She was worrying herself over me.'

'Nonsense!' her husband cut in. 'There's always a chance it was going to happen anyway. You lost a couple, Gracie . . .'

'Yes, but they were both only a few weeks into the pregnancy. Kate was nearly five months. She shouldn't have lost it now, Ned . . . it was the grief and the worry over me. I doubt she'll forgive me.'

'Mum! Kate loves you,' Georgie cried. 'She won't blame you. It's not your fault they . . .' He broke off as he saw the look in her eyes. 'Sorry . . .'

'Nay, lad,' his father put in as Grace bowed her head again. 'We've lost Derek and we've lost Tom. All I pray is that Kate will be all right.' He looked round anxiously as the nurse entered the kitchen. 'How is she, nurse?'

'I think she ought to be in hospital for a few days so I'll arrange an ambulance for her. She needs to rest and she'll be given sensible advice there – better than being here. You've enough sorrow and trouble as it is, Mr and Mrs Greene. I was sorry to hear the news.'

'Thank you,' Mr Greene replied. Grace said nothing. She just sat stony-faced, her tears drying on her cheeks.

The nurse refused a cup of tea and left them, saying the ambulance would be along shortly. For a moment there was silence, then Georgie asked if he could go up to Kate.

'She'll be sleeping,' his mother told him. 'The nurse gave her something . . .' She wiped her cheeks. 'You

108

shouldn't be here, Georgie – though it was a good thing you were. You can stop tonight and go back in the morning. You're better off down there, for now at least. I'm still afraid of an invasion – and I can't cope. I need to be quiet.'

'Can't I wait for Tom's funeral?' Georgie sent an appeal to his father.

'You'd best do as your mum tells you,' he said. 'It isn't the right place for a lad.'

'I'd like to say goodbye . . .'

'So would we all!' Grace looked at her husband bitterly.

'He was gone before I got there,' Mr Greene said and tears began to trickle down his cheeks. 'I saw him but I couldn't tell him how sorry I was – how much I loved him.'

'I'm going back to bed,' Grace said just as the door opened and Jenny walked in. 'She'll make your tea for you.'

Jenny stared after her as she walked out, then looked at her grandfather and then her uncle. 'Where's Kate? I've got something to tell her!' There was a smile in her eyes that disappeared when Georgie told her that Kate's baby was lost.

'No! That's not fair,' she cried. 'Not Kate's baby, too!' She sat down and burst into tears. 'What will she do? Oh, she was so looking forward to being a mum . . .'

No one answered. No one knew what to say.

CHAPTER 13

'Dad wrote to someone and asked for a message to be sent to Steve,' Jenny said as she sat by Kate's hospital bed two days later. 'Perhaps he'll get leave and come home.'

'He might but he can't do much,' Kate replied. Her face was pale and her eyes were red-rimmed but she was getting better. She no longer felt as weak as she had when she was admitted. 'I know he'll be sorry for my sake – but he wasn't really ready to have a family. Perhaps it was a blessing in disguise . . .'

'You don't mean that!' Jenny cried, shocked. 'I know you don't. I've seen the little things you were making and collecting.' She hesitated, then, 'I packed them in a tin trunk and Grandad put them in your attic. We thought that best . . . they will keep nice for the next time.'

'Poor little girl, to be just a memory before she ever drew breath . . .' Kate's face screwed up with grief and she gave a small sob. 'It isn't fair that she never got a chance to live. I know it happens. I know small children die – but it still isn't fair.'

'No. It isn't,' Jenny agreed with her. 'Georgie sent you his love but Gran packed him off to Mum the next day. He argued and tried to persuade her but she wouldn't let him stay, said she wanted to know that at least one of her sons was safe.'

'That's Mum,' Kate said with a wry smile. 'Is she better now – up and doing things?'

'She gets up . . .' Jenny was hesitant. 'She doesn't do much, Kate. She didn't even get Grandad's tea last night. I fetched him pie and chips from the shop. I've been doin' a bit of housework for her – but she hardly knows I'm there some of the time. Sits in a daze, until Grandad mentions the funeral – and then she gets angry with us both. She says she won't go. She couldn't have a grave for Derek so she won't have one for Tom.'

'Oh dear.' Kate sighed. 'Dad will have to go on with it alone but I will be there. I'm going home tomorrow. You can come or stay at home with your Gran but I think we should have the funeral tea at mine if Mum doesn't want anything to do with it. It will just be us and a few close friends, but why shouldn't Tom have a little send off?'

'That reminds me,' Jenny said. 'I was at your house this morning, checking the milk and the post. I brought you these letters – and I took the milk to Gran's rather than waste it. Well, while I was there a man in RAF uniform came to the door and asked for you. It's that friend of Steve's who's been in hospital . . .'

'Oh, poor Chuck,' Kate exclaimed. 'I was going to visit him but in all the bother I completely forgot about him.'

'I told him you'd lost the baby and were in hospital.

I think he might visit you this evening.' Jenny looked concerned. 'I hope I did right? I wasn't sure if you'd want him to know?'

'Everyone will know in the end,' Kate said, a sigh escaping her lips. 'It doesn't matter, Jenny. I should like to see him – to apologize for not visiting.'

'You've had too much to do,' Jenny said. 'Gran blames herself for what happened to you, Kate.'

'No! That's daft,' Kate exclaimed. 'She mustn't. She really mustn't. It wasn't her fault – I'd been upset over losing Derek and when Dad told me about Tom . . . and then Mum was ill. You won't blame her, will you? She needs all our help—'

Kate broke off as they heard a terrific bang. They looked at each other in concern. 'What was that?' she asked, her hand shaking a little. 'A gas main or . . .?' The two young women looked at each other in dismay. Had it started at last, the bombing they'd all feared for months?

Jenny heard the commotion on the streets as she headed back home. Rumours were flying about what had happened but it seemed that on this lovely September afternoon the enemy had dropped several bombs on civilian areas. As yet no one appeared to know where they'd fallen, though the trails of dark smoke drifting across the East End of London seemed to indicate that they had been concentrated in the area, perhaps aimed for the busy dockyards, where ships and goods formed the lifeline for Britain. Sirens were blasting as she hurried home, not bothering to wait for a bus. Her jumping nerves calmed as she saw that Kate's house –

in fact the whole street – was still standing. She passed it by and started to run as she saw that there was smoke coming from just a few streets further on. Was it her grandparents' house? Her heart was thumping and her breath short as she turned the final corner and saw a scene of disaster before her. Two houses were on fire, but as her eyes searched and she counted frantically, she saw that their home was still standing; two doors away from the houses that had been hit, it looked as if the windows had smashed and the front door was hanging by a hinge.

'Gran!' Jenny gave a glad cry of relief as she saw her grandmother standing in the street in her slippers and pinny over a floral cotton dress. 'Oh, Gran dearest, are you hurt?'

Grace looked through her. She didn't seem to recognize Jenny and was obviously shocked. As Jenny reached for her hand, a woman in uniform came up to her. 'Is she your mum?'

'She's my gran. Her name is Grace Greene and my grandad lives there, too – but he'll be out at work. He drives trains . . .'

The woman nodded. 'It's good you arrived. Your gran is in shock and we'll be taking her to hospital. You'll need to get some stuff for her – and see about someone fixing your door, otherwise your house may be looted. It shouldn't happen, but it might.'

'How . . .?' Jenny asked but the woman was leading her gran to the ambulance. She went with her calmly, seeming almost childlike in her trust. Jenny looked around and then she saw someone she knew. 'Mr Simpson!'

Jeff Simpson came to her at once. 'Good thing your gran got out. Your neighbour caught it.'

'Nellie?' Jenny stared at him in horror. 'Was she killed?'

'Yes,' he said briefly, shaking his head in sorrow, and looked towards the Greenes' house. 'I'll fix the door for you and nail up the windows. Are you all right to go in and fetch a bit of stuff out, lass?'

Jenny could hardly take it in. Nellie dead?

'Y-yes. I'll take some to the hospital for Gran – and take Grandad's things to Kate's. He might want to stay here, but I shan't.'

'No, you'll be better orf elsewhere – not that any of us is safe now.' He suddenly crossed himself. 'God protect us. This is just the start of it!' He walked off, shaking his head and muttering to himself.

Jenny approached the house. An air raid warden appeared and asked what she wanted and she explained. He let her go in but told her not to take too much. 'Watch where you step, there's broken glass about, but it's safe enough otherwise. I don't reckon as you're a looter but we can't be too sure, miss.'

'Mr Simpson is going to board up the broken windows and secure the door for us,' Jenny said and he nodded gloomily, making no further attempt to stop her.

She trod on a bit of broken glass as she went in, but although some things had fallen down from shelves and the mantelpiece, there wasn't much damage. Jenny went up to the spare room and found some cases. She packed clothes for her grandmother and a few towels and soap; then she packed another case for her grandfather. She found his gold watch in the drawer beside his bed and her gran's handbag with her little bits of jewellery and some money under the bed on her side. She packed her gran's valuables in with her grandad's things and carried the cases outside. The air raid warden glanced at her and nodded but was too busy to speak to her again.

Jenny walked slowly back towards Kate's house. She had no idea how to let her grandfather know what had happened, but thought that once he saw his house he would come round to Kate's in search of her. Grandad would know that Jenny would go there. It would be a bit crowded if they all lived there – but would any of them wish to return to the house that had been home to them for so long?

CHAPTER 14

Kate was sitting up in bed, trying to persuade the nurse in charge to let her leave a day early when a man in RAF uniform walked in. He was carrying a large bunch of beautiful and fragrant roses, which he presented to Kate with a smile.

'Oh, Chuck, thank you so much. They are lovely,' Kate cried, her face alight with pleasure at the thoughtful gesture. 'Can you help me persuade this nurse that I'm fit to go home?'

'Are you?' he asked, smiling at her once more.

'Yes, I am – and I'm worried. There were bombs today and someone said they were in the area where we live. I need to see if Mum's all right.'

Chuck looked at the nurse. As he turned his head, Kate saw that there was a burn mark on the side of his face, also a red scar across his left eyebrow. He looked winningly at the nurse. 'Would it be at all possible for my wife to come home this evening if I promise to look after her?'

Kate was a little shocked at his audacity but as he

turned back to her and winked, she laughed. 'Please, nurse. He has to go back to his base soon . . .'

'Well . . .' The nurse looked from one to the other. 'I'll go and ask Doctor Brock. He's usually persuadable – and if your husband has to go back to duty, well, we have to look after our heroes . . .'

Chuck looked at her as the nurse went off to seek permission, anxious now. 'Was that all right, Kate? I thought it might work – and I'm sure Steve would understand.'

'Of course it was,' Kate replied and laughed. 'I just want to get out of here.' She picked up her roses, inhaling their beautiful scent. 'This is so kind. I was going to visit you in hospital, but things went wrong . . .'

'Yes, I know.' The smile left Chuck's eyes to be replaced by sympathy. 'I was sorry to learn about your brothers, Kate – and the baby, of course. That was really too much for anyone to bear.' He hesitated, then, 'I wasn't sure if I'd be in the way, but if there is anything I can do . . .'

'I'll be writing to Steve. If you could give it to him personally?'

'Yes. I would be glad to do it,' Chuck agreed. 'Oh, nurse is coming back and she looks pleased '

Kate looked and saw the nurse approaching. 'You can go,' she said. 'We need the beds – another influx of wounded is on the way. Just be careful and see your own doctor if you bleed or feel unwell.'

'Yes, I shall,' Kate told her. 'I'll be fine – thanks to your nursing.'

The nurse flushed and glanced at Chuck. 'Make sure

she takes it easy for a while – and no marital relations yet. She can't for a while.'

Kate flushed, but Chuck looked grave and nodded, thanking the nurse for her advice. 'Sorry. That's what we get for lying,' Kate said after she'd moved away. Pull the curtains, will you? I need to get dressed.'

'I should wait outside . . .'

'I may need help with my zip,' Kate said. 'You can turn your head until I'm decent – and I'll want your arm please. I might still be a bit shaky.'

'Are you sure you should go home?'

'Quite sure. I would've discharged myself if she hadn't let me go!'

Kate breathed a sigh of relief as she saw lights on in her house. She opened the door and went in, hearing both Jenny and her father's voices. Her heart quickened with fear, because it was unusual for her father to be here. Hurrying into the kitchen, Chuck lingering uncertainly behind, she saw them sitting at the table drinking tea, the remains of a meal spread before them.

'Dad?' she said breathlessly. 'How is Mum?'

'Kate, you're home!' Jenny said, jumping up to touch her hand. 'You look a bit pale. Should you be out of hospital yet?'

'I heard about the bombing . . .' Kate's anxious eyes met her father's. He nodded and looked sad.

'Grace is in hospital suffering from shock. It was next door that was hit – and poor Nellie caught it.'

Kate felt weak and dizzy of a sudden. She sat down with a little bump. 'Nellie – is she dead?'

'Aye, she was gone before they could get to her,

trapped under the rubble,' Kate's father confirmed. 'I reckon it must have been quick – I pray it was. She was a decent woman and your mother relied on her often enough.'

'She was Mum's best friend. Does Mum know?'

'Not sure. I visited her earlier but they'd given her something and she was sleepy. I think she knew me but . . .' He sighed and shook his head. 'Those two were friends before you were born, Kate. Grace will take it hard when she knows.'

Tears trickled down Kate's cheeks. 'It's never ending, Dad. One blow after another. I'm not sure Mum can cope.'

Chuck had moved forward, causing both Kate and her father to look at him. 'I'd best leave you,' he said in a quiet voice that was deep with sympathy. 'I'll call back tomorrow for that letter, Kate.'

Kate gave him a grateful glance. 'Thank you for everything. I'll visit Mum in the evening, Chuck, so best come as late as you can . . .' Seeing her father was staring at him oddly, she said, 'Dad, this is Chuck – a friend of Steve's. He visited me in the hospital and brought me home in his car.'

Her father stood up and offered his hand. 'I think I did meet you briefly when you stayed with Kate and Steve,' he said, smiling as they shook hands. 'Thank you for looking after her. I would've visited her later, but . . .' He shook his head.

'Naturally, you had to visit your wife,' Chuck said, smiled and took his leave. 'I can see myself out, Kate.'

'Nice chap,' her father said when he'd closed the door behind him. 'Sensible sort.'

'Yes. And I think he's clever. Steve said he helped him with his exams and he's a flight lieutenant.'

'So . . .' her father said. 'What are we goin' to do now, love? I slept on your sofa last night, but your mother needs her home.'

'Was it much damaged?'

'Windows smashed and front door blown off. We can use the back entrance. I'll go round in the morning and tidy up, get someone to put new glass in the windows, fix the front door a bit better. Trouble is, I'm not sure your mother will want to go back there. Nellie's house is a wreck – there was a fire and I doubt they can do much except pull it down.'

'We'll have to see how she feels when she's ready to come out of hospital. Perhaps she'd like to go down to the country – somewhere near Vera and the kids?'

'I don't know. She vowed she wouldn't leave me. I tried to get her to go when the others went, but she wouldn't . . .'

'I don't want to go to the country,' Jenny put in. She looked anxiously at Kate and her grandfather. 'Mum won't make me, will she?'

'She might once she knows the bombs are falling,' Kate replied. 'It might be safer for you, Jenny.'

'I'd hate it there. I'll only come back again.'

'Well, you can stay as far as I'm concerned, but Vera is your mother. If she says you've got to go, I can't pull against her.'

'I'll put in a word for you,' Jenny's grandfather said. 'Tell her how helpful you've been – gettin' me tea and lookin' after things.'

'She'll let me stay if you say you need me,' Jenny smiled. 'I am a help to you both, aren't I?'

They agreed she was, but looked at each other anxiously. Both Kate and her father knew that this was only the first day of bombing and it was bound to get worse. As if to confirm their fears they heard the siren start to wail.

'We'd best look for shelter,' Mr Greene said, jumping up and reaching for his jacket. 'The pub in the next road has a cellar they might let us take cover in.'

As they emerged from the house, they saw the street was filled with people; some looking anxiously at the sky. Now they could hear the ack-ack of guns in the distance and the roar of many planes headed their way.

'Where are you headed?' one of Kate's neighbours asked.

'To the Green Man pub,' she answered.

'They can only take a dozen. We're goin' down the underground . . .'

'We'd best go there then.'

Kate, her father, and Jenny ran as fast as they could, as the drone of planes got louder and then they heard a tremendous explosion and saw smoke over the docks.

'Looks as if they're catchin' it tonight,' her father said as they ran down the stone steps to the underground station.

The platforms were already crowded but he found a space for them and spread his jacket for Jenny to sit down. Kate joined them, placing her coat on the ground and making room for her father to sit next to her. As she glanced around, she saw that some people had brought food with them and also blankets.

'We may have to start doin' that too,' her father said and put an arm about her shoulders. Kate leaned against him. She felt tired and weak. She'd wanted to leave hospital but she'd thought she would sleep in her own bed rather than on the platform of an underground station.

CHAPTER 15

'There you are,' Vera exclaimed as she read the details of what was happening in London in her newspaper that weekend. 'Now you can see why I wanted to come to the country. It must be terrible back home these days.'

'I hope Mum and Dad and Kate are all right,' Georgie said. 'What did Kate say in her letter, Vera?'

'I told you, she just said that the house next door had been hit and Mum was in hospital. Kate'd just come out after her miscarriage and the siren went so they had to shelter in the underground . . .'

'I think I should go back if Mum isn't well,' Georgie said. 'She might need help – Kate, too.'

'If they wanted you, they'd have said.' Vera looked cross. 'You can't leave, Georgie. I need you here for shopping and fetching the milk and stuff. You know I do.'

'You can manage. Mrs Baker would look after the baby if you were sick.' He gave her a mutinous look. 'I only said I'd come down for a while . . .'

'Oh, stop being a nuisance,' Vera said as the baby wailed. 'I've got enough to do without you playing me up. It isn't safe for you up there. I'd tell Jenny she has to come back, but Kate says she needs her to help for a while so I suppose I must let her stay – but I don't like it.'

'I'm goin' out,' Georgie said and went. Billy followed him and they walked down the drove towards the farm in silence for a few minutes.

'You won't go and leave me alone with Mum?' Billy asked in a small voice. 'Please, Georgie. You promised.'

Georgie sighed. He *had* promised and he didn't like breaking his word. The summer had been good on the farm. He and Billy had enjoyed roaming the countryside, climbing trees, and helping in the fields when they were needed. Georgie was already proficient in milking, and Billy liked feeding the animals. He'd got into a few scrapes, riding on the back of the sow and running round the field after the farmer's horses, but he hadn't yet got one of them to let him ride it. He'd fallen out of a tree, but luckily hadn't broken any limbs, just felt bruised and sore for a few days. Overall, they'd both done more good than harm.

Now, the school holidays were just a happy memory and they were back to school. Neither of them liked it much, preferring the freedom they'd had for those long weeks. Now it was a rush in the morning to do their chores, pick up their sandwiches for school and eat their breakfast before catching the bus into Chatteris. Mostly, they ate a piece of toast as they walked, unless Georgie rode the bike he'd borrowed from the farmer with Billy on the handlebars. They parked it in a hedge near the road for the day and no one ever touched it. Georgie reckoned it was pretty safe because hardly anyone but the farmer and his family even passed by.

Georgie had ridden all over on his borrowed bike. He'd been as far as Mepal, a nearby village, to swim in the river. The airfield was close by and he'd walked up to the guard on the gates, asking if he could look at the planes, but wasn't allowed in. He'd lain in an adjacent field in the sun and watched the planes as they flew out on a mission; it was warm in the sun and the grass smelled sweet and fresh, insects buzzing and chirping round his head.

Billy really wanted a cycle of his own so that he could come too, but no one knew of a suitable one he could borrow. Mr Barker had suggested Billy's mum might buy him one for Christmas, but she'd said it was far too expensive.

'Billy can use Georgie's when he grows a bit,' was all she'd said when he'd pestered her.

Georgie took Billy with him for rides into the fens. He sat on the handlebars and they careered through fields of long grass and collapsed in a heap to lie amongst the daisies, laughing at each other as they ate jam sandwiches and drank orange squash from bottles.

The work on the farm was hard. Georgie had done the job of a man, using a pitchfork to help stack first corn and then straw after the threshing. Threshing was hot dusty work and his face got black when he was put on the dirty job of filling the chaff sacks, bits flying all over him, in his hair and his eyes. After his day's work was done, Mrs Baker had given him rock buns and a glass of cool lemonade before he went into the cowshed to help with the milking. He'd slept well that night.

Billy had spent that day helping Mrs Baker to weed her vegetable garden and had carried home a basket of lettuces, tomatoes, spring onions and radishes, together with half a dozen eggs from the hens. His mother had been very pleased with him. Georgie had given her half his wages, which she'd thanked him for, but money didn't buy much these days, because the food wasn't in the shops. You could only buy the meagre rations everyone was allowed, which was just a few ounces of meat, butter, sugar, and lard. So it was the vegetables, from Mrs Baker's garden, and the gift of a trapped rabbit, pigeon, or a piece of a pig's innards that was so valuable and eked out their sparse diet. It was the same for everyone, and Vera made the most of whatever she got. Georgie couldn't fault her for cooking, but she often seemed cross for no reason that he could see.

He wasn't sure she liked living in the country any more than they did. The only time he'd seen her perk up and laugh was when Jock came down on the Bank Holiday Monday and stayed overnight. He'd slept on the sofa in the living room, and the next day he'd taken them into March, a nearby town, and bought them all lunch at a pub. The adults had eaten inside, but Billy and Georgie had their ham and chips followed by ice cream at a table in the gardens at the back of the pub. The landlord had a dog, which was friendly and begged for food so they gave him some chips and a small piece of ham. There were also guinea pigs and rabbits in cages. Billy fed them bits of grass.

When Georgie mentioned them later, Vera grimaced and told them the animals weren't pets. 'He keeps them for food, I expect,' she said, and that made Billy cry.

Georgie's thoughts came back to the present as Billy grabbed him by the arm, pointing to a field. He looked and saw a horse lying down, but it seemed to be struggling, and it was making a noise – an odd sound, as if it was in pain.

'That's Mr Baker's best mare,' Billy said. 'She's in foal – do you think she's all right?'

Before Georgie could answer, Billy had jumped the ditch and was in the field. He knelt down and stroked the horse's flank and then looked at the back of it, which looked swollen and bloody.

'I reckon she's havin' her foal and can't manage it,' he called to Georgie. 'You'd better go and fetch Mr Baker. Run, Georgie! She's struggling!'

Georgie ran faster than he ever remembered and was gasping for breath when he got to the farm gate. Mr Baker was in his car, about to drive off, but Georgie jumped in front of him, waving his arms frantically. Mr Baker screeched to a halt and jumped out of the car, shouting at him.

'What the hell are you playing at, lad? I could've knocked you over.'

'It's the mare!' Georgie gasped. 'We reckon she's strugglin' to have her foal.'

'Right, jump in then,' the farmer said, and as soon as Georgie was in beside him, he set off back down the drove. Billy was still next to the mare, stroking her and talking to her as she kicked and struggled, clearly having trouble birthing her young. 'Well, blow me down . . . I'd never have thought she'd let that rascal do that to her.'

Mr Baker was out of the car and striding towards the stricken mare. He bent over it and then turned back to Georgie. 'Run back to the farm and tell my wife to telephone for the vet – tell her it's an emergency.'

Georgie nodded, not bothering to answer. He'd only just got his breath back, but he ran almost as fast as the first time. Mrs Baker was in the kitchen and she looked at him in surprise as he burst in on her, but listened and nodded. She told him to sit down and catch his breath while she went into the hall and made the call.

'He'll be here straight away; he's only just up the road,' Mrs Baker said. 'It's a good thing he hadn't gone out on his rounds – another few minutes and we'd have missed him.'

Georgie smiled, still panting a bit. She nodded and gave him a bun and a glass of squash. 'Good thing you were passing and saw, Georgie,' she said. 'The mare might have died otherwise. You and young Billy have been a godsend these past weeks. We were promised a land girl but she went down with a burst appendix so we never got her – and they haven't sent a replacement yet. I hope you won't be going back to London – not that anyone would want to at the moment. I feel so sorry for those that have to live there.'

'My mum's neighbour got killed,' Georgie said. 'She was a nice lady – and Mum's upset. I want to visit her, but my sister says I'm needed here.'

'Well, that's quite true. You are. My husband said you worked as hard as any man when they were threshing. You're a good lad, Georgie.'

Georgie grinned, finished his drink, and set off back towards the field where the mare was giving birth. As he walked, he was passed by a rather battered-looking Land Rover he knew belonged to the vet; Georgie had seen him around the farm a few times, giving injections and treating the cows and pigs.

By the time Georgie got to the field the vet was in action. He'd got his arm inside the mare and was turning the foal, while she snorted and tried to rear but was held by Mr Baker and Billy, who was now stroking its nose and watching everything avidly.

In a few minutes it was all over. The foal had been assisted into the world and was lying, covered in its birth sack, next to its mother, who miraculously seemed to have recovered and was no longer rolling her eyes or snorting. She started to lick the foal free of the membrane, and then, within minutes, the miracle happened and the little creature was up on its spindly legs, nuzzling at its mother.

Billy hadn't left the mare's side. He was pressing his face into her neck, gentling her as she gave a snort of alarm and tossed her head; at his voice, she quietened and turned to nuzzle him before returning to her foal.

'Thank you,' Mr Baker said to the vet. 'I reckon we could have lost her if you hadn't been home.'

'You need to thank this young lad too,' the vet said and smiled at Billy. 'He kept her quiet and saved her from getting in a worse state. I reckon he's a natural.' He looked directly at Billy. 'You should consider becoming a vet, young man. I think it's your calling.'

Billy turned pink but didn't say anything for a minute, then, 'I just wanted ter 'elp her.'

'Aye, lad. That's what vets do.'

Georgie glanced at Billy. He seemed as if he didn't want to leave the mare, even though she was fine now. Mr Baker turned to look at them.

'Would you lads fetch her a bucket of warm bran mash? I reckon she needs a treat?'

'Yes, I'll go,' Georgie offered.

'I'll come,' Billy said. 'I know how she likes it.'

The two of them set off towards the farm and were passed, first by the vet and then by the farmer in their vehicles. In the yard they set about making the warm bran mash with some hot water from the kitchen. Georgie looked at Billy, who seemed a bit quiet.

'It was like a miracle what that vet did – and then the way the foal suddenly stood up on those spindly legs.'

'Yeah, a miracle,' Billy said, looking at him in awe. 'She was so frightened when I started talking to her, but then she seemed to listen to me and I told her the vet would come and make her well.'

'He said you should be a vet, Billy.' Georgie looked at him. 'You need a lot of schoolin' for that.'

'I know. I don't reckon I'm clever enough.'

'You might be if yer tried. You knew what to do, Billy. I thought she'd bite yer or kick out at yer – but she trusted you.'

'Yeah. I liked that.' Billy smiled at him. 'I like livin' on the farm – or near it. I hated it at first but now I reckon I could stay in the country. I could work with animals on the farm, even if I couldn't be a vet.'

'Maybe you could, if you work hard,' Georgie said. 'Tell you what, Billy. If you promise to work hard in class, I'll stay here with you. I might go and visit Mum when I can – but I'll come back.' He looked hard at his nephew. 'You've got to promise to get good grades, though.'

Billy was silent for a moment, then, 'All right then. I'll try and we'll see what happens.' Georgie grinned at him. 'Race yer back. We've got egg on toast for tea tonight!'

CHAPTER 16

'How is your mother?' Chuck asked when he called to collect the letter for Steve. Kate asked him into the kitchen and made a cup of tea. He looked at her uncertainly. 'I was sorry to intrude yesterday . . .'

'You didn't,' Kate told him. 'I was very grateful for your help. I'm glad to see you safe after last night's raid. I wondered how you'd got on. We all rushed down the underground when the siren went, but it seems they were after the docks.'

'Yes, pretty mess they've made, I expect,' Chuck said. 'My hotel had a cellar prepared so some of us went there to shelter.' He took the letter she offered and placed it in his breast pocket. 'I'll make sure Steve receives this but I'm not sure he'll get leave, Kate. We're going to be pretty busy. The bastards will savage London and as many of the big cities as they can so our fighters will be up constantly, trying to fight them off – and the bombers will be retaliating over their cities. All leave has been cancelled.'

'Yes, I understand. It's all right, Chuck. I can manage. I have my dad and Jenny – and Mum was conscious

132

when I saw her . . .' Her voice broke slightly and he made a move towards her, as though to comfort her, and then checked himself. 'She isn't quite sure where she is or what's going on . . .'

'I'm so sorry. I wish I could tell you everything will be fine, but I can't . . .' His blue eyes rested on her face. 'All I will say is that if you and your loved ones should feel you need to escape all this – my family would be glad to take you in and help you settle. You could stay in Canada until the war is over.'

'In Canada?' Kate was astonished at his offer. 'That is so kind of you, Chuck. It is really lovely of you but I think we'll try and see it out – though that is a lovely thought.'

'I . . .' he faltered, giving his head a slight shake, visibly wanting to say more. 'The offer is there if things get too hard.' He smiled oddly, half shy, half something else she wasn't sure of. 'I must leave. I have to catch a train in an hour. Please take care of yourself, Kate. I'll be seeing you . . .'

She went with him to her door, watching as he walked away. Somewhere in London a bombing raid was happening. It sounded quite far away. She'd heard the siren and the ack-ack as she'd walked home from the hospital but she hadn't run for the shelters. Somehow, she'd felt safe, as if she knew it wouldn't be her area that night. They seemed to be peppering London and the South East with bombs at the moment, but they weren't the only ones to be raided. Other big cities were getting it, too.

Kate turned back into the house and shut her door. Her father was on night shift but she wasn't sure where

Jenny had gone. Perhaps she'd headed for the shelter of the underground when the siren sounded.

Kate was tired but her body no longer ached all over. She was still sore inside but knew it would be a while before she healed. The physical pain was bearable but now that she was alone, with nothing particular to do for the moment, the grief hit her. Her baby had gone, torn from her womb too soon because of the worry and stress over her brothers and her mother.

'When you suffer an internal trauma like yours,' the doctor had told her, 'your body will need a long time to heal properly. You may seem fine, but inside may not be all that it should – and I think it likely that you might not fall for another child until you are really over this. It may take years, if ever . . .'

Kate had held back her tears then, but now they came thick and fast as she curled up on the sofa and wept. She'd wanted her child, had been so happy. It wasn't fair that she'd had to lose it when you thought of all the unwanted children there were. Why couldn't she have kept it warm and cosy inside her its full term?

Her tears dried at last and she got up, going into the cloakroom to splash her face with cold water. She was lucky to have a downstairs toilet as well as one upstairs. Her mother didn't have that luxury.

Kate's thoughts went to her mother. Grace had looked at her daughter almost vacantly when she'd visited the hospital, as if she wasn't truly seeing her, even though she'd spoken her name.

What were they going to do if she didn't recover?

*

Kate wasn't surprised when Georgie turned up on her doorstep a few weeks later on the first day of school half-term. She opened her door to him, inviting him in and then suddenly hugging him to her fiercely.

'Vera wouldn't let me come before,' Georgie told her. 'She said I shouldn't miss my classes and I'd only be in the way – I shan't, shall I?'

'Of course not.' Kate ruffled the top of his head. She noticed that he'd grown a lot since he'd started living in the country. He was past her shoulder now and filling out, too. If she hadn't known he was fourteen, she would have taken him for sixteen at least. 'You'll have to sleep on my sofa – unless you want to go home at nights. Dad is sleeping at the house now but Jenny won't stay there at night. She goes round and does a few jobs, makes some tea for Dad – unless they both come here.'

'Mum is still in hospital?' Georgie looked at her anxiously. More than a month had passed since the first full-on air raid on London, during which time Georgie had fretted inwardly but stuck to his promise to stay with his nephew. 'Can I see her? I've only got a couple of days. I promised Billy I wouldn't stay longer.'

'Mum is in a kind of nursing home,' Kate told him. 'The hospital needed the beds for patients who are physically ill. There are so many wounded soldiers these days that they fill the hospitals to overflowing.'

Georgie nodded; he read the papers and knew what was happening. 'Why can't she come home?'

Kate hesitated, then, knowing he had to be told. 'The doctors say she is suffering from mental trauma. She isn't ill in her body, Georgie, but her mind is . . .

135

well, the best way I can describe it is that she's lost somewhere – in the past, I think. Sometimes, when I visit, she knows me for a few minutes; she smiles and asks me how I am, sensibly, the way she always was – but then she starts talking like I'm still a little girl. She thinks I'm still in school and she talks about Derek and Tom as if they were still boys.'

Georgie's eyes widened. He was silent for a long time, then, 'Poor Mum,' he said. 'That's awful, Kate. What does Dad say?'

'Not much. You know Dad, Georgie. He thinks a lot but doesn't say very much. He misses her terribly, of course he does, but we look after him – and he'll be happy to see you. I think it's his day off tomorrow.'

'Great! We can spend some time together.'

'I'll take you to see Mum this afternoon,' Kate said. 'We'll try to get her some fruit if we can, or perhaps some nice biscuits – but she doesn't look at magazines or books so no point in taking them.'

'What does she do all day? She was always so busy looking after us kids, Kate.' His eyes were wet but he scuffed the tears away.

'I believe she just loses herself in the times when she had all her family and she was happy. We were a very happy family, Georgie.' Kate reached out and took his hand, squeezing it. 'Don't ever lose sight of that, love. What has happened these past few months is more than Mum can bear. I hardly know how to cope when I think Derek and Tom won't ever come home – so imagine how hard it is for her.'

Georgie nodded. 'I miss them too. They were

smashing brothers – looked after me when I was a youngster, showed me all sorts.'

'Yes.' Kate smiled at him. 'Remember how they taught you to play football, Georgie? Hang on to the good things. We'll get through these hard times and be happy again, and we'll never forget those we lost.'

'No, we shan't,' he agreed.

'We're lucky. We still have family – we have each other.' Georgie nodded and then smiled at her.

'Billy needs me,' Georgie told her. 'I look after him at school. Some of the older boys tried to bully him when I wasn't around but I sorted them. They leave him alone now.' He flashed a grin at her. 'I reckon he's goin' ter be a vet when he's old enough. He helped when a foal was born and the mare was in trouble – and now he's studying hard so he can go to college and become a vet.'

'Well, that's wonderful,' Kate said and looked at him thoughtfully. 'What does Vera think of that idea?'

'She doesn't know yet. Billy hasn't told her . . .' Georgie hesitated, then, 'Vera gets cross a lot these days. She was only happy when Jock came down and stayed overnight . . .'

Kate saw the uncomfortable look in his eyes. 'What is it, Georgie? What are you afraid to say?'

'Vera hasn't heard from Bob in a long time. I believe she thinks he's dead . . .' He hesitated, then, 'If – if she did something wrong, would Bob be very angry? I mean I suspect, but I don't know . . .' He flushed bright red. 'I like Bob. It isn't right . . .'

'Georgie! You don't think Vera is – is—'

'Betraying her husband,' Georgie said and looked straight at her. 'I think she is, Kate. I reckon I heard them when Jock stayed overnight. He was supposed to be on the sofa downstairs but when I went down for a glass of water he wasn't there – and I heard them laughing in her room.'

'Oh, Georgie! You haven't told anyone else?'

'Nah, 'course not,' Georgie said. 'I wouldn't let on to Billy and I hoped it wasn't true – but she was all happy and smiling the next day, and now she's miserable again, because he can't get down at the moment.'

'That does sound . . . but we mustn't jump to conclusions and nor should we judge. I don't know what Vera and Bob's marriage was like before the war. I thought it was sound but . . .' She sighed. 'In a way, I understand, Georgie. I haven't seen Steve for months now and I doubt if I shall for ages, because the pilots just don't have the time to come home. He rings me now and then at the phone box on the corner and I write long letters to him – but he hardly ever writes back; he's never been one for that, not even Christmas or birthday cards. He'll buy me a present or bring me flowers now and then – but sometimes he just gives me money to get what I'd like. It doesn't mean he doesn't love me; he does, but he isn't into sentimental stuff much.'

Georgie nodded. 'Steve's OK though, isn't he? He wouldn't go off with another woman?'

'I'd kill him if he did,' Kate said and laughed, but then her laughter died. 'Bob has a temper. If he ever suspected Vera and Jock were having an affair . . .

138

but perhaps there was a reason he was in her room – catching a mouse or something.'

'I'd never tell Bob,' Georgie declared. 'I think it's mean of her, though. I might be wrong but I'm pretty sure I'm not.'

Kate nodded. 'Just keep it to yourself. It might be just a fling and Vera will be fine when Bob comes back – as we all shall.' She looked sad. 'I don't know when it will end. It all seems a bit hopeless at the moment – we're not getting on as well as we all thought.'

'I know. People pretend we're winning, but we might lose. The Germans are much stronger than the government expected – and we weren't ready. That's what my teacher says anyway.'

'She might be right,' Kate said and hesitated as she heard the wail of a siren. 'Damn them! Not again!' She looked at Georgie. 'Shall we run for the shelters or just go under the stairs?'

'Let's go under the stairs,' he said. 'I'm hungry – can we take some food with us?'

His expression made Kate laugh. 'Let's grab the biscuits and buns I made earlier. I was expecting you, you see, and I saved my rations to use this weekend.'

The raid was a short one and didn't come near them. When the all clear sounded and they came out from under the stairs, Kate made them a light lunch of tomato sandwiches and then they set out for the nursing home, which was across the river in Southwark. It was a big, old house, set in grounds close to a peaceful spot on the river. Autumn sunlight was playing on the water and the trees had just begun to turn gold and brown.

They were told Mrs Greene was in the common room – a large, comfortably furnished lounge overlooking the river. A big window looked out at the gardens and the river in the distance, but Grace was sitting in a corner, her back to the pleasant view, eyes closed.

'Mum?' Georgie reached out and touched her hand. She opened her eyes, stared at him for a moment and then smiled.

'Tom,' she said. 'You look well, lad. Have you been playing cricket?'

'Mum! It's me, *Georgie*,' he said, his eyes moving to Kate's face. She smiled at him reassuringly.

'You like cricket, don't you, Tom,' Grace said calmly and patted his hands. 'Derek likes football best but you like your cricket. Your dad will be home for his tea soon. Put the kettle on, love.'

'She doesn't know me,' Georgie's voice caught with a hint of tears.

Kate reached for his hand and squeezed it hard. 'You do look like Tom did at your age. It's all right, Georgie. She hasn't forgotten you in her heart, it's just her mind playing tricks on her.'

Georgie swallowed hard. 'It's all right, Mum,' he said and bent to kiss her cheek. 'I love you. I always will.'

'That's a good boy, Georgie,' she said and for a moment she smiled as she looked at him. She closed her eyes, appearing to doze off again. Georgie stroked the back of her hand. She'd known him briefly. It was like Kate said, she was still his mum, even if she wasn't the same.

A nurse brought them a cup of tea each. She left one for Grace with a plain biscuit. 'She does this all the time,' the nurse said brightly. 'She'll wake in a minute – but if she doesn't just give her a nudge. She needs to drink her tea and eat if she will.'

She went away and Grace opened her eyes. 'I'll have me tea,' she said and then looked at Kate. 'What are you doin' here, love? You should be home looking after your man. The baby will be here soon don't forget . . .'

A flicker of pain passed across Kate's face. 'The baby has gone, Mum,' she said with a catch in her voice. 'How are you today?'

'I'm all right.' She looked at Georgie. 'Tom was here just now . . . You should be with Vera, Georgie. Too dangerous in London . . .' A tear squeezed from the side of her eye.

'I came to see you, Mum. I love you . . .'

'Love you, too,' she said. She sipped half her tea and then handed the cup back to Kate; she hadn't touched the biscuit. 'When is Derek coming? I haven't seen him for ages . . .' She closed her eyes again.

Georgie looked at Kate. 'Is she always like this?' he asked in a whisper.'

'Pretty much,' she replied. 'Yes, I'm afraid that's probably the most she'll say today.'

They sat with their mother for another half an hour but she didn't open her eyes again, and, after kissing her cheek and telling her they would come again, they left. They both looked back as they left the ward but her eyes were still closed. Neither of them could see the single tear that slipped down her cheek as they turned away.

'Is she really asleep?' Georgie asked as they went out into the now chilly air to catch a bus.

'I'm not sure,' Kate replied. 'Some of the time perhaps – but I think she just blocks us all out, because she'd rather live in the past. Whether she's conscious of doing that I don't know.'

'Will she get better?' Georgie was battling his tears and Kate put an arm about his shoulders.

'The doctors think she will in time. I certainly pray she will,' Kate gave him a hug. 'At least she knew you for a moment.'

'It's not fair!' Georgie said in a burst of sudden anger. 'Why did they both have to die?'

'I can't tell you. It seems senseless to me.'

Georgie laid his head against her shoulder for a moment. 'I hate this war.'

'So do I,' Kate said. 'Come on. Let's see if we can find anything nice for tea.'

CHAPTER 17

They found some crumpets and a pot of honey. Kate scooped them up with glee and they hurried back to her house. She put the kettle on and made up the range, then they opened the door and toasted the crumpets one by one on a long fork in front of the fire. When they'd toasted four, they were spread with margarine and some of the honey. Warm and dripping they tasted wonderful and they'd just about finished theirs when Jenny came in, her cheeks glowing from the cool breeze that had sprung up.

'Crumpets! Wonderful! I hope you've saved some for me?'

'We've got two for you and two for Dad,' Kate told her. 'We've had a pot of tea but we'll have another one now you're in. Don't throw the old leaves out, Jenny. Just add another spoonful and it'll make a decent pot of tea again. I have to be bit careful, even though Dad gave me his ration. We can't use Mum's rations because she's in hospital.'

'You've got mine, though,' Jenny said. 'Mum did send them to you?'

'Not this month – not yet anyway,' Kate replied. 'It doesn't matter. We'll manage as long as we're careful. I'll remind your mum I need your new ration book when I write to her.'

'I bet she's using mine,' Jenny said and took off her coat. 'Well, I got myself a job!'

Kate stared at her. 'You're not fifteen yet. How did you manage that?'

'I lied. I'm fifteen next week so it's near enough. I'm going to be working in Peacocks from next Monday. I'm on the jumpers and cardigans counter.'

'Well done!' Kate said, looking at her in surprise. 'You haven't even got your school leaving certificate yet – though I'm sure you'll pass your exams. I looked at your answers and they were all correct.' She hesitated, then, 'I thought you wanted to be in a dress shop – a nice one in the West End?'

'I do – but I'll have to work elsewhere first for a while,' Jenny told her. 'I tried three shops last week and two the week before and they all said I was too young or needed experience in the retail business. So today when I came away from the canteen I've been helping out in – the one for injured servicemen you told me about – well, I saw this job advertised in the window.' Jenny grinned, clearly pleased with herself. 'I told them I'd finished my education at home and sat my exams – and they asked a few questions, then said if I could start on Monday the job was mine.'

'If it's what you want?' Kate smiled at her. 'I'm glad you just went out and got yourself a job, Jenny. I was going to talk to you about it, see if I could help you – but you didn't need my help.'

'I doubt I'd have got it if you hadn't helped me finish my studies and put me in for the postal exams.' Jenny looked pleased with herself. 'I thought I might have to go in the jam or biscuit factory when they all turned me down – but now I don't have to.' She hesitated, then, 'It isn't much money yet. I get thirty shillings a week for the first six months and then it goes up to two pounds and five shillings. After a year I could be a senior assistant if they're satisfied with me and then I would get nearly three pounds.'

'I doubt you would've got more at the dress shops in the West End,' Kate said. 'That's a good starting wage, Jenny.'

'I know. They thought I was bright, clean, and honest,' Jenny said with a little giggle. 'It's the nice dress you helped me make, Kate. And the fact that they really need assistants. Most of the girls are signing up for the Women's Forces or the factories – unless they're goin' for nurses. So shops like Peacocks are finding it hard to get more experienced girls. I told them I'd been doing volunteer work and they were very impressed – and that's all because of you, Kate. If you hadn't let me come and live with you, and told me what to do, I might not have got the job I wanted.'

'I'm glad,' Kate said and gave her a hug. 'Your mum will be proud of you when I tell her.'

Jenny shrugged. 'She might, but it doesn't matter. I'm happy here – oh, and they'll give me a nice dress to wear as a uniform. It's grey with a white collar. I'll need to buy another dress like it and make some white collars to change, though.'

Kate put the crumpets in front of her and she bit

into one with pleasure. 'It's better than a birthday,' she said and Kate smiled.

'We'll go to Lyons one day to celebrate. When is your half day?'

'On Mondays,' Jenny replied. 'You have Monday off sometimes, too, don't you?'

'I can change my afternoon off when I want,' Kate told her. 'My colleagues all change when they want to go somewhere. That way we keep the library open six days a week.'

Jenny nodded, still munching. Georgie looked at his sister. 'Do you miss teaching, Kate?'

She was pouring a fresh cup of tea and hesitated, then made a wry face. 'Yes, I do, Georgie. Quite a lot actually. The library is a nice place to work and we hold a few classes sometimes in the evenings for adults who didn't get much schooling – but I miss seeing the children's faces.'

'I wish you were our teacher in Chatteris,' Georgie said. 'I suppose you wouldn't think of coming down?'

'I have thought of it,' Kate said, glancing up as they heard a faint wail. A siren was going off somewhere but not close by. 'It isn't very pleasant or safe here at the moment, but my home is here. I don't want to give it up – and there's Mum and Dad and Jenny . . . and one of these days Steve will get leave.'

'He didn't come home after you were ill?'

'All leave was cancelled,' Kate told him. 'He rang me after he got the letter . . .' A spasm of grief passed across her face. 'He was sorry, of course, and worried about me. He sent me some flowers – well, got a florist to bring them. I suppose he must have rung them up.

146

Don't know how he managed it, but I got a lovely bouquet, and a note telling me when he would ring.' She smiled and shrugged. 'Steve thinks there's plenty of time for us to start a family and I expect he's right—'

She broke off as another siren suddenly sounded, this one much closer. 'Perhaps we should all get under the stairs – bring your crumpets, Jenny!'

They all scrambled into the hall and squeezed into the cupboard. It was just big enough for the three of them to sit on the cushions and rugs Kate had placed in there.

They could still, very faintly, hear the ack-ack of guns going off somewhere not too far away and knew that a fleet of planes must be in the vicinity. Suddenly there was a huge explosion and the house shook, which meant the bomb might have exploded either in this street or the next. Jenny put her hands over her ears and leaned up against Kate. She put her arms around them both, holding them close as they waited for the next big bang.

It didn't happen. After ten minutes or so they stopped huddling together, just waiting. They could hear sirens going off, but they belonged to the ambulances and fire engines that would be needed after a raid.

'It wasn't our street,' Kate said after a bit. 'The sirens aren't close enough.'

A few minutes longer and they heard the all clear. Georgie scrambled out first and ran to the front door to look out. He could see a pall of smoke off to the right and came back as Kate followed him to the door.

'It was Coal Street,' he said. 'You can see the smoke. Are you going to 'ave a look?'

147

'No. I can't do anything to help and I'd only be in the way,' Kate told him. 'If you want to see you can, but be careful. There may be holes in the ground and shattered glass everywhere.'

'I'd like to take a look,' he said. 'Don't worry. I'll take care not to get in anyone's way and I won't hurt myself.'

Georgie ran off without waiting for his sister's reply. He'd been frightened when the raid was happening, fearful a bomb would fall on them but it hadn't happened, so now he was curious.

When he got to Coal Street, just round the corner, he saw that two houses were on fire. One looked as if it had been a direct hit but the flames had jumped to the next terraced house and were spreading along the communal roof. It would be lucky if the fire engines could stop it taking the whole terrace.

Everyone was out in the street, watching as the firemen fought the flames. Two ambulances were there and men were digging at the ruins of the house that had taken the full blast. It belonged to a family called Smith . . . Smoke and bits of debris were everywhere. Georgie saw the men digging bring up a body – it was a child's . . . and now they were trying to get a woman out.

'She's dead, too,' someone shouted. And then a bit of burning roof slid down and the men digging had to move back in a hurry.

Georgie turned away. His eyes were stinging from the smoke and he felt a pain in his chest, wanting to cry for the two who had died. He suddenly ran back to his sister's house, wanting to be with her.

She looked at him as he rushed in. 'Is someone hurt bad?' she asked.

'It's little Lily Smith and her mum,' Georgie said. 'They pulled them both out of the rubble but they were dead.'

'Oh, poor Lily – poor Betty,' Kate said. 'I was talking to Betty last week. She said she was thinking of going to stay with her cousin at the seaside but didn't want to leave her home . . .'

'Too late now,' Georgie said and to his horror he burst into tears.

Kate crossed the room swiftly and enfolded him in her arms. 'I know, love. I know,' she comforted, stroking his hair. 'It hurts. It doesn't matter whether it's our family or friends. It just hurts . . .'

'And Mum,' Georgie mumbled into her chest. 'It hurts to see her that way, Kate. It isn't right. This bloody war just isn't right.'

'I know that, my darling,' Kate said and kissed his forehead.

Jenny came to put her arms around him and they all hugged each other, eyes meeting in shared grief. It didn't matter who died, it was all the same, pain and grief for everyone.

Georgie sniffed and broke away first, rubbing his eyes. 'Sorry. I wanted to see but now I know. I hope I never see anything like that again.'

'Dad will be home soon,' Kate said. 'Why don't you let him take you back to the country on the train?

You can talk and have something to eat somewhere, before you catch a bus to where you live. There's no need for you to be here, Georgie. You're happier and better in the country, aren't you?'

Georgie was silent for a moment, then he lifted his head and looked at her. 'Yes, I am,' he said at last. 'I thought I would hate it but I don't. I like the farmer. I help out with chores and his wife is kind – and it's safer there. I just wish you were all with us.'

'I don't think we'd all get into your cottage,' Kate said and laughed. 'I tell you what – I'll take a day off tomorrow and come with you. We'll all get away from this for a few hours – what about you, Jenny? Will you come, too?'

'Yes, all right. Mum can't make me stay there now I've got a job – and we can collect my new ration book, too.'

CHAPTER 18

Vera wasn't in when they arrived at the cottage, but Georgie knew where the key was and opened the door so they could go in and make a cup of tea for themselves. 'I expect she's helping Mrs Baker at the farm. I'll run down and tell her we're here for a short visit.'

'I'll come with you,' his father said. 'I'd like to see Mr and Mrs Baker – just to thank them for taking you in, lad. It's done you a lot of good working on the farm.'

'I like it, Dad,' Georgie told him. 'I thought it would be awful and when it's cold in the mornings, I don't always feel like getting up to do my chores – but once I'm up and on the farm, I'm – I'm happy.'

'That's good to know,' his father replied and put a casual arm across his shoulders. 'You'll be fifteen next year, Georgie. You could leave school if you want the life of a labourer. Have you thought about what you'll do when you're grown up?'

'I'm not sure,' Georgie said seriously. 'Billy wants to be a vet – and I think he could if he can stay on and pass all the exams. I don't know what I'd like yet.

I thought I wanted to be a soldier but now I'm not sure. If I was eighteen, I'd be fighting now and I'm not sure I'd like that, Dad.'

'No one with any sense likes it, my son – but at the moment it's a matter of duty, of loyalty to our country and our people. We can't let that bastard beat us. We have to fight – and our boys gave their lives for us, Georgie. Never forget that.' He gave Georgie a hug. 'I pray it will be all over before you can join up – and I pray our John will make it home alive. He's overseas somewhere and I haven't heard from him in months, but I believe in my heart he's alive.'

'I pray too, Dad – for all of us.'

'Good. We'll be all right then.' Georgie's father ruffled his hair. 'You give the future some thought, lad. I like my work on the railways but there are plenty of other good jobs. If I were you, I'd train for something – an apprenticeship is a good idea.'

Georgie hesitated, then, 'I don't know if it's a daft idea, Dad, but I think . . . I think I might like to be a doctor, or if I'm not clever enough, to work in a hospital somehow – even if I was just a porter it would be helping folk.'

His father stopped walking and looked at him. 'Where did that come from, lad?'

Georgie shrugged. 'I'd like to help people – I wanted to help Kate when she lost the baby but I couldn't. And I can't help Mum – or those people who died – but I'd like to know how.'

'Well, that is a fine aspiration,' his father said. 'And it has me flummoxed for the moment, Georgie. None of our family has ever looked that far up – but

152

I'll encourage it if you want to go for it. I'm not sure how long but you need to study for years to become a doctor.'

'I think it's about five years,' Georgie told him. 'That's if you pass all your exams at school.' He shrugged. 'I don't come top in anything, Dad, but I'm not bad at most things. So I might stay on and take the exams – see how I do. I'd get a better job if I did, wouldn't I?'

'Yes, you would, son.' His father chuckled. 'There was me speculating you'd turn into a farmer and you thinking about being a doctor! Well, blow me down, if that's not bloomin' wonderful.'

Georgie smiled. 'If I'm not clever enough I could be a nurse – men can be nurses, too, did you know?'

His father shook his head. 'Where did you get all this stuff from, lad?'

'The school had someone come in and talk to us about what the lads want to do. They have lots of leaflets and I took one of each.' Georgie shrugged. 'Probably won't pass all the exams, but I'll try.'

'Good on you,' his dad smiled at him. 'Well, looks like we've found your sister Vera – isn't that her hanging out the sheets?'

'You know it is,' Georgie said and called to her. Vera turned, stared, then gave a cry of pleasure and came running to hug her father.

'I didn't know you were coming down, Dad.'

'Thought we'd all come for a quick visit,' he said and kissed her cheek. 'Your sister and Jenny are at the cottage. We thought we'd have tea with you and then the girls and I will catch the late train back to town.'

'I'll finish this and come,' Vera promised, looking happier than Georgie had seen her for a while. 'Mrs Baker has just given me a nice piece of home-cooked gammon. We'll have it for our tea with some salad and the bread I made this morning.'

Georgie cycled to the end of the drove to see his family catch the bus that would get them to the station in time for their train. He was sorry to see them go, but his dad gave him ten shillings and a big hug before he left.

'I'll see you at Christmas if not before,' he told Georgie. 'I was thinking that Billy could do with a bike of his own – what about if I buy him an early Christmas gift?'

'He'd love that,' Georgie confirmed with a grin. 'Vera says they're too expensive, but if you gave it to him that would be all right.'

'I'll get a secondhand one and do it up, and then I'll come down one weekend and bring it on the train.' Georgie nodded his agreement. 'Anything you particularly want?'

'Nah, I'm all right,' Georgie said. 'Billy needs a bike then we can have more fun together.'

'I'll think of something for you,' his father promised and touched his shoulder. 'Keep being just the way you are, son. I'm proud of you.'

'I'm proud of you, too,' Georgie said. 'Take care of yourself, Dad.'

He watched his father board the bus, following Jenny and Kate. Waving to them as it drew away; then he turned back, cycling towards the farm.

'I'm going to help with the milking,' Georgie said to Billy. 'Are you coming or going home?'

'I'll ask if they need me for anything,' Billy replied. 'I'm glad you're back. It was lonely without you – even though it was all right on the farm. Mr Vester called by and we had a long talk about being a vet.'

'Is that his name?' Georgie asked and Billy nodded. 'Do you still want to be a vet?'

'Yeah, I do,' Billy said. 'He told me it's hard work but very rewarding, and he said if I don't pass all my exams enough to qualify as a vet, he'd take me on as his assistant, because he says I have a natural way with animals.' Billy turned innocent eyes to his uncle. 'What are you goin' to do?'

'Me?' Georgie grinned. 'Be a labourer on the railways like as not or a train driver like Dad – but I might not. I might be a doctor.'

Billy laughed. 'Me a vet and you a doctor – pigs might fly.'

'Yeah, and they probably will before we get to be what we want,' Georgie said. 'Let's try though, shall we?'

'Yeah, we'll both try,' Billy said and laughed as Georgie made the bike swing. 'I wish Mum would get me a bike for Christmas but she says they're too much money.'

'I know, but maybe she'll change her mind,' Georgie replied. He wanted to tell his nephew he would have a bike before Christmas but didn't want to spoil the surprise. 'If not, we'll think of something before next summer.' He stopped the cycle. Billy got off and Georgie parked it against the gate before they both walked into the farmyard.

*

Jock came down to stay the next day. He told them he had a couple of days off work and would stay two nights. Both Billy and Georgie liked him, or at least they tolerated him, because it made Vera happy to have company. He'd saved his sweet ration and brought the boys a big bag of treats; pear drops, humbugs, black liquorice chews and some sherbet.

'I'm going to take your mother to the cinema for a treat this evening,' he told them. 'Will you boys be all right here on your own for a few hours? Mrs Baker is going to have the baby overnight.'

They agreed they would fine. It was darker at night now and they didn't have much time on the farm after school, but they were used to negotiating the drove in the dusk now and it held no fears for them.

'You can have egg sandwiches and a treacle tart I made for your tea,' Vera told them. 'We're going to the early showing so we'll be home before it's too late – but in case we aren't, go to bed at your usual time. Lock the door and take the key out. I've got my spare so we can get in when we get back.'

The boys said they would, nodding to all their mother's instructions. As soon as Jock's van had driven away, they ate their tea, even though it was only three o'clock. After they'd eaten, they went out and rode the bike down to the farm. Mr Baker welcomed them and gave them a job straight away.

They helped with feeding the cows and pigs and then Georgie helped with the milking, while Billy went to do some jobs for Mrs Baker. When they emerged from the cowsheds, Georgie saw that a pile of wood had been built in the field behind the yard. He asked what it was for and the farmer smiled.

'It will be Guy Fawkes night soon,' he said. 'We're not going to light the bonfire at night, because that might attract enemy planes, but we're having a bit of fun on the Sunday afternoon. We'll roast jacket potatoes and have hot cocoa – several of our neighbours are coming, and you're all invited, too.'

'That should be fun,' Georgie said and grinned. 'Dad took us to a bonfire one fireworks night, but there weren't many fireworks.'

'No, and there won't be this time either,' Mr Baker said. 'There's none about that I know of and folk have better things to spend their money on – but we had this old wood and thought we'd have a little party, just to lighten the atmosphere a bit. It's been hard times all round of late I reckon.'

'Yes, very hard,' Georgie said, his face twisting with grief. 'We lost two of my brothers early on.'

'I know,' Mr Baker said with a look of sympathy. 'Vera told us. I was very sorry to hear it, Georgie, but I thought there was no point in mentioning it.'

'No, not really,' Georgie said, because someone saying sorry didn't help much. 'Have you heard from your son recently, Mr Baker?'

'Yes, I have. He's fine at the moment and hopes to get leave at Christmas.'

Georgie smiled as the farmer's face lit up. 'That's good then. I hope he comes home. My dad's coming down before Christmas and bringing a bike for Billy but it's a secret so don't let on to him.'

'I shan't. I told Vera I could find one for a few pounds but she wasn't interested.'

'Well, Dad will do one up for him,' Georgie said. 'He's good with stuff like that.'

They walked into the large, homely kitchen together. Mrs Baker had just taken a big pie from the oven; it smelled gorgeous and Georgie's stomach rumbled. She looked at him and laughed.

'That sounds as if you're hungry. I've made a steak and kidney pie with mushrooms, more of them than the meat, but enough kidney to make it tasty, and there's mashed potatoes, and cabbage to go with it – the baby's asleep in the other room so would you boys like to stay and share it?'

'Yes, please!' they chorused together. Mrs Baker smiled and set two extra plates, giving them a generous share of the pie as well as lashings of fluffy potato and vegetables. 'That tastes wonderful,' Billy said and he popped a piece of her gravy-laden pastry into his mouth. 'I've never had pastry like that before.'

'Aye, I've a light hand with the pastry,' Mrs Baker said, looking pleased. 'Eat up, boys. There's an apple crumble for afters.' She sat down at her own place, beginning to eat. Looking up as she swallowed her first bite, she said casually, 'Where has your mother gone, Billy?'

'Her friend Jock has taken her to the pictures,' he replied. 'She left us some tea but we ate it straight away.'

'As if that isn't always the way with growing lads. You boys have got hollow legs, I reckon.'

'That's what my mum used to say when she was well,' Georgie said and a look of sadness passed across his face. 'The war has made her ill but Dad says she just needs a nice rest and then she'll be fine.'

The farmer and his wife glanced at each other but didn't answer. Mrs Baker encouraging the boys to eat a bit more pie and the farmer looking thoughtful.

'How are you getting on at school then, Billy?' he asked after a few moments.

'I came third in class for science and biology, fourth for maths and second for English language,' Billy said, shooting a look of triumph at his uncle. 'My teacher said I've made a vast improvement in the last month or so.'

'That's since he decided he wanted to be a vet,' Georgie said, clearing his plate of the last morsel. 'That was the best dinner I've had in a long time, Mrs Baker. Thank you. It's good of you to share with us.'

'You're very welcome, both of you,' she said, smiling at them as Billy chimed in and told her it was all lovely. She brought the apple crumble out hot from the oven, gave her husband a big helping and then divided the rest between the boys.

'Don't you want any?' Georgie asked, not touching his plate until she shook her head.

'I've had enough for now,' she told him. 'Now, as a rare treat, I have a little fresh cream to go on that crumble. I don't often skim the cream to use. Mostly it's kept for butter – but today I thought we'd have a little treat . . .' She brought out a jug from the pantry and poured cream on all three portions.

'Are you sure you don't want any?' her husband asked. 'I've got more than enough, Muriel.'

'I'm having a cup of coffee with sugar and cream,'

she told him. 'That's my treat – and what I'd really like.'

After that they all tucked in. Mrs Baker made herself a cup of Camp Coffee and poured in a generous dollop of cream. Georgie saw her sigh with pleasure as she drank it so he didn't feel guilty about finishing off the last piece of crumble.

After their delicious meal, the boys asked politely if she would like any help with the dishes. Mrs Baker allowed them to clear the dirty plates and cutlery to the sink but then shooed them away. 'Get off home now, lads,' she said. 'It's dark but you've got a torch?' They nodded and thanked her again, leaving her to her chores.

'She's a lovely cook,' Billy remarked as they cycled home. The bike light was shaded so that it showed the ground in front of them but didn't flare up into the sky and alert an enemy aircraft. Not that they'd actually seen any more since the day of the dogfight and crash. Sometimes they heard distant sounds of guns and thought perhaps one of the airfields in the area was being attacked but they hadn't seen or been told of any big explosions so perhaps the ack-ack had successfully prevented the enemy dropping their bombs.

Both boys knew it wasn't as peaceful in London. They heard bits of news at school and were shown newspaper headlines; Mrs Baker had a wireless and Billy had heard snatches of news when he was helping her with chores. Mr Baker sometimes told them things, too. Hardly anything came via Billy's mother. Vera had shut off from the war and didn't want to know anything about it.

The cottage was in darkness when they got home, but Georgie lit the oil lamps and soon had the range made up so it was warm in the kitchen. The boys settled down. Billy was doing a jigsaw puzzle, which he kept on a large wooden tray so that he could put it to one side when his mother needed the table. Georgie was making a balsa wood plane and painting it air force grey with a blue and red circle on its wings. They enjoyed what they were doing so the time passed and neither of them realized how late it was until Georgie glanced at the mantle clock.

'It's nearly ten o'clock,' he said to Billy. 'We need to go to bed or we shan't be up in time to do our chores.'

'Why aren't they back?' Billy asked, looking up from his puzzle. 'If they went to the first showing they should have been home ages ago.'

'Your mum said to lock the door and take the key out if they were late,' Georgie said and got up to do just that. 'Come on, Billy. Leave your puzzle now. I'm going to bed.'

Billy followed him up the stairs. They took a candle each but left the oil lamp burning on the kitchen table for their mother and Jock when they got back.

Georgie was in bed first as Billy struggled into pyjamas that were on the small side. His mother said they would have to do as she couldn't buy any new ones, but they were a bit tight and uncomfortable about the crotch. He climbed into the other single bed – they'd pushed the two together so they were close, because they liked to just lie there and talk quietly to each other before they went to sleep.

'I wish we could eat with Mrs Baker all the time,'

Billy said on a yawn. 'Mum doesn't cook half as good as she does.'

'Yeah, I know.'

'Where do you think they are?' Billy asked sleepily. 'Do you reckon Mum's sweet on him, Georgie?'

Georgie hesitated, then, 'She might be,' he said. 'I ain't sure – but even if she is, don't tell your dad. It would hurt him.'

'Not as much as if she runs off with Jock,' Billy murmured. 'If Dad knew I think he'd give her a clout!'

Georgie didn't answer. He thought Bob would half murder her if he found out she'd been messing about with his best friend. He just hoped it would all be over by the time his brother-in-law came home.

CHAPTER 19

'I am sorry we were late back last night,' Vera told the boys at breakfast the next morning. They'd been to the farm, done their work and come back before she was downstairs. 'Jock's van got a puncture in the rear tyre and it took ages to change it – but you were all right. You had your tea and went to bed at the proper time.'

Billy was about to say they'd had their tea at the farmhouse, but Georgie kicked him. Billy looked at him in surprise but kept quiet until they had finished eating and were on their way back to the farm.

'What did you do that for?' he asked. 'I was only going to tell Mum how nice Mrs Baker's pie was – and she's always saying what a good cook Mrs Baker is.'

'I know but that's her sayin' it,' Georgie remarked. 'Sometimes, it's best to keep quiet, Billy.'

'Yeah, all right,' Billy lapsed into silence. 'What are we doin' today?'

'Mr Baker is digging ditches and clearing brambles,' Georgie said. 'Most of the land work is finished until the spring. He has all his hay and straw stacked in the yard, and there are just a few roots in the ground to get up, but he says he needs the hard frost for that so he's maintaining, that's what he calls it.'

'What can we do?'

'Not much. Maybe cart a bit of rubbish to the dung heap,' Georgie said. 'We'll ask if he needs us. If not, we can take the bike somewhere – go into Chatteris. I've got a couple of bob in my pocket. We can get some sweets.'

'Or some fireworks if there are any in the shop,' Billy suggested. 'Mr Baker would like a few fireworks for his party, wouldn't he?'

'Yeah, he would,' Georgie agreed. 'We'll see if we're needed and then go in and see what we can find.'

The farmer was dressed in long boots way past his thighs, a heavy waxed jacket and a knitted wool hat pulled down over his ears. He smiled at the boys but shook his head when they asked if they could help.

'Not with this, lads. Be back for the milking.'

They nodded, said they would and went back to pick up Georgie's bike. Billy rode on the handlebars all the way down the drove and then the couple of miles up an almost deserted country road into the small town. It was called a town but was really just a large village, with a handful of shops, a Post Office and a doctor's surgery. The boys were only passed once by a car; the driver waved at them in a friendly way as he drew ahead. They saw a stallion being led towards the farm and knew that Mr Baker had a mare that had come into season quite late. The stallion man would bring his champion to the farm, let him rest, and then put the two together in a paddock. Hopefully, they

164

would produce another beautiful foal about the same time next year.

There was a newspaper shop at the top of the High Street. The boys had been there for sweets before and they entered now, finding it empty apart from one old lady, who purchased a magazine and a packet of mints. She smiled at them as she went out.

'Hello, lads,' the newsagent said. 'What can I do for you today?'

'We wondered if you had any fireworks?' Billy said. 'Mr Baker is having a bonfire party and we thought he'd like a few fireworks.'

'I'm afraid there isn't . . . just a packet of sparklers left over from last year, if that's any good?'

'Sparklers?' Billy's face lit up. 'Can I see please?'

The newsagent held up not one but two packets of something he'd recovered from under the counter. 'I'd forgotten about these,' he said. 'They'll be a bit of fun, but no bangers or rockets, I'm afraid.'

'They're all right,' Billy said. 'How much please?'

'Sixpence a packet.'

'We'll have them both – one each,' Georgie said, grinning. 'That leaves us a shilling to spend on sweets, if you've got any?'

'Have you got ration cards?'

Georgie's face fell. 'I forgot about those,' he said, disappointed.

'Well, seeing as it's you two – nice polite youngsters – how about I forget the coupons for once? You can have some sherbet lemons or these Tom Thumb Drops – or the blackjack chews?'

They settled on a quarter of each sweet and four

chews each, leaving Georgie with two pennies in his pocket when they left. The sparklers went in the bike bag on the back, the sweets in their pockets. As they started to cycle back towards the main road heading in the direction of the farm, they saw a milk cart drawn by a horse by the side of the road. On the cart were bottles of milk with shiny silver tops, also little bottles of orange squash.

Georgie stopped the bike and asked how much the orange squash was. 'Tuppence,' the man said. 'If you return the bottle, I'll let you have the next one for a penny.'

'Thanks, mister. I'll leave it at the end of Farm Lane,' Georgie said, knowing that the milkman passed the drove twice a day on his rounds.

'I shan't forget you – Georgie and Billy, isn't it?' The milkman nodded and smiled. 'I've seen you helping on the farm. Down from London, aren't you?'

'Yeah, just for the duration,' Georgie replied. 'My sister thought it was safer.'

'Well, poor old London is catching it now,' the man said. He got back up behind the horse. 'Must be on our rounds. Dobbin likes to keep to his routine.'

The boys sat on a gate to a field and drank their orange squash, passing it back and forth until it was finished. The sky had suddenly become dark as they got back on the bike and cycled back up the drove, having placed the bottle in a safe place by the hedge.

'I reckon it might rain,' Georgie said as they passed the farm. 'Pity if the wood gets too wet; it might not burn.'

'We'll still have the sparklers,' Billy said. 'Let's hope it's only a bit of a shower.'

When they got back into the cottage, no one was in the kitchen. 'I'll make us a drink of cocoa,' Georgie said and filled the kettle. He heard a slight sound upstairs as he put the kettle on to heat and a couple of minutes later, his sister came downstairs. She looked a bit flushed and her normally neat hair was ruffled.

'I thought you'd be out all day,' she said, almost accusingly.

'Mr Baker didn't need us so we went into Chatteris,' Georgie said. 'Got a few sweets – but it's spitting with rain now so we came home.'

'Well, I'll make your cocoa then,' she said. 'I just took some clean towels up for Jock. He used your bedroom to have a wash. You don't mind, do you?'

'No, Vera.'

''Course not.'

Billy looked at Georgie. Neither of them believed her but they knew better than to question her.

'Jock tried to get you some fireworks yesterday but there was none in the shops,' Vera said as she made the cocoa. Jock came downstairs then. He looked fresh and clean so a part of what she'd said was true anyway.

'I thought I might get a few but they all said they hadn't got any,' Jock said. 'I bought you some sweets instead. I left them upstairs on your beds.'

'Thanks, Jock.' Georgie nudged Billy, as it was obvious they were supposed to go upstairs and see what he'd left. Billy went first and Georgie caught a whisper as he followed.

'Do you think they suspect?' Vera asked in a soft voice.

'Nah, shouldn't think so – why should they? We've been careful, Vera. Don't worry, love.'

'Bob would kill me if he ever found out.'

'He'd have to kill me first . . .'

There was a rustling sound as though they embraced and then Georgie went into their shared bedroom and closed the door behind him. He could see from the look on Billy's face that he knew what had been going on and he was upset – angry and upset.

He picked up the packets of sweets lying on his bed and threw them on the floor where they landed with a clatter. 'Bloody bribery!' he said savagely. Tears stood in his eyes as he looked at his uncle. 'How could she? I know Jock is nice looking and he's got a bit of money – but how could she do this to Dad?'

'Beats me,' Georgie said and sat on the edge of the bed. He felt like throwing his share of the sweets at the wall but didn't. 'I like Bob. I don't reckon it's right.'

'It's dirty, that's what it is,' Billy yelled and then burst into tears. 'I hate her, Georgie. I bloody hate her!'

'Keep your voice down. You don't want them to hear us.'

'Why? I'd like to hit them both!' Billy's eyes were wild with temper. 'She promised to love Dad forever. If she goes off with Jock I won't go with them. I swear I'll run away first.'

'Don't be daft. Where would you go?' Georgie asked. 'Mum isn't well so you can't go there – and Kate has Jenny staying with her. We have to stay here, Billy.'

'I don't!' Billy stared at him. 'Don't take her side.'

'I'm not. I wouldn't – but you can't just run off. You need to work hard, Billy. You're doing so well at school now. Remember you want to be a vet. Don't throw all that away just because—'

'It's all right for you!' Billy snapped, forgetting in his distress that Georgie was his best and only real friend. 'Your mum never did anything bad.'

Billy suddenly snatched up the sweets from the floor, wrenched open the bedroom door and pounded down the stairs. Georgie followed an instant later, standing on the bottom stair as his nephew burst into impassioned speech.

'I don't want your rotten sweets!' he yelled and threw them across the kitchen. 'I know what you've been doing with Mum and I'm going to tell my dad the minute I see him.'

'Billy!' Vera cried angrily. 'What are you saying? Don't be so rude to Jock. Apologize this instant or I'll give you a good smacking.'

'I hate you!' Billy cried.

'Billy, don't,' Georgie called and walked swiftly into the kitchen just as Billy bolted out of the door. 'Billy, don't be daft!' The door slammed shut behind Billy.

Georgie sent his sister an accusing look and followed his nephew outside, but Billy had picked up the bike from where they left it, and was cycling wildly down the drove. His legs were hardly long enough to reach the pedals so he was standing on them, careering from side to side and out of control.

'Go after him, Jock,' Vera said as she came to the door and saw her son disappearing down the drove.

'No. You've done enough damage,' Georgie said coldly, looking from one to the other. 'Leave him to me. I'll see if I can calm him down.' He set off down the drove, running but was unable to catch up with his nephew. Georgie was seething with anger inside. His sister and Jock had clearly been having an affair and Billy had understood what was going on and was upset and angry.

Georgie thought it was a rotten trick. Bob had trusted Jock to look after his family while he was away fighting and he'd taken an unfair advantage. He didn't even want to think about his sister. It was a betrayal of her marriage vows and her husband's trust. If they'd been his parents, he'd feel just the way Billy did; to him it was something to frown at but no more – but Billy must feel that his world was falling apart. Not only had he been sent away from his home and his grandparents, whom he loved, his mother didn't love his father and that meant his life would never be the same. His mind must be whirling, wondering what would happen when his dad came home and discovered what had been going on. Bob would never stand for it. Either he or Vera would leave – and it would most likely be Bob, which meant Billy might not see his dad much – if at all – in the future.

Georgie had seen kids at school where their parents had split and he knew that it almost always ended with neglect and misery for all concerned. How could she do it to her family? Georgie was angry with his sister, but for Billy's sake and the baby, who might grow up never knowing her dad. He didn't think Jenny would care too much. She would live with Kate or her grandparents – that's if Georgie's mum ever came home from the hospital.

He was panting by the time he reached the farm

gate. There was no sign of Billy and it was nearly time for the milking. Georgie had hoped that his nephew would head for the farm but he'd kept going and it was useless to search for him. Shrugging, he walked towards the cowsheds just as he saw Mr Baker and Benny bringing the beasts in from the field. It would soon be too cold to turn them out and then they would just stay in their sheds with nice warm beds of straw for the winter.

'Ah, Georgie,' Mr Baker smiled at him approvingly. 'Good lad. I wondered if you would come when I saw the young one go racing by on that bike. It's far too big for him so I hope he doesn't come a cropper.'

'I know. He shouldn't have taken it but he was upset over something,' Georgie said. 'I ran after him but he wouldn't stop. If he falls off it might teach him not to take other people's bikes.'

'You two haven't fallen out, have you?'

'No, sir. Billy's cross with his mum, that's all.'

'Ah, I see. Well, let's hope he comes back shortly and no harm done.'

'I hope so,' Georgie said and followed him into the cowshed.

The milking was done in less than an hour and Georgie looked for Billy when he left the farm. It was dusk but there was just enough light to see his way home. He didn't have his shaded torch or the bike so he walked in the centre of the road, away from the deep ditches on either side. As he got closer to the cottage, he could see all the windows were lit and that made it easier to see the door without bumping into anything.

'There you are!' Vera cried as soon as he went into the cottage. 'Did you find him? Where is he?'

'I couldn't catch up to him,' Georgie replied. 'It was time for the milking so I stopped and helped because I didn't know where Billy had headed for.'

'Jock should have gone after him in the van and brought him back,' she said, sounding annoyed. 'He wouldn't because he said Billy needed time to sort his head out.'

Georgie glanced round the kitchen. 'Where is Jock?'

'He left. He had to get back. I wanted him to stop and look for Billy but he said he needed to get back to his job.'

'I suppose he does,' Georgie shrugged. 'Billy wouldn't have come back until he was gone anyway.'

'What do you mean? What has Jock done to upset Billy – or you?'

Georgie raised his eyes and looked at her. He didn't say a word but it was all there in his eyes and she flushed bright red.

'You don't understand, either of you. You're too young.'

'Billy loves his dad,' Georgie said, angry now that she meant to dismiss them as silly kids. 'He doesn't want his dad to go off when he knows—'

'Knows what?' Vera demanded her voice shrill. 'What have you put in my boy's head? Have you been making up lies about me and Jock?'

'I haven't made anything up,' Georgie said. 'I'm not daft and neither is Billy. We're only in the next bedroom and we heard—' Vera's hand snaked out and slapped him hard across the face.

'How dare you insinuate such things! It's a lie – nothing happened like that. Jock just helped me get something from the top of the wardrobe. We're just friends.'

'If you say so.' Georgie looked at her defiantly. 'I don't care who you have it off with, Vera – but Billy does. If you've hurt him, he'll be a long time forgiving you.'

'How dare you!' she began but then the cottage door flew open and Billy rushed in. 'Billy – where the hell have you been? Worrying me to—'

'Georgie, you've got to come,' Billy said, his face white and scared. 'The haystack is on fire and I don't think Mr and Mrs Baker are home.'

'I'm coming,' Georgie said and picked up his jacket, shrugging it on as they ran out, ignoring Vera's commands to come back and stay away from it. 'What happened?' Georgie asked as he picked up the bike and Billy hitched up on to the handlebars. 'How do you know it's on fire?'

'Because it was my fault,' Billy replied over his shoulder. 'I hid in the haystack when you were in the cowsheds . . .'

'I didn't see the bike?'

'I hid that too, behind the muck heap,' Billy said, a sob in his voice. 'I heard you talking to Mr Baker but I didn't want you to see, because I'd been crying.'

'So how is the fire your fault?' They were getting close to the farm now and Georgie could see black smoke issuing from the yard. 'That hay is important for keeping the animals fed all winter . . .'

'I know.' Billy gave him a scared look as he jumped down the moment his uncle braked, running ahead of

Georgie to the stack. 'I didn't mean to start a fire. After I saw Mr and Mrs Baker leave in the car, I went into the shed and found some matches. It was getting dark so I lit a candle they keep there – and then I remembered the sparklers . . .'

'Oh, Billy, no!' Georgie said. He could clearly see that one side of the large stack was burning, flames shooting into the sky. 'We've got to put it out – come on, help me! There's a hose we use for washing down the sheds and some buckets. You can throw buckets of water on while I fetch the hose.'

Billy ran to the tap that was used for all kinds of things and had two buckets filled when Georgie came back with the hose. While Georgie fixed the end to the tap, Billy carried one bucket and threw it over the burning stack. He ran back for the other as Georgie turned the hose on to the stack. Instead of aiming it on the fire as Billy had, Georgie turned it on the other side of the stack. He wasn't sure there was enough force of water to put the flames out, but perhaps, if he made a lot of it wet, it wouldn't burn.

Billy was holding the hose now, helping him direct it at the stack. They worked their way round, damping it all as thoroughly as they could, but it looked as if their efforts to save it might be in vain. The smoke was thick and black and choking but it seemed to Georgie that the heat from the flames was dying down a bit as they spread and encountered wet hay.

'It's no use!' Billy cried, tears streaming down his face. 'We can't stop it.'

'Hold the hose here. Keep the water on that spot, Billy. I've got an idea.'

Billy did as he was told. Georgie ran to pick up a long-handled fork they used for pitching the hay. He rushed back to where the flames were fiercest and thrust it into the stack, pulling a large heap of burning hay away from the rest and towards him. It fell on the earth just near his feet and he raked at it, seeing the fire die as it encountered mud and water. Going in again, he pulled another great lump of burning hay down and then another and another as fast as he could. Showers of hot sparks and bits of burning hay went over his feet, legs and arms. By jerking backwards, he managed to keep it out of his face. He didn't have time to see if his idea was working, just forking it down as fast as he could and then he heard a shout and a car door slamming and Mr Baker was there.

'Good lads!' he said, sounding out of breath. He grabbed another pitchfork and started raking it down the way Georgie had, stamping on any flames, and kicking them out. Mrs Baker came and joined in, the three of them pulling the entire side of the stack down. After a few minutes the water started to run through the stack, black and filthy, floating with bits of burned hay. There was plenty of dark smoke hanging about, but Georgie couldn't see any more flames. Benny had fetched another hose and had water running from the kitchen into buckets, which he was throwing over the stack as fast as he could.

'My God!' Mr Baker said as he forked some soaking wet hay down that was untouched by the fire. 'I think we've done it, lads. When I saw the smoke, I thought we'd lose the lot – but there's a good half of it left and it will dry out if we take it inside the barn.' He walked round the stack several times, poking his pitchfork in to make sure that the fire wasn't still smouldering inside where they couldn't see it.

'I have to thank you boys,' he said as he came back shaking his head in wonder. 'What you did, Georgie – that was quick thinking. If you hadn't come along when you did – the barns might have gone too.'

Billy looked at him. His face was black from the smoke and stained with tears. Suddenly, he turned and ran off.

'He's upset,' Georgie said and took off after him. On foot, Billy was no match for his uncle and he caught him halfway down the drove. 'Billy, stop it. It's not your fault,' he said as he caught hold of him and brought him down with a rugby tackle. 'You helped put it out. It wasn't deliberate.'

Billy sobbed against his shoulder. 'They won't want me on the farm ever again,' he said. 'It was me that started it, Georgie. You put it out.'

'You helped,' Georgie said and gave a wince of pain as he scraped his hand on the earth. He couldn't see his hand properly even though the moon had sailed out from behind the clouds, but he thought it might have been burned. It was starting to sting a bit. 'Come on. We need to get home.'

Billy stood up, swallowing a sob. 'I have to tell them it was me,' he said and set off towards the farm.

Georgie followed reluctantly. He didn't want Billy to tell Mr Baker, because the farmer would be angry. If he didn't want either of them on his farm again, it would spoil everything.

Mr Baker was still forking hay, still checking that

no smouldering embers remained. He turned to look as Billy walked up to him.

'What do you want, Billy?' he asked and smiled.

'It was me, sir,' Billy said tearfully. 'I didn't mean to. I lit a sparkler so I could see better. I didn't think it would do any harm. I don't know if it was a spark or when I threw it down . . .' He faltered as the smile disappeared from the farmer's face. 'I didn't know what to do so I fetched Georgie and he . . .' Billy came to a fearful halt. 'I'll work and pay for the damage.'

'You did this?' Mr Baker looked at the mess all around him. 'All the work that we put into gathering the hay and stacking it? You must have known how important it is to us? Without the hay we might have to slaughter some of the beasts – and it could have been the whole farm!' His rage suddenly erupted and he grabbed Billy by the shoulders, shaking him until his teeth rattled. 'You stupid boy! Don't you know better than to play with fireworks near a haystack?'

'Don't hurt him!' Georgie said, pushing the farmer away and standing in front of his nephew. 'I bought the sparklers for your party. Billy didn't mean to do any damage. It wasn't deliberate.'

'That's what we get for taking evacuees in,' Mrs Baker said angrily. 'After all we've done for you? This is how you repay us?'

'Come on, Billy.' Georgie took his nephew by the arm. 'We're going.'

He pushed Billy in front of him. When they got to the discarded bike, he hesitated and then walked past it.

'What about the bike?' Billy whimpered.

177

'It ain't ours,' Georgie said. 'Come on. I shan't come where I'm not wanted.'

The boys walked back to the cottage in silence. Vera was sitting at the kitchen table, drinking a cup of tea. She looked up. 'What have you two been doing? You're filthy, the pair of you.'

'The haystack was on fire,' Georgie said. 'We put it out – or we started to and then Mr Baker came.'

'You'd best put some water on to heat. You'll need a bath. You can have it together.' She came towards them, grabbing at Georgie's hands. 'Just look at the state of you. Why you had to get involved I don't know. It's their haystack, not yours. We do quite enough for this miserable little place.'

Georgie winced and his sister frowned. She looked at his hand and her frown eased. 'You've burned yourself, you foolish boy. Come here, let me put a little marge on it. I suppose that will work as well as butter.'

She took him to the sink and poured cold water over his hand, then patted it dry. 'You're lucky. It's just scorched. You could have done much worse.' She shook her head at them. 'I'll get the bath and you can both wash yourselves and then I'll bind your hand up.' She dropped it carelessly. 'You'll live. What about you, Billy? Did you burn your hands?'

'No.' Billy stared at her coldly. 'Not that you'd care – you only care about you and him!'

'Now don't cheek me or you'll get a smack,' Vera said crossly. 'You don't know what you're talkin' about. Jock was merely lifting something down from the top of the wardrobe. Do you hear me?' She gave him a little shake. 'Did you hear what I said?'

'Yes . . .' Billy looked at her sullenly. It was obvious that he didn't believe her but was too subdued after the episode at the farm to say more. 'I don't want to stay here. I want to go home to Gran and Grandad . . .'

'Well, you can't,' Vera said. 'Do you want us all to die in our beds?'

Billy shook his head. 'Well, that's what might happen if we went back while all these bombing raids are happening. We have to stay here,' his mother told him.

'Don't want to,' Billy said and kept his eyes down.

'Neither do I,' Georgie gave her a look. 'We want to go back to London. Dad's on his own. We should be with him. You could look after him . . .'

'Do you think I don't know that?' Vera asked. 'I wish we were there, too. I don't like it here much either – but it is safer. Or it would be if you two didn't go charging off in the dark to put a fire out.' She shook her head. 'I called you back but you ignored me. I had no idea what you were up to.'

Georgie looked at her and her eyes dropped. She *had* known but she hadn't bothered to come after them. Billy was right. The only person Vera cared about was herself. He wasn't even sure she really cared about Jock . . .

CHAPTER 20

'Mum?' Kate bent to kiss her mother's cheek. She was sitting by her bed, looking out of the window towards the river but she wasn't enjoying the view. 'How are you now?'

Grace turned her head slowly to look at her. 'I'm the same as I was last time,' she said. 'How do you expect me to be when I've got nothing left to live for?'

'Oh, that's not fair,' Kate exclaimed. 'What about Dad? He's a good husband. You've never been knocked about or seen him drink his wages away down the pub. He's a good man – and he loves you so much. He never complains, but, Mum, he does miss and need you.' Kate reached for her hand, but she drew it away. 'Don't you think you should make an effort to get well and come home?'

'What for? Your dad's all right. He's got his work and his friends – and you. I'll just sit at home and do nothing. I might as well stay here and do the same.'

'You used to enjoy keeping things nice,' Kate said, feeling desperate. 'Why can't you think about the things and people you still have? Perhaps if you came home,

Vera would bring the boys back. I don't think they're happy down there now.'

'Oh, why?' Grace glanced up, curious for a moment. 'I thought they were enjoying the farm?'

'They don't go there anymore. Apparently, Billy set fire to the haystack, and although Georgie helped to stop it spreading, the farmer was angry and they daren't go back. Vera still helps but she says the farmer's wife has changed towards her – doesn't give her any extras now.'

'That's daft,' Grace said, sounding more like her old self. 'Billy didn't do it on purpose. I know that boy and he's too scared.'

'It was a firework. Probably a spark or a dropped sparkler.'

Grace shook her head. 'They should move elsewhere. Must be somewhere else they could go.'

'Why don't you tell them so?' Kate suggested. 'Vera might take notice of you.'

'Huh,' her mother snorted. 'First time in her life if she did. You go down and tell her yourself, Kate.'

'I might visit them,' Kate replied. 'I've got some Christmas presents for the boys – and it's too expensive to post things these days. Dad's going to take the bike for Billy next week so I might go with him.'

'What bike?'

'Dad got an old one and did it up for him. He's sprayed it and it looks as good as new. You should see it, Mum.'

Her mother looked at her for a moment then sighed. 'You won't be satisfied until you get me out of here, will you?'

'The doctor said you're a lot better, Mum. He thinks you would improve faster at home – and we all miss you. *I* miss you . . .'

'I suppose . . .' She gave a little shudder. 'Has next door gone completely, then?'

'Yes. The rubble has been cleared and there's just the foundations. I know it will be hard, Mum. Dad could find you another house if you'd rather?'

'No! If I'm coming home, I'll come to my own home.' She looked at Kate and suddenly the tears were trickling down her cheeks. 'I miss them . . .' she said and sniffed. 'I miss my boys, Kate.'

'I know, Mum. I miss them too . . .' Kate felt her own cheeks wet and leaned in to kiss her mother. 'I know it hurts, Mum – but we all need you so much.'

'I've let you down,' Grace said sadly. 'You lost your child and you were ill and I wasn't there to comfort you.'

'You helped when I lost the baby, don't you remember?' Grace shook her head. 'You were there with me, Mum. It was at yours.'

'I forget things,' Grace admitted. 'Sometimes I remember things and then they go. You've suffered too much, Kate. I do love you, you know.'

'I love you, too. We all do.'

'Talk to Sister Jones before you go,' Grace said. 'I'll come home tomorrow – but I'll need you with me.'

'I'll take a couple of days off work,' Kate promised and squeezed her hand. 'Thanks, Mum. Everyone will feel better if you're home.'

Kate caught the bus and then walked the last few yards

to her home. She felt much lighter in spirit. For a while it had looked as if her mother would crack under the strain, never be herself again, but these past couple of weeks she seemed to be getting better.

Once she was home things might begin to get really better. The war was still raging and the bombs were falling most nights, but Grace was no safer in the nursing home than in her own house. All kinds of buildings had been hit and it sometimes seemed as if the enemy just dumped their load wherever and didn't care whether it was a school, a church, a home, or a factory they hit; they were just intent on causing as much damage and heartache as they could.

As she walked into her own house, she had a sudden sense that something was different – cigarette smoke and . . . cologne?

'Steve!' she cried and rushed to the foot of the stairs. 'Steve, is it you – are you home?'

Steve appeared at the top of the stairs. He was in his shirt sleeves and a pair of old corduroy trousers, his hair still wet. His face lit up as he saw her and he ran down to catch her up in his arms and kiss her passionately.

'Kate, my love,' he murmured against her ear. 'I've missed you, wanted you so much . . .'

'Oh, Steve . . .' She was crying and hugging him all at the same time, lifting her face for his kiss. 'I can't believe it. How long have you got?'

'Just twenty-four hours. I have to be back by seven tomorrow evening.'

'Oh!' Kate felt the disappointment. 'So soon? I have to fetch Mum from the hospital some time tomorrow.'

'Can't that wait for another day?' he asked, sounding irritated. 'I haven't seen you for months. I was planning on spending most of the day in bed . . .'

Kate laughed, but felt a little nervous. She had healed after the miscarriage but still didn't feel quite right. Making love was something she'd always enjoyed but she couldn't help wondering if anything had changed inside after her miscarriage.

'Why don't we start now then?' she said, banishing her doubts as she looked up at his handsome face.

Steve took her at her word, scooping her up and carrying her up to their room. He started to strip, his eyes never leaving her face. Kate took her things off. She could see the hunger in his eyes as she moved into his arms, willing herself to feel it too. She'd always adored him, always thrilled to his touch, but it wasn't happening. Her heart caught with grief as she realized that she felt nothing.

'Well, that wasn't exactly welcoming home the hero,' Steve drawled, a note of sarcasm in his voice as he sat on the edge of the bed in his underwear and lit a cigarette. 'What's wrong with you, Kate? You used to enjoy it – now you're like a bloomin' frigid virgin.'

'I think I'm a little bit sore after losing the baby,' Kate said weakly, but she hadn't been, not really. 'I'm sorry, Steve. It will be better next time.'

'I don't want you to force it,' he said roughly. He looked angry. 'I was told it was only for a few weeks that you couldn't have sex.'

'The doctor said it varies,' Kate said. She didn't know why she felt like crying. 'Who told you that?'

Had Chuck told him? She wasn't sure why that felt like a betrayal.

'A mate of mine whose wife had the same thing happen. I thought you'd be over it by now or I wouldn't have bothered . . .'

Kate felt the shock of his words like a pail of cold water in her face. She stared at him in disbelief – was that the reason he hadn't come home? Because she couldn't have marital relations? She'd thought it was because of the Blitz but suddenly she wasn't sure. Something had changed since he'd been away – something had changed, either in Steve or in her.

'You haven't mentioned the baby,' she said, her throat tight with misery. 'Or how I felt . . . how I feel . . .'

Steve's head came up. 'We talked about that on the phone after it happened. I couldn't get leave then, Kate. Of course, I was sorry – but you know I didn't want it. We weren't ready for kids. It wasn't what we planned, was it?'

'No, it wasn't what we'd planned,' Kate said and felt the coldness spreading through her. 'It was beautiful, though, growing inside me. I felt it kick . . . *her* kick. She was a little girl, Steve, a real baby – and she died because she came too soon.'

'Well, that wasn't my fault, was it?' he said and there wasn't a shred of caring in his voice.

Kate stared at him, as if she were seeing him for the very first time. Steve, her big handsome husband, who was handy with his fists with any man that upset him, and had swept her off her feet – but he was a selfish man, who didn't or couldn't enter her feelings.

Losing their first child meant nothing to him and everything to her. She realized that this distance had been creeping over them slowly ever since he hadn't come home when she'd needed him. Kate had listened to his excuses on the phone, but she knew that other men – even the pilots who were fighting so desperately to keep Britain's skies free of the enemy – had managed the quick visits home. With a sick lump in her breast, she understood that Steve hadn't wanted to visit. He hadn't wanted to be around her when she couldn't give him satisfaction; he hadn't wanted to see her crying and offer her comfort – or shed a few tears for his child himself.

Steve stood up and finished dressing in his uniform. 'I'm off to see a few mates. I might be late home. Don't wait up.'

'Steve! Please – don't be angry. I'm sorry . . .'

Steve didn't answer. He just walked out. Kate sat down on the bed and bent her head. All at once, deep sobs shook her. She'd loved him so much, so very much – but it had been a young girl's love. Kate realized then that it was her who had changed. Losing her baby had made her more aware – and the boys, too. Her mother's illness . . . all of it, living with the bombs falling all round, losing her job as a teacher. So many little drops. Tiny drops of water falling on a stone will wear a hole in it, and that's how she felt – hollow inside.

Steve had always been a selfish devil. Handsome, bold, brave – all the things that make a young girl's heart race, but a woman wants and needs compassion, understanding and love. The ability to be gentle when

186

it was needed. Steve didn't have that. He was a young lord of his neighbourhood and he expected to get what he wanted. Kate had been the prettiest girl – and all the boys had been after her. She'd been a trophy, though a willing one. Steve had been her hero.

The tears had dried now and Kate felt strangely better. She washed, dressed, and put some make-up on. When Jenny came in from work a little later, she was able to smile and ask her about her day at work.

'It was good. I sold twenty pounds' worth of knitwear,' Jenny said. 'My superior was very pleased with me. She says I'm one of the best salesgirls they've ever had.'

'That's wonderful, Jenny,' Kate said and smiled. 'I'm so pleased for you.'

Jenny looked at her. 'I thought you'd be dancing round the room,' she said. 'Someone told me that Steve came home. Is he here?'

'He was – but he went out to see some friends,' Kate said, avoiding her niece's sharp gaze. 'Oh, Mum might come home tomorrow. I spoke to the Sister at the nursing home and she said it was up to the doctor but she thought it likely he would agree.'

'I've got the morning off,' Jenny said. 'Do you want me to fetch her? I've swapped with a girl who wants next Monday off . . . if you want more time with Steve?'

'Yes, thank you. I'll ring and see if she can come home and what time in the morning and let you know.'

Jenny nodded. 'Are you going out this evening? I thought I'd go round and cook Dad's tea. He should be home about eight.'

'I don't think so,' Kate replied. 'I'll see what time Steve gets back – but you could stay over at Dad's tonight, if you don't mind?'

'Yes, that's what I thought. Give you some privacy,' Jenny said. 'Are we having those muffins for tea? They smell lovely.'

'Yes. I bought a pot of strawberry jam too. Wasn't I lucky?' Kate said brightly. 'They'd just come in and the shopkeeper was rationing them – one per household. I managed to wangle one for Dad as well. He likes a bit of toast and jam for his breakfast and so does Mum.'

'I'll take it with me,' Jenny said. 'Oh, blow it! Why do they always go off when we're ready to eat?'

The wailing of the siren was closer than expected and as they grabbed their buttered muffins and the pot of jam, the drum of several planes in the distance could be heard. Under the stairs, with just a torch and a blanket to sit on, they munched the sweet treat, shuddering as the house seemed to shake and tremble.

'That was close,' Kate said. Jenny's face looked pale and scared in the torchlight and she expected hers did, too. 'Perhaps we should have run for the underground?'

They heard another explosion but it was further away. The thrumming noise had gone and they looked at each other in relief; it seemed the planes had moved on. They weren't the main target for that night . . .

CHAPTER 21

'I'm sorry, Kate.' Steve sat up, stretching and bleary-eyed. He'd come home drunk and slept on the sofa in the front room. Kate was strained, silent as she brought in a tray of tea and toast the following morning. 'For what I said yesterday . . . It was probably my fault for rushing you. I didn't mean it to be like that, and I *do* care about you . . .' She thought he meant his apology and the tension went out of her.

'It is all right. I told you – I'm just not quite healed; sorry I disappointed you.'

Steve got up and came to her, taking her hand. 'I can be a pig at times, I know – but things have been hectic and never knowing whether you'll come back from a mission, never being sure it won't be you next . . . There are so many of us dying, Kate.' He shuddered, looking so frightened in that instant that she instinctively put her arms around him, kissing him softly on the mouth. 'I'm so sorry. I don't want to lose you . . .'

'You won't,' she told him. 'We've both changed a bit, Steve. We've had to grow up in our separate ways.

It must be terrifying for all of you every time you go up.'

'You've had so much worry and grief . . .' He touched her face with his fingertips. 'I can see it's aged you, Kate.'

She laughed. 'That's not much of a compliment!'

'You're still the most beautiful woman I've ever seen,' he said and his voice broke a little. 'I always wondered why I was lucky enough to get you, Kate. You could have had anyone.' He smiled, half-amused, half-jealous. 'Even Chuck is in love with you . . .'

'Don't be daft!' she said and shook her head. 'Of course he isn't. He's just kind and caring and thoughtful—'

'All the things I'm not?' Steve said and for a moment she saw real anger and jealousy spark in his eyes. 'Have you fallen for him?'

Kate looked at him in astonishment. 'Why on earth would you say something like that? I hardly know him. He was kind when I was ill – but I don't think of him as anything but your friend.'

'That's OK then,' Steve said, a note of possessiveness in his voice. 'You belong to *me*, Kate.'

She felt as if he'd slapped her and something inside her woke up. 'No, I don't,' she said and she felt calm and strong as she spoke. 'I belong *with* you, Steve, for as long as I want to be and we love each other – but I don't belong *to* anyone. I'm no one's possession.'

Steve looked at her for a moment and, in his eyes, she saw something that sent a shiver down her spine. He didn't say anything, but then he got up and went to drink the tea she'd poured.

'What do you want to do today?' she asked as she sipped her own tea.

'You had to fetch your mother,' he muttered, eating a slice of toast.

'Jenny will do it if . . .'

'Fetch your mother,' Steve said. 'I'm going to wash and shave and then I'll catch the next train. I might as well be at the base as here.' He sounded like a sulky child refused a treat.

'Steve, don't be like that,' Kate protested. 'I don't want to quarrel. I love you . . .'

'Do you?' His eyes blazed suddenly. 'I doubt it. I doubt it very much – but don't let it worry you. I don't need sex with a block of ice. I can find as many willing women as I need.'

'I'm sure you can,' Kate replied. Her heart felt as if it had turned to ice. She expected to feel pain but she was too numb. 'Have you? Is that what this is, Steve? You want to be angry with me, because you've found someone else?'

She read the answer in his eyes as they failed to meet hers. 'Who – who is she?'

'There isn't anyone,' Steve muttered. 'I'm only saying there could be if I wanted.' Now he was lying and they both knew it.

'I see . . . Well, thanks for telling me,' Kate said. She went out into the kitchen and put her coat on, wrapping a scarf around her throat. Picking up her handbag, she left. She didn't call out to say she was leaving, she just went. Steve could go to the devil for all she cared at that moment.

'Kate! Come back . . .' she heard him call as she left

191

but walked on. At that moment she didn't care whether she ever saw him again, though she knew the regrets might come later.

Kate fetched her mother from the hospital and took her home. She stayed with her all day and then Jenny came to join them. 'I'll make tea and look after her if you want to go home, Kate,' she offered.

'I'll pop in tomorrow after work,' Kate told her mother as she kissed her cheek. 'If I can, I'll come for a few minutes in my lunch break.'

'There's no need,' Grace said and smiled sadly. 'Come when you can, both of you – but don't make me a burden. I'll be all right here alone.'

'Are you sure you feel comfortable, Mum? Dad will be home soon.'

'So he will,' she agreed. 'What have we got for his tea, Jenny?'

'I bought some sausages earlier,' Kate told her. 'There's some nice carrots and a cabbage, potatoes, too.'

'Your dad will like that,' Grace nodded to Kate as she put her coat on. 'You get off home, love. I think I'd like a bit of toast and that jam you gave me earlier for my tea.'

'I could get you a sausage,' Jenny said, nodding to Kate as she left. She didn't wait to hear her mother's reply. Jenny was growing up fast and would try to persuade her gran to eat a proper meal, but if she only wanted toast, it was all she would have.

Walking home, Kate felt a little flutter in her stomach. Would Steve still be there, waiting for her to get back so they could have another row – or had he left early as he'd threatened?

When she got in the house was silent. She looked for any sign of him but he'd taken his kitbag, so he wasn't planning on returning just yet. Kate went up to the bedroom. She knew she was half-looking for a letter, just a brief note Steve might have left to say he was sorry and there was no other woman in his life, but of course there was nothing.

She sat down on the edge of the bed feeling drained. As if she hadn't had enough to cope with these past months. Why had Steve felt the need to go with another woman? It was months since they'd been together, because of her pregnancy and miscarriage, but Kate hadn't even considered a mild flirtation with another man. Yes, she hadn't been as responsive to Steve when they made love as in the past but she still loved him; it was just that her body had suffered a deep trauma – wasn't it?

Kate wrapped her arms about herself. She felt very alone and miserable. All these months she'd longed for Steve to come home and then he had and they'd quarrelled. Was it all her fault – or had he done it deliberately to hurt her and make her angry?

Steve had a conscience. Kate knew that for certain. If he had found a new relationship near where he was stationed, he would feel guilty about breaking his marriage vows. Why would he, though? Was it something lacking in her? Or had it always been going to happen? Perhaps it was just the long separation and the war?

A lot of marriages had suffered because of the

enforced separation. Kate knew of young women who had found love – or simply amusement – in the arms of a man who was not their husband. It had never occurred to her. Steve was her husband for life – or that was how she'd seen it.

Did she still love him? Kate wasn't sure and that upset and bewildered her. Had she changed so much that, instead of thinking him her hero, she had begun to see him as a rather arrogant and selfish man?

She scolded herself for the thought. Steve had been upset because she'd held back when they made love. Kate wasn't sure why, except that she'd been afraid it might hurt. Yes, it had been a little uncomfortable, because she was still a bit tender, but it hadn't hurt much. Yet she hadn't experienced the pleasure that their love-making had once given her. Her eyes felt moist with tears but they didn't fall. It was just sad that her marriage had lost its glow but perhaps that happened to a lot of couples.

Sighing, Kate went downstairs to cook her own tea. Life went on whether she was happy or not.

It was a few days later that Kate had a letter from Steve. She opened it with trepidation, unsure of what he would have to say. It was so rare for him to write that it must be important.

Dearest Kate
   Forgive me. I do love you. You know I do. I don't want our marriage to fail. So you have to forgive me.
   I won't lie to you. There was another woman,

*but it only happened once. We'd got back from
a raid that scared the hell out of me. I really
thought I was going to die, Kate. I got drunk
and this woman threw herself at me at the pub.
I don't even remember her name. I'm sorry. It
won't happen again.*

*Please don't be angry or hate me. I know
you've been through a lot. I said some rotten
things. I didn't mean them. Please let me know
it's all right.*

Love Steve xxx

Kate closed her eyes. She refused to cry. She wouldn't.
Reading the letter again, she wasn't sure whether she
was happy or sad. The perfect thing that had been her
and Steve had gone. Once upon a time, a confession like
this would have seen her leaving him in outrage at his
infidelity, but she was older and wiser now. Sometimes
you had to admit that something wasn't perfect, but it
was still worth having.

For now, Kate thought, perhaps she still had enough
of a marriage to try to save it. The alternative was to
go back and live with her parents and give up the home
she loved. This house was in Steve's name and she
didn't earn enough to keep it going without the part of
his wage he gave her.

It was a fact of life that as a woman she couldn't
hope to earn a wage that would give her a home of her
own, unless she was married. A wry smile touched
her mouth. She wouldn't be the first to stay in a broken
marriage for the sake of a house – and if it proved to
be intolerable, she could always go to her parents. Her

father would welcome her and so would her mother. They would both be on her side, which wasn't always the case. Some folks insisted that a woman stayed within her marriage, even if her life was unhappy.

Kate put the letter aside. She would answer it and she would forgive him, but not just yet. In the meantime, life had to go on. They were all going down to visit Vera and the boys that weekend, even her mother who seemed to have picked up a little now that she'd faced life again.

'Yes, I'll come,' she'd told Kate when she asked her. 'It will do me good and I always did like a nice trip on a train. We'll pack ourselves some food and then we can eat when we're hungry. Do we need to get a bus when we leave the train?'

'I think we change trains at Ely and then a short bus ride – or perhaps a taxicab . . .'

'No, we'll go in style,' her father said when he got home that evening. 'I've arranged to borrow a friend's car and he's got enough petrol coupons saved to get us there and back. I reckon he got some of them on the black market, but for once I don't care!'

CHAPTER 22

They started out early in the morning so as to miss the traffic in town, stopping once on a quiet country road to eat their elevenses. It was too early for lunch and they expected to have a late one with Vera, or a high tea, before they drove home again. They were all feeling excited and happy in their various ways, because it wasn't often that they got to do something like this as a family, especially since the start of the war. A couple of times they heard the drone of planes overhead, but when Mr Greene stopped and stuck his head out to look up at the sky, he said they were British.

Perhaps it was being away from the now constant sight of smoke drifting across the city or the fear of a bomb dropping on their homes, but as they got further away from London, the mood seemed to lighten. Even so, Kate was surprised when her mother started singing. First of all, she sang, 'Daisy, Daisy, give me your answer do, I'm half crazy, all for the love of you.' Then she sang 'Danny Boy' and followed it with some of Harry Lauder's popular numbers.

At first, they let her sing alone. Grace had a lovely clear voice but after the first two songs they joined in, enjoying the feeling of being carefree and on holiday.

'I didn't know you could sing all those songs,' Kate said when they stopped at a roadside pub and went to have a drink: lemonade for Grace, Mr Greene, and Jenny. Kate asked for cold water and some ice. Her throat felt dry and the water was cooling.

Kate's father looked around at them as they sat in the cosy little taproom, a log fire burning brightly in one corner. 'I could stop here all day,' he said and there's food cooking – but we promised Vera so we'd best get on.'

They got to Cambridge some twenty minutes or so later and then found their way to Haddenham and from there to Mepal, a tiny village but with an airfield used by both American and British planes. After that they were directed towards Chatteris and eventually discovered the drove leading to the farm cottage. Georgie and Billy were on watch at the opening to the long and slightly muddy drove. They jumped up and down as they saw the car coming and rushed to greet their grandparents and Kate when they got out.

'I said it was you because it was a different number plate – a London one,' Georgie said triumphantly. 'We don't get many with that sort of plate here.'

'Do they have different number plates for different areas?' Kate asked doubtfully, but Georgie was certain they did so she didn't argue.

Her father went to the back of the car, where Billy's bike was strapped on. He'd covered it with a tarpaulin and Billy cried out in delight when he saw the shiny red cycle, staring at it in disbelief. 'Is that really for me?' he asked and gave a yell of triumph when it was confirmed. Climbing on, he went cycling off as fast as he could back to the cottage. Georgie mounted his and followed, his grandfather following behind in the borrowed car.

Mr Greene saw the farmer at his gate and waved. Reluctantly, it seemed, Mr Baker lifted a hand in return. 'What's wrong with him? He was friendly enough when we came down last time, Kate.'

'Billy set fire to the haystack,' Kate said. 'Naturally, he didn't mean to but I think Mr Baker was angry and yelled at them.'

Her father frowned. 'The boys apologized, didn't they? And they helped put out the fire.'

'Yes, but they haven't been to the farm since,' Kate reported. 'Vera still goes to help but the boys don't. I imagine they're afraid to in case he shouts at them and tells them to clear off.'

'Hmm. I think I'll walk down, and have a word before we leave,' Mr Greene murmured, as much to himself as the others

Then they were at the cottage and Vera was standing at the door. She welcomed them in, kissing her parents and seemed pleased to see them all, including Jenny.

'You look very smart, love,' she remarked to Jenny. 'Where did you get a dress like that?'

'Kate and I made it,' Jenny told her. 'We do lots of stuff in the evenings – help out at a canteen for wounded soldiers, take first aid classes – and make clothes while we listen to the wireless.'

'Sounds as if you're having more fun than I am,

stuck down here and hardly ever seeing anyone unless it's work.'

'It was your choice,' Grace said, a sharp note in her voice. 'I'll admit I thought it a good choice – but not one I'd make myself.'

'I wanted your mother to come down, find herself somewhere pleasant away from the bombs but she says if they've got your name on them, they'll find you wherever you are – and if it's not meant you'll survive the worst attack,' Ned Greene said.

'I suppose that's right, but I still worry they'll invade,' Vera said. 'I might not like it here that much, even less since the boys upset Mrs Baker. She seems as if she half blames me.'

Kate saw Georgie flash a look at Vera that spoke volumes. Something had caused the incident at the farm – something that had made Billy careless with a firework. Was it something his mother had done? Kate wouldn't put it past her sister to upset her son enough so that he didn't think what he was doing. Obviously, she would deny it, so Kate didn't ask, she just sent an understanding look at Billy.

Vera had ham, hard boiled eggs, and lettuce and onion salad, for their tea, grown by Georgie in their garden at the back, with a jacket potato, followed by fatless sponge spread with jam and eaten with warm custard. It was filling and the ham was tasty, though the pudding wasn't particularly nice.

After they'd eaten, Mr Greene left the women to sit and talk over a pot of tea while he walked down to the farm. He hadn't quite reached the gate when he saw the farmer coming towards him.

'Mr Greene?' he said politely. 'Can I help you?'

'Yes, I hope so. I wanted to talk to you about the haystack . . .' He paused as Mr Baker looked as if he might say something but he stayed silent. 'I'm sure you know that Billy wouldn't have set the fire on purpose. It was careless and stupid – and I'm prepared to pay you for your loss – but please don't let the boys go on believing they are some kind of criminals.'

'Well, we lost half the hay, which is a nuisance, because there isn't any going spare so we'll have to buy in oats to feed the horses – but that isn't a problem this year, thankfully. And I'm not asking for compensation. In fact, I wanted to apologize . . .' He cleared his throat. 'My wife was very angry and her tongue ran away with her – fear of what might have happened, I suppose. However, she blamed both lads and Georgie certainly didn't do anything wrong. His quick thinking saved some of the hay and I had intended to reward him – then Billy told us about the firework and I'm afraid I was cross and the wife was sharp with them.'

'Ah, women!' Mr Greene said with a friendly nod. 'They do get carried away when they're upset.' He nodded to himself. 'I'm glad that's cleared up.'

'I'd like them to come back to the farm,' Mr Baker said. 'Georgie in particular is very helpful. Bright lad, your son. Billy is good with animals, too. He wanted to be a vet. Pity if a silly accident turned that ambition sour.'

'My Georgie wants to help folks,' Mr Greene told him. 'He might be a doctor or some such thing if things work out – but while there's bombing raids on London every night, I feel safer with him here. If I know he's still welcome – otherwise I'll take the boys back with me.'

'Oh, no,' Mr Baker replied swiftly. 'Ask them if they'll come and give me a hand in the morning. The cows are under cover for the winter now and that makes extra work.'

Mr Greene nodded his agreement. 'I'll tell them we've had this chat – unless you want to come back and tell them yourself?'

'I'll leave it to you,' Mr Baker murmured. 'They might react one way and then think it over. I reckon they listen to you.'

'Yes, mostly,' Mr Greene said with a smile. 'I had four boys and two girls and I never lifted a hand to any of them. A quiet word would usually do the trick, even though our Kate was a trifle headstrong when she was Georgie's age. Come to think of it, she probably still is!'

The two men laughed, shook hands, and went their separate ways.

Billy and Georgie were outside kicking an old leather football about when Mr Greene got back. Georgie aimed a kick at him and he headed the ball back to him. The lads laughed to see their grandfather demonstrating his skill with the ball and then quietened as he told them of his conversation with Mr Baker.

'He was very angry that day – justifiably so, I think, wouldn't you say?' Both lads nodded their heads and looked shamed. 'However, he knows that Billy didn't mean to do it. It was an unfortunate accident – and because of Georgie's quick thinking a lot less damage was done than might have been. So he's willing to forget it, if you two are – and he would like you to go back to your jobs on the farm.'

'I ain't goin'!' Billy yelled. 'She was nasty to me, Grandad, and I said I was sorry. I never meant to do any harm.'

'I think Mr and Mrs Baker know that,' his grandad said with a smile. 'If you don't want to go, Billy, you don't have to, of course – but I thought you enjoyed looking after the animals?'

'I do . . .' Billy kicked the ground, looking miserable.

'I like helping with the chores,' Georgie said. 'They'll be riddling potatoes soon and I was promised a bag if I helped. I enjoy the milking, too. I think I might go back, if he's sure.'

'Oh yes, he praised your quick thinking in saving the stack,' Mr Greene assured him. 'I thought it was very clever and very brave of you, Georgie. If a lump of that burning straw had fallen over you, you could have been badly burned.'

'I pulled it down rather than too far out,' Georgie told him, looking proud. 'I did get a few small burns on my hands but it was all right.'

'Well, I think you acted cleverly and bravely,' his father said. He looked at Billy, who was still kicking at the ground and looking as if he would burst into tears. 'Are you man enough to accept an apology and go back to doing what you like, lad?'

'I don't want to,' Billy said stubbornly. 'You didn't see the way she looked at me – and hear what she said. She hates me, so I'm not going near.'

'Well, I'm sorry for that,' Mr Greene said. 'It would please me if you tried to overcome your anger, Billy.

I understand why you don't want to – but it would make things better for everyone if you did.'

Billy shook his head. He turned his back on his grandfather and Georgie and went into the cottage. When they followed him in a little later, he'd gone upstairs to his room.

'Why is Billy sulking?' Vera asked but no one enlightened her.

Mr Greene glanced at his silver pocket watch. 'I think we'd best be on our way, Vera. I hope you'll like the Christmas gifts we brought – because I doubt, we'll see you again before the spring. I was lucky to borrow the car for this visit.'

Everyone kissed and wished each other a Happy Christmas, even though it was still some weeks away. Kate looked at her sister before they left.

'If there's something wrong, you can tell me,' Kate said. 'If I can help I will.'

'I doubt anyone can,' Vera said moodily. 'Unless you can influence Mr Hitler and make him leave us alone so that everyone can go home.'

'Don't I just wish I could,' Kate said. 'I expect we all do – but we have to carry on as best we can.'

'That's what I do every day,' Vera said but didn't smile. She looked at Jenny. 'You think yourself so clever getting a job up there – but come the invasion you girls will probably be rounded up and sent to one of those work camps we know they have over there. Or maybe worse . . .'

'My manageress says that talk is traitorous,' Jenny told her defiantly. 'She's got a gun under the counter and she says she'll die defending us – but she doesn't think it will happen. She says we're goin' to win, no matter what the papers say.'

'Oh, well, you've made your bed so you can lie on it,' Vera muttered. 'I don't have a Christmas present for you. I'll send you a postal order when I can.'

Jenny walked off to catch up with her grandparents without another word and Kate gave her sister a speaking look. 'That wasn't necessary, Vera. She's a good girl and she helps her gran – me too when I need her.'

'Oh, well, I suppose you think you know best,' Vera said, then, a little shamefacedly, 'It was nice of you all to come down. You didn't have to.'

'We wanted to,' Kate said. 'If you don't want to lose your daughter entirely, Vera, I should find something pretty for her for Christmas and mend your fences.'

Vera looked at her for a long moment, then inclined her head. 'I might, if I can. There isn't much to choose from in a small town.'

'Why not go into Cambridge on the train?' Kate said. 'It isn't my business, Vera – but have you fallen out with Bob?'

'Who told you that?' Vera demanded.

'No one – but you seem so unhappy. It was your choice to come down here, Vera. Unless there is a good reason, it seems to me that if you drive us all away you'll end up a bitter and lonely woman.'

Kate walked out, leaving her sister to stare after her in a mixture of frustration and fury. Billy came down the stairs, yelling for his grandad to wait. He rushed after them and Mr Greene wound down the window to say goodbye to him.

'I'm sorry,' Billy said. 'Thank you for my bike and I know you told me right – but I just can't go back there.'

'That's all right, lad,' his grandfather said and smiled. 'I just want you to be happy. You're my grandson and I love you – don't ever forget that, Billy. Even if it seems that the world is against you, I'll be on your side.'

'Thanks, Grandad,' Billy said and put his head through the open window to kiss him. 'Bye, Kate, bye, Gran – Jenny. I love you all!' He stood back with Georgie, waving as they watched the car drive slowly away. It had just started to rain again.

'Is there room in the shed for my bike with yourn?' he asked Georgie. The borrowed bike had been left outside the cottage a couple of days after the incident at the farm, and, because he needed it, Georgie had accepted it. He'd known he ought to say thank you but until his father settled things he hadn't dared to go near the farm.

'Yeah, plenty,' Georgie said. 'Let's put them away and then we can make a start on the new puzzle Kate brought us. They brought us several parcels for Christmas too.'

'We can't open them yet, can we?' Billy said, grinning at him.

'Nope but we know we've got them,' Georgie said. Billy glanced at him as they locked the shed door.

'Are you goin' back to the farm in the mornin' then?'

'Yes, I reckon I shall,' Georgie said. 'I like the jobs I do and I earn a little bit. We can do things if I've got some money in my pocket.'

'I miss the animals,' Billy confided, sniffing. 'I wish I could come, too – but I can't.'

Georgie looked at him. 'No one will be horrid to you, Billy. I wouldn't have gone back if Mr Baker hadn't spoken to Dad. If they were nasty to you, I'd leave again and I would never go back. In fact, if they were nasty, I would go home.'

'Even though the bombs are fallin' every night?' Billy looked at him in awe. 'I'm feared of the bombs, Georgie. Nellie next door got killed and I liked her. She used to give me jam tarts and a quarter of sweets every Saturday if I put her bin round the front for her on a Monday.'

'Yeah, she was all right. I bet Gran misses her,' Georgie said. 'You'll be fed up on your own while I'm working, Billy.'

'I'll be all right. I found some books in the school library about bein' a vet and stuff. I borrowed them, so I'll sit and read them in my bedroom . . .'

'I shall only be an hour or so at night,' Georgie promised. 'I wish Mum and Dad lived nearer . . . and Kate.'

'I wish Kate was my mum,' Billy said suddenly. 'I wish the war was over and my dad would come home.'

'Yeah, me too,' Georgie agreed. 'You won't tell your dad about your mum and Jock, will you, Billy? It will just make things worse so promise you won't tell.'

Billy looked at him and shrugged. 'I won't but I'll bet he knows.'

Georgie inclined his head. 'We can't stop him finding out – but don't be the one to hurt him. He's goin' to be very upset and angry too.'

'Do you think he will ever come home?'

Georgie looked at him. 'Steve's a pilot and they're working night and day to stop the air raids but he got a short leave – so don't see why your dad wouldn't and it might be soon. It might even be for Christmas.'

Billy grinned at him. 'That would be good. I miss him, Georgie.'

'Yeah . . .' Georgie gave him a playful punch. 'Yer still got me, mate!' Laughing, they went into the house together.

CHAPTER 23

Christmas arrived but no word or cards from Billy's father, though the mantle was filled with pretty cards from family and friends. Vera had put a few trimmings up to make it festive, but no tree, because she didn't have her decorations, which were all still in London, packed away in the attic. On her recent shopping trip to Cambridge, she'd found a few puzzles, colouring books, and a model plane for Georgie to build, as well as some sweets and tangerines. For breakfast they had toasted sandwiches made with streaky bacon, a rare treat these days.

Mrs Baker had invited the family down to Christmas dinner and they all went, walking together down the long drove dressed in their Sunday best, because Vera said they wouldn't get a roast dinner if they didn't. It was frosty and the drove was hard beneath their feet, uneven with ruts made by carts and the hooves of horses, but the air was clear and the surrounding Fens had a stark beauty all their own.

Billy hung back when they entered the farmhouse kitchen, which was toasty warm and smelled of baking and something nice cooking in the oven but he was welcomed along with the others. The baby, who was now walking a little, caused a lot of hilarity by constantly falling on her bottom.

Vera mostly just called the little girl Baby and Mr Baker asked her why.

'Well, she hasn't been christened,' Vera said. 'I was going to have her done when my husband came home but he hasn't had leave since before she was born.'

Mr Baker shook his head over it but said no more. There was a big cockerel with stuffing, roast potatoes and three vegetables for dinner, followed by a suet pudding with jam and custard. Mrs Baker apologized because she hadn't been able to make a traditional pudding. There was just no dried fruit around.

After dinner they had a cup of tea and the adults listened to the wireless and a speech by the King. Then Benny took the boys outside and they walked round the farm, looking at the animals. It was chilly and what little sun there had been early on had gone, becoming cloudy and dull, making them shiver. It was warmer in the stables and Billy asked if he could give the mare and her foal some bran mash that Benny had made and he laughed as the horse remembered him, nuzzling his hand.

'Give her this,' Benny said and held out a piece of apple. Billy fed it to the mare and she whinnied her appreciation. He was smiling as they all headed back to the house and the warmth of the big kitchen.

Mr and Mrs Baker and Vera were playing a game of cards, just for fun and having a laugh. Mrs Baker looked up as she saw the boys.

'Enjoying yourselves, lads?' she asked. 'You'll stay

for tea – my daughter is coming. She went to her in-laws for lunch, but we've got a special treat. I made an iced sponge. I couldn't make a fruit cake but I'd got some icing sugar in the pantry.'

The boys played a noisy game of Spillikins, and then Snap with the cards the adults had abandoned in favour of a chat. Tea was slices of fresh bread with farm butter, sticks of celery from the Fen with a taste all their own, pickled onions, some leftover cockerel – and a tin of red salmon that Mrs Baker had been jealously guarding for Christmas.

Vera had taken the family a bottle of sherry she'd bought on her shopping trip to Cambridge and a box of chocolates. When the boys and Vera got up to leave after tea, Mrs Baker handed them all a parcel each.

She looked directly at Billy. 'I hope you'll like your gift, Billy – and I want to say I'm sorry for shouting at you the way I did. If you want to feed the animals or just see them, you're welcome to come whenever you wish.'

Billy blushed bright red and then he rushed to her, put his arms about her wide hips and pressed his face into her body. 'I'm sorry, really, really sorry,' he said and he was crying. 'I never meant to do it.'

'Hush, then,' she said, patting his shoulder. 'No tears on Christmas Day. I have forgiven you – will you forgive me?'

Billy raised his head and looked at her, his face wet. 'Yes, I will,' he said. 'And I *will* come and feed the animals if – if it's all right?'

She nodded, smiled, and ruffled his hair. Vera, the baby asleep in her arms, called to the boys and they were moving towards the door when someone knocked. 'Well, who's that on Christmas night?' Mrs Baker said.

Her husband answered the door and a tall man walked in. 'Dad!' Billy screamed and flung himself at the man in naval uniform. 'I asked God for you to come and He sent you!'

'That He did, my son,' Bob Rush said and bent to scoop his son up in his arms, swinging him high above his head. 'I reckon it was your prayers that kept me safe all this time . . .' He glanced towards the farmer and his wife. 'Sorry to intrude. I'd hoped to get here earlier but I was . . . delayed in London.' He glanced at his wife, his eyes like cold steel. 'Are you ready, Vera?'

'We were just leaving,' she said, looking flushed and nervous as she turned to the farmer and his wife. 'Thank you so much for everything – the welcome and the food, and the presents.'

'You're very welcome, Vera. We'll see you tomorrow as usual – unless you want time with your husband,' Mrs Baker said, smiling at them. 'Come back when you're ready.'

Bob was standing waiting. He had an arm about his son's shoulders, but his expression was hard to read. Vera was ushered out to a car that waited in the drove. Bob held the doors open for her and then the boys to climb in. He said something to the boys over his shoulder, greeting Georgie and asking if he'd had a good day, but to his wife he said nothing.

At the cottage they all got out. Vera rushed ahead to open the door, taking Sally to the tiny room her cot was in and then lighting the lamps so that there was an inviting glow when the others trooped in.

'Do you want cocoa, boys?' she asked and they shook their heads. 'Why don't you take your presents upstairs? Your dad and I want a word together, Billy. Georgie, look after him.' She sent them an agonized look.

The boys needed no telling. Billy ran up the stairs. Georgie followed. They looked at each other but neither of them said anything; they were waiting for the shouting to start and it did, almost at once.

'He knows,' Billy said, biting his lips. 'I didn't tell him, honest.'

'I know . . .' Georgie heard the voices raised in anger. 'Open your parcel from Mrs Baker, Billy. See what you've got . . .'

He opened his own and found a beautiful fountain pen. He didn't think it was new but the nib had never been used so perhaps it had lain in a drawer. He looked at it, smiled and tucked it in his school satchel. Billy had found a book in his parcel. He gave a little cry of glee.

'It's a vet's dictionary,' he cried in pleasure. 'It tells you all the things that animals get wrong with them – cows, horses, sheep, pigs – and dogs and cats, too.'

'That's useful,' Georgie said, trying to sound enthusiastic but he could hear the sounds from downstairs getting louder and louder – and then there was a crash, followed by a scream and the sound of a door slamming. They looked at each other as they heard the car start up and drive away.

'Dad!' Billy yelled and pelted down the stairs to the kitchen. His mother was just getting up off the floor and as Georgie followed him into the room he saw her holding her face. It was obvious that Bob had hit

213

her hard. Her eyes were full of tears and she looked scared. 'Where has Dad gone?' Billy demanded. 'What did you say that made him go?' He looked at her accusingly.

'He hit me . . .' Vera sat down, sounding dazed and shocked. 'He's never hit me before.' She gave a little sob. 'Someone told him . . .' She leaned forward, burying her head on her arms on the kitchen table as her shoulders shook.

'He'll come back,' Georgie said, though he wasn't sure who he was trying to convince. 'He's angry. Angry and hurt – but he loves you, Billy. He'll come back for you.'

Billy looked at him, then turned and ran upstairs. They could hear his loud angry sobs as he threw himself on the bed.

'He *will* come back, Vera,' Georgie said and she raised her head to stare at him.

'I hate him!' she said. 'I don't want him back – and if he thinks he can take Billy and the baby, I'll fight him tooth and nail.'

'Is that what he said?' Georgie stared as she nodded. 'He didn't mean it. He has to go back to sea. He can't take them with him.'

'Oh, he'll find a way,' Vera said bitterly. 'But I gave birth to them. They're mine and I won't let him have them – not any of them!' A hard look came into her eyes. 'I'll tell him I'm finished with him. I'm going to be with Jock and I don't give a damn what anyone thinks . . .'

Georgie stared at her, then turned and walked back up the stairs. Billy was lying on his bed, face buried in his pillow. Georgie sat by him, touching his shoulder gently. 'Your dad will come back for you, Billy.'

Billy shrugged his hand off, but didn't say anything. Georgie didn't know what to say. Bob was very angry and he didn't blame him. It would have been bad enough if Vera had had a fling with a stranger – but she'd chosen Bob's best friend so Bob must feel doubly betrayed. He'd been at sea, facing all the hardships that both the weather and the war could throw at him – and his wife had been sleeping with another man.

His arrival should have made Christmas for Billy, but instead it had brought the world crashing down around his head. Georgie wished he could make it better, but there was nothing he could do. He prayed that Bob would come back the next day and make it up with Vera. Otherwise, Billy would go on grieving and hating his mother.

Georgie didn't see what happened, but his brother-in-law did return the next day. He'd waylaid Vera on her way to the farm and taken her off somewhere. Georgie was making a plane at the kitchen table when his sister walked in later that afternoon. Billy was sitting on the floor reading. They looked up at her and then beyond her to the man standing there silently in the doorway. Billy gave a glad cry and jumped up, running to his father.

'Dad!' he said, clinging to his legs. 'I want to come with *you*.'

Bob reached down and ruffled his head. 'That's just what you're goin' to do, lad. I'm taking you back to London with me now. Go up and pack your things.'

'Bob, don't do this,' Vera said and looked tearful. 'I've told you it won't happen again. He's safer down here with me.'

'You'll keep the baby,' Bob said gruffly. 'And Jenny is happy where she is but Billy is going to live with his gran until I come home for good.'

Billy looked from one to the other and then rushed up the stairs. Georgie looked at Bob. 'Can I come with you?' he asked.

'I'll take you if you want,' Bob replied. 'But your mum says she wants you to stay here so I think she'll send you back again, but I'll take you.'

'I'm coming,' Georgie said and looked at his sister. 'I want to see my mum – and make sure Billy is all right. I'll come back in time for school to start.'

Vera nodded silently. Her face was tear-stained but she was subdued and wouldn't look at her husband.

Georgie ran upstairs and fetched a few things he needed. Billy was busy packing all his stuff, thrusting it into brown paper carrier bags and his school satchel.

'Are you comin', too?' he asked, looking uncertain.

'For a visit. I don't think Mum will let me stay, though.'

'Good. I'm glad you're comin'. Maybe your mum will let you stay if we both ask her.'

Georgie shrugged. He knew he would most likely be sent back by his mother. He was surprised that she'd agreed to let Billy live with her, but perhaps Bob would have taken him away to strangers if she hadn't.

When they returned to the kitchen, Vera had gone and taken the baby.

'Your mother has gone to the farm,' Bob said. 'She didn't want to say goodbye, Billy, but she said to tell you she loves you.'

'I hate her!' Billy said fiercely and his father grabbed him and put his arms round him, holding him tight.

'So do I at the moment, son,' he said gruffly. 'Although I expect we'll forgive her in time.' He glanced at Georgie. 'Sorry about all this, old chap. It wasn't exactly the Christmas surprise I'd planned. I've got presents for you both in the car.'

Georgie nodded. 'I'm sorry about what happened, Bob. We didn't like it but we couldn't do anything.'

'Yeah, I know.' His brother-in-law smiled at him. 'I reckon your mum will give me a rare roasting for bringing you both back to London – but I can't leave Billy here with her.'

'I wouldn't stop,' Billy told him. 'If you hadn't come back for me, I would've run away.'

'Well, I want you with your gran and grandad,' his father said. He led the way out to the car and opened the door for them to get in the back and then loaded all their stuff in the boot, including Billy's bike. Billy and Georgie looked at each other. Billy grinned and Georgie nodded back.

Billy was pleased with the way things had turned out, but Georgie thought the regrets might come later. Aunt Vera wasn't the most caring mother, but she did her best and deep down inside Billy loved her. His life had changed forever, because he would never have his mother and father together again. Georgie felt sorry for him, but didn't let it show. He couldn't imagine

217

how he would feel if his parents got divorced, but felt a warm glow inside because he knew that would never happen.

'Georgie! What are you doing here?' Grace demanded when all three of them trooped in. She looked at Bob and there was sadness in her tired face. 'So it was true, then? I'm sorry, lad. I didn't believe it when I heard rumours – suppose I didn't want to.'

'She admitted it was going on even before I went to war – and the baby is his . . .' There was a choking sound in his throat.

'She told you that?' Grace looked at him oddly. 'I never thought Vera could be that cruel. I know she's a bit on the selfish side – but this beats everythin'.' She shook her head. 'I don't believe her. That baby's yours, Bob. I reckon she told you that so you would let the baby go . . .'

'You might be right,' he said. 'But I couldn't take the baby. You couldn't have the worry of that, Grace. I feel bad enough about asking you to look after Billy.'

'He's my grandson and I'll see he's looked after – but he'll be in danger here in London. We all are.'

'I know, and I would've taken him somewhere safer if I could.' Bob ran his fingers through his dark hair. 'I can't bear the thought of him being with her after—' He shook his head. 'He's better off here with you, Grace. I don't trust her.'

'Well, I'll do my best for the lad,' Grace promised. 'To be honest, I'd do the same in your shoes.' She held her arms out to Billy and embraced him. Then looked at her son. 'Well, Georgie, what am I going to do about you?' She hesitated, then, 'I can't force you to go back to your sister if I'm willing to keep Billy – so what do you want to do, love?'

Georgie grinned and went to hug and kiss her. 'You're well again, Mum! That's great. I wanted to come and make sure you and Billy would be all right – but I'll go back after the Christmas holidays.'

'Are you sure that's what you want?' Grace asked, looking surprised.

'Yes, just for a while anyway,' Georgie said. 'Mr Baker really needs my help on the farm and I'm doing all right at school, Mum.' He paused, then, 'And she might not deserve it, but Vera needs help, too. She can't manage there all by herself.'

His mother nodded and leaned forward to kiss his forehead. 'That's my Georgie. Always looking to help others. I'm proud of you – and so is your dad. He says you think you might want to be a doctor one day. What made you think that, Georgie? It's a lot of hard work, love. You'll need to study for years.'

'Yeah, I know,' he replied and grinned. 'If I'm not clever enough I could do something else in the hospital, though. I just think people need help when they're sick or down.'

'Yes, they do,' Bob said and smiled. 'Thanks for looking out for your sister, Georgie; like you said, she might not deserve it but she needs it. And I hear you want to be a vet, Billy?'

'I'm goin' to be one day,' Billy said, glowing in his father's look of praise. 'I came top in most things at school when I tried . . .' His smile faded. 'Where will I go to school here, Gran?'

'Kate will set some lessons for you and we'll do them here,' his grandmother told him. 'One day they'll open the schools again. You're not the first evacuee to come home, lad. Some of them went to strangers who weren't kind to them and they ran away or asked their parents to bring them back.'

'We were lucky,' Georgie said. 'The farmer and his wife are really nice. I like helping them – and they gave us a smashing Christmas lunch and tea, didn't they, Billy?'

'Yeah, they did,' Billy agreed and looked at Grace hopefully. 'I'm hungry, Gran. Is there anything to eat?'

She laughed and nodded. 'I'll be cooking tea later – omelette and chips, though it's only powdered egg, but quite nice. I've made vegetable soup to start, but I can give you a bit of bread and dripping now if you're starving?'

'Oh yes,' both boys chorused together. Grace's bread and dripping was smashing and they hadn't had any for months and months. 'Please!'

'Can I have a slice, too?' Bob asked and went to put the kettle on. He smiled but there was sadness behind it. 'I'll stop for a cup of tea and a bite – and then I have to report back to base. I was lucky to get even a short pass the way things are.'

'We'll all have somethin' now,' Grace said, smiling round at them. 'I feel a bit peckish myself . . .'

CHAPTER 24

'Are you sure you feel up to having Billy live with you?' Kate asked when she came round later that evening and the boys were tucked up in bed. 'I'll do what I can to help you, Mum, but I have to work.'

'I know that and I'm fine now.' Grace gave her a wry smile. 'It seems that you don't die of a broken heart, Kate. You just go a little mad for a while – at least, that's what happened to me.'

'Oh, Mum,' Kate said and hugged her. 'I'm so glad you're well again. I was very worried.'

Grace smiled and stroked her cheek. 'You're a good girl, Kate. I wish Vera was as sensible as you. She's got herself in a proper mess.'

Kate nodded. 'Did you know? I wasn't sure until you told me that Bob had found out and was going to take the kids away from her.'

'Not properly. She was always a fool,' Grace said. 'What did she want that other bloke for when she'd got Bob? I shall never understand it.'

'I don't know, Mum. I suppose . . . I suppose people

sometimes fall out of love.' Kate bit her lip. She hadn't told her mother of her quarrel with Steve and wouldn't. 'Anyway, is Georgie staying too?'

'I gave him the choice. I couldn't keep Billy and send him back but he says he intends to go for a while, anyway. He thinks Vera needs help – and this farmer he works for.'

'I'm not sure I approve of the boys being expected to work on the farm,' Kate said. 'Why doesn't this farmer have some land girls?'

'Apparently, the one he was allocated went sick and somehow he didn't get another.' Grace shrugged. 'I don't think it was hard work. They haven't been mistreated, as some of the kids have. Several have come home, you know. I was talking to someone at the market and she says her daughter was made to scrub the kitchen floor every night.'

'That is so wrong!' Kate exclaimed. 'People were supposed to look after them, to keep them safe – not exploit them.'

'I believe most have been treated fairly,' Grace said. 'You'll always get that one or two who take advantage.' She laughed. 'I'm afraid I've taken advantage of you, love. I told Bob that you would set lessons for Billy. I hope you don't mind, but he needs to keep up with his education if he's to be a vet one day.'

'Why would I mind?' Kate said, smiling at her mother. 'I'm a teacher. I wish they would open some more of the schools in London again. I'd go back like a shot.'

Her mother nodded. 'I thought you would say that.' Grace looked at her. 'Are you all right, Kate? You've been a bit on the quiet side lately. Nothing worrying you?'

'No. I'm fine,' Kate lied. Her mother hadn't liked the idea of Vera and Bob splitting up. She would be shocked if she knew that Kate's marriage wasn't perfect either. Kate had no intention of telling her or anyone. For the moment she would just carry on as if nothing had happened, because Steve was away. He was in danger every time he flew a mission, and that was day and night at the moment.

There were dogfights in the skies over Britain constantly as the RAF struggled to repel the fleets of bombers bringing devastation to the cities all over the country, but mostly to London. Infidelity seemed to Kate to be nothing compared to the fact that none of them knew what would happen next. Hitler was trying to break them and then he would invade.

Kate might have a bruised heart but she also had a family and she was determined to be there for them. Her mother was well again now and that was good, but Kate wouldn't give into her inner distress. She had to be the strong one, for Jenny, her parents, and the boys.

'Have you heard anything more from John since his last letter?' she asked, changing her mother's train of thought.

John's letter had arrived for Christmas. He hadn't been allowed to say much, because his words had been censored, but they'd gathered that he was overseas and somewhere warm.

We're very busy, Mum, Dad, he'd written. *Life isn't easy but it's OK. Just want you to know I am all right*

223

and thinking of you. I'm warmer than you are right now. Love to everyone, John.

That bit of his letter was as much as they'd been allowed to read, all the rest had been thoroughly scored out. It had been enough to lift everyone's spirits, though Grace had looked sad after she put it away, clearly remembering the two sons who couldn't send her greetings.

Kate thought the wound Derek's and Tom's deaths had dealt her mother would never quite heal, but it was becoming a little less sharp with the passing of time.

Kate saw her younger brother off on the train back to Chatteris, where he could either walk or catch a bus to the farm. She'd packed him sandwiches and a piece of seed cake to eat on the way, also a cold sausage.

'Take care of yourself, love,' she told him, wanting to kiss him but holding back because Georgie wasn't a child any longer. He was in that in-between stage, a gangly youth but strong because of the exercise he did working on the farm and cycling everywhere. 'If you want to come home, please just come, Georgie. You've got enough money?'

'I've still got the pound you gave me when I went the first time,' he said and grinned. 'And I've earned a bit on the farm and I don't spend much – so yes, I could come home if I needed to, Kate. Don't worry about me – look after the others.'

'I shall,' she promised. Watching proudly as her brother walked confidently to the train and got on, she felt a pang of regret that he was going away. He looked back once and waved and that was it.

Kate waited until the train moved off. Some young men were hanging out of the windows waving to family, but Georgie didn't appear. Making her way from King's Cross Station and then catching a bus home, Kate was thoughtful. In one way she was glad that Georgie would be safe down in the countryside but in another she was sad. Their family had split apart because of the war and it would never be the same again.

Georgie took the piece of string from his pocket and started to practise tying knots. It kept him busy for half an hour or so, then he put it away and stared out of the window. He wasn't hungry yet but he was bored and wished he'd brought a book to read. Billy read his veterinary dictionary all the time these days, but Georgie didn't have any medical books. He'd only seen comics on the newspaper stand, nothing he was interested in.

Thinking that he might eat simply for something to do, he was about to reach for his satchel when a man in uniform entered the carriage. He hesitated for a moment, staring, then smiled, 'Georgie Greene?' he asked. 'You're Kate's brother.'

'You're Chuck!' Georgie cried and then flushed. 'Sorry – I don't know your proper name. Steve just said you were Chuck.'

'My given name is Charles Durrant,' Chuck said, smiling. 'Flight Lieutenant if you want the full title – but I warn you, I only answer to Chuck.'

Georgie laughed. 'That's funny,' he said and Chuck sat next to him. The only other passenger, an elderly lady sitting on the opposite seat glanced at them and then away. 'Where are you going? I'm on my way back to Chatteris – I'm staying there with my sister for a while and I help out on the farm.'

'Like that, do you?' Chuck nodded. 'I live on a farm back home in Canada. It's a good life, plenty of fresh air – and sometimes you can ride for miles and not see anyone.'

'I like the freedom of the countryside,' Georgie told him. 'I enjoy milking and feeding the animals – and the harvesting was good, too.'

'Is that what you intend doing when you leave school?' Chuck asked. He took a packet of chewing gum from his pocket and offered it to Georgie.

'Thanks . . .' Georgie popped a piece in his mouth, enjoying the peppermint flavour. They chewed in silence for a few moments, then, 'I'm not sure if I want to work on a farm or be a doctor.'

Chuck smiled. 'There's a great big divide between the two, Georgie. If you choose the farm, it will be hard, back-breaking work all your life – if you choose the medical path you'll have to study for years.'

Georgie nodded. 'I know. I think I'd like to help sick folk but I'm not sure I could pass all the exams.'

'You seem a bright lad to me,' Chuck said. 'If I were you, I'd work as hard as I could at school and then see what happens. There are lots of different ways of helping people, many different jobs in a hospital, and others in the community. I don't see why you shouldn't find one that suits you, even if you don't make it to the top.'

'That's what I hoped,' Georgie agreed. He grinned.

'Nothing to stop me having a big garden and keeping animals if I want, is there?'

'Have the best of both worlds,' Chuck agreed. 'In Canada you'd be able to do that, Georgie. A lot of people keep a horse or a dog – or some chickens – out back. We have plenty of land, but we're not all farmers. My people started out as farmers but they do other things. My sister runs a clothing store but she lives on a smallholding and keeps her horses and some pigs, special ones – rare breeds. It's her hobby. My elder brother is in the other family business – and I'm going to be a mechanic when this is all over. I learned to fly before I joined the RAF, because Canada is a big country and it's easier to get around that way.'

Georgie looked at him in awe. 'That sounds wonderful,' he said. 'I never knew there were places like that in the world. Until I went to the country with Vera, I pretty much thought London was the world.'

'To some folks it is,' Chuck agreed and laughed. 'My people feel the same about their land. I think I could live anywhere, if I had the right people around me – the ones I loved.'

Georgie nodded. 'People are what matters, aren't they? My mother got sick when my brothers were killed and I didn't know what to do. I was worried she might die, but she's a lot better now.'

'Is that why you want to be a doctor, if you can?'

'I'd like to help anyone who was sick.'

'It's a good thing if you can do it,' Chuck said. 'So, have you been home on a visit?'

'Yeah . . .' Georgie hesitated, then, 'Billy's mum and dad fell out so he's gone to live with my mum – she's

227

his gran.' Chuck nodded. 'Kate says I can go home if I'm unhappy – but I promised I'd help on the farm and Vera can't manage all alone with the baby.'

'So you're going back . . .' Chuck was silent for a moment. 'Did Kate see you off? I wasn't sure but I thought I saw her walking away after the train got going.' He looked thoughtful. 'I had to stand in the corridor for a while, until some passengers got off – and then I found you. It's good to have company on a journey.'

'Yes, Kate came to make sure I got the right train.' Georgie grinned. 'She and Mum think I'm still a kid – but it doesn't matter.'

'You're not, though, are you?' Chuck said, looking at him seriously. He hesitated, then, 'If you ever think Kate's in trouble for any reason and I might be able to help, will you tell me?'

'I might . . .' Georgie replied. 'You're Steve's mate, aren't you?'

'We're friends – though I've been relocated to a new unit so I shan't be seeing him much now. Why?'

'You wouldn't steal Kate from him, would you?' Georgie gave him a straight look. Chuck met it easily without blinking.

'No, I wouldn't do that,' Chuck reassured him. 'I admire your sister but I would never try to come between her and Steve – even if I could, which I doubt.' He smiled oddly. 'I'm not her type anyway. Nothing like the man she chose to marry.'

'No, you're not, but I like you,' Georgie told him. 'Kate could have had anyone. All the local lads wanted her – but she chose Steve.'

'I'm not surprised. He's good-looking and confident,' Chuck said. 'They make a good couple.'

Georgie nodded. He was thoughtful. Chuck seemed the sort you could trust – and he'd never trusted Jock. He turned his head to look into Chuck's eyes. What he saw there decided him. 'If I thought Kate – or any of us – needed help I would tell you.'

Chuck smiled and offered his hand. 'Thanks, Georgie. I appreciate your trust. The more so because it wasn't given lightly.'

'You're all right,' Georgie said. 'My sister Vera broke up with her husband Bob and I wouldn't like it to happen to Kate.'

'It won't because of anything I do,' Chuck said and offered him some more chewing gum.

'I've got somethin' better,' Georgie said, producing the brown paper bag Kate had given him. 'She made me some sandwiches – there's cheese and pickle or spam and pickle.' He offered the packet. 'Go on, have some. I shall have a meal when I get home.'

'OK,' Chuck chose a spam and pickle sandwich and bit into it. 'That's good. I'll buy us a drink and something to munch when they bring the trolley round, if they do on this train.'

'They do sometimes,' Georgie told him and tucked into his food.

'Do you play cards?' Chuck asked as he finished his sandwich and wiped his fingers on a white handkerchief. 'I've got a pack in my kitbag. We could play something to while away the journey.'

'Yeah, that would be fun. Are you going all the way?' Georgie asked surprised.

'I'll be stationed not too far from you,' Chuck told him. 'Maybe come out and see you sometimes.'

'Yeah, that would be all right,' Georgie said and offered him the packet again. 'Go on,' he urged as his companion hesitated. 'Kate makes the best sandwiches.'

'Yes, she does,' Chuck replied and took another.

Georgie wondered at the fleeting look of sadness in his eyes. Was Chuck a bit sweet on Kate? He hoped not because Steve would never let her go and he didn't want his new friend to be unhappy.

CHAPTER 25

Georgie was lucky enough to catch a bus when he left the train in Chatteris. Chuck was headed in the same direction but going further so they sat together until Georgie got off at the end of the drove. He walked to the cottage, passing the farm but not stopping. Vera might not have anything for tea and he was hungry now. If he got there early enough, he could perhaps cycle into Chatteris and fetch some shopping if need be.

When he got to the cottage, it was empty, the door locked. Georgie looked for the key and found it, opening the door to go in. It was cold and felt strange. He went to the sink, filled a kettle but then muttered in frustration as he realized the range was out. That was so strange because his sister always kept the fire going.

Georgie ran upstairs to his room and stopped on the threshold. It looked different. All his things – his model planes – everything he owned had gone and there were different covers on the beds, which had been pushed apart. Feeling oddly frightened, Georgie went through to his sister's room and then he knew – she wasn't here. She'd left while he was visiting his mother.

Georgie went back down to the kitchen and picked up his satchel. Going out, he locked the door, replaced the key where he'd found it and began to trudge back towards the farm. His stomach was rumbling and he felt anxious. What was he going to do now? Had he come all this way only to return to London?

He knocked at the farm kitchen door and was invited to enter. Mr Baker was sitting at the table eating his tea. He looked surprised, then frowned, before smiling.

'I didn't think you were coming back,' he said, sounding annoyed. 'Your sister said you'd gone back to your home with Billy – before she left with that friend of hers, the one who brought you all down here.'

'Jock?' Georgie sensed their disapproval. 'I know what she's done isn't right, Mr Baker. When Bob came home, he found out and they quarrelled but I didn't know she'd go off with Jock. I came back to help her – and to help you on the farm, but I can't stay there on my own.'

'No, I'm afraid you can't,' Mrs Baker put in. 'We need the cottage now, Georgie. We have two land girls starting any day now and they want their own rooms.'

'Oh, you won't need me then . . .' Georgie's heart sank.

'You've been a big help,' Mr Baker said with a glance at his wife. 'You could have stayed here with us but my daughter . . . well, she's having another child so she's decided to move in with us until it's here. We don't have a bed for you, Georgie. Even if I put a camp bed in Benny's room it wouldn't be suitable. He snores and he's up all hours.'

Georgie knew they didn't want him to stay with

them. He would be just one more mouth to feed and they had enough help now. Hesitating between leaving immediately and asking if he could stay one night, he just stood there feeling as if the breath had been knocked out of him. 'I'll get the train back . . .'

'You can stay tonight,' Mrs Baker said, 'and have some supper. I'll be bound you're hungry.'

'I'm sorry, lad,' Mr Baker said, 'but I was told you wouldn't be back.'

'I told Vera I would be,' Georgie said. 'And thank you, I would like to stay tonight and I'm hungry. I can go home but . . .' He clamped his mouth shut. He wouldn't beg.

'There's an alternative,' Mrs Baker said suddenly. 'I wonder . . . would you mind looking after an old lady and a little girl for a few weeks, Georgie?'

'You're not thinking of old Mrs Seward?' Her husband looked at her and frowned. 'You can't send the lad there – she'd shout at him and it's no job for a young boy.'

'I'm not a boy anymore,' Georgie said. 'If I go back to London I can't go to school because there's none open – and Kate can't teach me what I need to know to take my exams. She can Billy but he's younger and maybe the schools will open again soon. Kate said there's been talk of it. But I don't want to take the chance.'

'Is it important for you to go to school?' Mrs Baker asked.

'Yes. I'll be taking important exams later this year and I really like my teacher where I am. Who is this lady?'

She beckoned him to the table and he sat down, eating the soup and bread she put before him.

'Jean Seward, her name is,' Mrs Baker said. 'She's elderly and a bit deaf so she shouts at everyone. Her husband died two years ago and she's been going downhill ever since. Her daughter Lizzie normally looks after her, shops, cleans a bit and makes sure she's all right – but she's in hospital having an operation and has left her eight-year-old daughter, Ellie, with her gran.' Mrs Baker took a deep breath, then, 'I went over there today and tidied up a bit. She isn't fit to take care of herself, let alone a small girl, but she refuses to ask for help and tried to put me out. I managed to do a bit but . . .' She shook her head. 'I don't have time to look after her, but if I go to the council and tell them, they'll put her in a home and take young Ellie to an orphanage.'

'You can't ask the lad to do it,' Mr Baker said firmly. 'It wouldn't be right.'

'I could try,' Georgie put in quickly. 'If she would let me. I'm not sure I can cook anything but . . .'

'I'll bring food a couple of times a week – and you can take home chips and a bit of fish to share,' Mrs Baker said. 'You'd be closer to school so could do a few chores in the mornings and shop for food that doesn't need much cooking. Besides, I think Jean might still cook a bit – it's just keeping herself and the child clean and the house. That kitchen was like a pigsty until I sorted it out.'

Mr Baker shrugged. 'It's up to you, Georgie. I don't think it's fair on you – but I can't think of anything else. We'll help you with the food as much as we can.'

'I'll see if she wants me,' Georgie said and grinned. 'She can only throw me out – and then I'll have to go back to London.'

'He'll be safer down here,' Mrs Baker reminded her doubtful husband. 'And we're here if he needs us.'

'Not far on your bike,' Mr Baker said and grunted. 'I'll take you in the morning. Your sister left all your stuff here when she left. Said she wouldn't be seeing you as she was going to family in Scotland.'

'That will be Jock's family,' Georgie muttered. 'How she thought I'd get all that stuff back on the train by myself! But that's Vera. She never thinks of anyone else.'

'Well, eat up,' Mrs Baker told him. 'I'll show you where to sleep – and then you can give a hand with the milking. Our girls don't start until next week.'

The next morning Mrs Baker went with Georgie to Mrs Seward's house. They rode their cycles into the small town, enjoying the ride despite the chill wind that tore at their clothes and turned their noses red. Georgie had brought just his satchel strapped across his shoulder, because there was no point in trying to take all his things if the elderly lady would not accept him, and Mr Baker would bring everything later if it was to be his new home for a while.

'I'll go in first,' Mrs Baker said. 'Follow behind and wait at the door while I tell her my idea.'

'All right,' Georgie said, frowning. He felt a bit uneasy now that he was here, wondering whether he should have gone straight back to London and studied at home. He could smell something not quite pleasant in the kitchen and wrinkled his nose, then he realized that the smell was not coming from the room Mrs Baker had entered, but behind him. Turning, he saw a little girl staring at him. She was small and thin, her fair hair straggling around her face and her cheeks stained with tears. She looked younger than eight, he thought. 'Hello, are you Ellie?' he asked.

'I didn't mean to do it,' Ellie said on a sob, fresh tears trickling down her dirty cheek. 'I've got tummy trouble and I messed myself.'

'Are you uncomfortable?' Georgie asked and she nodded. 'Is the toilet upstairs?' She nodded again. 'Shall we go and clean you up?'

'Yes . . .' she whispered and inched towards him, looking at him curiously. 'Who are you?' she asked shyly.

At that moment Georgie made a lifetime decision. 'My name is George,' he said. 'I've come to look after you, if your gran will let me.'

'She will if I ask her,' Ellie told him, working her way closer. 'I need someone to look after me, because she can't – but she loves me.'

'Of course she does,' George said and held out his hand. 'If we get you out of those dirty clothes, we can have you all nice and clean again – if you'll let me help you. We'll do it together.'

Ellie took his hand, leading him upstairs to the bathroom. It was tiny, but at least it had a bath, a basin, and a toilet. She had obviously been unable to control the emptying of her bowels for the mess had gone on the floor as well as the toilet seat and her clothes.

George found the water was warm, though not hot.

He filled the basin for her and a flannel and soap. 'Can you wash yourself, Ellie?'

'Of course I can,' she said. 'I was just upset because of the mess I made.'

'Wash yourself in this nice water and I'll clear up the mess here,' George said. There was some torn-up newspaper on the tiny windowsill; many folk had to use that these days because toilet rolls were scarce, as were so many other things people had taken for granted. Turning his back while Ellie removed her soiled under things and washed herself, George went down on his hands and knees and wiped the floor. He flushed the paper down the toilet and frowned. 'It needs a wet cloth. I'll have to find one in the kitchen.' At that moment he heard Mrs Baker call him. 'You find a clean dress and I'll come back and finish up here.'

'Thank you for helping me!' Ellie called as he went back downstairs.

'Where have you been?' Mrs Baker asked. 'I thought you'd changed your mind and run off.'

'I wouldn't do that without sayin',' George said. 'I was helpin' Ellie – she had a bit of trouble.'

Mrs Baker raised her eyebrows but George didn't enlighten her. She tutted and pushed him into the kitchen. It was big but very untidy. Food scraps and dirty crockery were left on the table and the drainer and there was a pile of saucepans in the sink. By the range sat an old woman dressed in black with a white lace collar about her throat. Her hair was as white as the lace and her eyes were a piercing blue that looked at him sharply.

'So you're the one,' she said and sounded cross. 'Well, what's your name then, boy?'

'It's George, and I'm fourteen so I'm not a boy any longer, Mrs Seward.'

'Why are you still at school then?' she demanded, her gaze stabbing at him. 'Why aren't you at work?'

'Because I want to be a doctor – or at least, work in a hospital – so I need to stay on at school and study hard so that I pass my exams and go to college.'

'Hah!' If anything, the old eyes brightened. 'Clever one, are you?'

'I don't know if I'm clever *enough*,' George said, 'but I want to try. And if I can't be a doctor, I'd like to do something at the hospital – to help people who are sick.'

'Are you a namby-pamby, boy?' she demanded. 'I can't stick those mealy-mouthed folk who try to tell me how I should live.' She glared at Mrs Baker.

'I don't think so, ma'am,' George replied. 'I'm not sure what that means – but I like to help folk.' His eyes moved to the overflowing sink. 'I could wash those pots for you – and the floor, if you wanted?'

'You could, could you? And what makes you think I can't? Tell me that!'

'Perhaps you don't quite feel up to it,' George replied. 'My mum was ill after my brothers were killed at the start of the war and I helped her but then she sent me to the country to keep me safe. Only, Mrs Baker can't keep me now and if you won't have me, I'll have to go home and miss out on my schooling.'

'Hah! Why won't she keep you?' The sharp eyes flicked to the farmer's wife. 'Is he a lot of trouble?'

'None at all,' Mrs Baker replied. 'I thought he might be a help to you, but if you don't want him, I'll take him home. We might be able to make him a camp bed up somewhere.'

'Who said I didn't want him?' the old lady barked. 'He can stay until Lizzie comes home from the hospital.' Her eyes moved beyond them to Ellie, who was now standing behind George. 'Come here, my love. How do you feel? Does your tummy still hurt?'

'It's not so bad now.' Ellie looked at her granny. 'I had the runs and it went all over everywhere. George helped me. He cleaned the floor and he's going to wash it. I washed myself when he told me . . .' She sniffed. 'Can he stay, Granny?'

'He can stay until your mother comes home,' Mrs Seward replied. She lifted her gaze and glared at the farmer's wife. 'Why are you still here? You've got enough to do at home.'

'Yes, I have,' Mrs Baker replied. She turned to George and smiled. 'Are you all right to stay, George?'

'Yes, thank you, Mrs Baker.' He grinned. 'Thanks for letting me stay last night and bringing me here. We'll be all right.'

'Then I'd best get back. The house won't clean itself and the men will soon be back for their lunch.' She nodded to Mrs Seward and then George. 'You know where we are if you need anything.'

'Thank you. I'll pop over one day when I can.'

Mrs Baker hesitated, as if unsure she was doing the right thing, but then she turned and left. The door closed with a snap behind her. For a moment there was silence, and then George said, 'I need a bucket and

239

cloth to wash the bathroom floor over. You're lucky to have such a nice bathroom, Mrs Seward.'

'My husband had it put in when our children were young,' she replied. 'You'll find all you need under the sink. But you should choose a bedroom – we've got two spare ones. I once had a big family . . .'

George looked at her, because he caught the underlying grief in her voice. 'Did you lose someone in the war, Mrs Seward?'

'In the first one. My three sons were killed on the Somme. Lizzie was just a baby. There was a lot of years between her and her brothers . . .'

'Same as me, or almost,' George said and went to the sink, looking behind the curtain that hid the space beneath it. It was dingy and worn, like the mats on the floor. Clearly, what had once been a large, special house, had suffered neglect for a few years now.

Mrs Seward didn't reply, and when he turned, he saw that she had leaned back in her chair with her eyes closed. Ellie sat on a little stool beside her chair and the old woman's bony fingers were stroking her hair. She put a finger to her lips and George nodded. He took what he needed as quietly as he could and left the kitchen. Going upstairs, he filled his bucket over the bath and added washing soda, then he got down on his knees and scrubbed the floor. It hadn't been done in a while and he changed the water twice.

After he'd finished, he poured the water down the toilet and decided to wash the sink, bath, and toilet with some Vim he found next to the bath. By the time he'd finished, it looked very much cleaner and he rinsed his hands in clean water. Leaving the bucket to the side of the upstairs hall, George went to look in the bedrooms. It was easy to see which two were not in use – they had clearly belonged to the lost sons and there was still evidence of the possessions those men had once cherished.

George chose the one overlooking the back garden. He'd never seen such a large garden and, inevitably, it was overgrown. From what he could see, there were three large old trees, perhaps fruit trees he thought, though didn't know for sure, but it looked to have been a vegetable garden once rather than just for sitting in. There was a path leading down to the bottom where the trees were and a small lawn to one side, but he thought it must have been mostly used for vegetables and small fruit bushes, which were still there but rambling and neglected. Whoever had tended the garden was no longer here to keep it neat.

George took his pail down to the kitchen. Mrs Seward was struggling to poke up the fire in the range. He went to her and laid a gentle hand on her arm.

'Let me make it up for you,' he said. 'I know how to do it.'

She nodded and sat back in her chair with a relieved sigh. 'It needs to be hotter so we can make tea and cook something – there should be some food in the pantry. The butcher and grocer deliver and Ellie puts it away for me. I can't do much at a time. I have to rest in between.'

'It must have been hard for you with your daughter in hospital, ma'am.'

'If you're going to stay here, call me Jean or Mrs Seward,' she said and there was a gleam of amusement in her sharp eyes. 'You make me feel old, calling me ma'am.'

George grinned. 'You're not old, just not quite well.'

'Hah! That's all you know,' she said and cackled. 'I'm old enough to be your grandmother, lad – but a lady never tells. I was a lady, you know. I had a maid to wait on me and another to clean, but that was before my Ernest died and by then the money was mostly gone.'

'I'm sorry you lost your husband . . .'

'So was I,' she said, her voice sharp with remembered grief. 'I've lived too long, that's the trouble – but if I'd died when I should have, who would look after Ellie now?'

'Have you no other relatives?'

'None. Her mother would never have left her with me if there was anyone more capable – but we won't have her sent to an orphanage. Nasty places. I've heard bad things about them.'

'She is definitely better with you,' George replied, glancing at Ellie's scared face.

'With *us*,' the old woman said unexpectedly. 'I thought you might bring in the coke and perhaps make a cup of tea if I wasn't up to it, I didn't expect you'd wash floors.'

'I can do most things,' George said. 'Mum taught me how to make up the fire and a lot of chores she said I could do. She said men should be able to look after themselves, if need be. I wasn't always happy about it, but Mum didn't see why I shouldn't be able to boil an egg and make a pot of tea. I cleaned windows for pocket money, too. Scrubbing a floor is only commonsense.

242

I'm not sure I could cook a pie, though – pastry looks more difficult to get right.'

'You won't need to do that,' Mrs Seward told him, her wrinkled features relaxing into a smile. 'I can just about make pastry on my good days. On my bad we'll eat toast or fish and chips from the shop.'

'I picked the room with the blue coverlet – is that all right?' George asked, changing the subject. He picked up his satchel as she nodded. 'I'll take this up and find some sheets. I can make my own bed, too.'

'Is that all your stuff?'

'Nah, Mr Baker will bring it later. We weren't sure if you'd have me, Mrs Seward.'

'I'd be a fool not to – and whatever I might be, I was never that.'

'No, I didn't think you were,' George nodded, picked up his satchel and went out.

She called after him, 'I'll have a pot of tea in five minutes – and then we'll think about what we're going to eat.'

CHAPTER 26

Kate was feeling happier than she had for a while that morning in March 1941. Her supervisor at the library had recommended her for a promotion, which would mean a few shillings a week extra and she'd managed to buy a lovely big pork chop, which she and Jenny would share for their tea. Kate normally got home an hour or so earlier than her niece, because the library closed at four. In normal times they opened again in the evenings for a couple of hours but because of fuel restrictions and the need not to show unnecessary lights at night, they were now opening mornings and afternoons only. In the summer they might open for two hours in the evening again.

As Kate entered her house, she saw a small pile of letters on the mat. She bent down to pick them up; two were just bills, but one was from George – as he preferred to be called now – and the other was from Steve. Carrying them into the kitchen, she filled the kettle and put it on the gas to boil. Once her tea was made, she sat down to look at her post, tossing aside the two small bills and opening the letter from her brother.

Dear Kate,

I wanted to tell you everything is fine here. Mrs Seward had a little turn the other week and I had to fetch the doctor quick. He sent her to the old people's infirmary in March and on this Sunday, I took Ellie to see her. She was very much better and they say she can come home this next weekend. The doctor said if I hadn't been there, she would've died, that I did all the right things – I did tell you I'd been to first aid classes, didn't I? Our teacher said it was a good idea so I joined and it came in handy.

Ellie's mother is still ill but they say she is getting better slowly. I got an A in my science test this time and my English has improved. Mr Baker says I speak better than when I came down to them. I don't go to the farm often, but every now and then I pop over. I helped with the milking on the previous Saturday morning, because their land girl had the stomachache. It was when I got back that Mrs Seward was first ill.

I hope Mrs Seward recovers because I like her. Sometimes she bites my head off if I say something she doesn't approve of, but she can be funny and kind and she loves Ellie. Ellie is my shadow and follows me all the time when I am in the house. She doesn't go to school much, because Mrs Seward says she is delicate – she had scarlet fever as a small child – so she does her lessons at home.

She is nervous and easily frightened but seems to trust me. I help her with her lessons if I get time, but I have a lot to do. Sycamore House has five bedrooms as well as three reception rooms and a huge kitchen and pantry. I don't clean it all, because Mrs Seward has someone come in once a week to do the scrubbing and dusting. Mrs Baker said she ought and so she did, but she doesn't have a lot of money to spare so I do lots of things for her. If it's fine I do a bit in the garden, too.

I still have time to study and my teacher says that the improvement in my work is remarkable. He says I can definitely try for medical school when I'm old enough, and he has offered to coach me for my exams. I think I would have to pay – about ten shillings a week. I'm not sure if Dad can afford that so would you ask for me, please? If he says it is too much it doesn't matter as I can study in my room. Mrs Seward gave me a desk to keep my things in. It's really nice. Very old. Antique, she says. I think some of her things might be worth selling if she needs money but she won't part with anything so I doubt she will.

Give my love to Mum and Dad, Billy, Jenny, and Steve. Love to you, Kate. Hope all is well with you,

  Best wishes,
  George.

Ps, I thought you might like to know. I saw Chuck two weeks ago. He had a few hours leave and he took me to the pictures in Ely. We had a fish-and-chip supper. He is really generous and kind. XX

'That was nice of him,' Kate said aloud, smiling as she put down her brother's letter. He was the only one of her brothers who had ever written long newsy letters and she looked forward to them coming about once a month. She always wrote back and told him all the news about the family.

Glancing at the clock, Kate saw she had loads of time to prepare tea so she opened her husband's letter. It felt like one sheet of paper and it was. Her eyes scanned the brief note and then again, as the shock of disbelief hit her.

Kate,

I don't think this will come as much of a surprise. We both knew it was over the last time I had leave. I've met someone and I've realized that I've never been in love before. What we had was just girl and boy stuff, as I think you knew before I did.

I shan't claim anything from the house other than my clothes and a few personal bits. I've made a list on the back. Could you pack them into a suitcase and I'll collect them next time I'm in London? I think it is best to end it swiftly rather than quarrel over little things. When the war is over we can get a divorce – or if you want to you can start it now.

Sorry,
Steve.

247

'Unbelievable!' Kate exclaimed as she stared at the flimsy sheet of paper. Turning it over, she saw that he'd written his list. He wanted all his clothes, his school prize – which was a book of poems – and his silver penknife, his football and boots, his tiepins, best watch, a wallet his mother had given him that he'd never used, and various other similar small items that she would find in his bedside drawer. And that was it.

For several minutes she stared at the paper, not truly taking it in. Was it really that easy to end a marriage? Kate had thought about it after that disastrous leave but decided she would carry on – that there was something worth saving – but it seemed that her husband had come to a different conclusion.

'Damn you, Steve!' Kate muttered.

For a moment she felt like tearing the letter up and his things with it. Why should she tamely pack a case for him, like a little mouse? It would serve him right if she ripped everything to pieces to see how he felt, because he'd just torn her life apart.

Kate was angry. No, she was furious, but it didn't hurt, not this time. As she began to think calmly, it came to her that maybe Steve was right – perhaps it had been over after his leave. Yet even if that were so, it still meant her life must change. For one thing, she couldn't afford to stay in this house without his help. That niggled at her. A woman who worked full time, who had a good education, should surely be able to have a home of her own. But even with the small raise she'd been promised, it would be too difficult.

Kate got up and walked into the sitting room, looking at the things she'd lovingly collected. Most of

248

it was second-hand, bought with her savings when she could afford it; some had been given her by her parents. It dawned on her then that there was nothing of Steve's in the room. He'd never added one thing to it.

She walked slowly up the stairs to the bedroom she'd shared with Steve. There wasn't very much of his here either, apart from the clothes he'd left behind when he'd joined up, saying he would mostly be wearing uniform, and the items in his bedside chest. All his brushes and shaving stuff had gone with him, of course. She opened his drawers and took out everything inside. Along with the items he'd named, there were pebbles, old tickets to football matches, a lighter that didn't work and other things that had just been thrown into the drawer.

In a sudden surge of anger, Kate tipped them all on the bed. Her heart stopped as she saw some small black-and-white photographs of her and Steve on their honeymoon. She caught back the tears, jumped up and ran down the hall to the box room. Three cases were stored there – two of them Steve's. Still feeling as if this was all unreal, she took them back to the bedroom, scooped the contents of his bedside chest into one and then began to pack his clothes. Everything fitted into the two suitcases.

When she'd finished, Kate sat on the edge of the bed and stared at them. Two suitcases – all there was to show for their marriage. It was Kate who had put their home together. Steve had made the house nice for them but everything else had been her. When she gave the house up, as she would have to eventually, someone else would benefit from those renovations.

All her dreams of a home and family were fading.

Kate felt an aching emptiness inside. Why? Why had it happened? They'd been so happy until the start of the war – or was it until she fell for the baby?

As she walked slowly downstairs, Kate realized that that was when it had started – their first real disagreement. Steve hadn't wanted a baby. He didn't particularly want a divorce – or not yet. Despite his talk of a big family, when it came to it, Steve didn't want responsibility for a child.

Kate shook her head, determined not to cry. She might be able to get a second job. Perhaps if she went out to work three or four nights a week, she could keep her home. Jenny was earning money now. She could afford to pay a small amount for her room, if it became necessary.

'Damn him! Damn him to hell!' she cried aloud.

'Who is that – not me I hope?' Kate's father poked his head round her kitchen door. He looked at her face. 'What's up, love? Something happened?'

'Oh, Dad!' Kate's voice shook with the anger that suddenly swept through her. 'Steve has found someone else. He wrote to me – wants his things – and he says we'll get a divorce when the war is over; or I can do it sooner if I like . . .'

'The rotten bugger!' Ned Greene's normally mild temper erupted. 'You tell him, if he wants a divorce he has to pay. He can't just swan off and leave you in the lurch, Kate. Supposing you'd got the baby? You couldn't have worked – or if you did, you would have to leave the child with someone. You should go to a solicitor and ask for advice. Make sure you get something for what he's done . . .' His eyes met hers, questing. 'You haven't given him reason, Kate?' She shook her head. 'I thought not. I wish you'd never married him. I wasn't convinced he was right for you – but you loved him.'

'I did,' Kate said with a wobbly smile. 'I know it was a mistake. It was first love, Dad. I thought it would last forever – but what is it? Not even three years?'

'It might have been better if the war hadn't happened.'

She was silent for a moment, then, 'He was my hero. I thought he was brave and clever – and he is very handsome.'

'Yes, I'll give him that – but brave and clever?' Mr Greene shook his head. 'If he had an ounce of sense, he would hang on to you for all he's worth – and only a coward ends his marriage with a letter.'

'Yes, it was a cowardly act,' Kate said. 'He could have told me to my face.'

'He should have.' Her father shook his head. 'Do you want me to go after him, Kate? I can't promise to thrash him; he's younger and stronger – but I'll guarantee to make him sorry for hurting you.'

'Please don't,' she begged. 'It isn't worth it, Dad – and it doesn't hurt much anymore. It's just that I don't want to lose my home.'

'You knew before this?' he questioned.

'Sort of. I knew he'd been unfaithful; he said just once and I thought we might still make it work. It happens to a lot of people and they go on.'

His eyes raked her face. 'You're not breaking your heart, love? Tell me the truth.'

'I'm sad and angry – but no, I'm not breaking my heart. I'll manage somehow.'

'I know you will – and I'll help as much as I can. I'm saving for George's future, Billy's too. He'll get nothing from his mother – she hasn't even written to him once and Bob will do as much as he can when he can – but goodness knows when that will be, if ever. Even so, I can give you a few bob to help out, Kate.'

'George needs ten shillings a week for extra tuition,' she said, giving him her brother's letter. 'Don't worry for me, Dad. I can get an extra job at nights. I've seen a notice in a pub window; they want a barmaid three nights a week. That could pay my rent.'

'Well . . .' Her father was indecisive. 'I promised George I'd see him through college but if you're short, Kate, I'll find the money. Promise me you'll ask if you need to?'

'Yes, I will, and thank you,' she said. 'I've been doing volunteer work in the evenings but I can take paid work instead.'

'Your mum won't like you working in a pub, Kate.'

'I know – but I'd rather do that than lose my home. If I just give up and come home to you, Steve wins. I won't let him do that to me.'

The pride was in her voice and her face. Mr Greene nodded and put his hand on her shoulder. 'I might get an extra shift if I put in for it,' he said. 'Keep strong, Kate. We'll get through this time together – and we'll speak to a solicitor. Steve is the one that broke the marriage, he should pay you something. You've got his letter as proof.' He ran fingers through his short grey hair. 'I think he wants you to go for the divorce – he's given you the means by writing this down.'

'Perhaps that's why he did it that way,' Kate said. She heard a noise and hushed him. 'That's Jenny now . . .'

He nodded and smiled as his eldest grandchild entered the kitchen. 'Oh, hello, Grandad,' she said. 'What are you doing here?'

'I came to invite you to Billy's birthday tea.' His next words were lost as the siren wailed. 'It's on Saturday. Right, I'd best get back to your mum, Kate. She's terrified of these raids.'

Jenny looked at Kate when he'd gone. 'Grandad looks tired, didn't you think so?' she asked and yawned. 'I'm whacked, Kate. We've been so busy. We had a big delivery of knitwear in today and we had to price it all up and list it. My manageress was so pleased. She was wondering how we'd keep going if we couldn't get the stock we ordered – but all of a sudden there it was. It's all English wool and it seems we've got plenty of that at the moment, because we can't export it.'

'I wish the same applied to the meat,' Kate said. 'If there are plenty of sheep, I don't know who gets all the chops. I haven't seen any for months – but I do have a pork chop we can share.' She glanced at the clock. 'Goodness! I haven't started the supper yet.'

'It doesn't matter. I only want a piece of bread and jam. I'm going out with a friend this evening – you eat the whole pork chop, Kate.'

'You went out last night and the night before . . .' Kate looked at her. 'Just who is this friend, Jenny? Is it a man?'

Jenny blushed. 'Yes, his name's Pete – and he's in the

army. Don't look like that, Kate. I know I'm only fifteen but he's nice and he doesn't try it on.' She laughed as she saw the look in Kate's eyes. 'No, really, he doesn't. He kissed me last night but he asked if he could and he didn't do anything else. I'd say no if he tried.'

'That doesn't always work,' Kate said. 'I don't think your mum – or your gran – would approve of you going steady.'

'He has to go back to his unit tomorrow. Don't say I can't go, Kate. Please, don't spoil it for me . . .'

'I won't, Jenny,' Kate assured her. 'But don't do anything silly. The last thing you want at your age is to have to get married quick – and with him away you'd be an unmarried mum before you could wed.'

'I know and I won't.' Jenny hugged her. 'You are the best aunt in the world, Kate!' She saw the letters on the table and picked one up. 'Is this from Steve?'

'Jenny don't!' Kate cried but it was too late. Jenny had read the few lines. She looked at Kate in horror. 'Oh, Kate, I'm so sorry.'

Kate shook her head and shoved her towards the hall as they heard the ack-ack start and then the drone of planes in the distance. 'Under the stairs, love – and just pray it isn't us!'

They came out of the cupboard two hours later, stiff and frozen, to the all-clear. Jenny looked at the kitchen clock and gave a wail of despair. 'I should've met Pete an hour ago.'

'Go now, as you are,' Kate urged. 'He'll understand and I'll bet he'll be on his way to meet you even now.'

'All right, I will,' Jenny said and dashed off, snatching

up her bag as she went. Kate smiled and started to prepare her supper three hours late . . .

The next morning Jenny came down to breakfast looking pleased with herself. Kate was making some toast and looked at her, smiling.

'So Pete waited for you then?'

'He went to the underground and came back when the all-clear sounded. I've given him my address now so we're going to write to each other.' She gave a little trill of laughter. 'He says he loves me, Kate. Says he's never met anyone like me and he wants us to get engaged on his next leave and then married when I'm seventeen.' She gave a little giggle. 'He says he'll wait however long he has to.'

'Well, if he's willing to wait for you, he must be serious,' Kate said. 'I don't know what your mum and dad will say to you being engaged, though.'

'Mum wouldn't care.'

'Perhaps she wouldn't – but there's your dad and your gran and grandad. You need to listen to what they say, Jenny. It doesn't always work out if you marry your first love.'

'The way you did Steve?' Jenny looked at her in apology. 'I'm sorry, Kate. I shouldn't have said that – he's a pig for what he said to you . . . the way he said it was horrid.'

'It was a bit stark,' Kate admitted. 'Things haven't been right for a while, though, Jenny. I don't like what he did – but I accept it.'

'I wouldn't. I'd go for him with my nails!' Jenny said savagely. 'Are you going to divorce him?'

'Dad says I should. I'm not sure – he might have to pay me something, a pound or two – but that would help pay my rent. I'm going to find an evening job if I can. Otherwise, I might have to go back home to live.'

'Oh, Kate!' Jenny looked stricken. 'I've never given you anything for my board – you never asked.'

'I could manage and you brought home some food now and then. You don't earn that much, Jenny. I don't want to take your money.'

'I'll give you five shillings a week,' Jenny offered. 'It isn't much but it will help pay the rent.'

'Yes, it will,' Kate agreed. 'It would be a big help, Jenny – if you're sure?'

'I'd have to pay a lot more for a room,' Jenny replied. 'And I wouldn't want to go back to Gran. I love her lots, but she wants to know what I'm doing all the time. You let me get on with it.'

'I trust you to be sensible,' Kate said with a smile. 'I have no right to dictate your life, love. We all have to do what we think best for ourselves and our families. As long as you don't get into trouble, because if you do, they'll all blame me.'

Jenny laughed. 'They would, too,' she said. 'How they think you could stop me doing something if I was determined to, I don't know – but I haven't been daft and I won't. I like Pete a lot. I might love him – but I'm only fifteen and I want to see a lot more of life before I start a family so I promise I'll be sensible.'

'Good.' Kate gave her a hug. 'I'm so glad you're with me, Jenny. Now, we'd both better get ready for work, because we mustn't be late.'

CHAPTER 27

Kate and Jenny went to Billy's birthday tea that Saturday afternoon. Kate had been saving to buy him a new pair of leather shoes and, despite her concerns about the rent, had got them for him while Jenny's present to him was a big bag of sweets. He'd invited a couple of lads from the next street to his tea. Like Billy, they'd been evacuees but had returned home; in their case, because they'd been treated unkindly by the couple who were supposed to take them in.

'They made us scrub the paintwork, sweep the yard, clean the windows and carry in heavy buckets of coal,' Jimmy said, rolling his eyes. 'It was horrible there. They only had a little fire in the kitchen and the food was awful. Not much of it, either.'

'I liked working on the farm,' Billy said. 'I helped deliver a foal and the farmer was good to us.'

'Why'd yer come 'ome then?' Jimmy asked.

'I wanted to live with my gran,' Billy said and then changed the subject. ''Sides, I'm studying hard and I can do that at home.'

'We've got ter go back ter school soon,' Jimmy said,

giving his little brother a nudge. 'Don't pick yer nose, Freddie. Ma will give yer a clout if she sees yer.'

'Are they starting school again, then?' Billy asked.

'Ma says so – but your aunt would know. Ask her.'

When applied to, Kate told them she'd heard rumours but nothing for certain. 'I'm sure they'll have to if more evacuees come back,' she said. 'I'd like to think I'd get my job back but I don't know anything yet.'

The boys tucked into their tea – ham and egg sandwiches, and strawberry jelly with tinned pears and a little evaporated milk on the top.

'This is lovely, Mum,' Kate said as she ate a ham sandwich. 'However did you find all this stuff?'

'I know the shopkeepers and they always try to find me a bit extra if I ask for something special.' Grace smiled. 'We used to have fifteen kids or more running around at our parties and a dozen different kinds of cakes and buns, sausage rolls, too, but this was the best I could do.' She looked sad for a moment. 'Georgie's fifteenth birthday is coming up soon, but I don't suppose he'll come up to London for it. He seems settled where he is.'

'I think he's busy most of the time,' Kate said. 'I'm proud of him for volunteering to do it, Mum, but he seems fond of the little girl there, who is sickly and needs looking after – and the old lady makes him laugh despite her sharp tongue.'

'He's happy, I know that,' Grace agreed. 'And he's safer there I suppose.' She sighed. 'They've left us alone so far today but I suppose we'll catch it later.'

'Don't tempt fate, Mum,' Kate said with a shiver.

'Georgie's much better off where he is and a little work won't hurt him. He's never done as well at school as now. I wouldn't take him away, even if the bombs stop . . .' She heard a wailing sound in the distance. 'Sounds as if the West End may be catching it this time.'

'I'm not going down the underground and leaving all this food to waste,' Grace said with a puff of annoyance. 'If it gets closer, we'll go under the table or the stairs.'

'They say it isn't safe under the stairs,' Kate said with a quirk of her brows. 'I only know I feel safer there than on the streets. It's all right when you're underground, but that few minutes before you get there is so vulnerable to attack.'

The boys had carried on eating tea, ignoring the siren. The all-clear sounded about six that evening and the guests went back home. Kate and Jenny walked back to the house together late that evening. It was dark and difficult to see where you were going, because there were no street lamps, just a flicker of light from their shaded torches. Cars had to drive by headlights that had bars across them and shone downwards. It was a wonder there weren't accidents all the time, but everyone was in the same boat and most people walked. It was hard to get coupons for petrol, unless you bought them on the Black Market and there was always a risk that they were counterfeit. Counterfeit money had been circulating too, so everyone had a habit of holding a note up to the light to check the watermark and the silver line were there. People said it was a conspiracy to make the citizens lose faith in their currency and bring down the Government. Kate's father said it was just some crooks trying to get rich at other folks' expense.

When Kate entered her house, the back of her neck tingled. Someone had been in. She looked to the spot where she'd left Steve's bags and cases and saw they had gone. His smell was still there as she went into the kitchen. She looked to see if he'd left her a note to say he'd taken his things but there was nothing. When she went to the pantry to get some milk for a cup of tea, she saw that two of the buns she'd made earlier had gone. Steve had obviously helped himself. She wondered what else might be missing, but didn't notice anything until she went up to her bedroom. The silver-framed photograph of their wedding had gone. The picture had been taken from the frame and thrown on the bed, but the silver frame had disappeared. It had been a wedding gift to them both from Steve's uncle so she supposed he was entitled to it if he wanted it, but it seemed a petty thing to have done. As she looked around the room, she saw that her alarm clock was also missing – and that had definitely been hers.

For a moment she felt annoyance but then she let it go. Neither item had been worth more than a pound or two, so what was the point in making a fuss? She reached for the wedding photograph, looked at it and then tore it across. Any lingering doubts that her marriage was truly over disappeared like the morning mist.

Kate slept better that night than she had for a while. She spent Sunday cleaning the house, but didn't notice anything else missing. In the afternoon, she washed her hair and curled up in her dressing gown and slippers on the sofa to read. Her mind was made up. She would try for the barmaid's job the following day. It was time to put the past behind her and move on. She would earn enough to pay her rent and buy the coal needed to keep the fires going. She would miss her volunteer work but she might still manage to do that one night a week.

Yawning, she stretched out on the sofa. It was too early for bed yet, but it had been a long day. She was just wondering if she ought to go up and have the one bath they were allowed to take each week, when she heard the door knocker.

'Who on earth is that?' Kate wondered aloud.

Getting up, she went to answer her front door, her hair still wrapped in a damp towel. For a moment when she opened it, she couldn't think who it was and then 'Chuck?' she said with a burst of pleasure as recognition came and she laughed. 'I wasn't expecting anyone. I must look a fright – but come in. I'll put the kettle on. Would you prefer a cup of tea or cocoa? I don't have coffee or anything stronger . . .'

'Cocoa would be fine,' he said, following her through to the kitchen, which was spotless and very tidy. 'I'm a coffee person but cocoa is good.'

'We can't get coffee very often these days,' Kate told him. 'I've been cleaning all day. I was at my nephew's birthday party yesterday – just two other boys and us, but it was nice. I didn't do any work then and I'm back to my job tomorrow.'

Chuck hesitated and then sat at the kitchen table as she made their cocoa with half milk and half water in a saucepan. 'I think this is the first time I've seen you alone in your house. Where is your niece?'

'Out with friends.' Kate laughed. 'She's fifteen going on twenty-five and already has a fiancé lined up, if she decides he's the one. She has a good job and is a sensible girl so I try not to nag her.'

'I doubt you would ever nag,' he said with a gentle smile. 'You're one of the most restful women I've met, Kate. Do you ever get angry?'

'Sometimes . . .' A flash of grief went through her. 'I was angry with God and the world when my brothers were killed. I hate this war and Hitler for starting it – but I do try not to be angry. It does no one any good.'

Chuck accepted his mug of cocoa and sipped it. 'That's good; it tastes like my mother used to make. I expect she still does . . .' He hesitated, then, 'We aren't suffering the way you are over here, Kate. And I know I've said it before – but if you were in trouble or couldn't cope, there would be a home for you there.'

'Oh, Chuck, that is so lovely of you,' Kate said. She sat down and sipped her cocoa, then raised her gaze to meet his thoughtful eyes. 'You know Steve has left me for another woman, don't you?'

'I know he's a fool,' Chuck replied. 'I've seen her – and he'll leave her when he's bored. She's nowhere near the woman you are, Kate.'

'Thank you . . .' She gave a shaky laugh. 'It did hurt a bit, though things hadn't been right for a while. I don't think Steve was ready for a family.'

'As I said, he's a fool.' Chuck finished his cocoa. 'You know I'm stationed near George? He's becoming a fine young man, Kate. I like him a lot.'

'He told me you took him to the pictures. He had

262

a good time, Chuck.' She toyed with her mug. 'I'll try to get down to see him before his birthday – but it will have to be a weekend . . .'

They heard the wail of a siren close to. Chuck's eyes widened. 'When we hear that we run for our planes – what do you do? Go to a shelter?'

'I go under the stairs,' Kate replied. 'Sometimes, if I'm out, I'll go to the underground or a shelter.' She heard the thrumming of planes and the ack-ack. 'Shall we go under the stairs?'

She led the way and they crouched in the confined space, sitting on the cushions there. Chuck laughed. 'I shall picture you here now,' he said. 'I often wonder where you are and what you're doing.'

Kate smiled in the gloom but didn't answer. Even if she'd known what to say, her answer would have been lost as a terrific explosion rent the air. 'That was close,' Chuck murmured and reached for Kate's hand. She allowed him to take it and they sat close together, waiting for the next, half-expecting it to be them.

Another explosion sounded, but a little further away. 'I'm glad you're here,' Kate said. 'It's worse if you're alone. If you'd just gone you would've been on the street . . .'

'Better here with you,' he said softly and his fingers tightened around hers.

They sat huddled together for the next hour until the all-clear sounded and then found their way out of their shelter and back to the kitchen. Different sirens were blasting now, ambulances and fire engines. Even though the windows were shut and the glass hadn't fallen out, there was a smell of smoke in the air.

263

'Wait here, I'll take a look,' Chuck said and she did as he cautioned.

He went out the front door and she washed their mugs while he was gone, filling her kettle, and making up the range. He came back, shutting the front door and then walking into the kitchen.

'A house at the far end was partially hit,' he told her. 'They're fighting the fire – but the people are unhurt. They were in the shelter.'

'And now they have to find a new home,' Kate said with a little shudder. 'I'm losing touch with people I've known for years, Chuck. They get bombed out and move away to the country or to stay with friends. I wonder how the men fighting will ever find their families again.'

'I suppose they might get a letter,' Chuck said, looking thoughtful again. 'If it happens to you, let me know, Kate. Please don't disappear out of my life without a word. I want to be your friend.'

'You are,' she said simply.

'Good.' He hesitated and then moved towards her. 'I hope you know that I think highly of you, Kate. If ever . . . but no, it's far too soon so I won't embarrass you. But Kate I care about you – and your family. If ever I can help, you must tell me – please?'

Kate met his searching gaze and then smiled. She'd always known that he liked her and would have liked to be more to her, but she was married to a man who had been his friend. It was far too soon for her to think of a relationship, but she knew that one day she would and then, perhaps . . . He was a good man.

'I think you're probably the best friend I have, apart

from my family,' she said softly. 'Is that enough for now?'

'Yes.' His smile lit up his face. 'It's all I want – for now, Kate.' He moved towards her and took her hands in his. She looked into his eyes and had he tried to kiss her, she would not have denied him, but he simply held her hands for a moment. 'I should go – but I shall think about you, dear Kate. I always do . . .'

And with that, he turned and left. A part of her wanted to stop him, to call him back. There was at that moment a wildness in her that would have cast commonsense to the winds, a longing to be taken in his arms, to be made love to – to be made whole again, the pain of Steve's betrayal washed away by a man's love. It was too late and he'd gone. Her head told her that it was a good thing, but her heart and her body denied it.

'Next time . . .' she whispered to the empty room. 'Next time I won't let you leave me without knowing that you're special to me, too.'

Kate smiled as she made herself a cup of tea and a slice of toast. It was too soon but now at least she knew that one day she would be ready to love again – love a very different man to the one who had let her down.

Kate was in bed, her hair in pins when she heard Jenny come in. The sound of running feet up the stairs and then hesitation. 'I'm not asleep, come in,' she called and Jenny entered.

'I'm sorry I'm so late,' she said. 'I was in the underground for ages and then I went to a friend's house – Mary wanted me to help her cut out a dress. It got late and there were no buses. There are great holes in the road and some whole streets have been cordoned off. I think they're worried about gas explosions now.'

'Yes, I expect so,' Kate replied. She hesitated, then, 'Jenny – if you had the chance to start a new life in Canada, would you take it?'

Jenny looked at her in silence and then shook her head. 'No, I don't think so. I mean, I can see the advantages: nowhere near so many bombs, though I think some of their ports have been attacked. Canada is such a big country. Lots of good food too – but everyone I care about is here.' She hesitated, then, 'You wouldn't go either, would you?'

'No – not right now,' Kate replied. 'Only someone offered and if you wanted to – perhaps Mum and Dad too . . .'

'Grandad would never move from London,' Jenny said and sat on the edge of the bed. 'Don't even think of it, Kate. You would hate not to be able to pop round the corner and see your mum, you know you would.'

'Yes, I suppose I would . . .' Kate lay back against her pillows. 'Have you heard any more from Peter?'

'Not yet – but I shall.' Jenny was smiling and happy. 'I'm going to ask Grandad if I can get engaged when Peter comes home. If he says yes, Dad will agree. Oh, we shan't marry – perhaps not until the war is over. I want to get promotion at my job first.'

'Sensible girl,' Kate said. 'Switch the light off in the hall as you go, will you?'

'Night then, Kate.' Jenny went out, closing the bedroom door. A little later the hall light went off. Kate extinguished her own and turned over in the big bed.

The bed felt empty and cold with just her in it, so

she pulled a pillow down to the arch of her back. That felt better, as if a warm body lay beside her. Jenny's words had made her think. Would she be happy if she married Chuck and went to live with him in Canada? A flicker of unease played on her mind. She'd begun to get fond of him, to like and respect him – but was that enough? She would have to find a new life in Canada.

'Daftie!' she told herself. He hasn't even asked you yet. She knew he would though, when the time was right, and a little smile touched her mouth. It was good to feel wanted. Steve had hurt her and damaged her self-confidence, but she wouldn't let him break her.

Tomorrow, she would get that evening job and she'd build a new life. The future could take care of itself!

CHAPTER 28

It was May 1941 and the Blitz in London seemed to be endless. For months the alerts had sounded night after night and thousands of people had died, their homes destroyed by Hitler's bombs. Even schools and shelters had been hit directly and the devastation in some parts of London was horrendous; other cities, too, like Cardiff, Coventry and Birmingham had suffered greatly. In fact, the whole country was reeling from the hammer blow of the Luftwaffe.

'The paper says that London suffered one of its worst raids,' Mrs Seward read aloud that bright morning. She looked up and over her paper, her glasses perched almost on the end of her nose. 'I'll understand if you want to go home and make sure your family are all right, George.'

'You won't go home, you won't!' Ellie said and threw her arms about his thighs, hugging his legs. Her little face pleaded with him as she gazed up at him. 'Please, George. Stay with us!'

'Your mother will be home next week,' her

grandmother told her. 'Let go of George, Ellie. It isn't seemly to hug him like that.'

Ellie obeyed but looked miserable. George was undecided. 'If I do go on a visit I'll come back. I shan't take my final exams until next year when I'm sixteen,' he said. 'If the war continues, I might get called up before I can go to college.'

'You have to be eighteen to join up,' Mrs Seward reminded sharply. 'Don't be foolish and think of lying about your age, George.'

'No, I shan't do that – though a friend of mine, Mike Smith's brother, did and they took him. He was only just seventeen, but big and strong. They signed him up and he went. His family haven't heard from him yet.'

'You wouldn't be that foolish, I hope?'

'You know what I want to do,' George replied. 'I can finish my education in London, though. Kate says they are definitely reopening some of the schools so I could go and live at home when your daughter's ready to look after you both.'

Mrs Seward nodded. 'That won't be for a few weeks, George – if ever. Lizzie has been very ill. I wasn't sure she would even recover, but it seems the doctors think she should come home.'

'You'll be glad of her company – and you'll be happy to have your mum home, Ellie.'

'Yes – but not if you go away.' Ellie's big blue eyes filled with tears as she pouted, and George laughed. 'I'll stay until your mum is properly well again. I'm taking some exams this week and, if I do well, I'll be given the chance to take my important ones next year. If I get good grades, I stand more chance of getting into a good school back in London and it's there I'll apply for medical school, if I can. So I shan't leave just yet – if I may stay on?'

'I hoped you would say that,' Mrs Seward said. She got up and went to the tall dresser at the side of the room, opening a small drawer, from which she took a box. She brought it back to the table, leaning heavily on her stick as she walked, clearly in pain. One of her bad days.

'I could have fetched that for you,' Georgie said. 'Is your rheumatism playing up today?'

'When doesn't it?' she asked drily and opened her box. She fished inside and took out a smaller blue velvet box, looked inside it and nodded, then closed the lid and held it out to him. 'This is for you, George. I don't have much money to spare these days, but I really have appreciated all your help these past months. I believe you can sell this for a few pounds when you're ready.'

She waited as George hesitated, then, 'Don't be a fool! I know you're not. I owe you far more than this trinket. Had you not looked after us, both my granddaughter and I would have been in homes by now.'

'I didn't do it for reward,' George said but she tapped her foot impatiently and he took the box. Inside was a brooch in the shape of a flower with small blue and white stones. Instinctively, he knew it was valuable and tried to hand it back. 'This is too much! I've only done what anyone would.'

'If you think that, you've lost your wits,' she cackled. 'It's a trinket. I had far better once but most have been sold to keep this house going. I should sell it and buy a small box to live in but I would hate that. Just take it, George, with my thanks.'

George nodded and slipped the box into his trouser pocket. He didn't like to ask but thought the stones might be diamonds and sapphires. Gran had them in her engagement ring, but much smaller.

'Thank you – but if you change your mind and want it back, just ask,' he said and looked at Ellie. 'Do you want a ride to the farm on my bike this Saturday?'

'Yes, please,' she said and giggled, her tears gone now. George had made a little trolley that he towed her in with cushions and a blanket to cover her legs and it was a way of getting her out into the fresh air. She had been used to just sitting at home. Sometimes she played in the garden but more often than not she just stayed in the house with her grandmother.

George decided to pay a fleeting visit to his home the following weekend. It was months since he'd had a letter from anyone. Kate normally wrote every few weeks and his mother sent him a couple of lines on the bottom of her letter. His father had sent him a postal order for five pounds to pay for his extra tuition but since then, nothing.

Ellie didn't want him to go but her mother was expected home on the Saturday and he thought it might be a good time to leave them to settle as a family again.

He had borrowed an Agatha Christie murder mystery to read on the train, which made the time seem shorter and he'd almost finished it when he tucked it into his satchel and prepared to leave the train. He took the underground to Angel Street and got out, walking through a district that he'd once known well but which now seemed almost unrecognizable in places. There were so many burned-out shells of buildings, craters in the road and some streets had all but disappeared.

George had a hollow sensation in his stomach as he walked, trying to remember where he was and often failing. At last, he saw a church he recognized and then, two streets away, he saw the road he'd grown up on. Dickon's Terrace had been two facing rows of houses, all with small backyards and opening on to the pavement. He felt a sick shock of horror in his stomach as he saw that it had been almost obliterated. Only two houses remained standing and they were damaged and empty. His parents' home had gone. Just a pile of rubble remained.

'No! Please no!'

Feeling rising panic, George walked towards the rubble. It looked as if much of it had been cleared; there was no sign of any personal possessions. George's throat was tight with fear. What had happened to his mother and father? Were they alive, injured or . . . dead? And why had no one told him?

As he turned away, he saw an ARP warden walking towards him.

'No looting, sir,' the warden said. 'We look on that very severely, young man.'

'My – my parents lived here,' George said, feeling frozen. 'I was just looking but there's nothing . . .' Suddenly, he looked at the warden. 'Do you know where they are?'

'Afraid not, lad. I've only just been given this area.

I can tell you it was bombed last week and there were several casualties. You should go to the council offices and ask; they might know – or try the hospitals.' He looked at George with pity. 'Just come back from the country?'

'Yes. I was sent because mum thought there might be an invasion.'

'Is there anyone else you can ask?'

'Yes, my sister. She doesn't live far . . .'

'You'd best go there then – good luck, lad. I hope you find your family.'

'So do I,' George said. He felt numbed, his eyes burning with unshed tears. He was too terrified, too anxious to cry. Where were Mum and Dad – why hadn't Kate written to him?

As he came to the corner where his sister lived, he stared in horror. Only two houses right this end were left standing. Kate's house was just a pile of rubble.

'Not Kate too,' George whispered. 'Not Kate and Jenny . . .'

He ran to where he thought Kate's house had stood, but it was difficult to tell. Here the rubble hadn't all been cleared and there were still a few pieces of personal property amongst the bricks and burned timber. He saw the pages of a burned book fluttering in the breeze and his heart caught. Kate had owned a lot of books. Tears came to his eyes and streamed down his cheeks. He sat down on a pile of bricks as the sobs broke from him.

His whole family gone? No, he couldn't believe it. He wouldn't accept it! Surely some of them had survived. He just had to find them.

George couldn't think what to do. It was a Saturday afternoon and the council offices would be closed. He wouldn't find any help there. Where could he ask if anyone knew if his family had survived?

A horrid little voice at the back of his brain kept telling him that if anyone was still alive, they would have let him know where they were and who was lost. For a moment he felt as if his whole world had come crashing down and he wanted to scream and shout like a child, but then he found the strength to control his panic.

His father had sometimes gone for a drink at the King's Arms. George had noticed it was still standing as he walked here. He turned and made his way back. The bars were closed until the evening, but he went round through the yard and knocked at the back door. George knocked loudly several times before it was opened by a red-faced woman with her head in a turban of towelling.

'We're closed for the afternoon,' she grumbled. 'I was washing my hair – can't a body have a moment to herself?'

'I've just come back from the country and my home has been bombed,' George said hastily, before she could slam the door. 'I wondered if you knew what happened to Mr and Mrs Greene at number ten Dickon's Terrace – my nephew Billy was staying there, too.'

'Are you Ned Greene's boy?' the woman said and hesitated, then opened the door to admit him. 'Come in, lad. I'm sorry I didn't recognize you – you'll be Georgie, studying to be a doctor your dad said.

He often came here to drink – but we haven't seen him since the bombs fell that night . . . a week or so ago it was.'

'Do you know if anyone survived? My sister's house was bombed, too?'

'I know there were some deaths and a lot injured,' the woman said sympathetically. 'Most folk who've lost their homes are being relocated, sometimes out of London. They've run out of anywhere to put them after these past months. If they survived and were uninjured, they will have been sent to temporary homes, lad. You should ask down the council offices. I can't tell you where they might be.'

'Yes, the ARP warden said to ask the council but they'll be closed over the weekend and I have to get back to school on Monday. I have important exams coming up . . .' George faltered. 'Besides, I have nowhere I can stay and not much money.'

'I'd find you a bed 'ere but we're full with folk who've nowhere to go,' she said. 'I can give you a bit of something to eat – and I've got the address of the council offices. You can write to them and ask them if they know where your family have gone. You would probably have to go back a few times, because half the time they don't know whether they're comin' or goin', in my opinion. I'm not sure they keep the records they should, but that's what I'd do. If you've got some coppers, you could try ringing a few of the hospitals. In fact, I'll do that for you on my phone. I'll make you a sandwich and while you eat, I'll see what I can do.'

George thanked her, relieved to find a friendly face in all this chaos and feeling hungry. He drank a mug of strong tea without sugar and munched a thick spam sandwich with a spoonful of pickle, waiting hopefully as his hostess went off to phone round the hospitals.

When she returned, she looked thoughtful. 'I wasn't able to trace any of your family, George,' she told him. 'I think you can be sure that they aren't in a hospital bed so . . .' Her words trailed away as she gave him an anxious look. 'Have you got anyone at all?'

George knew what she was saying. If his family were not in hospital, it left two options. Either they had been relocated or they were dead. George knew that Kate would have written as soon as she could and that gave him a hollow sensation inside.

'I've got somewhere I can go in the country,' he said. 'Perhaps I'll get a letter soon – and I *will* write to the council and ask them.' He stood up. 'Is there anything I can do to repay you for your help, Mrs . . .?'

'I'm Suki,' she replied. 'Bless you no, lad. I only wish I could do more.'

'I'd better go,' Georgie said. 'I should catch the last train home if I'm quick. Thank you for the food – and for ringing the hospitals for me.'

'You're welcome, lad,' Suki said. 'Will you write down your address for me in the country? If I should hear anything – and I'll ask around – I'll write and let you know.'

George's face lit up with a smile. 'Thank you. Someone may know something. If you hear anything I'll come back another weekend and look for them.'

'I'll do my best for you, lad.' She gave him a pencil and a piece of paper and he wrote down Mrs Seward's address and his name. She glanced at it and placed it in her apron pocket. 'Get off and catch your train then – and don't give up. A lot of folks have been given up for lost when they're only misplaced. You keep looking, Georgie.'

George said he would and thanked her, then took his leave. As he walked away through the war-torn streets his heart sank. What had happened in these streets was devastation. How could anybody survive this chaos? Yet he knew miracles happened – and perhaps his family had sought shelter in the underground.

George caught the tube back to King's Cross. He was jostled and pushed and squeezed between hurrying commuters, but finally arrived at platform nine to see his train just pulling out of the station. He wouldn't be getting home that night and he didn't have enough money to go to a hotel. Thoughts of returning to Suki at the pub were dismissed swiftly. All her rooms were full and she'd already helped him. He would just have to find a bench to sleep on and hope the night wasn't too cold.

CHAPTER 29

Billy knuckled the tears from his eyes as he was herded onto a bus with a lot of other children and some adults he didn't know. The past few days had been a nightmare for him. His gran had sent him to the market to buy some vegetables for her. She'd given him money and told him what she wanted and he'd gone happily, proud to be trusted to do his gran's shopping, and thinking of the penny bar of chocolate he'd been promised as a reward.

When the bombs started falling, Billy had run to the nearest shelter with a lot of other people who had pushed him ahead of them. He'd stayed there while the raid lasted, which seemed like hours. When it stopped, it was late afternoon. His gran would be worried and cross, too, because she'd wanted her vegetables to cook for their tea. Billy had hurried through streets that were fast becoming dark, because of the pall of thick smoke that hung over everything and got in your throat and choked you. His heart was racing and he'd been terrified as he'd neared his home and then discovered that it was no longer there. Ambulances and fire engines were there and lots of people – but there was no sign of his gran.

'Have you seen Gran? Where did the lady from this house go? Have you seen Mrs Grace Greene?' Billy had gone from one person to the next but none of them seemed to know anything.

'A lot of people have been killed or injured,' a woman dressed in some kind of uniform took notice of him at last. 'Was this your home?'

Billy nodded, his throat too tight to answer, then, 'I live with her and Grandad . . .'

'I'd better take you to one of the help centres,' the woman said. 'What did you say you name was?'

'Billy. Billy Greene.' In his fluster he'd given his grandmother's name instead of his own.

It had all seemed like a nightmare when he was taken in a stranger's car to a church that was being used as a refuge centre. Inside were more strangers who took Billy's details and then he was given a cup of tea and a bun and told he would be found somewhere to live as soon as possible. When he tried to ask about his grandparents all he'd got was the same answers. They hadn't been brought to this centre but his name was on the list so when someone came looking, they would find him.

Billy had found a corner to sit in. He'd been cold, miserable, and hungry; the bun that was slightly stale did nothing to help but he ate it, wrapping his arms about himself and rocking to keep warm.

At various times during the past week someone had come to ask him questions; he'd been fed and given something to drink, and one kind woman had brought him a blanket. There was a temporary toilet set up behind a screen but there was always a queue for it and Billy had gone outside to relieve himself behind one of the mouldering old gravestones. He hadn't been able to wash or change his clothes and he felt dirty, lonely, and abandoned.

After six or seven days had passed most of the people sheltering in the church had gone, finding family or new homes, but Billy was still there. He'd wondered if he should leave and go to Kate's house, but he was in a different part of London and he wasn't sure he could find it. So he stayed where he was and then, on the next morning, a man came in and said he was taking all the children who had lost their homes. Billy shrank back but was beckoned forward. There weren't any other children in the church, but when he was taken outside to the bus, he saw several waiting to board. He was given a packet of food and a bottle of water, and told to take a seat inside.

'Where are we going?' he asked of the man who had come for him.

'Somewhere safe,' was all the answer he got.

Once everyone was on the bus it drove off. Some of the children seemed to know each other and chattered, laughing as if it was an adventure. Billy sat silent and anxious. Where was he being taken and why had no one come looking for him?

When the bus stopped at Liverpool Street Station, Billy hung back. He didn't want to leave London and all that he knew. No one had asked him what he wanted and he felt a surge of rebellion, hanging at the back of the group as they were taken on to a platform to wait for their train to arrive for Newcastle – a destination unknown to Billy.

Looking about him in desperation, he sought a friendly face or a way of escape, but everyone seemed in a hurry. Then he heard a Tannoy announcement, 'The next train departing from platform nine terminates at Cambridge . . .'

Cambridge was where his mother had gone Christmas shopping! Without thinking it through carefully, Billy slipped away and ran as fast as he could to platform nine. He ran straight past the ticket inspector who was too busy to notice immediately, and jumped on the train seconds before the doors were slammed shut and the train moved off down the line.

Billy found himself a seat in an empty carriage. He had never been to Cambridge in his life and had no idea how far it was from the farm where he'd stayed, but, somehow, he would find his way there. George didn't live there now but the farmer or his wife would know where to find him.

Billy had some food and water, and the change from his gran's shopping in his pocket. He didn't know if the few coins would be enough to get him to George's home but he could walk some of the way. His panic and doubts of the past week resolved themselves as he thought of his uncle. He would find him and George would know what to do.

A woman entered the carriage and sat down, but after one glance she ignored Billy and took out a book to read. He settled back in his seat. His stomach rumbled, because he'd only had one piece of bread for his breakfast and very little for the past few days. Still, he wouldn't open his food packet yet, because it might have to last him a while.

George had arrived back at Mrs Seward's house just after lunch, his train leaving an hour earlier than the one Billy caught. Mrs Seward looked surprised but pleased to see him, then became concerned as she saw his expression.

'What happened, George?' she asked. 'Are your family all safe?'

'I can't find any of them,' he said. 'Mum's house has gone and so has Kate's – most of the houses in their streets caught it. I asked after them but no one knew anything. I was told to try down the council offices, because they should be on a list, but they're closed all weekend so I came back.'

'What about the hospitals?' Mrs Seward asked, looking concerned.

'Someone rang round for me and said no one by the name of Greene had been admitted . . .' George took a deep breath. 'It could mean that Mum got out all right and went off somewhere but . . .'

'Don't start thinking the worst – not yet,' Mrs Seward said. 'This council office – do you know whereabouts it is?'

'Sort of,' George replied. 'I've never been there but I know Mum did and . . . but . . .' He let out his breath. 'I'll go back again next weekend and see if I can find anything out, but I have exams this week so I had to come back – and I don't have enough money to stay in a hotel.'

'I've none spare to offer you,' Mrs Seward replied.

282

'But you could sell the brooch I gave you, George. You should get enough to cover your journey back and forth, because you may need to go a few times.'

'I won't do that unless I have to,' George told her. 'I still have a bit of the money Dad sent for my extra tuition. I didn't take it with me, but I will next time. After I take my exams there's no reason why I shouldn't take a few days off school and search for them—' He broke off as a woman entered the kitchen. She was tall and thin, her skin very pale and her eyes red-rimmed.

'Mother . . .?' The woman stared at him and George sensed faint hostility.

'Lizzie, this is George – the young lad who has been such a help to me,' Mrs Seward said. 'He was just telling me his family has been bombed out of their homes and, so far he can't find them.'

'I'm sorry to hear that,' Lizzie said but in a cool voice that sounded uninterested. 'I came to tell you that I feel very tired, Mother. I shall go to bed. Can you look after Ellie? She's been clinging to me and it's exhausting.'

'Ellie?' Mrs Seward looked at her daughter. 'She's just happy to see you home.'

Ellie came running into the kitchen. She paused on the threshold and then rushed to George, flinging herself against his legs. 'You're back! I thought you might not come. Mummy said we didn't need you anymore.'

'Ellie!' her mother reprimanded sharply but a red flush crept into her cheeks and it was obvious that she had said something of the sort.

'I make the decisions here,' Mrs Seward spoke

softly but in the voice of command. 'George is still very necessary as far as I am concerned.' She sent him a look filled with apology. 'I hope you will consider this your home until you can find your family, George. I know you thought you might go home once these exams were finished – but now I'm not sure what you should do for the best.'

'I refuse to believe they've all gone,' George replied. 'Thank you for the offer, Mrs Seward. Mr Baker might let me sleep on his sofa if necessary.'

'It will *not* be necessary,' she said and looked at her daughter. 'Why don't you go to bed, Lizzie? You'll feel better for a rest.'

She left without a word. Ellie, leaning against George's leg, looked up at him. 'You won't go away yet, will you?' she asked in a small voice.

'Not just yet – if your gran can put up with me.'

Mrs Seward gave a harsh laugh. 'My daughter is a fool. She was always a fool. She married to disoblige me and look where that left her!' George glanced at her and she shook her head. 'She regretted marrying him almost immediately – not rich, you see, so couldn't wine and dine her, buy her the falderals she wanted and she quickly discovered that love didn't make up for that.'

'I don't want to be the cause of friction between you,' he said. 'I can go to the farm. Mrs Baker's daughter has gone home now her baby's born and she's on her feet again.'

'Leave me with the child and a sickly daughter to look after, would you?' She glared at him.

'No, you know I wouldn't.' George inclined his head. 'I'll stay if I can help – until I find out what has happened to my family. They may need me . . .'

'I understand that,' Mrs Seward agreed. 'And if you need money, sell that trinket I gave you. I daresay a jeweller will give you a few pounds for it.'

'If I have to . . .' George smiled at her. 'Thank you. I'm hoping a letter will come soon, giving me some news. My father wouldn't have been at home when the raid happened. I can't understand why he hasn't let me know . . .'

'That is a bit strange,' Mrs Seward said. 'Mind you, if he's trying to find a new home for them all, and sorting things out, he might not have thought it urgent. Probably thinks you're all right here.'

'Yes, that might be so,' George said. His father would be reluctant to pass on bad news, but that thought only made it all the more worrying. 'I'll send a letter to the council offices in Poplar and then I'll try a few more. It was all such a mess; they might be listed anywhere.'

'Yes, they could have been taken to a refuge miles away. Especially, if they were injured or dazed.'

'I think Mum would have been frightened and confused,' George replied. 'She was ill for weeks after the first time a bomb landed in the street.'

'I expect she's recovering somewhere and your father doesn't want to worry you with your exams so imminent. Depend upon it, a letter will come, George, and then you can make your plans.'

'In the meantime, I'll try not to upset your daughter, Mrs Seward.'

'Just ignore her,' she replied. 'I am the mistress in my own house and if I say you can stay that's the end of it!'

George carried on doing all the jobs he'd done before Mrs Seward's daughter returned from hospital. For her part, Lizzie chose to ignore him. She spoke only if she was forced to and called sharply to Ellie every time the child tried to go to George, which made Ellie look at her in a puzzled way. Clearly, she was happy to have her mother home, but didn't understand her hostility towards the person who had looked after her for many weeks.

George spoke to her politely but otherwise followed her lead and ignored her. He wrote several letters to London, to the council offices he'd heard of and others he'd looked up in a London telephone book. He also cycled over to the farm the evening after he'd taken his exams and asked if any letters had come for him there.

'No, lad,' Mrs Baker told him. 'We would have brought them over for you – but your family know where you are, don't they?'

'Yes. I just thought, if the address got lost, they might remember this one . . .' George shook his head. 'It was just a chance, Mrs Baker. I don't really know where to start looking for them. I'm thinking of going back to London this weekend and stop a day or so. I've written to some places but if I'm actually there I can ask around – someone might know something.'

'I would've expected your father to contact you – unless he was caught up in it, too?'

'Dad would've been at work, unless he had a day off for some reason.' George couldn't hide his anxiety.

'Each day I think there's sure to be a letter but there never is. I don't know what I'll do if I can't find them.'

'Will Mrs Seward let you stay on there – at least until you go to college, if you do?'

'I think she would – but her daughter seems to resent me.'

'Lizzie was always a bit strange,' Mrs Baker said. She was thoughtful for a moment, then, 'If you get stuck – well, I'm sure my husband would welcome you back. We've got a bed for you now, George, and those land girls . . .' She made a wry face. 'One of them – Maureen – she does her share, but Wendy, she's a lazy little— Well, least said, soonest mended. You'd do a far better job than her!'

George laughed. 'I'd be happy to help, Mrs Baker. If Mrs Seward's daughter gets her strength back, I'm sure she won't want me around. I had planned to go home – but I don't even know if I have one any longer.'

'Ungrateful wretch! After all you did to help her mother. They would never have managed without you.'

George nodded. 'Can I ask you something, Mrs Baker?'

'Of course you can?'

George took the velvet box from his jacket pocket and opened it, showing her the brooch inside. 'Is this very valuable?'

Mrs Baker took the box and looked at the contents, her eyes widening. 'That looks like diamonds and sapphires – where did you get it, George?'

'Mrs Seward insisted on giving it to me for helping her. She says I can sell it if I need money but I think it's too much. I'm not sure I ought to keep it.'

'I can see what you mean,' Mrs Baker replied and looked at him thoughtfully. 'Most people would just take it and do what they wanted with it – but you don't feel comfortable with that, do you?'

'I could do with the money,' George admitted. 'Yet Mrs Seward doesn't have much money and I don't feel right about taking it from her. She says it's a trinket, but it isn't.'

'No. I think that might be worth a hundred or two – perhaps as much as three hundred pounds, George. It would cost more than five in a jeweller's, I'm certain.'

George nodded. 'I'll give it back, then, if she'll let me. I only went there to help – and this is far too much.'

'That's very honest of you,' Mrs Baker said. 'Only she may be offended.'

George looked rueful. 'Yes, I know – but I think I should. Perhaps I'll just put it back in her drawer and say nothing.'

'Yes, that would save any embarrassment. She might have given it to you and then regretted it, George.'

He agreed, deciding that he would simply slip it into the dresser drawer and say nothing. It was far too valuable for him to keep, though the money would have been very useful. Perhaps once school was over, he could find work on the farm and earn a little money to replace what he needed to spend on his search for his family.

CHAPTER 30

Billy got off the train in Cambridge when it terminated. He'd avoided the ticket inspector on the train by going to the toilet when he heard him asking for tickets. At the station in Cambridge, Billy tagged on with a group of soldiers and other passengers and managed to get through the barrier without being asked for proof of payment.

Outside the station, he stood looking about him. He had no idea where he was or how to get to where he wanted to go. Was there a train headed for Chatteris? He thought there must be, but wasn't sure and was afraid to ask. Perhaps it wasn't too far. He might be able to walk it.

Seeing a man getting on a bike, Billy went up to him and asked if he knew the way to Chatteris.

'Never heard of it, lad,' the man said and cycled off without looking at him.

Billy hesitated, then approached a lady. She was plump and carrying a suitcase and she had a trench hat pushed down hard on her dark curls. For a moment he thought she would ignore him, too, but then she gave him a straight look.

'If you're begging I shan't give you anything – but if you really want to get to Chatteris, there is a train leaving for Ely in twenty minutes. I don't think it is far from there.'

'Thanks, missus,' Billy said but she'd walked away to a car that had drawn up and was getting into it.

He looked back at the station. Ely wasn't far from where he'd lived for a short time – well, only a bus ride away. His hand went in his pocket, fingering his few coins. Billy didn't want to spend all his money, because he was already feeling hungry and his packet had just one rather dry sandwich left inside.

Fortune had favoured him on the train ride from London, but would he get away with it again? He could see the ticket inspector checking people's tickets as they went on to the platforms and thought about it. Then, remembering a machine that sold platform tickets for a penny, he grinned.

Billy bought a platform ticket and showed it to the inspector at the entrance. 'Meeting someone?' the man asked, eyeing him suspiciously.

'My dad is coming home today,' he said. 'He's in the Royal Navy.'

'Go on then – but no joyriding on trains or you'll be in trouble!'

Billy ran off before he could change his mind. He heard the announcement for the next train to Ely and ran to platform nine. Boarding the train, he went into the toilet and locked the door, staying there until the train started moving. When he came out the seats were mostly full, but he found one carriage with just one passenger – a man in RAF uniform. The man looked at him and smiled as he sat down, but didn't speak. Billy eyed him curiously, noting the small scar on his left brow and cheek.

Someone came round to offer refreshments. The RAF officer bought a packet of cheese sandwiches and opened them. Billy's tummy rumbled and the officer looked at him.

'Hungry, lad?' Billy nodded and was offered a sandwich. He hesitated and then took it, biting into it hungrily.

'Thanks, mister,' he said. 'It's good.'

'Not bad,' the officer replied. 'Are you travelling alone?'

'Yeah. I'm going to visit my friend George,' Billy said and the man stared at him for a minute and then he laughed.

'I thought you looked familiar! I'm not sure I'm right – but are you related to George Greene?'

'Yeah.' Billy stared at him in surprise. 'He's my mother's brother but much younger so I think of him more as a brother; he's the one I'm going to stay with.'

'Does he know you're coming? Only, I'm not sure Mrs Seward will be expecting another young man in her house.'

Billy finished his sandwich. 'How do you know about George and where he lives?' he asked.

'I'm Chuck – I don't know if he's ever mentioned me?'

Billy hesitated, uncertainly. 'He might have . . . are you from Canada?'

'Yes, I am.' Chuck smiled encouragingly. 'I know George quite well but I haven't seen him for a few weeks because I've been busy with a training course. I'm just on the way back to my base now.' Chuck frowned. 'Are you in trouble, lad?'

'Oh . . .' Billy took a deep breath and then it all came pouring out of him in a rush. 'Mum's house has gone and so has Kate's . . .'

'Kate was bombed too?' Chuck looked startled and then sat forward, anxious all at once. 'When did this happen?'

'Just over a week ago. I was taken to a shelter and I stayed there for a week, because I didn't know what to do. Then a man came and they were going to take us up north somewhere and so when I heard there was a train leaving for Cambridge I ran off and got on it.'

'And then you got on this one?' Chuck said and Billy nodded. 'No ticket?'

'No. I hid in the toilet on the way to Cambridge.'

'Better not do it again,' Chuck said. 'If an inspector comes, I'll pay your fare. Tell him we were in a hurry and didn't have time to buy a ticket – I've got a pass, you see.'

'I suppose it was wrong,' Billy said. 'I don't have much money but Gran would say it was dishonest.'

'She would be right – but in this case I'm glad you chose to do it, Billy. If you'd been sent off up north somewhere you might never have been found. Probably have billeted you in an orphanage or something.'

'Don't want to go there. I want to find my folks.'

'Of course you do.' Chuck offered him the last sandwich. 'Bit of luck I caught this train. I was due to catch an earlier one but I was delayed.' He laughed. 'I met George on a train returning from London once. Must be fate.'

'Will you help me get to Chatteris?' Billy asked.

'Yes, I will,' Chuck promised. 'When we get to Ely, I'll pick up my car – I only bought it a few weeks ago – and I'll drive you there. I need to talk to George. He may know what has happened to Kate and your grandparents.'

'My sister, too. She lived with Kate.'

'Yes, I remember.' Chuck took his cigarette case out and selected one, lighting it with a gold lighter. He drew deeply and Billy saw that his hand shook a little as though he was upset. 'I wonder if anyone has been in touch with George?'

True to his word, Chuck drove straight to Chatteris and to Mrs Seward's house. It was almost four in the afternoon and just as they were about to knock, George came cycling towards them. He threw his bike down and rushed to Billy, giving him a tight hug.

'Thank God! I thought you were all dead.' Billy wriggled and he let go, staring at him. 'How did you get here?' George demanded. 'Where are the others? Are they alive?'

'So you don't know either,' Chuck said, looking at him, his face drawn with anxiety. 'I was hoping you might have heard.'

'Come into the kitchen,' George said. 'Mrs Seward

won't mind. Her daughter might but I think she may be at the doctor having a check over this afternoon.'

He led the way inside. Mrs Seward was drinking tea and Ellie had a glass of milk. She raised her eyebrows, then recognized Chuck but looked pointedly at Billy.

George gave a rueful laugh. 'He looks as if he needs a good scrub,' he said, 'but it's Billy. He's my nephew but we've always been like brothers. I think he has a story to tell us . . .'

Billy went through his story again and Mrs Seward nodded, looking thoughtful. 'Well, at least you survived, lad – and it was very clever to get yourself here, though I don't know what we'll do with you. I suppose you could sleep with George if need be.'

'I don't think your daughter would approve,' George told her. 'I think Mrs Baker would take him in – just until I can sort things out.' He looked at Chuck. 'I'm trying to trace them but I haven't had much luck yet.'

'Well, I'm back now and I'll help,' Chuck told him. 'Did you try to contact me, George?'

'No. I knew you were away, because you'd told me . . .' George frowned. 'I'm going up to London again this weekend. I want to ask around a bit – see if anyone has heard of Kate or my parents.'

'I'll make some calls when I get back to the base,' Chuck promised. 'I'm due a couple of days leave and I'll see what I can do.' He looked at Billy. 'I can take you to Mr Baker's place if you direct me, George – but I don't think Billy has any clean things. I suppose you don't have anything to fit him?'

'I think my stuff is too big, but he can try.'

'I have a few bits that might fit at a pinch,' Mrs Seward told them. 'In the room you use, George, there's a locked trunk . . . I'll give you the key.' She went to her dresser and searched and then gave a little cry of annoyance. Returning, she handed George a key. 'See what you can find – and what is this doing in my dresser?'

George looked uncomfortable. 'It's too valuable, Mrs Seward. I couldn't take it so I put it back . . .' She opened the box and they both stared, because it was empty. The beautiful brooch had gone. Her eyes met George's. 'You put the brooch back, not just the box?'

'Yes, of course!'

'I see . . .' She frowned but said no more. 'Take Billy with you and see if there's anything to fit of my son's . . .'

George gave Billy a little push ahead of him. He could hear Mrs Seward talking to Chuck but didn't stay to listen.

'I'm glad you came, Billy. I wish you could stay here, but Mrs Seward's daughter doesn't like me – and she wouldn't want you here.'

'I don't like it 'ere,' Billy said. 'It's creepy. I'll be better at the farm.'

'That's all right, then. I'll come when I can. I want to earn some money this summer.'

After a pair of long trousers, a couple of shirts and a pullover had been sorted for Billy, the boys went back down to the kitchen. Chuck was drinking a cup of tea at the table and there was silence, but, George thought, a harmonious atmosphere. Mrs Seward wished Billy well and slipped half a crown into his hand before he left.

'I'd have you here, lad, but my daughter has been ill and I don't want to upset her.'

Billy thanked her and left with Chuck. George followed them on his bike, so by the time he arrived at the farm, Mrs Baker was making tea and offering both Chuck and Billy a slice of bread and honey and a rock bun. Billy accepted with alacrity but Chuck refused.

'I need to be on my way,' he told them. 'I have to report back but then I have some free time due – so I'll do what I can.' He looked at George and then Billy. 'I once offered your sister refuge with my family if she felt it was needed – and now I'm telling you. If you've nowhere else to go and you like it, I can arrange for your passage out to Canada.'

George grinned. 'That's champion,' he said. 'We'll be all right for a while – but thank you for the offer. W-we might need to take you up on it . . .'

After he'd gone, Billy looked at George. 'I don't want to live in Canada, do you, George?'

'I don't know,' George said thoughtfully. 'It might be good. It's a big country – much bigger than ours. I think it might be fun to travel one day – but our family is here, Billy. We need to find out what happened to them before we think about the future. Meanwhile, you help Mr Baker all you can on the farm and we'll both work hard for our exams.'

'I lost all my stuff,' Billy said mournfully. 'My medical dictionary for animals – everything.'

'Yes, I know.' George looked sadly at him. 'I'd buy

you a new one if I could, Billy. If I can earn a bit I'll see if I can find one for you.'

With that promise, George left his nephew to settle in at the farm and cycled back to Mrs Seward's house. As he opened the door into the back hall, he heard Mrs Seward quarrelling with her daughter.

'You took that brooch, Lizzie! Don't lie to me. I know it was you.'

'I haven't seen it, I tell you,' she replied. 'Why don't you blame that scrounger you took into your house? He's from London – a cockney – and they're known for thieving.'

'That is a disgusting thing to say. You shame me, Lizzie.' Mrs Seward sounded angry and disgusted. 'The reason I know he didn't take it is that I gave it to him to pay for all the help he has given me – but he returned it to the drawer because he didn't want to accept a valuable jewel.'

'He's just playing on your sympathy, hoping for more,' her daughter said bitterly. 'You've put him in my brothers' place – I've always come last!'

Horrified at overhearing such a personal argument, George went out and re-entered, banging the door so that they were bound to hear him. As he walked into the large kitchen, he could feel the atmosphere and the tension. Lizzie glared at him but he ignored her.

'Is there anything I can do for you, Mrs Seward? If not, I'll go up to my room. I have some letters to write.'

'Thank you, George. Go and do whatever you wish. I'm going to make some toast later and we can grill some tomatoes – those lovely big ones you got from the market the other day.'

297

'I'll come when you call me,' George said and went through into the hall and up the stairs. He could hear their voices as the argument resumed but the words were no longer clear.

Shutting the door to his room, George sat down and wrote more letters to places and people he thought might have heard of his parents. He'd been going through the London telephone book, picking out all the official offices that might have a list of displaced victims of the bombing. In the morning, after he'd done his chores, he would post them and then cycle to the farm and see how Billy was faring. There didn't seem to be much point in Billy enrolling in the school again, because it was almost the end of term. School summer holidays were longer since the beginning of the war, especially in country areas where young lads were needed to help get in the harvests.

His letters written, George got out his school books. He intended to study, but found his thoughts wandering. Billy had turned up miraculously. His nephew had known where to find him and if a young schoolboy could get to him, despite not having any money in his pocket other than a few coppers, why hadn't his parents or Kate sought him out?

There was a sick feeling in his stomach and an icy shiver at his nape. It looked as if the worst might have happened and they'd all been killed in the bombing raid.

For a moment George felt close to despair. He couldn't imagine life with the people he'd loved and trusted gone forever. It choked him and made his eyes burn with the need to cry, but he held the tears back.

Crying wouldn't help him now. He murmured a silent prayer. He'd already lost two brothers in the war and his sister Vera had gone off with her lover. If his parents and Kate had gone, that made him responsible for Billy. So he couldn't cry and let this terrible grief defeat him. He had to be strong.

Yet somewhere inside there was a little voice that refused to believe they had all gone. Fate could not be cruel enough to rob him of almost his whole family.

CHAPTER 31

It was July now and the sun was beating down on their backs as they gathered the sheaves of golden corn ready for the threshing. George wiped the sweat from his eyes, arching his back to ease the ache. It was hard work and he'd been up since early in the morning, milking, and then following the cutter to gather up the ripe corn into sheaves, and now they were standing them in the field to let them finish drying for a few hours before taking them into the yard where the stack would be built.

'Time for a rest,' Mr Baker said and brought out a pail. It was filled with cold water and bottles of beer were cooling in it. The men all accepted one gratefully. The farmer hesitated and then offered one to George. 'You've done a man's work today, lad. You can have a man's drink – if you want it?'

'I'll try it.' George grinned. He would have gladly drunk cold water but none had been sent, so he accepted his opened beer and took a swig. It was his first ever and he thought it tasted bitter, wondering why men liked to drink it. However, there was nothing else but the water in the pail and that had bits floating in it so he drank the beer. It was strong, and as its warmth spread through his gullet into his stomach, he felt his tiredness fading and his strength returning.

Mr Baker laughed as he returned the empty bottle. 'You'd best eat something before you cycle home,' he said. 'Don't want you falling off your bike and into a dyke.'

George was about to deny its effects, which though pleasant, were also slightly disorientating, when he saw a man walking across the fields towards them. He knew at once that it was Chuck and he sensed something had happened. He started running towards him, his heart racing wildly.

'Chuck – is there news?' he asked, breathless from the run and his sudden fear.

Chuck looked at him and he felt ice at his nape. 'There's some news, George,' he said. 'I haven't traced your parents but Kate is in hospital. She's been badly hurt and she's still unconscious . . .'

'But we tried the hospitals!' George's throat tightened with tears. Kate badly hurt. Unconscious. Yet alive. 'Can I see her?'

'I'm going up to London this evening,' Chuck told him, 'but you're under the age they normally allow into hospital wards, George.' He hesitated, then, 'Why don't you let me go first? I'll come straight back and tell you everything. You can come with me if you want but they may not let you in.'

George struggled with his feelings. Kate was his sister. He should be the one to see her, but he knew that Chuck was right. Drawing a deep breath, he said, 'You care about her a lot, don't you?'

'Yes, George. I care as much as it is possible to care for anyone.'

George nodded. 'Then you go. If Kate wakes up, she might know . . .'

'I'm still trying to find your parents, and Jenny. I haven't given up, George, and I shan't.'

'It's a long time for her to be unconscious – just over a month . . .' George looked at him anxiously. 'She's very ill, isn't she?'

'I shan't lie to you,' Chuck said. 'She might not pull through, lad – but I'm going to see if I can get her moved somewhere better. Perhaps nearer to us so that we can visit her more.'

George bit his lip, his chest tight with emotion. 'I can't thank you – I don't have the words . . .'

'I don't need thanks,' Chuck told him and smiled. 'Let's face it, we both love her. We just have to do the best we can for her.'

'Yes, I know.' George fought his tears. 'You will let me know?'

'You have my word.'

Hearing a shout behind him, George turned to look. 'I'd better get back. I'm needed.'

'I'll be in touch soon,' Chuck promised. George nodded. He longed to go with him, but he knew he had to wait and to trust in his friend. Chuck wouldn't let him down.

A telegram arrived the following day when George returned from the fields.

Kate now conscious. Still very ill. Arranging to have her brought to a nursing home in Cambridge. She doesn't know what happened to your parents. Chuck

The message was brief but telegrams were expensive. It was enough for the moment. George stared at it for several minutes. His prayers had been partially answered. Now he had to pray that Kate would recover and his parents and Jenny would be found alive.

Mrs Seward looked at him as he put the telegram away. 'How is she, George?' she asked sympathetically.

'She's conscious now. Chuck is having her transferred to a nursing home nearer to us – in Cambridge, he says.'

'That's very expensive,' Mrs Seward said. 'However, I daresay he can afford it. I think he comes from a good family.'

'They just have a farm, like Mr Baker,' George said. 'He thinks a lot of Kate so that's why he's doing it.'

'Yes, I gathered that,' she said and smiled. 'You needed a bit of good luck. When your sister's out of hospital and well again, you might want to live with her, George.'

'Yes, perhaps,' he admitted, hesitating, then, 'Am I in the way here now, Mrs Seward? I think you've quarrelled with your daughter because of me and I'm sorry. Perhaps I should find somewhere else to live now?'

'Not until you're ready. This is still my house – and this belongs to you.' She took out the velvet box from her skirt pocket. 'Lizzie had borrowed it . . .' George

303

made no move to take the box and she frowned. 'If you refuse, I shall be very offended.'

'Very well,' he said, smiling ruefully. 'I just think it's too much for what little I've done.'

She gave a harsh laugh. 'I was in danger of losing my home and my granddaughter. Had you not come along, I would have been in a home and only God knows what would have happened to Ellie . . .' She sighed. 'Her mother has always been selfish, George. Thankfully, her father adores her. I pray that he comes back hale and hearty and claims her one day, because I don't want to die and leave Ellie to her mother's mercies.'

'You're not going to die,' George said and grinned at her. 'You're as strong as a horse.'

'In mind and spirit,' she admitted. 'The body is weaker than I'd like, George. I hope to see this wretched war out and Ellie safe with her father – but . . .' She sighed and shrugged. 'We're all in the lap of the gods, are we not?'

'I suppose,' George said. 'I pray to God my parents are still alive. Do you think He listens?'

'I'm sure he does,' she replied. 'Providing that He exists.' Seeing his shocked look, she laughed. 'Take no notice of a bitter old woman, George. No doubt when I'm on my deathbed I'll pray for forgiveness like the rest of them.'

George nodded, then wrinkled his brow in thought. 'If my father is alive, why hasn't he written to me? I just don't understand it. He must know I'd be worried. Yet, he would almost certainly have been at work when it happened, so surely he must be alive?'

'It is a mystery,' Mrs Seward agreed. 'Unless . . . well

with all the chaos, it's just possible that his letter went astray.'

'Yes. I hadn't thought of that,' George said and impulsively kissed her cheek, which startled her and then made her laugh. 'Thank you – and, if you're sure, I'll sell the brooch. It will help Kate to get better – and to find a home for us somewhere.'

'Now that's talking like a sensible man,' Mrs Seward said, looking at him with approval. 'You've grown up a lot these past months, George. You were still an uncertain youth when you came to me, but now you seem to me to be a young man. I think you'll do well, whatever you do in life.'

'Thank you again,' he said. 'It's been a privilege to look after you these last few months.'

'Get off with you, no flummery,' she said but looked pleased all the same. 'You can make the range up for me if you will – and scrape those new potatoes you brought from the farm. It's a job I can't abide. You brought them so you can do them!'

George laughed. She might pretend to be harsh and order him about, but he knew her secret; she had a tender heart that had been badly bruised at various times and the harshness she projected was a measure of protection.

Chuck found George on the farm that weekend. They'd been working from dawn to dusk to get the harvest in and now all the wheat was stacked and most of the oats and barley, too.

'Ah, Mrs Seward said I'd find you here,' Chuck said. 'Have you got a few minutes?'

'I've just finished for the day,' George said, his heart racing. 'How is Kate?'

'Very tired at the moment. The journey knocked her back a bit – but she'll be better where she is now. The wards of the infirmary where she'd been taken were crowded and noisy and she'll have more peace here.'

'That's good. What's wrong with her exactly?'

Chuck hesitated, then, 'She has broken ribs, a fractured ankle and she's lost two fingers of her right hand . . .' He drew a deep breath. 'She was also burned, her arms and legs – and the right side of her face.'

'No!' George stared at him in horror. 'That must hurt terribly. Poor Kate . . .'

'She's being treated, George. I've seen a lot worse, but there will be scars. I know it sounds horrendous, but Kate is alive – she's still with us, and she'll get well again. I promise.' He touched the scar at his temple. 'We learn to live with them, George.'

'I don't notice yours – but you're a man and a hero. It will be worse for Kate,' George said, a catch in his throat. 'I don't care. I love her – but I know she'll care. She was the prettiest girl in the street – anywhere.'

'I know,' Chuck agreed. 'She still is to me, George. I don't see the scars – just the bravest girl I've ever known.'

George swallowed hard. 'I'm glad she has you, Chuck. Steve let her down – and he wouldn't want her now, because she isn't perfect. He's rotten!'

'I agree but he doesn't matter. I'm sure her divorce will go through – as you said, Steve won't try to hold her now.'

They looked at each other in silence for a moment,

then George said, 'It will cost a lot of money for Kate's treatment. I've got a brooch to sell. I've been offered two hundred and fifty pounds for it – and I want you to use it for her treatment, please.'

'That's a lot of money. Did Mrs Seward give it to you?'

'Yes. I didn't want to take the brooch. I gave it back but she insisted – and now I'm glad. It's for Kate.'

'You can give it to her when she's well,' Chuck replied. 'I must ask you to allow me to pay for her treatment, George. I know she's your sister – but I need to do this for her.'

George met his eyes for a moment and then he nodded. 'She'll need money to get back all she lost when she's better; besides, I know you love her as much as I do.'

'Yes. I did almost from the first time I saw her. I knew she would never look my way – why should she? Her marriage was good, or so I thought then, but I wanted to help her and now I can.'

'Then I thank you,' George said and held out his hand and they shook solemnly. 'Still no news of the others?'

'None,' Chuck replied. 'I'm sorry, George. I'm beginning to think the worst – but we shan't give up. We'll keep trying.'

'Yes.' George nodded as Chuck turned away. He ran after him as he reached his car. 'Will they let me visit her?'

Chuck turned and smiled. 'Yes. Not for a couple of weeks yet – but then, when she's had a small operation, I'll come and fetch you.'

George nodded and stood back. He had finished work for the day, but returned to ask Mr Baker if he was needed the next day.

'We've done until the threshing – and then we'll be lifting the roots,' he said. 'I'll want you for the milking at the weekend; the girls are off on their holidays so it will be just us again. I'll have your wages for you in the morning . . .' Mr Baker smiled. 'If you decide a life in farming suits you, I'll take you on full time when you leave school.'

'If I stay on to take all my exams they'll want me in the army,' George said. 'I'll see how well I've done when I get my results. If I've passed everything I'll try for a year at college before I join up – if they let me . . .'

Mr Baker nodded sorrowfully. 'Aye, by the looks of things it might drag on a few years yet. Still, you never know. I think you're right to try your best, George – but there's always a job for you here.'

George thanked him. It wouldn't be a bad life working on the farm, but more than ever now, he wanted to do something that would help others.

CHAPTER 32

Kate lay in bed staring out of the window to her side. Her view was of a pleasant garden, lawns, and neat flower beds, and in the background, a stand of cherry trees that would be beautiful in spring. In late July they were a mass of brown-tipped green leaves. She could feel the soreness of her skin on the right side of her face and a similar discomfort on her legs and arms, and she knew she'd suffered burns, because she'd been told so, though she had no memory of being in a fire.

She thought she remembered being at home when the warning sounded. Her tea had been on the table and, as the siren sounded distant, thought she might as well finish it but then . . . after that there was no memory. She couldn't recall the bomb hitting her home, nor lying in the wreckage. She had no memory of being hit by falling debris, none at all of her first weeks in hospital; they were just a dark blur of pain and being floating somewhere, neither alive nor dead. Then, one day, she'd heard a voice begging her to wake up, and for some reason something in her had responded. She'd woken to find herself looking up into a face she knew and cared for.

'Chuck?' she'd whispered, her throat dry and hurting; it was still sore from the heat of the smoke she'd inhaled.

'Don't try to move, my dearest one,' he'd said gently. 'You were hurt in a raid but you're alive. We've been searching for you, George and I.' He'd smiled and held her hand and she'd been aware of feeling safe, and then the mist had returned and she'd fallen into that strange state again. After that she was aware of doctors and nurses talking to her, gentle hands tending her pain, and then, gradually, the awakening. She'd known she was in an infirmary and that she was being moved by her husband.

Kate had frowned over that. She didn't recall seeing Steve and something wasn't right. It was only when she was comfortable again in a clean, fresh-smelling bed that she began to think clearly, and then she knew that it was Chuck who had arranged for her to be moved. She was in a nursing home somewhere outside the City of Cambridge so that she could be near him and her family. He'd been to visit her several times and then he'd brought George. They'd both sat by her bed and told her they loved her, but no one had mentioned her parents.

Kate had a feeling of sadness. Were they dead? Billy was with George now, or at least living close to him; they saw each other most weekends. Still no one had spoken of her mother, father, or Jenny.

Jenny hadn't been with her when the raid started. She would have been at work. Kate prayed that she was alive and well but no one had mentioned her. Were they afraid of upsetting Kate – or didn't they know?

She felt her lashes wet. They had been singed but were growing back now, so George said. She'd asked him how she looked and he'd said she was still pretty, but she knew the side of her face had been burned; it was numbed and sometimes itchy now rather than stinging as it had for the first weeks after her injury. There were no mirrors in the toilets. Kate had asked for a mirror but so far no one had obliged her – as if she would throw a fit of hysterics at the sight of herself!

Kate knew she couldn't look as pretty as she once had, but she was alive – and for the moment that was all that mattered. Aware that she needed to go to the toilet, she swung her legs over the side of the bed. Her other injuries were all healed now but the burns to her legs had been more severe, which was why she was still in hospital. However, although they stung as she moved to a standing position, she no longer had deep pain, and she felt that she wanted to leave this place of refuge, even though it had given her the peace and calm she so badly needed at the start.

She walked to the toilets and relieved herself. As she returned to her bed in the ward, where only three other female patients were being cared for, a nurse came to her, looking puzzled.

'Mrs Silvester?' she inquired. 'There's a man here claiming to be your husband – but he isn't the one who visits you regularly.'

'Steve . . .' The name was on her lips. 'That would be my husband, nurse . . .'

'Ah!' The nurse looked relieved. 'Did you want to see Pilot Officer Silvester?'

'Yes, if he wishes to see me,' Kate gave her permission. As the nurse left the ward, her hand went to her hair, knowing it must be a mess. She put a brush through it when they helped her wash in the mornings, but it hadn't been washed or set for ages and felt greasy. Yet what did it matter?

Kate returned to her bed, pulling the covers up over her chest. She was wearing a hospital nightgown of some thick cotton stuff that tied at the neck and had no lipstick or powder on.

Her heart caught as she saw Steve enter the ward. He stood at the far end, looking for her, and she saw the shock in his eyes as he saw her. It seemed to her that he hesitated, wondering whether to come forward or leave, but after a moment or two of indecision, he walked to her bed and stood looking at her. The horror in his eyes told her that as far as he was concerned her beauty had gone.

'I'm sorry, Kate,' Steve said lamely. 'I . . .' He averted his eyes. 'I had the divorce papers and I thought I should speak to you before I signed them . . .'

'Oh . . . I haven't had mine,' Kate replied. 'Someone has arranged to have my letters sent to his address so no doubt he has them.'

'I wanted to discuss the terms . . . but I think they're fair enough in the circumstances,' Steve said. 'You'll need a bit of money to get on your feet again.' He hesitated, then reached out to touch her face. 'It's rotten luck for you, Kate. I'm truly sorry.'

'It doesn't matter. I'll live.'

'But . . . Yes, I suppose that's the way you have to look at it,' he muttered and looked embarrassed. 'So I'll sign them then. I daresay you'll be glad to be rid of me. I wasn't good enough for you, Kate. This . . . is goodbye then. I doubt we'll meet again.'

'How did you know I was here?'

'Chuck phoned me,' Steve said. 'He thought . . . well, he said if I wanted to visit, I should come here. I wouldn't have known where to find you, otherwise. I thought you were dead and so did your father.'

'You've spoken to my father?' Kate sat forward, suddenly tingling. 'Where is he? *How* is he? What about my mother and Jenny?'

'Oh, I thought you must know. He said he'd written to George but hadn't heard from him . . .' Steve looked uncomfortable. 'I'll speak to Chuck – he can tell you.'

'No!' Kate's hand shot out and gripped his wrist as he turned away. 'Don't be a coward, Steve. Tell me!'

He shrugged off her grasp. 'Your father's all right – looks haggard – but your mother died in the raid and he hasn't been able to trace Jenny or you. He believes you both dead . . .'

'Poor Dad,' Kate said with a little sob. 'Do you know where he's living?'

'In a seedy little dump in Holborn,' Steve said. 'A boarding house, he said but I don't know any details, just that he hated it and wanted to move as soon as he could – but surely he must have written to George?'

'He hasn't heard anything,' Kate replied. She forced a smile. 'Thanks for coming, Steve. You've helped me, even though it wasn't your intention. We can find Dad now we know he's alive.'

'Kate – I came because I thought perhaps . . .' He shook his head. 'It wouldn't work. I couldn't . . . sorry . . .' Steve walked off abruptly, leaving Kate in no doubt of his feelings. He'd just admitted he couldn't live with her after seeing her injuries.

She lay back and closed her eyes as he walked away, tears trickling down her cheeks. Kate wasn't sure why she was crying. It didn't matter to her that Steve didn't want her now she wasn't perfect. He'd hurt her once but that was over. She might be crying for her lost mother or her father who was suffering a terrible burden of grief – or perhaps because she was so happy that he was alive.

The nurse came back into the ward. She approached Kate's bed. 'Are you all right, Mrs Silvester?'

'I'm Miss Greene now my divorce is almost final,' Kate said, because it soon would be. Steve wouldn't contest it now. He wouldn't risk being tied to a woman he couldn't bear to look at. 'And would you be kind enough to bring me a mirror please, nurse? I'd like to get dressed and do my hair. I want to leave as soon as I can . . .'

'Flight Lieutenant Durrant is coming tomorrow to fetch you home,' the nurse replied with a smile. 'You could have left a few days ago but he hadn't found a nice place for you to live and now he has.'

'Thank you. Will you bring me that mirror please?'

'Yes, if you wish.' The nurse nodded and went off, returning within a few minutes. She handed Kate the mirror in silence.

Kate looked at herself. Her forehead was still slightly red and the right side of her face was puckered, the skin red with white patches where it had begun to heal

314

over. Her eyelashes were barely there and it made her eyes look strange, her mouth was a little swollen, but otherwise she was herself.

'It will get better,' the nurse told her. 'You were lucky, Miss Greene. Some burns are so deep they need several skin grafts but yours will heal really well in time. You may have some patches of discoloured skin but the puckering is going – it was much worse than it is now.'

Kate looked her in the eyes. 'Is that the truth? Or are you just being kind?'

'We don't do that,' the nurse replied. 'Your burns were only first degree because you were pulled out of the wreckage so swiftly. As I said, you were lucky.'

'Yes, I know,' Kate said quietly. 'I've just been told my mother is dead and my father is worn to death with grief; my niece is still missing and my father thinks both she and I are dead. I have an idea where he is now and I need to get a message to my family so they can contact him . . .'

Chuck went up to London soon after he got Kate's message telling him that her father was in Holborn in a boarding house somewhere and she'd asked if he could find him. He'd asked for leave and been granted seventy-two hours.

It was late when he reached Holborn. The first thing he did was to book into a small hotel and ask for a register of boarding houses. The receptionist was taken aback but when he explained she immediately became helpful and found a book with hotels and boarding houses in the area listed.

'These are the best ones, Flight Lieutenant,' she told

him, pointing out some that had been marked. 'We've had lots of inquiries from people wanting somewhere cheap to stay – but these with the cross against them are not recommended. I understand they're not particularly clean.'

'Then they may be what I need,' Chuck said. 'I've been given to understand the person I'm trying to find is in a place that isn't pleasant and he wants to move.'

'If he can find anyone with a spare room,' the receptionist agreed sympathetically. 'All our rooms are permanently taken these days – apart from the one you have. We do keep one available for temporary military guests.'

Chuck thanked her, declined the offer of dinner, and armed with his book, set off to visit the first few on his list. It was eleven o'clock by the time he'd crossed three off his list and by then he knew he had to postpone until the morning. The doors on these boarding houses were locked by ten or eleven at the latest. He returned to his hotel, asked for some sandwiches and coffee in his room and went up.

In the morning, Chuck was up early and after breakfast set out again. He checked every one of the cheaper rooming houses on the list and found nothing. No one had a Mr Greene staying, nor did they have any record of his being there. Chuck took a break for a quick lunch of a pint and a pie at a public house and asked the landlord if by chance a Mr Ned Greene had been in for a drink. He shook his head, but said there were several pubs in the area that had rooms to let, though most were full. It seemed that the citizens of

London were seeking accommodation in their locality rather than heading out to the country.

Chuck left and checked out a few pubs until they closed for the afternoon; then he went back to checking boarding houses and then small hotels. His thoughts went constantly to Kate, who was staying with Mr and Mrs Baker at the farm. Chuck had found a house for her and arranged for the basic furniture to be delivered, but it wouldn't be ready until the following weekend and so Mrs Baker had offered to look after her until her new home was ready. It was just down the road in Chatteris so George and Billy could live with her and continue to go to school there.

Chuck wished that he could have spent time with her but instead he'd arranged for George and Billy to fetch her home. Mr Baker had driven them to the hospital and then taken them all back to the farm. It wasn't how Chuck had planned it, but it was more important that he should discover the whereabouts of Ned Greene. By the time it was beginning to get dusk, Chuck was wondering if whoever had told Kate about Ned's present whereabouts had got it wrong and he felt disappointed because he knew how much it would mean to the family to find him.

He took time out for a sandwich and a cup of tea at a café and then found his book to consult the list; there were only three more he hadn't checked. As he turned left towards the underground, a girl shrieked his name and he stopped, wondering whether he'd heard right, and then she came flying towards him.

'Chuck – is it you?' she cried. 'Do you remember – I'm Kate's niece!'

'Jenny! By all that's wonderful! I'm here looking for your grandad – and I find you!'

'I've been looking for him, too,' she said. 'I've been to most of the boarding houses in this part of London – and I just missed him. Yesterday. They said he'd left but they didn't know where he'd gone . . .' She gave a little sobbing breath. 'I know Gran is dead. I found her on a list – but I can't find Kate. I wanted to find her and Grandad before I go to Georgie. Billy went missing, too; they were sending him up north . . .'

'Billy's at the farm and Kate's there for the moment,' Chuck said. 'She was badly hurt and has just come out of hospital. I've found a lovely house for you all to live in – but we heard your grandad was in Holborn.'

'He was – at the Chester Hotel,' Jenny said. 'It's a boarding house but it calls itself a hotel and is a horrid, dirty little place, I'm not surprised Grandad didn't want to stay there.'

'Come and have a cup of tea,' Chuck said. 'Then I can take you down to the farm and you can help Kate settle into the house.'

'I'll have a cup of tea,' Jenny replied, 'but I won't come just yet, Chuck. I'm staying with someone – and I want to go on searching for Grandad. I'll come down one weekend soon . . .'

Chuck led the way back to the café he'd just left and bought her a pot of tea and a cake. 'Are you all right, Jenny?' he asked as she started to eat. 'We were all worried about you. Why didn't you write to George?'

'I did,' Jenny said looking startled. 'I told him I was searching for them all and would come down when I'd found out whether they were alive or dead.'

'He didn't get your letter,' Chuck said. 'He's been writing letters to all sorts of places and I made lots of inquiries about your grandparents and you. Billy went down to George as soon as he could.'

'After I saw both houses were gone, I didn't know what to do,' Jenny told him. 'Then . . . Well, I'd arranged to meet my boyfriend who was home on leave. I met him and he took me to his mum – and I've been living there. She got me a new ration book – and I told you, I wrote to George straightaway. I even gave him my address but he never replied.'

'Because he didn't get it,' Chuck said and looked at her.

'I'm sorry. I did wonder but I thought it would be best if I could find them before I wrote again. Is Kate very ill?'

'She had some injuries and a few burns . . .' He touched his right cheek. 'On her legs and arms too – but she was lucky. They say they will heal in time.'

'Will she be scarred?'

'I expect a little – but it doesn't matter. She's still Kate, isn't she?'

'It doesn't matter to me,' Jenny said but her eyes watered. 'Tell her I love her and I'll come soon – whether I find Grandad or not . . . but at least we know he's alive.'

'Yes, so Kate was told.'

Jenny sniffed. 'Poor Gran. She was so scared of the bombs and she died alone. Billy must have been out when the house was hit.'

'Yes, shopping for her.' Jenny's eyes filled with tears. Chuck gave her his clean handkerchief and she mopped them. 'I thought I was getting over it but it hurts . . .'

'Yes, I know,' Chuck said. 'I care about all your family, Jenny.'

'I know you love Kate – and I'm so glad.' She offered his hanky back but he shook his head with a gentle smile and told her to keep it. 'You'll look after her?'

'Yes, I shall – if she'll let me. I hope and pray she will . . . But first we have to find her father,' Chuck said sadly. 'She'll need him in the coming weeks and months.'

'Yes. Losing her mum will hit Kate hard,' Jenny agreed. 'We lost Derek and Tom – and now Gran . . .' A sob escaped her. 'When will it end, Chuck?'

'I wish I could say soon,' he replied, 'but that would be a lie. I think this war has a long way to go . . .'

CHAPTER 33

George was driving the cows towards the milking sheds when he heard Mr Baker call his name. He was waving to him, signalling for him to come and Benny was walking towards him.

'I'll take them from here,' he said. 'You're needed up at the house, George.'

George nodded and started to run, his heart racing wildly. Had Kate taken a turn for the worse? He ran as fast as he could and was panting when he entered the kitchen.

'Kate . . .' he spluttered, gasping for breath and then saw that she was on her feet and her face was glowing. He looked at the man she was gazing at and got a shock. It was his father – but looking grey and ill, years older than he had the last time George had seen him. 'Dad – oh, Dad,' he breathed, moving towards him. He put his arms around his father, holding him, feeling how thin he was. Looking up into hollowed eyes he saw the pain of a grief so terrible that it could scarcely be borne. 'Dad . . . I know . . .' Tears streamed down George's face as his father held him, his face nuzzled into his neck. It was as if he were the boy and George the father. He felt his father's body tremble. 'We all loved her . . .' he mumbled through his own tears.

'I thought I'd lost you all,' Ned Greene said at last. 'I saw Grace. She looked peaceful. I didn't expect that – but she'll be with her lads now . . .'

'I didn't know you were alive,' George told him. 'Chuck and me have been looking everywhere, writing and phoning. He's in London looking for you right now – why didn't you write to me, Dad?'

Ned pulled back and looked down at him. 'I did write two letters – and you didn't reply so I feared the worst and I came looking. Mrs Seward told me you were here so I came – and here's my Kate, too.'

'What about Jenny?' Kate asked. 'Have you seen or heard from her?'

'No. I tried some of the guesthouses and small hotels but no sign of her. She isn't on any lists of dead or injured or relocated. She has just . . . disappeared.' Ned gave a little sob. 'Apparently, quite a few children have done that – and they don't know whether they're alive or dead.'

'We'll go on looking for her,' George promised. 'Chuck won't give up – he found Kate for me and he's still looking for you, because Kate was told you were in Holborn.'

'I was for a while but I moved a couple of times. I wondered if my letters to George had got lost so I came down to find him.' A huge smile lit his face, banishing the tiredness for a while as he looked at Kate and then George. 'And just look what I found!'

'Chuck has discovered a nice house, big enough for

us all,' George told him. 'We're moving in next week –
the three of us, Billy, too – and you. You'll come, Dad,
please. You can get a job driving trains this way.'

'Yes, I can,' Ned agreed. 'Nothing to keep me in
London now. I'll visit your mum now and then, but
I'll still be on the London run, just a different base.' He
nodded, looking from one to the other. 'I thank God
for giving me this happiness.'

'We're lucky,' George said and smiled. 'We're
together – and perhaps we'll find Jenny soon.'

CHAPTER 34

George was thoughtful as he cycled back to Mrs Seward's house that evening. It wasn't likely that two letters from his father would just go astray – so who had taken them? And why?

His father had been offered a place to sleep on the Bakers' couch for the night. He'd one suitcase with him, which was all he had. Nothing from his home remained, but he'd been given extra coupons to buy some clothes and a few bits and pieces he needed. His savings were safe in the Post Office and so he'd been able to manage, but finding a home in London would be hard, which made it easier for him to join his family. Together, they would pull together the pieces of their lives.

George put his cycle in the back garden and went into the kitchen. Mrs Seward was sitting at the table alone. She looked up and smiled.

'Did you see your father, George?'

'Yes, thank you. He looks ill but it's grief. He'll be better now he's going to relocate down here with us.'

'So you'll be leaving us soon?'

'Yes, but if you need me, I can pop in and do things for you, Mrs Seward.'

'I'll like you to call as a friend,' she admitted. 'Lizzie can do most things now – but you never know. I hope we shan't lose touch.'

'I shan't be far away . . .' He hesitated, then, 'Dad wrote two letters to me – it's odd they both went astray, isn't it?'

She looked him straight in the eye, then took two unopened envelopes from her apron pocket. 'I believe these might be them,' she said. 'It wasn't me, George, but when your father told me he'd written to you I had my suspicions – and I was correct: Ellie had them. She was afraid you would leave us . . .' Mrs Seward sighed. 'It was very wrong of her and I'm sorry for all the suffering it caused you, George. She didn't understand . . .'

George nodded. 'I wondered if that might be the way of it.'

'Do you want her punished?'

'Why?' George smiled. 'She did it because she loves me – and I care for her. I've got my father and Kate back now – and please God we'll find Jenny. I don't want Ellie punished, Mrs Seward – so please don't tell her mother. Just tell Ellie that it was wrong but I forgive her – and say I will visit as much as I can.'

'You're a lovely lad,' Mrs Seward said. 'Lizzie was right – you *have* become a son to me, and I've made my decision. I don't need this great big house. I'm going to sell it and buy a small one that will be easy to look after. I shall use the money to make our lives better – and, if you ever need money for your education, George, please ask me. I think your ambition to help others in whatever way you can is wonderful. I just wish you were mine.' She stood up and gave him her hands. George took them and kissed her cheek.

'I shan't need money. Living together we'll manage and my dad is saving for my education if I go to college – but I thank you for the offer and for the brooch. I shall always think of you as a dear friend.'

'Now look what you've done,' she sniffed and dashed a tear from her eyes. 'I've got some shallots in the pantry – and you can peel them. We'll have some nice pickled onions for the autumn and Christmas . . .'

George turned away to hide his smile. It was typical of her to hide her emotion behind a command but he'd enjoyed his stay here. It had cemented his determination; he was going to be a doctor or bust.

CHAPTER 35

'You still want to stay in London?' Kate asked, looking into her niece's face. Chuck had persuaded Jenny to come back with him and see everyone and the tears had run all round as what was left of their family came together. 'There will be plenty of room in the house we've been lucky enough to rent. There are four bedrooms and three reception rooms, as well as a kitchen – and a proper bathroom.'

'It sounds lovely,' Jenny agreed and hugged her again. 'I'm so happy both you and Dad are alive – and Billy. I want to come and stay sometimes, Kate, of course I do – but I have a job in London and Pete's family have given me a home. It's easy for him to visit when he gets leave and . . .' She smiled shyly at Kate. 'We got engaged on his last leave and I'd like to get married next spring.'

'Don't you think you're still a bit young?' Kate asked but she shook her head.

'I know what I want,' Jenny said. 'If you agree, Grandad will too. Mum never writes – I know she wouldn't have the address now, but when she did, she never even sent a postcard. You and George, Billy and Grandad are my family now – so please wish me happy.'

'John too,' Kate told her. 'Dad wrote to him and he had a letter back. He's still alive – and don't write your mum off, either. She did send your gran one letter so Dad knows her address. And when you're ready to get married, we'll invite her to the wedding because it's wrong to hold a grudge, Jenny. Your mum is your mum, even though she let you all down.'

'All right, if you think we should,' Jenny said, her eyes shining. 'I was happy that Pete loves me, but when I thought I'd lost all of you, it threw a shadow over everything. Now I can really look forward to the future.'

'Yes, we all have to do that,' Kate replied, her face shadowed by grief. 'As a family we've lost too much, but we mustn't let it break us. We have so much to be grateful for – and to live for.' She shook her head, as if to banish her pain. 'I've made up my mind to go back to teaching and I've seen a post offered in a school in one of the villages. I could cycle in every day if I get it.'

'You won't go back to work yet, surely?' Jenny said, shocked. 'You're not well enough, Kate. You ought to rest and get strong again first.'

'It won't be until the autumn term,' Kate told her. 'I should be back to normal by then . . .' She touched her cheek. 'As normal as I can be . . .'

Jenny looked at her, sadness in her eyes. 'You were hurt badly, Kate,' she said, reaching out to touch her hand. 'Does it hurt where you were burned?'

'It is a bit sore and stiff still,' Kate replied. 'It will

get easier – my legs are the worst; I doubt the scars will ever fade, but I can cover them with stockings.'

'You still look lovely to me,' Jenny told her. 'It's just a reddish-brown mark, Kate. I think it must have been very painful but it looks fine now.'

Kate smiled and shook her head. 'I know what I look like,' she said. 'Steve pitied me, but I won't be pitied, Jenny. I have my life and I have some of my family. I'm lucky.'

'Oh, Kate!' Jenny burst into tears and ran to her arms. Kate hugged her, soothing her. 'I love you so much and it isn't fair!'

Kate kissed her cheek and held her back, looking into her eyes. 'No, don't upset yourself, dearest. I told you – I won't be pitied. I know I can't be beautiful again, but that isn't the end of the world.'

'You're beautiful inside,' Jenny said and wiped her tears. 'I hate Steve for the things he's said and done to you!'

'I don't hate him,' Kate replied. 'Life moves on, Jenny. I've changed but he hasn't. If we'd stayed together, I think we would have been very unhappy – trapped in a marriage that no longer mattered. It was best that he wanted his freedom.'

'But what about you? Who's going to take care of you?' Jenny asked, staring at her.

'Dad and George – and you, and my friends,' Kate replied with a smile. 'I'm loved and I love. I can work and make a new life.'

'What about the love of a husband?' Jenny said a little awkwardly. 'You wanted your own home and a family.'

'That's for the future,' Kate said. 'I can't think far ahead, Jenny. For the moment I've found the family I thought lost and I shall have a home with them and one day, perhaps . . .' She shrugged her shoulders. 'Don't talk about it anymore, love. I just want to be happy that you're here with us and alive . . .'

Kate glanced around the house they had begun to move into. It was a large, square building with big bedrooms and spacious sitting rooms and a long dining room/ kitchen overlooking a huge back garden. After the small terraced houses she'd been used to, it seemed like a mansion, and definitely needed a family to fill it.

They had been given some furniture by the local Red Cross and Mrs Seward had sent the beds from her sons' bedrooms, together with chests of drawers and wardrobes.

'She's already put her house up for sale,' George told them. 'She won't be needing these and she knew we hadn't got anything from our old homes. It isn't easy to buy new at the moment, Kate. It's old-fashioned but good quality.' He'd looked at his sister anxiously, as if afraid she might reject the gift.

'It's beautiful stuff,' Kate told him. George had insisted that she and her father should take the beds Mrs Seward had sent, and he and Billy had a pair of twin beds with iron rails and horsehair mattresses from the second-hand shop. They'd also found an oak settle that had once belonged to a church that went well in the huge kitchen, a pine dresser that Mr Greene had stained to match the settle and a long pine table. The chairs were a hotchpotch of styles, none of them matching. As yet, the big sitting room wasn't furnished at all, but since the kitchen was the place where they spent most of their time it didn't matter for now.

'Mrs Seward will be selling more of her furniture when she moves,' George told his father. 'She'll sell it to us, if we want it.'

'I must go and thank her,' Mr Greene said. 'She has been more than kind – and I understand she isn't well?'

'She suffers a lot of pain in her limbs and her back,' George confided. 'She makes out it's nothing but I've seen how much it hurts her when it's bad. She would be better off in a nursing home with folk to look after her, but she wants a home for Ellie, because she doesn't trust her mother, Lizzie, to look after her.'

'That's a shame, son,' Mr Greene said. 'You'll keep visiting her, won't you?'

'Yes, I shall.' George smiled. 'We're lucky, Dad. So we need to look out for others who aren't as lucky as us.'

'George is right.' Kate had heard their conversation. 'I'd like to meet your friend, George. She sounds like a lovely lady.'

'She has a sharp tongue,' George laughed. 'But if she likes you, she likes you.'

'Then, when we're settled, you must invite her to tea.'

George beamed. 'I think she might like that – but Ellie will have to come and we should invite her mother too . . .'

'Of course,' his father said. 'We'll invite them all on Sunday. We'll have the house straight by then.'

Kate nodded to herself. The house had begun to look like a home; she would buy cushions and begin to collect books, and . . . a sigh issued from her at the memory of all her lost books, some she'd kept from childhood. In time she would have more. She'd heard about a second-hand bookshop in March, the small railway town a short distance away. She would take the train and do some shopping: a few cushions, some material for curtains if she had enough coupons – and bits and pieces.

By the end of the week Kate had worked a small miracle. On her trip to March in search of books, she'd discovered a junk shop. Inside, were all manner of wonderful things. The family now had two very comfortable, if shabby, armchairs placed near a window at the end of the long kitchen. The wooden bench was piled with bright velvet cushions, also from the junk shop, old but clean and vibrant in gold and crimson. There were books on the shelves in the smaller sitting room and one big chair that Kate could curl up in to mark exercise books when she got her new job, with a small oak wine table beside it.

She'd seen a lot of other bits and pieces she'd wanted but could not yet afford; they would come piece by piece once she was working again. Moving into the house, buying things for it and enjoying putting them in place, had made Kate begin to feel like herself again. If she didn't look in the mirror, she could almost forget the pain, fear, and suffering of the past months.

That first weekend they'd invited Mrs Seward and

her family to tea. Mrs Seward and Ellie came, in a car that a neighbour owned. He brought them and promised to fetch them at eight. They delivered gifts wrapped in tissue – a pretty lace tablecloth and a silver-plated teapot, sugar bowl and jug.

One of Kate's purchases had been a Shelly bone china tea service so she was able to offer the old lady her tea in a pretty cup and saucer. They'd bought eggs, milk and salad items from the farm and some sliced ham from the butcher, who had taken a shine to Kate and suddenly produced it from under the counter.

Kate had made rock buns and jam tarts, also a fatless sponge with a little fresh cream whipped up, soft and delicious, plus some plum jam to fill it. After some initial shyness on Ellie's part and a little reserve from Mrs Seward, they got on well and talked about the war and how marvellous George was, making him escape to the kitchen with a tray of used dishes. He stayed to wash them up, returning only when he felt it must be safe.

'Why did you run off?' his dad asked after the guests had gone. 'They both had only good to say of you, son.'

'It's embarrassing, Dad,' George said. 'I only did what you taught me was right – you and mum.'

His father ruffled his hair. 'Well, I'm proud of you – and because you've made me as proud as Punch, I've got something for you.'

He produced a parcel in brown paper. George took it and tore off the wrappings, giving a cry of delight. 'It's a medical book!' he told Kate, who was looking on and smiling. 'It's got lots of pictures and things showing you the insides of folk and telling you about what goes wrong.' He grinned at his dad. 'Thanks, Dad. It's what I've been wanting. I can start studying medicine before I go to college.'

'Kate found it for you but I paid for it, because I wanted to give it to you myself,' his father said and looked fondly from his daughter to his young son.

'Well, thanks both of you,' George said. 'It's great.'

'I thought you'd like it but I couldn't afford it so Dad gave me the money.' Kate smiled at him. 'I like your friends, George. I can see they're both fond of you. It's a pity Lizzie was unable to come with them.'

'Oh, she didn't want to,' George said. 'She doesn't like me. I think she's jealous because Mrs Seward and Ellie care about me.'

'That isn't a nice thing to say, George,' his father reprimanded.

'It's true, Dad. Mrs Seward wouldn't say it, because she thinks her daughter is rude to me – but she knows.'

'Even so, you must try to like her. I hope you aren't rude back, George?'

'No, Dad. I just avoid her as much as I can.'

His father nodded, but clearly didn't like what George had told him.

Kate smiled at him. 'Thank you for washing up, George. It's saved me a job – and Chuck is coming over this evening. About nine he said, he can't get away earlier, and we might go for a walk.'

George nodded. 'I'll go up and study for a while,' he told his father. 'Thanks again for the book.'

He went out, not quite closing the door behind him. 'Do you think he's right when he says the daughter doesn't like him?' he heard his father ask.

'George doesn't lie,' Kate said. 'Billy only went there briefly but he said Lizzie wasn't very friendly.'

'That's a shame,' Mr Greene said. 'You can see both the little girl and her grandmother adore him.'

Kate's answer was lost as George took the stairs two at a time to his room. Billy was already there, sitting on his bed, reading. He looked up and grinned as George entered. 'Kate said I should come to bed while you were in the kitchen, 'cos I've got exams in the morning. It was a good tea, wasn't it?'

'Yeah, it was,' George replied. 'I'm going to read for a bit – tell me if you want to get to sleep and I'll put the big light out.'

'I'm all right,' Billy said. 'Grandad's going to write to Mum and ask her to visit. Do you think she'll come?'

'Don't know. Will you like it if she does?'

Billy shrugged. 'I'd like it if my dad did,' he said. 'Grandad says I can write to him. He knows where to send it.'

'Yeah, you do that,' George said. 'Now, shut up – I want to read!'

Billy tossed a pillow at him, laughed, and lay back on the bed, his eyes shut. George grinned and opened his medical encyclopaedia at page one.

CHAPTER 36

'I'm sorry I couldn't get over before,' Chuck said as he helped Kate into her light jacket. It wasn't cold out but the breeze could be cool now that they were into early September. 'I used up all my leave and I've been pretty busy.'

'That's all right,' Kate replied and smiled. 'I know you took a lot of leave when you were helping me and searching for my family.'

'It was what I wanted,' he said simply. 'We were all very worried about you – and your family, Kate.' He looked into her eyes as they paused outside the door for a moment. 'I'm sorry about your mum . . .'

'Dad has taken it hard,' Kate replied. She tucked her arm through his as they began to walk. 'For a while I wondered if it had broken him, but he seems to be recovering now, slowly. He's taking an interest in his football again, thinking about the new season.'

'Ned's tough,' Chuck said. 'He'll grieve in his own way – but he has you and the boys now, Kate. That's given him a reason to live again.'

'Yes, it has. He's very proud of what George did, looking after Mrs Seward and Ellie.'

'He's proud of you, too,' Chuck told her with a loving glance. 'And so he should be. I'm glad you went out and got yourself a new job, Kate. You're a born teacher and it's what you should be doing.'

'I do love it,' she agreed. 'I'm looking forward to starting next week.' She touched her cheek a little self-consciously. 'It isn't as red as it was – I hope the children won't find it repulsive.'

Chuck caught her hand and held it. The back was discoloured by burns but she was lucky that her hands had healed well. 'Don't even think it,' he said and raised her hand to lightly kiss the scarring. 'You are brave and beautiful, Kate. Yes, you do have scars and some will never quite go – but that doesn't make you ugly.'

'I see people staring when I shop,' she said, meeting his gaze. 'I know what I look like, Chuck. The scars aren't pleasant. Children aren't always kind so I'm prepared for some comments.'

'You'll live with it because you have to,' he told her. 'In time they won't see the scars, Kate. They'll learn to love you for who you are and then they'll just think of you as Miss Greene their teacher who taught them so much.'

'I hope so,' she said and smiled. 'I don't mind that I'm not pretty. Looks aren't everything, are they?'

'But you are beautiful,' Chuck told her and traced the outline of the burn. 'This is just a beauty spot – your eyes and your mouth and the tip of your nose are all perfect.' He bent his head and kissed her, first very gently on her cheek, then her nose and then her mouth. Kate just stood still and let him, her heart racing as she felt a longing to be in his arms, and yet she held back. 'I see the inner you and that has always been perfect,' he murmured.

'Oh, Chuck,' Kate whispered. 'You're so kind and generous and . . .'

He touched a finger to her lips. 'I'm not asking for anything, Kate. I think you know that I love you . . . so very much, but I know you need time, dearest. You've been through so much.'

Kate held his arm tighter, her throat choked with emotion. Inside, she was torn, her heart telling her to give in and tell him she loved him, tell him she would marry him, and, when the war was over, go back to his home in Canada as his wife. Yet her head was buzzing with all the reasons why she should let him walk away. She was scarred, both inside and out, and she didn't know if they would heal enough to make her fit to be his wife – and there was her father, George, Billy, John, if he made it back home and Jenny. They were her family and needed her. She thought perhaps she needed them, too. Once before she'd given her heart to a man, given her promises and left her home for him – but that dream had ended in bitterness.

How could Kate be sure that this time the love would last?

'Don't answer,' Chuck said softly. 'I won't rush you, Kate. Your happiness is everything to me.' He smiled down at her. 'Let's just enjoy the walk . . .'

Kate looked up at him, grateful that, as on other nights, he'd accepted that she just couldn't commit –

not yet. She was wounded and she needed time to heal. The war didn't just ruin the lives of fighting men, it left an indelible scar on the hearts of all it touched.

Kate felt some trepidation as she began her first class in the little village school. It was only four miles or so from her home and for young children up to the age of eleven, and her class had seven pupils. She could hardly believe it when she walked into the classroom and they all stood up quietly and waited for her to tell them to sit down. She saw their innocent faces as they looked at her and smiled. So different to the children she'd taught in London and yet so much alike.

'I'm Miss Greene,' she told them, because she had reverted to her maiden name. 'I'm going to take you for reading, writing, and history but first of all I think we should get to know each other. Where do you live – and what does your father do?'

Kate pointed to a girl with fair plaits. The girl blushed and giggled and then stood up. 'I'm Betty Smith and my father is in the army. He drives a tank and he says it's just like a big tractor!'

'Don't be daft,' one of the boys said. 'Tanks are much bigger and heavier and they shoot guns.'

'They are sort of the same,' Kate told him. 'They can go over rough land just like tractors – I expect that's what Betty's father meant. Thank you, Betty – now, who else?'

All hands shot up and the next half an hour was both informative and fun. It was playtime before they had finished getting to know one another – and then Ben Grundy asked Kate a question.

'Miss,' he said, 'you asked about us – can we ask about you?'

'Yes, of course,' Kate replied. 'What do you want to know?'

'How did you get that mark on your face?' he asked. Betty hissed at him that he was rude and he went bright red. 'Only asking . . .'

'Yes, and I'm glad you did,' Kate said gently. 'I was in a house that was bombed in London. It caught fire and I was briefly trapped before someone pulled me out – so I was lucky because other people in the same road died.'

'Cor blimey,' Ben said loudly. 'You're a brave one, miss. I'm glad you got pulled out alive.'

'What's it like up there?' another lad asked. 'Mum says it must have been awful.'

'It wasn't good,' Kate told him. 'It was frightening at times and a lot of people were killed. Thankfully, it seems that the worst of the bombing is over – at least for now.'

'You'll be safer down here, miss,' Betty said, but before Kate could answer they heard an almighty bang and the whole of the building shook, a crack appearing in a pane of glass. The children started to scream, in Kate's class and the other next door.

'Keep calm, children,' Kate said. 'I don't think it was a bomb. I believe it might have been a plane crash up on the aerodrome. You may file out behind me into the playground, but no one is to run off or go home without permission . . .'

340

The children stood and followed her outside, everyone moving to the side of the road so as to look towards the hill. Fields sloped gently to the aerodrome, which was spread over many acres of what had been prime farm land and, sure enough, a column of black smoke was drifting up into the air. The second class of slightly younger children had followed the other teacher into the playground and she came across to Kate.

'I think a plane must have missed its landing,' she said in a quiet voice. 'It happens now and then if they've sustained damage on a mission – mostly the crew get out all right, but it looks as if this one exploded on touchdown.'

'Yes . . .' Kate felt fear clutch at her heart, because she knew that Chuck could well be in that plane. 'I wonder if the pilot got out . . .'

'I'd ring but I know they won't tell us, Kate. I have a friend and he might tell me when he gets off-duty – but for now, we should take the children in and talk to them. I think all together in the hall . . .'

Kate saw that some of the smaller children were crying and scared. They all looked white and stared at her with big eyes. 'Yes, let's give them their milk and talk to them, Sheila.'

The children were ushered into the hall and Sheila talked to them about the plane crash, her words calm and reassuring, but without lying as she told them that it was possible someone had been hurt.

'All of you know there is a terrible war going on,' she said. 'Some of you have relatives fighting – and we all know of some who were killed. Brave men who

341

went to war to keep us safe. They knew they might be hurt or killed but they still did it for us – and so we shall pray for them all. We shall pray that all our brave men come home safely and if they do not, we know their souls will be forever in Heaven. We love, honour, and respect them, and we shall never forget them. Now all of you – God Bless and keep you . . . Amen.'

'Amen . . .' the children echoed her and then Kate handed out their bottles of milk.

'We shall play inside today,' Sheila announced. 'What about a game of pirates?'

'Yes please!' the hall echoed with cheers and laughter and Kate nodded. Sheila wasn't the senior mistress here for nothing. A noisy game of pirates in the gym was a good way to turn children's minds from the terrible and frightening accident up on the aerodrome. However, as she handed out sashes and helped organize the two teams of opposing pirates, who had to swarm up ropes, climb bars and vault a wooden horse before the battle, her own thoughts were not so easily calmed.

Chuck could easily be the pilot in that crashed plane and the awful thought that he might be killed and she would never see him again shocked her to the core. No! No, he couldn't die – he *mustn't* die. Kate had never told him how much she loved him. If he died in that crash, she never would . . .

It was a long day, even though her class was a delight to teach. Kate struggled to keep her mind on her job because suddenly, all her doubts meant nothing. Chuck was the kindest, most generous, loving man she'd ever known and she couldn't bear the thought that she might not see him again, might never kiss him. And she did so want to hold him in her arms and kiss him, to melt into his warmth and feel the strength of his love surround her. She'd hung back, let silly fears keep her from telling him and now she was torn with regret.

Just before school ended, Sheila came into the classroom. 'I have an announcement to make,' she said gravely. 'We all know that a plane crashed this morning and I have just been told that it carried a full crew of six men. Two have been badly hurt – and one has died. I understand he was the pilot. We will remember those brave men in our prayers tomorrow morning, children. I've told you, because it's best that you know the truth and your parents will wish to know. I have a note for you to take home . . .'

She placed some envelopes on Kate's desk, nodded and walked out. Betty started crying. Kate went to her and put a hand on her shoulder.

'It is very sad,' she said. 'But remember that the pilot was a brave man and he died doing his duty – for the sake of his country and for us.'

'I know,' Betty sniffed. 'My uncle works up there – he doesn't fly but he helps rebuild the planes.'

'Yes? Then he's a brave man too,' Kate said. 'You should be proud of him, Betty.'

'I am . . .' She sniffed again and wiped her nose with the back of her hand. Kate handed her a handkerchief and she blew her nose. 'I like you, miss. I'm glad you've come to teach us – and I think you're very pretty . . .'

Kate smiled. 'Thank you, Betty. Off you go home now – and take your note. I expect your mum will want to know what happened this morning.'

'Mum works on the land. She might have seen it,' Betty said and ran off.

Kate watched her and the other children leave. She picked up her jacket and a pile of exercise books and took them out to her bicycle. Sheila followed her out and locked the school door.

'What will you do in the winter?' she asked. 'There is a bus but you'd have to come in early. I can get a key for you so you can make a cup of tea before we arrive.'

'Oh, yes, I may well catch the bus when the weather turns nasty,' Kate said. 'I suppose you didn't get any names – the pilot in that crash?'

'No – just the facts,' Sheila told her. 'Do you know one of the pilots?'

'Yes, I do,' Kate said. 'He's a Canadian . . .'

'Ah, yes, we've got all sorts – Americans, New Zealanders, Australians and Canadians. They're all brave lads. It throws a shadow over things, doesn't it?'

Kate agreed that it did, got on her bike and pedalled off. She went as fast as she could around the corner and up the long straight road that led eventually to Chatteris and her home. It seemed an effort and, after she'd been going for a while, she was forced to stop, because her eyes were filled with tears. She sniffed and looked for her handkerchief, then realized that she'd given it to Betty and wiped her face with her coat sleeve. She longed to turn round and go up to the base to ask if Chuck was safe, but knew they wouldn't tell her. It was surrounded in security, because it had to be. News would leak out eventually – but if Chuck had been involved would anyone think to tell her? She wasn't a relative, and she wasn't his wife – they weren't even going out as a couple.

The thought that it could be weeks or months before she knew anything filled her with fear and dread. 'Oh, Chuck,' she whispered. 'Please, please be alive. I can't bear to lose you!'

CHAPTER 37

George left school but didn't go straight home. He
didn't know why he headed for Mrs Seward's house,
but something in his gut told him he was needed. As
he approached the house, the front door opened and a
small figure came flying towards him.

'George! Come quickly!' she said. 'Granny's ill – I
think she's dying!'

'Where is she?' George asked, his heart catching as
he saw the terror in Ellie's eyes.

'On the kitchen floor. She went all funny after
she quarrelled with mum – and then, just now, she
crumpled up and fell to the floor. Her face is all twisted
and there's stuff on her mouth . . .'

George rushed into the kitchen ahead of her. He saw
the figure on the floor and knelt down, feeling for a
pulse. It took a minute to be sure, because he'd only
practised on himself and Billy, but then he was certain
it was there – very slow and weak. But Mrs Seward
was alive. He turned to Ellie.

'Is she dead?' she asked fearfully.

'No, but she's very ill. Get me a little warm water,

Ellie, and a cloth. I'm going to bathe her face and try to sit her up. If I can make her comfortable, I'll get the doctor – but where's your mother?'

'She quarrelled with gran and then she left. She took all her things with her and she says she won't come back.'

'Are you sure she said she wouldn't come back?' George asked and Ellie nodded. So there was going to be no help from Ellie's mother then. He thought furiously. 'Your gran needs to be in hospital, Ellie. I'll take you home with me once we get her somewhere she'll be looked after.'

Ellie brought him the water in a little bowl. It was cool but not cold. George gently washed the vomit from around her mouth. He had already cleared it from her throat while Ellie was getting the cloth. He heard her moan slightly, her eyelids fluttering. He beckoned to Ellie, showing her how he wanted her to support her gran once he lifted her, and then he managed to hoist the old lady over his shoulder and moved her to the sofa, laying her down so that her head was on the cushions. Mrs Seward moaned slightly, her eyes flicking open and then shutting.

'You're going to be all right,' he told her. 'Ellie will hold your hand while I run to the phone box and ring for the doctor. I'll come straight back and we'll soon have you comfortable.'

Ellie looked frightened but George told her she had to be brave. 'Just hold her hand while I phone for help and then I'll come back. Don't worry, Ellie. It will be all right, I promise.' Ellie nodded and took her granny's hand, talking to her as George had in a soothing voice.

George left her and ran to the phone box just on the corner. He was lucky and got the doctor's wife immediately. She said her husband was in surgery but she would ring for an ambulance for Mrs Seward.

George would have preferred the doctor to come straight away but of course he had other patients and in twenty minutes – although it seemed more like forever – the ambulance arrived. The two men listened to George's tale and followed him to the kitchen. Mrs Seward was just about conscious but clearly helpless and very ill.

'We'll have to take her to the hospital,' one of the men said. 'Looks like she had a stroke. What about the girl?'

'She can stay with my family,' George said. 'Kate will look after her – and there's my dad and Billy. She'll be all right . . .'

Ellie moved closer to George. 'I want to go with him. He's my friend . . .' she said and reached for his hand. George took it and held it.

'OK – someone from the council will be in touch,' the man said and then they carried Mrs Seward out to the waiting ambulance.

'We'd better get some clothes for you,' George said, leading the way upstairs. Ellie's bedroom was untidy and it looked as if no one had bothered to clean it for ages. George shook his head. Her mother should be ashamed!

He packed her things into a satchel and some paper bags, then carried them downstairs. 'We'd better lock up,' he said. 'I'll take the key with me, because your gran won't come home alone without us knowing. I'm not sure—' He stopped, because he wasn't certain Mrs

348

Seward would ever be well enough to live on her own again. Ellie couldn't look after her and if her daughter had gone . . .

'You did the right thing,' George's father said when he got home. 'Hello, Ellie. George will show you your room – Jenny stays sometimes and uses it, but she won't mind sharing if she comes.'

After George had taken Ellie upstairs, he went to his father in the kitchen. 'I didn't know what else to do, Dad. Mrs Seward fought tooth and nail to keep her from an orphanage and if she can't come home . . .'

'I don't see why she can't stay with us,' his father said. 'Mrs Seward could come, too, if she's well enough. We don't need that huge sitting room. It could be turned into a bedroom come sitting room for her . . .'

'Who would look after her?' George said. 'Kate works – and you do long shifts. Billy and I are at school . . .'

'Ellie should be at school during the day, too,' his father said. 'I know she used to be delicate, but I reckon she would be better for a bit of fun with other girls. It ain't right to keep a young girl with an old lady all the time. 'Sides, we'll face that when we come to it. Her gran might get well again. Maybe not to live on her own – but, as I said, we've got that front room doing nothing.'

'Ellie would love that, to live here,' George said and grinned. 'Thanks, Dad. I'll help as much as I can.'

'We all will – and we're doing all right now. We might get a nice woman to come in and help a bit while Kate's at work.'

George nodded. 'Yeah, it might work but . . .' He was going to ask what if Kate wanted to get married again, but his father had got out his evening paper.

George frowned. He knew Chuck loved Kate and wanted to marry her but he wasn't certain how Kate felt. However, he didn't think it would be fair to make her feel she had to stay around to look after them all. Perhaps it hadn't been such a good idea to bring Ellie here – and yet the alternative was unthinkable. He just hoped and prayed that her grandmother would get well again, though he'd seen how bad she was and he knew that was asking for a miracle.

CHAPTER 38

For a week Kate heard nothing and she kept her worries to herself, fretting inside. She knew that it was often a week or more before Chuck had free time, but couldn't help fearing that he'd been on board the crashed plane. However, there was too much going on for her to give way to her sorrow and fear. Ellie was nervous and upset for the first couple of days. She kept crying and wouldn't stop, even for George. It took several days for Kate to win her confidence.

'Will they put me in an orphanage?' she asked, her eyes wide with terror when Kate finally manged to get her to talk. 'Granny says they're terrible places . . .'

'I don't know much about them,' Kate admitted. 'But your gran isn't dead, Ellie love. I rang the hospital and she's stable. That's all they told me – and we won't let them take you away. I don't see why they should but . . . I think you should start school. You could come with me on the bus in the mornings and find friends to play with – and then it's more likely the council will let you stay with us.'

'Gran taught me things,' Ellie said. 'She says I'm too delicate for school.'

'You were but I think you're much better now. Shall I give you some lessons at home first – and then we'll see about school?'

Ellie agreed, and Kate soon discovered that she was a bright child and knew lots of things that older children might not – but there were serious holes in parts of her education. She decided that it would be best if she coached Ellie at home until after the Christmas holidays and then enrolled her for the spring term.

Having Ellie as their guest at home and learning to know her pupils at school helped Kate to get through the days and nights of wondering whether Chuck was alive, injured, or dead. She cried into her pillow for several nights, praying that he would come soon, or send her a letter, but nothing came and the fear grew in her heart.

After the weekend, Kate was reluctant to leave Ellie at home alone, for although she was no longer the helpless little girl George had taken to his heart, it would be a long day for her alone. So she rang Sheila from the phone box and explained, and was told she could bring Ellie with her and let her join the class unofficially.

Ellie was a bit anxious but the children Kate taught were well-behaved and did not tease her. Ellie was unable to follow in the maths lessons at first, but Kate showed her how to do the multiplication in the evenings and by the end of the week she had learned and was getting most of her sums right. When it came to reading, Ellie was streets ahead of the others in class and could read long words without stumbling; she could spell and write simple sentences, but had no idea how to play rounders or any of the team games. However, when it came to music, she could play several notes on the recorder and her voice was in tune when they sang hymns.

Sheila came in and observed the class from time to time, and she spoke to Kate about Ellie. 'She's an unusual child,' Sheila said. 'So advanced in some things and completely without education in others. Her grandmother clearly did what she could for her.'

'Yes, and she loves her dearly,' Kate replied. 'She's learning fast, Sheila. It was good of you to let her join in, even though she's not up to our standards in many things.'

'You were in an awkward position and I perfectly understand that you don't wish to let Ellie go to an institution. She would have a terrible time and could not stand up for herself in that kind of environment. Our children are mostly gentle. One or two of the boys can be little monsters, but they all respect us and only need a look or a warning.'

'Yes – they're much easier than the class I took in the East End of London,' Kate said with a smile. 'Many of them were rough in speech and manner.' She looked curiously at Sheila. 'Have you not had any evacuees here at this school?'

'We had two lads but they now go to Chatteris school,' Sheila replied. 'I think they have more in Sutton . . .' She hesitated, then, 'Have you heard from your pilot friend yet?'

'No.' Kate looked at her anxiously. 'Have you heard any more?'

'I was told he wasn't British – one of our overseas friends . . .' Sheila shook her head. 'That doesn't help you much, Kate. I would ask my friend but he says he isn't allowed to talk about it.'

Kate nodded. 'My worry is that no one will think to contact me if he *is* injured. He has no relatives in this country – and any telegram would go to his family in Canada.'

'That is upsetting for you,' Sheila said. 'I'll ask again but I may not get an answer.'

Kate thanked her. She tried to put her anxiety out of her mind, but the thought that she might not know if Chuck was ill or dead haunted her and she lay awake night after night, thinking and fretting.

In the end, her father noticed that she looked tired and drawn. He sat looking at her across the breakfast table and then asked what was troubling her.

'You were getting better, Kate. Now you look drained – should you go to the doctor, love? I don't like to see you this way.'

To her consternation, Kate started crying. Her father came to comfort her, listening as she told him of her fears. He patted her shoulder and then stroked her hair as she fumbled for her handkerchief.

'How long has it been since the crash?' he asked.

'Over a week,' Kate replied through her tears. 'I know he doesn't always have time to visit and unless we arrange a time, he can't ring me at the phone box on the corner – but I'm worried, Dad . . .'

'I don't think Chuck would have neglected to

arrange for you to be informed if anything happened to him,' her father said as she blew her nose and wiped her cheeks, gulping back her tears. 'He thinks the world of you, Kate.'

She looked up at him. 'Did he tell you he wants me to marry him?'

'No, but you can see how he feels every time he looks at you,' her father said. 'I can't tell you for certain that he wasn't in that plane, but I *am* sure he has friends who would let you know if something happened to him. Chuck thinks of you as his girl, even if you haven't given him cause – and his friends must know about you, Kate.'

'Oh, Dad!' Kate dried her eyes and looked at him gratefully as he went back to his breakfast. 'Thank you. I hadn't thought of that – but I believe you're right. Chuck sometimes mentions a friend called Bart – so perhaps he has just been very busy.'

'I'm sure that's it,' her father said. 'You're going to marry him, Kate. It would be foolish not to when you love him. Don't let what happened before stop you . . .'

Kate put a hand to her cheek and he shook his head. 'I meant Steve's betrayal. Chuck isn't like him. I wish you'd met him first, Kate – or someone like him. You deserve the best.'

Kate's eyes filled with tears again but she smiled and shook her head. Her father's wise words had made her feel better and she felt a spark of hope. If Chuck was just busy, he would come when he could – and when he did, she would tell him what was in her heart . . .

CHAPTER 39

George and his father went to visit Mrs Seward in the hospital. It was a small cottage hospital and the wards had six patients, most of them elderly. She was sitting up in bed and looking very much better when the nurse directed them.

'Yes, she's getting on well. She had a nasty turn and we thought we might lose her, but she's a strong spirit and she fought her way back – though it'll be a week or two yet before we can think of letting her go home . . .' The nurse frowned. 'I understand she lived alone with her granddaughter?'

'They're both going to be living with us now,' Mr Greene told her. 'That's one of the reasons we're here – we want her to know she has a home to come to.'

'Is there anyone at home to look after her?' the nurse asked.

'Not all the time. Kate – my daughter – works as a teacher, and I'm on shift work. I shall be putting in for as many late shifts as they will give me so that I'm around when the others are out. In the evening they will be there – two lads and her granddaughter and

Kate. However, I've made inquiries and I've found someone who is able to pop in and look after her for a few hours when we can't. She should be all right on her own as long as she doesn't have to get meals and hot drinks – for an hour or two?'

'You seem to have thought of everything,' the nurse said. 'I'll talk to Matron and the doctors and I'm sure they'll agree she's better released to your care than an old folks' home.'

'Well, it's what I think she would want,' Mr Greene said. 'We're going to ask her now, aren't we, George?'

George agreed and they walked to the bed. Mrs Seward looked at them in silence for a moment. 'It's you I've got to thank for being alive,' she said, looking at George oddly. 'I suppose I should thank you . . . though I might as well be dead.'

'Now then, Jean,' Mr Greene said, 'you mustn't talk such nonsense. Ellie wants you home and so do we.'

'Well, I can't live in that mausoleum any longer,' she announced. 'If I had a bungalow I might manage it, but the house is too much for me.'

'You're not going there. We have a big downstairs room we never use and with your permission we're going to get your bed and some other bits and turn it into a bed-sitting room. You can live with us, just like Ellie does now . . .'

'Live with you? But how . . .?' She stared at him, a mixture of hope and disbelief in her eyes. 'You can't want an old woman like me . . .'

'Yes, we do,' George said. 'Ellie wants you to come with us and I'll help look after you, but Dad's going to work nights and early mornings – and there's a nice lady who will come in to make you drinks and get you a sandwich when we're all out. Besides, you'll be able to get up and dress soon – and next term I can study at home sometimes if I want.'

Jean stared at them, a tear sliding down her cheek. 'I thought my life was over when I woke up here. I don't remember much after the quarrel with Lizzie. She took the last of my good jewellery and went off with some man she'd met.'

'Well, she's gone now,' Ned Greene said. 'And your home is with us – if you'll accept?'

'I'd be a damned fool if I didn't!' she said a glint in her eyes. She looked at George. 'I can see where your kindness comes from now, lad. Yes, I'll come, and thank you. I'll pay for my keep – and whatever the costs are for my care. Once the house is sold I'll have money again, though I'll put half of it by for Ellie when she's older.' She sniffed. 'I've left everything I have to Ellie – that was what put her mother in a temper. She'd found my will and read it – tore it up, actually, but it was just a copy. My lawyer has the original in his safe . . . Cartwright and Son.'

'Yes, well, that's your business,' Ned told her. 'But we'll look out for Ellie when the time comes – and it isn't yet so just set your mind to getting better, not buried.'

Jean gave a cackle of laughter, her eyes sparkling. 'Doesn't mince his words, your dad,' she said, looking at George. 'I think I'm going to enjoy my time with your family, lad . . .'

*

358

'Mrs Seward likes you,' George said as they left the hospital and went to their bus stop. 'I'm grateful for what you've done, Dad. I would've felt bad if she'd had to go into a home.'

'We look after folk when we can,' his father replied. 'It was your mother's maxim and we must never forget that. Your friend helped you when you needed it, and we'll help her.'

'Yes. It helped a lot, living at her house so I could continue my studies.' He smiled at his father. 'I did so well in my exams this time that my teacher says he believes I really will get into medical school if I keep working as hard.'

'That is wonderful, son!' His father looked at him, his eyes moist. 'Your mother would be so proud of you. She missed you when we sent you to the country with Vera, but she believed it was the right thing – and, if you'd still been in London, you might have died, too.'

'I know,' George sighed. 'If the war is still happening when I'm eighteen I'll have to enlist, Dad – but I hate the thought of it. It isn't right that people kill each other. Life should be peaceful and good for everyone.'

'I agree with you, but there are times when we have to fight, George. Two of your brothers died fighting for their country and we honour them – and all the brave men who have died or are still fighting.'

'I do – but I still think war is wrong,' George said. 'I won't be a pacifist and refuse to join up when the time comes, but I have my own views.'

His father stopped and looked at him. 'You've grown

up a fine young man, George. I know you're not sixteen yet but all you've been through has made a man of you. I pray that in another two years the fighting will be over – but when I look at the newspapers, I can't see it ending for a while.'

'I know,' George replied. 'I hope John gets home for Christmas. It's over two years since we've seen him.'

'His last letter hinted that he might be home soon, so we'll just pray you get your wish.'

Kate was preparing their evening meal when they walked in, the smell of a pie in the oven making their mouths water. She turned to look at them with a smile.

'Ellie has been making the pastry for us. Her grandmother taught her quite a bit of cooking and she has a light touch so I think we're in for a treat.'

'What's in the pie?' her father asked. 'It smells delicious.'

'I was given a brace of rabbits today by the father of one of my pupils. He's a farmer and he says they're pests but they make good eating. I've never skinned one before but Ellie was quite good at it.'

'Well done, Ellie,' Ned said and looked at the girl who was smiling, pleased with Kate's praise. She was looking much better these days and he thought her new way of life was doing her good. 'We'll enjoy our supper this evening.'

'Your gran agreed to come and stay,' George told Ellie, who had gravitated to his side, as always. 'She was a bit worried about you, but knows you're fine now.'

'I read to the class today,' Ellie told him. 'And I can play pirates now in the gym . . .'

'Those two get on well,' Ned said to Kate, giving them an amused glance. 'She follows him like a little puppy.'

'I think Ellie really loves George,' Kate replied with a smile. 'The pie will be ready in—' Before she could finish there was a knock at the door. 'Answer that for me, George, please.'

Kate brought the pie to the table and then turned to drain and mash the potatoes with a little milk and margarine but she stopped and turned with a cry as she heard a man's voice.

'Chuck!' She put the pan back on the stove and rushed towards him, her voice caught with emotion. 'Oh, Chuck – you're all right! You're alive!'

Chuck caught her in his arms and held her, looking down into her face that was filled with joy – and then he kissed her. It was a long, passionate kiss and drew all eyes in the room. Ned took over the potatoes and started to whip them up with the margarine and milk, a look of satisfaction on his face. He then drained the vegetables while Kate and Chuck continued to look into each other's eyes.

'They sent me to another base for a few days,' Chuck told her. 'I didn't know about the crash until I got to my quarters this morning – and I knew you would be worried so I came as soon as I could.'

'I thought it might be you that was killed,' Kate said in a choking voice. 'Oh, Chuck, I couldn't bear it!'

'My dearest, dearest love,' he said and smiled down at her. 'Don't you know I lead a charmed life?' He laughed as she gazed up at him, stroking the arch of a fine eyebrow with his fingertip. 'I have too much to live for, Kate. Besides, I'm going to be around a lot more now. I've been promoted to Wing Commander and made senior tutor for young pilots, which means I won't be flying missions for a while. It seems they think I've done my bit for now and will be more use teaching younger men how to fight and live longer.'

'That's wonderful!' she said and hugged him. 'You'll be—'

'If you love birds don't mind, we want our dinner,' Ned said. 'You're welcome to stay, Chuck – but either way, the rest of us are going to eat.' He was laughing and Chuck grinned, letting Kate go. 'It smells delicious,' he said. 'I will stay if that's all right – and then we'll leave you lot to do the washing up.'

Ned gave a shout of laughter. George grinned, Billy whooped and Ellie smiled. 'We're family,' George told him. 'You're a part of our family now – that's if you're going to ask Kate to marry you?'

'Oh yes,' Chuck said. 'I intend to do that – but if you think I'll do it now, you're mistaken, you rogue. That will be in private.'

'Yeah, well we all know what the answer will be,' Billy said. 'She's been mooning about this past week or more, looking like she lost a pound and found sixpence.'

George gave him a good-natured cuff round the ear and told him to mind his manners, but Billy only ducked and laughed. Kate went to serve up their food, her cheeks pink, but Chuck looked as if he was enjoying himself.

*

362

'You have quite a family,' Chuck said when they were at last alone, walking away from the house. 'Your dad and George are as alike as two peas in a pod.'

'Yes, they are,' Kate agreed. 'Derek was like Dad too – but Tom took after Mum. John does, too.' She smiled up at him. 'They're getting over losing Mum and the boys but there's a way to go yet . . .' She looked shyly at him. 'I couldn't leave them – not yet . . .'

'You shouldn't think of it,' Chuck said and held her hand tighter. 'I want us to be together for the rest of our lives, and if that means I live here – then it's what I'll do. I love you, Kate, and I want you to be my wife – will you?'

'You know I will,' Kate said and he pulled her close, his lips against her hair. 'I love you so much. I didn't know how much until I feared I might never see you again – never be able to tell you how much you mean to me . . .'

'I'll never leave you,' Chuck vowed. 'Even if they send me away, I'll be with you, Kate, in my heart and mind. I'll never hurt you, never break your heart . . .'

'I know,' she said and lifted her head for his kiss. 'One day they'll be strong enough and then I'll come with you to your home. I want to see it, Chuck – to meet your family.' She raised a hand to touch his cheek. 'But we can be married here, can't we?'

'Yes, we can and we will,' he said. 'I have to sort out a few formalities and then we'll be married, as soon as I can arrange it.' He smiled and kissed her softly on the lips. 'Thank you for trusting me and for loving me, Kate. I think I loved you almost from the first moment I saw you but I knew you could never be mine – but someone up above was looking out for me, and now you'll be my wife and my love, partners, and friends for always.'

'Oh yes, please,' Kate said and knew she had found her safe haven, her love, and her happiness at last. 'We were friends first before we were lovers and I believe that's the way it will always be . . .' She laughed. 'I think it might be that way for Ellie and George, though he doesn't know it yet and it will be a long time before he thinks that way – but she knows. I've seen it in her eyes and I hope it will come right for her, too.'

'She certainly adores him,' Chuck said. 'If he needs help to get him through college I'll be there, Kate – and for all your family. I like them all, though there's some I haven't met yet?'

'We hope John will make it home for Christmas,' Kate told him. 'As for my sister Vera – well, she hasn't been in touch for a long time. I hope one day she will, if only for Billy's sake, but his father writes to him so at least he has him.'

'That's good,' Chuck said and put his arm around her. 'Do you have any idea where we're going? Shall we get on a bus and go to the pictures or have a drink at the pub?'

'Let's just walk for a while,' Kate said, smiling up at him. 'And then we'll go home and tell them . . .'

'What they already know,' Chuck said and they both started laughing.

Life had been hard for a long time. Life had been sad and full of hurt, but now Kate could only think that life was going to be happier than she'd ever known it.

She knew that up above in the Heaven her mum had believed in, Grace would be watching and smiling as her family rebuilt their lives.

'Yes, because they are family and they love us, even those who are no longer with us,' she said and he nodded. Because he understood, too.

Not the end, the beginning . . .

Turn the page to discover more of Cathy Sharp's
heartwarming Orphan stories . . .

CATHY SHARP

Can he find
a new family?

3

Step
out
in Stylo FASHION
SHOES

ALL CARS
STOP HERE

THE
Lonely
Orphan

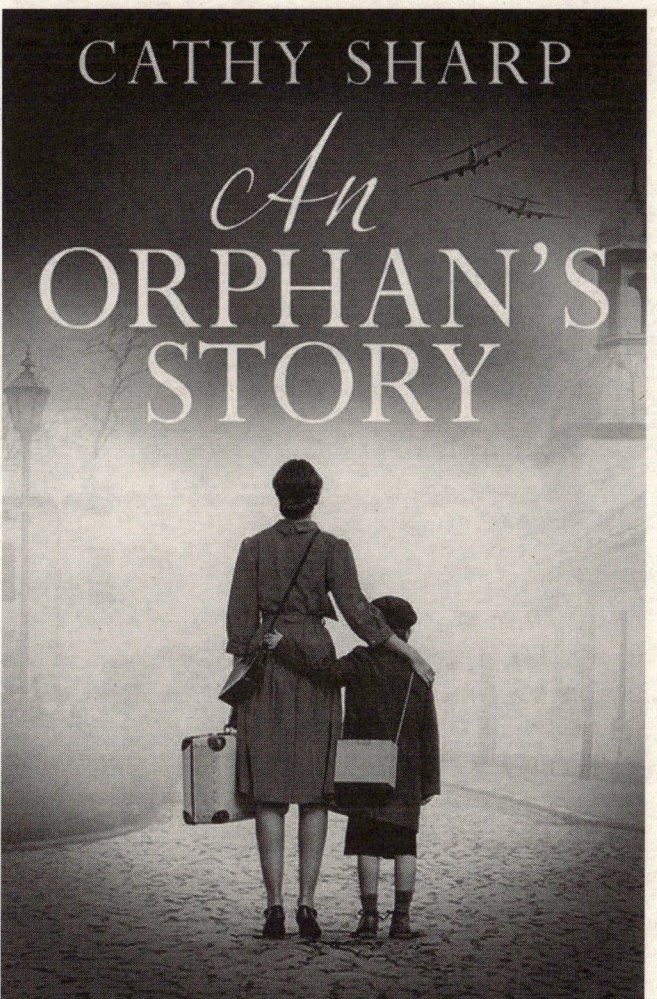

CATHY SHARP

An
ORPHAN'S
STORY

CATHY SHARP
THE BOY
with the
SUITCASE
He must travel a long road to find his way home...
'A story which touched my heart'
Glynis Peters

CATHY SHARP

THE
Lost
EVACUEE

Her journey's end
is just the beginning…

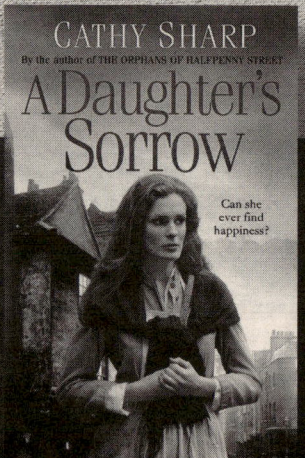
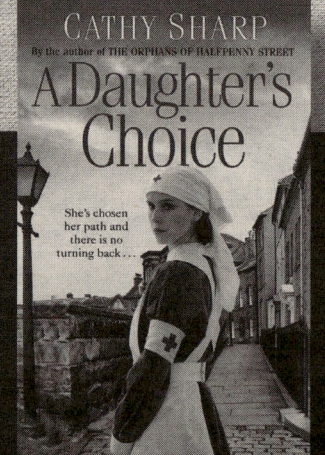

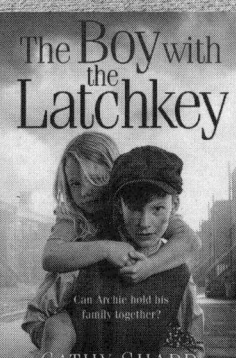